*T*HE WINNERS OF NINE BOOK AWARDS transcending the genres of science fiction, environmental fiction, and action-adventure, *The Girl Who Rode Dolphins* and *Dolphin Riders* have proven themselves thrillers with a labyrinth of spellbinding twists, turns, and thunderous action that takes readers on a roller coaster ride of nail-biting suspense and explosive adventure.

Upon its original debut, *The Girl Who Rode Dolphins* received the following multiple awards:

- *Winner of Best Epic Adventure of 2008*
  BooksandAuthors.net

- *Winner of Best Science Fiction Epic Adventure of 2008*
  BooksandAuthors.net

- *Winner of Science Fiction Genre*
  2009 Green Book Festival

- *Finalist in Action Adventure Category*
  2009 National Indie Book Excellence Awards

- *Winner of Environmental/Green Fiction Category*
  2010 International Book Awards Competition

- *Winner of the Talking Category*
  2015 Animals, Animals, Animals Book Festival

- *Honorable Mention Awardee in Science Fiction Category*
  2015 London Book Festival

Dolphin Riders, the sequel to *The Girl Who Rode Dolphins*, is an ensuing adventure combined with political intrigue that promises to captivate readers with enthralling action and mysticism on a scale every bit as intense if not greater than the first book.

- *Official Selection Winner of Action/Adventure Category*
  2016 New Apple Summer eBook Awards

- *Finalist In Action/Adventure Category*
  2016 Beverly Hills Book Awards

Following their original debuts, both books were re-released in 2023 by Seaworthy Publications, Inc. as a five-part cliff-hanger series as follows:

The Girl Who Rode Dolphins, 2nd Edition

- Part One - Gaia's Intervention
- Part Two - Gaia's Heartbeat
- Part Three - Retribution

Dolphin Riders, 2nd Edition

- Part Four - Creation
- Part Five - Survival

Retribution

Part Three
of
The Dolphin Riders Series

The Girl Who Rode Dolphins
2nd Edition

Retribution

Part Three
of
The Dolphin Riders Series

The Girl Who Rode Dolphins
2nd Edition

by

Michael J. Ganas

SEAWORTHY PUBLICATIONS, INC.   •   MELBOURNE, FLORIDA

Retribution
Part Three of the Dolphin Riders Series
The Girl Who Rode Dolphins, 2nd Edition
Copyright ©2023 by Michael J. Ganas

Published in the USA by:
Seaworthy Publications, Inc.
6300 N Wickham Rd.
Unit #130-416
Melbourne, FL 32940
E-mail orders@seaworthy.com
www.seaworthy.com

Library of Congress Cataloging-in-Publication Data

Names: Ganas, Michael J., 1946- author. | Ganas, Michael J., 1946- Girl who rode dolphins.
Title: Retribution / by Michael J. Ganas.
Description: Melbourne, Florida : Seaworthy Publications, Inc., 2023. | Series: The dolphin riders series ; part 3 | "The girl who rode dolphins 2nd edition." | Summary: "With the help of Destiny and several friends, Jake Javolyn must break into Haiti's National Penitentiary to rescue Amphitrite and Jacob's cousin, Emmanuel Baptiste, from the clutches of Colonel Ternier and his vengeful mother, Erzulie, an evil voudun sorceress. Having now obtained an ancient amulet containing the spirits of their ancestors, the colonel and Erzulie are more powerful than ever. In a race against time, Javolyn and the girl must stop an insidious plot aimed at obtaining a catastrophic weapon lying in the ocean depths near Navassa Island. A stunning roller coaster ride of epic adventure, Retribution, is the third book in this blockbuster series, an ecological saga that will leave readers spellbound and enthralled with its superb mix of intense action, environmental activism, and mysticism"-- Provided by publisher.
Identifiers: LCCN 2023020770 (print) | LCCN 2023020771 (ebook) | ISBN 9781948494731 (paperback) | ISBN 9781948494748 (epub)
Subjects: LCSH: Dolphins--Fiction. | LCGFT: Ecofiction. | Action and adventure fiction. | Fantasy fiction. | Novels.
Classification: LCC PS3607.A4385 R47 2023 (print) | LCC PS3607.A4385 (ebook) | DDC 813/.6--dc23/eng/20230804
LC record available at https://lccn.loc.gov/2023020770
LC ebook record available at https://lccn.loc.gov/2023020771

Dedication

To my gemstone, Harriet.

Facts

$\mathcal{H}$aiti is currently the poorest country in the Western Hemisphere, a Caribbean nation beleaguered by economic strife, dismal squalor, and political instability, a land of defoliation and ecological ruin. It is a place with a violent past, punctuated by a succession of bloody rebellions and previously governed by a long line of statesmen and dictators whose policies were either inept, ineffectual, unpopular, corrupt, or oppressive. The Duvalier dictatorships of father and son, however, proved to be the most corrupt, oppressive and violent, and under their brutal regimes Haiti suffered deeply.

Francois "Papa Doc" Duvalier ruled Haiti from 1963 until his death in 1971 when his son Jean-Claude "Baby Doc" Duvalier took over the reins of power. Under the Duvalier governments, the population was kept in a state of fear, terrorized by the regime's secret police force, the Tonton Makout. They were also known as the VNS, Volunteers of National Security, and Papa Doc referred to them as his "civilian" military, while the citizens called them "the bogeymen." They were recruited mostly from Haiti's slums and were used to crush all opposition, often imprisoning without trial, torturing, and even killing individuals considered enemies of the state.

An estimated 60,000 Haitians were murdered at the hands of the Tonton Makout, which had a standing force of roughly 10,000 loyalists. Papa Doc made sure his secret police outnumbered the Haitian army by a factor of two in order to assure that he did not get overthrown in a coup. Both Francois Duvalier and his son also took advantage of the people's strong belief in voodoo to control the population. Consequently, much of the citizenry believed them to be voodoo spirits. To this day, voodoo, merged with Catholicism, is the religion of choice embraced by most Haitians.

Misappropriation of government funds amounting to hundreds of millions was common practice under Baby Doc's tyrannical rule, and in the wake of intense political unrest and pressure from the United States to step down, he was finally forced from power in February of 1986, whereupon he fled to France. A wealth of evidence shows various drug cartels to be firmly entrenched in present-day Haiti, where the political climate, endemic poverty, and a breakdown in civil rule makes it an ideal staging area for the transshipment of illegal contraband, where public officials are often threatened or corrupted by bribery to keep a blind eye to drug trafficking.

Navassa Island is a small, uninhabited island, which lies in the Caribbean Sea between Haiti and Jamaica. The island originally belonged to Haiti before being claimed in 1801 as an unorganized, unincorporated territory of the United States, which currently administers it through the U.S. Fish and Wildlife Service.

Malique is a fictitious fishing village that lies roughly midway between the real cities of Saint-Marc and Gonaives along Haiti's western coastline. It has been created solely for the purpose of this novel.

Al Qaeda is an actual present-day organization of Islamic extremists bent on the destruction of the United States and its allies. To this day this terrorist group continues to flourish despite the loss of its originator and leader, Osama Bin Laden, who was killed by a team of U.S. Navy Seals when they stormed his hideout in Pakistan during a bold raid that occurred in 2011.

All mention of Haiti's former leadership and historical events, both past and modern day, are based on documented history and are used as a backdrop for the writing of this novel. In this way, history has been merged with fiction.

All characters, creatures and unusual settings that play a key role within the novel's plot are entirely fictitious and have been created solely for the reader's intrigue and entertainment.

Michael J. Ganas

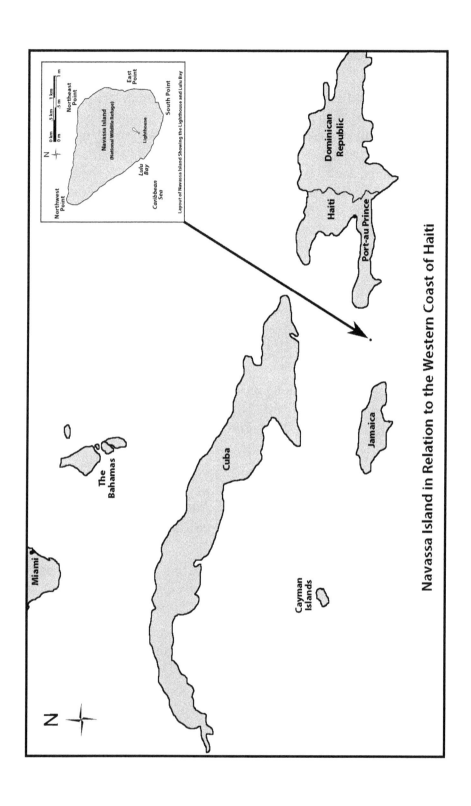

Navassa Island in Relation to the Western Coast of Haiti

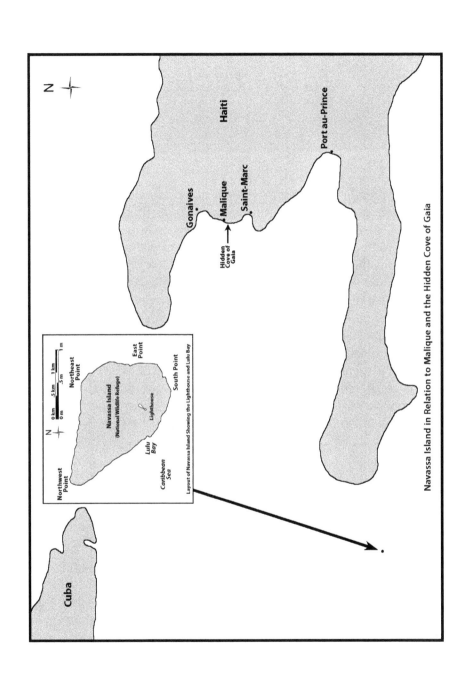

Navassa Island in Relation to Malique and the Hidden Cove of Gaia

Introduction

*A*fter rescuing Destiny from the vicious Colombian drug runners, Jake Javolyn follows the girl and her mentor, Jacob, back to a hidden cove along Haiti's western coastline. Arriving there, he is amazed to find the place pulsating with life, a place that Jacob calls Gaia, and within its clear waters Jake comes upon a strange organism that produces a constant flow of hydrogen gas and is able to harvest gold in great quantities. Jake is immediately puzzled, wondering how such a pristine environment can exist in the midst of a land ravaged by ecological ruin. Even the nearby coral reefs appeared to be on the rebound and teeming with life. According to Jacob, the organism is the cause of this incredible occurrence. Smitten by Destiny's compassionate but naïve persona, Jake's life quickly undergoes a profound change as he bonds with Achilles to become the pod's protector, and he is inexorably drawn into a world of mysticism and the supernatural, an alternate reality where anything is possible as long as you believe in it strongly enough.

The plot, however, takes an unexpected turn when Islamic terrorists led by an old foe operating from a submarine attempt to hijack his boat. But with the help of Destiny and the dolphins, Jake is able to foil the attempt, capturing one of the terrorists in the process. In the meantime, the sadistic Colonel Ternier and his evil mother, Erzulie, have plans to take control of the Haitian government by forging an unholy alliance with the vicious Cardoza drug ring and the Islamic terrorists, but they need an ancient amulet imbued with the mystical power of the rada in order to make this possible. Having a rough idea where it can be found, Ternier sends Chester Hennington on a discrete mission to recover it.

Chapter 1

Jake sat next to Destiny at the north end of the cove near the fish pen, their location farthest from the waterfall. At this distance, the sound of the plummeting water was only a dull susurration, allowing him to speak in a quiet tone. "Pardon me for bringing up the subject, but I'd like you to explain to me why these dolphins refuse to fight back against people trying to hurt them. I would think their extraordinary intelligence could be used as a weapon." He paused uncomfortably, waiting for her to say something.

Destiny gave a minute shrug. "It's not in their nature to fight back. They're incapable of aggression."

Something registered in the back of Jake's head, realizing she had said the same thing the night before. The idea puzzled him. For a creature to avoid striking back in self-defense was a concept altogether unique from his point of view. "You've led a sheltered existence, living in this cove all your life. The world beyond this place can be mean and nasty much of the time. If these dolphins are going to survive, they've got to learn to defend themselves in a proactive way."

Jake stared at Destiny's face closely, trying to see if he was getting through to her. Her expression seemed filled with empathic understanding, like that of a teacher patiently listening to the complaints of a stubborn child. "Causing harm to others is not in their nature," she reiterated softly.

The girl's reply prompted a montage of past battle skirmishes to go flashing through Jake's mind. Defending himself and others was an inborn trait that came naturally, never requiring much in the way of thought on his part. By nature, he was a man of action, seldom given to deep reflection. "Sooner or later we all must do things we don't like…that is, if we choose to go on living. Keeping your skin intact from an aggressor doesn't necessarily mean you have to injure or kill that person." For emphasis, he eyed Achilles floating leisurely nearby. "Back at Navassa I saw a member of your pod make an incredible aerial leap to intercept and toss aside a grenade thrown from that helicopter attacking us. That action prevented anyone from getting hurt, including the bad guys."

Destiny's face remained soulful, her eyes holding his gaze and infused with seemingly limitless compassion. Delaying a response, she reached out and stroked Jake's cheek with a gentle tenderness. "It was Hermes who did that," she finally said. "He was protecting your vessel and crew."

The girl's touch was soothing, and Jake felt his inner frustration quickly defusing.

He sat quietly for the moment, enjoying the light caress of her fingertips, vaguely mindful that those same appendages were capable of miraculous healing. A familiar stirring suddenly took hold of him, and it took all his will to fight off the urge rapidly consuming him. To conceal his embarrassment, he wrestled for words, practically choking them out. "Are you telling me these dolphins are only capable of protecting others, but not themselves?"

Destiny withdrew her hand slowly, looking at Jake strangely. "We must always be aware of the consequences of our actions. Even when we think we are justified in what we are doing, the act can sometimes cause unintended suffering."

Jake caught the inference. "You mean like when I kayoed Frank Loomins?"

Destiny stared back blankly, innocently. "I'm not familiar with that word."

Jake's surprise lasted less than a second, giving way to a wry smile. He should have automatically assumed the girl's sheltered life among the gentle creatures she lived with would have left her ignorant of terms descriptive of violence, and 'kayo' was one such term used to describe it. "Kayo means to knock out, to render someone unconscious with a blow to the head."

The girl nodded uneasily, and out of the corner of his eye, Jake saw the water splash as Achilles flinched.

Jake thought it necessary to explain himself further, remembering something he had gained from perusing books on existentialism. Destiny had mentioned that, among the diverse subjects Jacob had educated her and the pod on, philosophy had been one such field of study. "Isn't the morally right thing to do in any situation governed by the consequences of the actions under consideration? Had I not done what I did, we might never have been able to save Hermes and Aphrodite. Sometimes there are no alternatives available to achieve the desired result."

Destiny's reply was nonjudgmental. "You acted in a manner consistent with who you are. You were only doing what you were meant to do. Your nature is to protect."

Jake found himself growing weary of such sinuous logic, not knowing what else to offer on the subject. The girl was obviously hopelessly naïve. He suddenly felt inclined to nudge the conversation in another direction. "Are you and your friends happy living away from the rest of the world in this secluded place?"

Destiny sniffed the air. "I have always sensed an inner peace within Gaia. Knowing that it pulses with the purity of life gives me and the others great joy."

Jake steered the conversation even further, planting his eyes on Achilles again. "Have you ever considered how much your life and the lives of these dolphins will change once Jacob's plan is set in motion? A plan like that is quite grand and far-reaching in scope."

Destiny elicited a weak smile, noting Jake's concern. "The plan is already in motion. It has been for some time now."

"Yes, I understand all that. But what happens when it begins to take on a fruition that becomes visible to the rest of the world? From what I gather, I'm the only one outside your tight-knit little group who has knowledge of this plan, and I'm honored by the trust Jacob has shown me in revealing it. But I also know this project will be perceived as a threat by some people once they get wind of it."

Destiny appeared unperturbed, and Jake wondered if it was her naivety that was showing again. Some elements of the human race could be quite ruthless and downright vicious when it came to protecting their own interests, particularly when some new innovative enterprise threatened the piece of the pie they had established for themselves. For one, oil companies and oil-producing nations would not be receptive to the idea of cheap, environmentally friendly forms of alternative energy, seeing it as disruptive to the monopolies they had so painstakingly set in place over the last hundred years. He had no doubt they would take whatever measures necessary to stop Tursiops Worldwide from achieving its goals. Then again, there was the potential terrorist aspect to consider. Sea-based energy-harvesting and mining operations that benefited the world would be viewed as economic targets by Islamic extremists and other militant groups seeking to make a political statement. Such sites would become fair game for sabotage and attack. And once the *thurentra*'s ability to siphon valuable precious metals from the sea became known, it would draw the attention of all types of unsavory characters, causing them to descend upon Gaia and other *thurentra* habitats like a school of barracuda. A foreboding coldness settled over him as he thought about how the lure of easy riches and gold had led to the destruction of the Tainos by greedy men.

"Both my mother and Jacob have foreseen such a possibility," Destiny acknowledged. "But they believe most of the world will embrace the goals we're trying to achieve."

"It's the people who don't share your views you have to be concerned about," Jake said bitterly, finding it difficult to disengage himself from the cynicism he felt.

"If there's any possibility of saving the planet, of making the lives of everyone that much better, then we would be derelict in not even trying to make such a thing possible simply because the risks were too high."

"Is that you talking, or is it Jacob?" Jake looked away. "I just don't want you and your friends getting hurt."

Destiny studied Jake's face, once again seeming to probe his inner being. "A moment ago, you asked me if I was happy existing in a place you perceive as being unaffected by the outside world." Her words flowed softly, mellifluously. "There is a connectedness that you don't see…that I wouldn't expect you to see-"

Jake cut her off, unable to suppress his growing frustration any longer. "You'd be surprised by some of the things I've seen. It would horrify you." He suddenly caught himself, ashamed of how harsh his words must have sounded. In a gentler tone, he added, "Take my word for it, you'll be exposing yourself to dangers you never even imagined."

Destiny's calm air remained unchanged. "What we see can often be deceptive. An object floating on the ocean surface can sometimes have a submerged portion that lays hidden and extends very deep. Eventually you will find that many of the things most visible to you are nothing more than illusions."

"The danger I'm talking about is no illusion. It's very real."

"There is also much good in the world," Destiny countered patiently.

"Yeah," Jake agreed halfheartedly. "But unfortunately, I don't see enough of it going around."

Destiny glanced over at Hermes and Hercules as they swam over to join Achilles, then turned back to regard Jake with balmy, enchanting eyes and the trace of a knowing smile. "Just because you're not able to see or feel something doesn't mean it's not there."

Jake wanted to tell her he only believed what he could see or experience with his other senses, but he pulled up short of saying so, aware that Destiny had lifted a hand to his temple. He lost sight of his thoughts, feeling oddly relaxed by the solace of her touch. The scent of wildflowers wafting down from the upper ledges seemed suddenly stronger, making him light-headed. He had slept somewhat fitfully the night before, and a bout of drowsiness seemed to be creeping up on him, leaving him momentarily speechless. With heavy eyelids, he was vaguely conscious of a soothing, melodious warbling coming from the nearby dolphins. The trilling commingled with the chirping of the songbirds filling the air. Lulled by the sound, he gazed dazedly, letting himself drift into the deepening pools of Destiny's eyes. Like a cloud of mist, they engulfed him. A feeling suggestive of the healing he had undergone two days earlier accosted him, accompanied by something even more profound than before.

A voice reminiscent of Destiny's and the ululations of Achilles, Hermes, and Hercules seemed to echo across the cosmos in a soft, comforting whisper. "Conjoined with the minds of my friends, here, I am able see and feel something far bigger than any one of us, something beautiful that has given us special purpose. We have a duty, an obligation to fulfill…there are things we were meant to do. Turning away from this responsibility would be tantamount to a grave injustice, one that would leave only misery in its wake."

Jake had difficulty responding, overcome by the somnolence rapidly consuming him. "Misery already exists everywhere," he murmured, the words spilling lethargically from his mouth like thick maple syrup. "Here in Haiti…it…is…especially….baaad."

"Then we must look to change it," the foursome chorused soothingly.

Jake stared mesmerized. Lying behind the words was a rainbow. Intrigued, he reached out to grab it, but came away with nothing. Confused, he tried to re-orientate his ethereal being and latch onto it again, only to find his hands come up empty a second time.

Do not try to grab the rainbow, Jay Jay! It was Achilles speaking to him. *You will never be able to hold onto it.*

It's right there! Jake insisted. *I see it!* Stubbornly he reached for it again, disregarding what Achilles was telling him.

If you think about it, Jay Jay, you will realize rainbows have no distinct location, nor distance. Paradoxically, they do have a direction. A rainbow is really a phenomenon, a good example of the duality all phenomena exhibit. In one sense, a rainbow certainly seems real, appearing as an arc of brightly colored concentric stripes, but in another sense it does not really exist because it is a by-product of light and the prismatic properties of mist.

But light is a form of energy, Jake pointed out, *comprised of electromagnetic waves. Isn't electromagnetic energy real?*

Relative to the perceptions of the sentience perceiving it, yes, Achilles agreed. *Condensed energy forms matter, and a particular pattern of matter lays the foundation for the building blocks of life. It is this wellspring of energy that gives the universe structure, an infinite realm of superimposed dimensionality in which all living organisms are part of the whole, including humans. In their current state of evolutionary development, most humans are able to perceive only an infinitesimal portion of the energy grid that comprises creation in its entirety. Because of this, it is difficult for your species to embrace the full spectrum of beauty that embodies nature. All living things are an integral part of this spectrum, interdependent on the other energy bodies.*

Jake realized the rainbow had vanished, replaced by the painting he had seen Achilles create. As he studied it, a heightened awareness took hold of his senses. *These paintings are very much like portals, aren't they?* he found himself asking, although he was certain he already knew the answer. *They give some of us a fleeting glimpse of the universal energy grid, a subtle sense of the big picture.*

You are very perceptive, Jay Jay, Achilles said. *Though we did not consciously intend for it to happen, it turns out our art can be used as a tool. For those it affects, it allows them to look deep within in order to see beyond themselves. We surmise we subconsciously embed a higher mathematics in the overall composition formed by the various colored paints that are given form and texture by the brush strokes.*

Albert Einstein tried to give mankind a simplistic picture of the universe through mathematics, Jake replied.

This time it was the voice of Hermes who answered. *Yes, Einstein was one of your great thinkers. He understood man's limitations in his perception of the world around him, believing reality to be an illusion, albeit a very persistent one. According to him, man experiences himself, his thoughts and feelings, as something separate and disconnected from other things and phenomena…a kind of optical delusion of his consciousness. This delusion imprisons him, restricting him to a personal affectation for only a few people near him. But Einstein also saw that man could free himself from this prison by widening his sphere of compassion.*

What led him to that conclusion?

Einstein believed interdependence to be a fundamental law of nature. Without compassion for all living organisms, the human species cannot possibly grasp the interconnectedness of all things. Feeling genuine compassion means wanting others to be free of suffering. Without compassion, humans are prone to focus on the distinct differences and individuality of other life forms and objects instead of seeing the integrated whole. All things on this planet are interrelated. The oceans, clouds, forests, mountains, and flowers are part of a system that is really one. *Everything survives through an interaction of subtle patterns of energy, causing phenomena to arise that are also connected with this dependence. Nothing exists separate from the whole, for if it did, it would quickly decay and dissolve. To believe ourselves as existing independent and autonomous from everything else is out of accord with true reality. Einstein saw through the illusion, knowing that such thinking lay outside the bounds of ultimate wisdom.*

But modern science has already discovered this interdependence, Jake argued. *Fields of study like oceanography, ecology, and eco-biology have made considerable advances in recent years.*

Your claim is valid, Hermes capitulated. *But unfortunately, the vast majority of humankind still remains detached and aloof of these facts in spite of acquiring such knowledge. The callous disregard for the environment shown by the most pernicious elements of your species is frightening. You only have to look at the damage your civilization has wrought on the earth by making the petroleum-based fuels your primary energy source. Even though humans are aware that burning such fuel can cause global warming and acid rain, most turn a blind eye to the harm done. Only by instilling compassion will they fully realize the consequences of their actions, the wrong they have committed. Bad deeds and, in some cases, even bad intentions have a way of coming back full circle on the entity responsible for it.*

So this is your mission, to broaden mankind's compassion?

Among other things.

Einstein tried to unify all the forces of nature in one simple equation and failed, Jake felt it necessary to say. *Have your kind also made such an attempt?*

Hermes did not immediately respond.

Jake grew impatient and tried to coax an answer from the albino. *With those superior brains, I have to assume all of you have tried.*

Hermes hesitated a moment longer before answering. *Just as Einstein had failed, so have we.*

But you must have gotten closer than Einstein to solving this mystery?

The puff of a collective sigh seemed to brush up against Jake's mind. *Mathematics is a nexus to the eternal beyond,* Hermes explained. *In its purest form, it is a bridge between visible and hidden worlds, a means of turning the mind away from transitory physical perceptions of matter which is really illusionary and leading it to the contemplation of truly existing constants that never change. Another of your great thinkers, Pythagoras, understood this. From our perspective, mathematical thought is the language of the divinity that resides deep within the consciousness of all sentient beings, a form of inner communion. This language makes use of abstractions that correspond to nothing in one's experience. It is a vehicle for transcending the world of illusion into a realm of universals, drawing the soul towards a domain of higher being. In using it to its fullest, the thinker must learn to feel this thought in a reverent way if he or she is to become one with the eternal. The thinker must be able to cast off all beliefs and biases, striving for an emptiness that lies beyond duality.*

Jake tried to grasp the wisdom being imparted to him. *What do you mean by emptiness?*

Emptiness is a melting away of the ego, the self. It was now the group talking in a collective voice. *It is a purified state of mind that rids itself of the qualities we normally assign to reality. In such a state, what we usually identify as normal perception is contradicted, replaced with no attachment to any preconception of what truth may ultimately prove to be. It is a frame of arcane ignorance, a final state of perfection in which the thinker is possessed by the ultimate truth, rather than the ultimate truth being possessed by the thinker.*

A clarity of mind the likes of which Jake had never before experienced suddenly gripped him, awakening him to a feeling of inner calm and happiness he had never known. He let the sensation wash over him, wallowing in its glow before continuing with the discussion. *So by failing to achieve complete emptiness, you're not able to mathematically unify the known forces of the universe?*

That is correct! Achieving absolute emptiness might be analogous to exceeding the speed of light in the four-dimensional universe your human brain normally perceives.

I'm not sure I follow you.

If your mind is already restrained with Einstein's premise that such a speed cannot be surpassed, then going beyond light speed in a realm consisting of only four dimensions, three of space and one of time, is impossible.

But Einstein mathematically proved its validity, that the speed of light was a universal constant.

Yes, he did. Referenced to a four-dimensional time-space universe, his logic was sound. But tied to a system consisting of higher dimensionality, such logic is flawed.

One of Jake's conversations with Jacob came flooding back. *Jacob is convinced higher dimensions actually exist, that what we believe to be reality is really a subspace of a much greater realm. He believes all of you are capable of seeing beyond this subspace when you're linked together collectively. Is this true?*

We are able to attain instances of exceptional insight into the true reality that pulses all about us, yes. Sometimes we are able to arrive at conclusions that are not just probable, but undeniable. On such occasions we soar to a place that is eternal, unified, and never varies. In such a place our sense of certainty is unlimited.

Yet, in unison, you're unable to achieve a state of absolute emptiness.

Yes. While it is possible to approach it asymptotically, we never quite get there.

Why is that?

Our motivations are not sufficiently pure. Our compassion for your species falls short of being utterly self-disregarding, and our seeking of ultimate truth is tainted with bias.

What kind of bias? In asking the question, Jake sensed a subtle change in the minds surrounding him.

We still believe in the good that lies within mankind.

Jake pondered what was being revealed to him, but quickly gave up, realizing he was trying to ponder the imponderable. These intelligences were endowed with a wisdom far more advanced than he.

We would like to show you something, the group said, interrupting Jake's perplexity.

What's that?

Achilles' painting floated before Jake's eyes again. *Do not try to make sense of what you see before you for the moment.*

For one fleeting instant, Jake perceived he was seeing beyond infinity. An upwelling of something suddenly came flowing from a singular point that he sensed to be the back side of a black hole, growing in luminosity and oscillating harmonically as it wended its way toward him. Tendrils of it shot out to loop around his being, imparting an overwhelming, yet vaguely familiar warmth that took his breath away.

The emission you perceive is composed of the true essence of hyperspace. It is what gives matter pattern and form.

Caught in its grip, Jake felt rarefied, barely able to gasp out his next question. *Is it pure energy I'm seeing?*

Look closer, Jay Jay! Feel it for what it is!

Baffled, Jake continued to stare. *If it's not energy, then what am I sensing?*

It is the very thing that binds the totality of nature, the unifying force that connects everything in existence.

The lucidity that suddenly struck Jake slapped up against him like a wave crashing against a levee. Dumbstruck, he realized he was sensing pure love. Aware that he was now linked to the minds surrounding him, he felt his base consciousness rekindled, the part of him that was intrinsically pure and unpolluted with blinding presumption. There was harmony here, a synchronous joining of spirits in which one consciousness hovered at the center of the globular cluster, the focal point about which the others spiralled. Drawn to the gravity well, he fell into orbit, feeling the tug of the glowing astral body that was Destiny.

A rapid dawning began to impinge on Jake's awareness, and he instinctively grasped the nature of the things he was seeing. The laws of physics were different here. Gravity assaulted him from multiple directions simultaneously, pulling and pushing in such a way as to cancel out the combined effect. He wasn't really moving at all. Time had no meaning where he presently floated, that is, if he could call it floating. As best he could tell, he found himself entwined in a vast dodecahedron, a volume of space bounded by twelve planes extending to infinity where they intersected.

Enraptured, Jake felt his being reasserting itself much like the sun reemerging from the clouds to overlook the landscape that had previously remained obscured. He now understood the power of healing, the awesome nature of the energy coursing through him. Properly evoked and channelled, it could mend the mind as well as the body. This was the stuff that caused what most humans deemed as miracles, phenomena that contravened normal occurrences in the subspace his lower mind had come to know. But miracles were actually shadows of phenomena from dimensions above that intruded into everyday experience. In this current realm, miracles were not impossible. In this place miracles didn't transgress any physical laws. Unconditional love was the luminous side of the cosmos, the positive energy that made all things possible, its purity able to strip away the physical deceptions that trick the unenlightened senses. Like sweet harmonious music, it filled the heavens, resonating between the stars with an astounding number of keys. It was so clear to him. Here was an ally, offering its limitless vibratory tones to the enlightened composer. How the composer chose to play those keys would influence the world, setting off chain reactions of cause and effect.

Jake was suddenly jolted by one particular bit of insight. *You can see the future from here, can't you?*

The answer that came back was encouraging, though not absolute. *Sometimes, but most future outcomes are too shrouded in mist to be predetermined.*

With utter joy, Jake turned back to ask another question, but as he did so the dodecahedron shrunk into a galaxy that spiraled away beyond his reach. Caught off guard by this unexpected event, he groped at nothingness, feeling stranded and helpless in the midst of the great void. Cut off from the light, he plunged headlong into the darkness that formed the negative half of creation, vaguely aware of the voice echoing back at him in recession. Overcome with despair, he listened as it faded toward the far side of existence.

Do not let the darkness deceive your senses, for it can easily lay the foundation for foolish presumption, the voice warned. *There is a danger in such presumption. It has a self-fulfilling power.*

Something nudged him gently from behind, and as he twisted around to investigate the cause of it, he found himself staring up into Destiny's face.

The girl seemed amused. "You fell asleep."

"How long was I out?" Jake said groggily.

"Not long. Just a few minutes. I thought it best to let you get some rest, but you started thrashing around and I decided to wake you."

"Sorry for conking out on you. That was pretty rude of me." Sitting back up, Jake realized the entire pod had assembled just off the shore, their permanent smiles turned in his direction. As he stared back, fragments of the dream tingled his thoughts like the ghosts of a distant memory. In that moment, he wondered if it had been a dream at all.

Through his informant in the U.S. Coast Guard, Sebastian Ortega had learned there would be no overflights of the island on this day. From past experience, he knew such information was highly reliable. Nonetheless, he kept a vigilant eye for the approach of any cutters or aircraft as the Bell Ranger set down at the prearranged landing site for the second time in the past fifty-six hours.

Hastily, Ortega jumped from the aircraft and scrambled over to the spot Omar had designated for exchanging messages. As the main rotors continued to beat the air behind him, he glanced in all directions. Satisfied that nobody was currently lurking about, he lifted the stone situated against the base of a nearby tree. Lifting the lid on the metal container that lay beneath, a scrap of paper awaited him. Snatching the paper, he stuffed it into a pocket before inserting his own note, then closed the lid and replaced the stone. Scanning his surroundings one more time, he got back aboard the helicopter and buckled himself in as the pilot pulled the collective. Within minutes, the island was well behind them as Fernando guided the aircraft directly for Port-au-Prince where the *San Carlo* still lay at anchor in the harbor.

Pulling the paper from his pocket, Ortega unfolded the note, his eyes roving hungrily over the contents. Several seconds went by before his face broke out in a malicious grin. Omar had come through for him. Carefully, he read the note again before resting his gaze on the numbers at the bottom of the message. Scrawled in red ink were the latitude and longitude of the place where his attacker had gone following the firefight.

Unable to contain his growing excitement, he reached for a chart of the Haitian coastline and unfolded it, tracing with a finger where the lines of reference met. Without him being aware of it, his jaw hung open at what he saw. To make sure he hadn't made a mistake, he rechecked the location, making sure his eyes weren't deceiving him. No. It was right there. The coordinates fell just a short distance below the small circle he had penciled in on the chart earlier. Though this was actually good news, he found it eerily strange that the rendezvous point given him by one of Ternier's men was so close to where he might find his quarry.

Ortega was almost tempted to have Fernando change course, swinging more to the east where a quick recon of the area could be made. But as he thought about it, he realized such a move might prove too shortsighted by taking away all element of surprise, and surprise was something he needed if he was going to capture the girl and those strange white dolphins he had seen. Performing an overflight might tip his hand, alerting those people that another attack would be forthcoming. In addition, it was important he get back to the *San Carlo* right away. The electronic Gatling gun had been delivered, and Fernando would need the remainder of the day and a portion of the night to get the weapon system fully retrofitted to the Bell Ranger.

As they continued to head south, Ortega could not keep the smile off his face. The revenge he had been hoping for was now becoming a certainty.

Chapter 2

$\mathcal{F}$ or most of the afternoon, Jake prepared the *Avenging Angel* for an early morning departure, checking and rechecking diving gear as well as weaponry. With what he had so far experienced near Navassa Island, taking the necessary defensive measures was his top priority. If they were attacked again, he would be ready. Earlier on, Destiny had left him to attend to personal matters, but already he missed her company.

Using the trawler's skiff, he had Zimbola, Hector, and Phillipe make several trips to the falls where they filled five 20-gallon canisters with fresh water each time, eventually topping off the potable water tanks aboard the *Angel*. Upon completing the task, they then assisted Grahm and his assistants in bringing back aboard the equipment the scientist had brought ashore.

Satisfied that everything was in full readiness, Jake cooled off by taking a swim, eventually angling toward the beach. On the way in, Achilles joined him, staying by his side until he was hip deep in water. As he waded onto the beach, Jacob came over to greet him.

"I would like to show you something," the Haitian said.

"You've shown me quite a bit already," Jake replied.

Jacob nodded, his expression serious. "It may seem to you that we are isolated from the rest of the world here in Gaia, that keeping current with world affairs is not possible."

Jake stared, wondering what Jacob was getting at. "Now that you mention it, the thought has occurred to me."

Jacob looked in the direction of his tiny dwelling. "I have at my disposal something that allows me access to all types of information."

"Like what?"

"If you will come with me, I will show you?"

Abruptly, Jacob turned and began walking. Overcome with curiosity, Jake followed. Stacks of books, magazines, and periodicals cluttered Jacob's cottage. The Haitian moved some of these things aside to reveal a laptop computer. "While this might appear to be a typical computer, I can assure you it is not."

Jake studied the contrivance, looking for oddities. A mass of wires and electronic components seemed to spill from the rear of the device, appearing to terminate in two dissimilar cables that extended to the ceiling of the abode where they disappeared through the thatched roof. "What makes it so special?"

Jacob allowed himself a wry little smile. "These dolphins have an exceptional grasp of modern electronics and computer technology. They have modified the hardware and circuitry comprising this computer. They have also taken the internal programming and made it more efficient. With this device, I can access the worldwide Internet where I can peruse any information of my choosing."

Jake studied the assemblage of parts. "Are you telling me they rewired this thing?"

"Yes."

"How do you power it?"

The smile on Jacob's face broadened. "Sunlight provides the necessary power."

Jake felt his jaw dropping. "You have a solar collector on the roof?"

"Not on the roof," Jacob said, staring up at the ceiling as if seeing beyond it. "At the top of these cliffs." He touched the thinner cable with a finger. "This cable attaches to the solar array and provides the electrical energy that powers the computer. The other cable connects with a transceiver that allows wireless Internet access."

"Very impressive," Jake uttered.

"Would you like to see how quickly the system is able to boot?" Without waiting for an answer, Jacob pressed one of the buttons on the keyboard. In less than three seconds, the screen showed the computer was fully engaged and ready for processing.

Jake was stunned. "I've never seen a laptop boot so quickly."

"From here, I can research any subject, keying the topic of my choice into the available search engines. At this point, the device functions like any other wireless laptop, only it processes at a much higher speed."

Jake lifted his eyes to scrutinize Jacob's face. "Why are you showing me this?"

The Haitian paused, drawing in breath. "I wanted you to see the exceptional genius of these creatures."

"They've pretty much demonstrated that to me already," Jake conceded.

"Yes, but their minds are like sponges. They are able to absorb the fundamentals behind any type of technology and then refine it further. Imagine what they can do for mankind."

Jake let out a dubious laugh. "I can imagine a lot. It's what some segments of mankind can and probably will do for them that troubles me." He shook his head sadly. "Governments all over the world would love to get their hands on these protégés of yours once they learn what they're capable of. First and foremost, they would regard these creatures as potential military assets, to be used as they saw fit. Dr. Grahm has already told me about a man who tried to take possession of Natalie back in the states. He thinks that man was affiliated with the U.S. Navy. What happened yesterday is only the tip of the iceberg. I would think that should be enough to convince you that there are people out there who will stop at nothing in order to capture these dolphins."

"These creatures are well aware of the risks that face them," Jacob said dryly.

The statement had a familiar ring, and Jake suddenly remembered Destiny telling him the same thing. "Are they? I don't think they've seen enough of man's dark side to make such an assessment."

The shadow of a smile rippled across Jacob's features. "That is why they have chosen you."

Jake gaped in disbelief. "Chosen me for what? There's nothing I can do for them that would amount to much. I'm just an average Joe trying to make his way in the world like everyone else."

"On the contrary, Mr. Javolyn. You have already shown yourself to be anything but average. Perhaps they see you as their champion, their protector."

"If that's the case, then their expectations of me are way too high. I'm just one man, a little guy without much in the way of resources to combat the forces that will ultimately come after them."

Jacob gave a commiserating nod. "Sometimes circumstances arise that are seemingly beyond our control, making us feel insignificant when we see what we are up against. Nevertheless, these same circumstances often dictate our true calling whether we like it or not."

"They've got me pegged all wrong. I'm not the guy they think I am."

"Then you would abandon them in their time of need?"

Though said softly, Jake perceived the question to be more of an appeal, almost as if Jacob knew it would hit a sensitive nerve within him. "I," he began to say, but quickly realized he had no answer within him worth giving at the moment. Flustered, he groped for a way out of the corner Jacob had trapped him in. "These creatures are far smarter than me. I would think they're clever enough to come up with defensive measures much more sophisticated than my meager Stone Age methods."

Jacob stared back quietly, a deep abiding intelligence residing behind his weathered exterior. "Do you remember the place they let you see?"

"The place south of here?"

Jacob sighed deeply. "No. I'm talking about a place where the laws of physics as we know them do not apply."

Abruptly, the dream Jake had experienced came flooding back. Stunned by the implication, he had trouble finding his tongue. "It wasn't a dream, was it?"

Jacob's reply came slowly. "No."

"Then you've also experienced it?"

Though Jacob's outward demeanor manifested graveness, an underlying kindness seemed to be lurking just below the surface. "Yes, I have also been there," he acknowledged reverently. His eyes glinted with the memory of wonder. "It is a place that only a few of us have been fortunate enough to see." He studied Jake closely, letting the revelation take root before continuing. "Do you know why these dolphins have taken to you?"

Having no answer, Jake could only shrug.

"They see a kindred soul, a being not unlike themselves."

All at once, the spell Jacob had cast was suddenly broken, replaced by a cloud of guilt. "Then they're wrong," Jake retorted. "I was a soldier. People have died because of me. I've killed more than a few. Unlike me, these creatures are incapable of hurting anyone."

Jacob smiled warmly. "Yet you are a man who has no reservations about coming to the aid of someone in danger, a person who will place the lives of others above his own."

Such praise made Jake feel uncomfortable. "You give me far too much credit. If anything, the things I did were nothing more than knee jerk reactions to the situations at hand. Unfortunately, I gave little thought to the consequences of those actions. As I told you before, my actions have probably compromised the safety of this place, doing far more harm than good."

"Then Destiny and these dolphins will need you all the more," Jacob persisted.

With Jacob's imploring eyes resting on him, Jake felt oddly defenseless. "I have several commitments which cannot be ignored," he said, looking to escape the way the Haitian was pressing him. "Dr. Grahm is one of those commitments. As you know, tomorrow I sail back to Navassa to search out a sunken vessel he believes is his. Both you and Destiny are welcome to come with us. I have additional space aboard the *Angel* that can accommodate the two of you."

Jacob's expression turned somber. "Thank you for the invitation, but I have business of my own which also cannot be ignored. Perhaps Destiny will accompany you, though I cannot speak for her."

Jake felt a need for further appeasement. "If that offer you made earlier is still open, I would like to see these other *thurentra* you mentioned."

"Achilles will show them to you."

To Jake, the connotation was clear. Achilles would be going with him in any event. Strangely, he liked the idea. He was growing used to the albino's company. "Tell me," he said, looking back down at the modified laptop, "have these dolphins provided you with any other innovations?"

A subtle brightening in Jacob's manner seemed to take place. "Let me show you," he beckoned, moving toward the door and leading Jake to the rear of the dwelling. Pulling back a large tarp, he exposed a dozen identical steel cylinders, each nearly five feet in height. Connected to the cylinders was a jumble of tubing of varying diameters that joined with other components, some of them pressure gauges. The Haitian said nothing as Jake studied the array of equipment.

Jake raised an eyebrow and looked over at Jacob. "Compressed air?"

Jacob shook his head. "Hydrogen gas! A second pipe tees off the one that feeds the cooking grill. It runs under the sand before connecting with the system you see before you. As the gas trickles in, it is compressed and stored in these cylinders."

Jake stared perplexed. "Where's the compressor?"

An amused smile was evident on Jacob's face. "The heavy machinery normally required for pressurizing gas is not needed here."

Jake eyed the system skeptically. "But how is that possible?"

"To be honest with you, I do not completely understand how it works myself. The dolphins have developed a process that utilizes nanotechnology at its core." Jacob pointed to one particular fixture. "It is here that the hydrogen gas is first subjected to a magnetic field where it is polarized, inducing Van der Waal forces within the molecules."

"I've heard the term before," Jake interrupted, "but I'd appreciate it if you'd refresh my memory as to exactly what a Van der Waal force is?"

"It is the weakest type of intermolecular force, caused by a skewed symmetry in the electron configuration of atoms. Once polarized, the molecules of a gas attract each other like magnets, though the effect lasts only a fraction of a second."

"I assume this makes the gas temporarily denser."

"Yes. By polarizing the gas, it is being prepared for what comes next." Drawing his finger further along the tubing, he indicated another component, this one appearing like a cone-shaped frustum. "This is the heart of the system. It is here the polarized gas passes through a specially fabricated filter. The filter has a nanostructure that further alters the configuration of the molecules, greatly magnifying the Van der Waals forces within them. This force draws the molecules much closer together so that they come out the other side of the filter in a liquefied state. The filter channels the hydrogen in only one direction and is able to withstand the huge pressure differential that gradually builds on opposite sides of it, because once the gas is on the downstream side, the binding forces immediately weaken and the hydrogen changes back over to a gas."

The filtering device held Jake's attention. "The dolphins fabricated the filter?"

"Grown would actually be a better description of how the filter is made," Jacob clarified. "The material that comprises the filter was grown in the sea."

Jake could only nod as he continued to marvel over the relative simplicity of the setup. Though he understood little about nanotechnology, he had read enough on the subject to know that the essential properties of matter were determined at the nanoscale where the atomic structure of substances could be customized to behave a certain way.

"What about the power needed to operate the system?"

"Same as before. Energy from the photovoltaic solar collectors on the cliff above provides the necessary power. Surprisingly, the system does not require much in the way of energy to work."

"Where did you get the solar collectors?" Jake asked.

Jacob smiled again. "The solar collectors are also unique in that, they too, were grown in the sea. Most photovoltaic cells on the market today are highly inefficient, typically converting only about five percent of the sunlight impinging on them into electrical energy. The material the dolphins have grown is able to convert better than forty percent of the sunlight hitting it into electricity."

Jake shifted his gaze to the cylinders. "What do you do with the bottled hydrogen?"

"Believe it or not, I give most of it away," Jacob replied.

"To be used how?"

Jacob let out a deep sigh. "For most Haitians, getting electricity on a routine basis is problematic in this country. In Saint-Marc and Gonaives, there are several cantinas that receive the bottled hydrogen every few days. The gas powers generators that have been specifically modified to burn hydrogen."

"I see," Jake said. "So these establishments don't have to rely on electricity coming from Haiti's power grid for their electrical needs?"

"That is correct." Jacob grinned. "Examples of the dolphin art you observed earlier are showcased in those cantinas. A deal has been made with the proprietors to keep those paintings on permanent display if they are to keep receiving the hydrogen."

Jake's admiration for the Haitian escalated a few more degrees as he thought about what the man was trying to accomplish. "Have you ever considered setting up a web site on the Internet for displaying the dolphin art?" he suggested. "I would think you could reach a much broader audience if you did that."

"It has already been done," Jacob declared, his expression reverting back to solemnity once again. Lifting the tarp, he placed it back over the gas cylinders and the system that filled them.

A sense of guilt continued to grip Jake as he watched Jacob secure the tarp. "I'll be sailing at first light tomorrow. If you should change your mind about coming, the offer still stands."

Jacob looked away, directing his gaze elsewhere. "As I said, Mr. Javolyn, I have duties that will require my attention."

Jake turned to leave but stopped short. "Would you do me a favor?"

"That will depend on what you ask of me."

"Please call me Jay Jay. Those whom I consider friends call me that."

Jacob abruptly turned and scrutinized him for several seconds. "Obligations often accompany friendships. Are you certain you want me to be your friend?"

As Jake stared back, he realized the Haitian did not take such a relationship lightly. "Yeah," he finally said. "I'm sure."

It wasn't until much later in the day that Jake decided to visit the outer reef beyond the cove. Towed along by Achilles, he was able to locate enough lobsters to feed everyone at dinner, stuffing nine of the crustaceans into the catch bag he had brought with him. While holding onto Achilles during the return trip, Jake removed the snorkel from his mouth, taking the opportunity to converse with the albino.

"Jacob showed me some of the inventions developed by your pod," Jake said. "They were quite impressive."

Achilles reduced his speed, coming almost to a halt. "We have other concepts that will eventually gain embodiment in fully functioning prototypes," the juvenile trilled back.

"Like what?"

"All will be revealed in good time."

"Jacob tells me you'll be going to Navassa Island with me."

"Yes, Jay Jay, I will follow your vessel."

"I don't suppose it will do any good to talk you out of it. As you've already discovered, Navassa is a dangerous place." Carrying on a conversation with the dolphin no longer seemed strange to Jake, though he perceived the albino's trilling speech to be somewhat childlike and incompatible with the extraordinary intelligence behind it. To him, Achilles' profound wisdom made the juvenile seem far older than his years would suggest.

"There is a path to be taken no matter what perils exist along the way."

Achilles' response was just as Jake had expected. Readjusting his grip on the dolphin's dorsal fin, he said, "Will the rest of the pod be coming?"

"Yes, Jay Jay."

"What about Destiny?"

"She will also be with us."

The news brought a sense of relief to Jake. He would much rather have her with him than leave her behind. As it was, the cove's sanctity had been compromised and, with him gone, would be vulnerable to intrusion by unwelcome parties. This particular thought made him think of the gold that lay hidden within the tiny realm, and he suddenly found it necessary to ask the dolphin another question. "There is something I must know, Achilles."

"You want to know why Jacob rejects the very things most of your species covets."

"You're reading my mind again," Jake said. He wasn't sure if he liked this. It made him feel violated.

"Your thoughts tend to be very powerful at times, Jay Jay. I seem to be naturally attuned to receiving them."

Jake wasn't sure if this was a statement of fact or an apology.

"Jacob sees such things as money and power as corruptive influences on one's moral rectitude," Achilles went on. "While they are a means to an end, they have no true value. To Jacob, only knowledge that is used unselfishly holds true value. Some of your greatest thinkers maintained this view. Albert Einstein was one such person who held no desire for material riches. For him, finding the answers to universal mysteries was his form of self-enrichment. And like Einstein, Jacob also believes that reality can only be grasped through pure thought."

"But Einstein's matter-energy equivalence led to the development of the atomic bomb," Jake found it necessary to point out. "By sharing this knowledge with the rest of the world, the consequences of the act proved to be a detriment to the entire planet."

"Einstein was not responsible for how the knowledge was used. He was averse to unleashing nuclear energy for destructive purposes. It is not nuclear weapons that kill, but the sentience using it."

"I can't argue that point," Jake concurred. He thought about Jacob's philanthropic goals. "Do you really believe the pod's plan for a sea colony will work?"

"From a financial perspective, yes. Already we have amassed enough of the metals humankind deems as precious to make it possible. Such a resource will provide us with more than enough options with which to carry out the objectives we have established for ourselves."

"I assume you'll also grow much of what you'll need in the sea."

"Your assumption is a good one, Jay Jay. Once we get beyond the initial startup costs, the ocean will provide the sea colony with everything it will require for it to be fully self-sufficient and autonomous."

"I only have one suggestion to-".

Achilles cut him off before he could complete the sentence. "You think we should put our minds to developing defensive systems for protection."

"I wish you'd stop doing that," Jake objected. "I find it rather discomforting having my thoughts thrown back at me before I'm able to utter them."

"I am truly sorry if I have offended you, Jay Jay," Achilles apologized, "but your thoughts sometimes come to me as though you have already spoken them. From this moment onward I will try to be more mindful of your wishes."

Jake sighed. "Forget it, okay." Hefting the catch bag above the water, he gestured toward the lobsters it held and grinned. "I'm starting to get hungry, my friend, and these little critters have an overdue appointment with a pot of boiling water."

Achilles let out a sound Jake could have sworn was a laugh. "That is the one thing about your species to which I have never grown accustomed."

"And what would that be?"

"Your need to cook the food you consume."

"Hey," Jake said in mock protest, "if you haven't tried it, don't knock it."

The juvenile emitted the analog of a snicker. "What makes you think I have not?"

Rendered speechless by Achilles' unexpected response, Jake had to hold on tight as the albino suddenly forged ahead and shot for the cove.

Chapter 3

The trip back to Navassa Island had gone without incident, with the most difficult part of the journey occurring at the outset. With the tide in his favor and the dolphins marking the way through the narrow passage in the reef, Jake had managed to keep the *Avenging Angel's* hull clear of the coral that lay in wait on both sides of the channel. Sea conditions had been especially cooperative, with virtually no wind to stir the ocean and a diluted azure sky welcoming onward both the vessel and its escort of white dolphins. At Jake's urging, Destiny had chosen to come aboard rather than ride Hercules, dividing her time between him and Grahm as Zimby took over at the helm.

Ten miles out to sea, the *Angel* had overtaken a 35-foot open boat making its way slowly to the north, its gunwales forced dangerously low in the water from the ponderous cargo it held. The sight was nothing new to Jake. Since coming to Haiti, he had seen many such vessels overflowing with Haitian migrants looking to escape the wretched poverty of their homeland. In looking upon the grave faces staring up at him, he knew their chances of reaching Florida's mainland were slim. As it was, their boat was unstable and would be prone to swamping or capsizing in the face of rising winds. And if the sea didn't take them, interception by the U.S. Coast Guard was another obstacle in their path. Feeling empathy toward the boat's passengers, Jake had watched it recede far behind as the white cliffs of Navassa gradually drew closer.

Upon nearing the island, no other vessels were in sight as Natalie scooted out in front of the *Angel's* bow, showing where the boat should be positioned if Grahm was to find the remnants of his old sloop. The fact that Natalie still remembered the exact location of the sunken sailboat astounded Jake, and as the *Angel's* anchor was being set, he couldn't help but wonder if such an expectation might be just a little overly optimistic. But then again, their present position was matching the coordinates Grahm had given him. With that in mind, he quickly suited up and, donning a scuba bottle, dropped over the side of the swim platform, eager to see what awaited him on the bottom. Aside from the dolphins, he would be the only one to make the initial dive on the wreck. Basically, he wanted to keep his stay near the island as limited as possible. Though Navassa and its surrounding waters were closed to visitors, Grahm had in his possession a valid permit issued by the U.S. Fish and Wildlife Service for performing scientific studies on the local ecosystem.

For Jake, diving under conditions of dead calm was extremely rare, and as Achilles swooped in to tow him to the sea floor, he took note of his surroundings. The ocean appeared to be composed of glazed glass, giving off a glossy sheen of variegated colors predominantly comprised of indigo and turquoise. A mid-morning sun hung in a cloudless blue sky, adding to the tranquility as it reflected off the mirror-like surface that was unmarred by wind or tide.

With Achilles pulling him downward, he glanced up, marveling at what he saw. At a depth of sixty feet, the air-water interface above appeared like a sheet of thin ice with a boat trapped motionless in its grip. As he descended deeper, he discerned Natalie and two other members of the pod hovering just above a bottom profuse with life. Colonies of healthy coral abounded everywhere, providing a craggy backdrop upon which multitudes of reef fishes darted and thrived. Drawn closer to the other dolphins, he suddenly became aware of a sunken vessel lying on its side, its hull and deck almost unrecognizable beneath a heavy blanket of encrusting coral and sponges.

Releasing his hold on Achilles, Jake swam alongside the vessel, trying to estimate its overall size. Dense groupings of damselfish and wrasses scattered at his approach, with several large parrotfish appearing unperturbed by his presence as they continued to feed on live coral. After a minute's worth of inspection, he was convinced he was looking at the remains of a sloop, though it was evident the boat's mast had been torn away. Floating adjacent to a section of railing encrusted with fire coral, he checked his depth gauge, noting that it read ninety-five feet. Adjusting his face mask, he gazed up toward the surface. A massive school of barracuda drifted lazily above him, the sheer magnitude of numbers giving the appearance of a passing storm cloud. Barely discernable above, the silhouette of the *Angel's* hull could be seen, draped by streaming shafts of sunlight that penetrated the depths like fat laser beams. As Jake stared, the cloud of barracuda abruptly parted, giving way to a creature of considerable size. Hercules had come to join him with Destiny clinging to his back. At his current depth, Jake was amazed that the girl was not wearing a scuba rig.

Turning back to the task at hand, Jake unclipped from his harness the chipping hammer he had brought with him. Subjected to almost four atmospheres of ambient pressure at his present depth, he had little time to waste. The maximum bottom time he would be afforded without having to undergo decompression would be limited to twenty-five minutes.

With practiced efficiency, he glided to the vessel's fantail and went to work, hacking away at the horny material stubbornly adhering to the hull. Within minutes he was able to expose the bronze nameplate Grahm had described. He had brought several other tools with him, one of them being a small crowbar with a wire brush taped to it. With this, he brushed away the softer growth, running a gloved hand over the plate's raised lettering. Satisfied with what he read, he inserted the tip of the crowbar behind the plate and applied leverage. He had barely begun to pull hard when one of the fastening bolts gave way. Jimmying the bar behind the plate in other locations, he was able to snap several more bolts until it hung loosely. Giving the bar one final yank, the plate came free, upon which Achilles rushed in, snatching it with one of his prehensile appendages before it could sink to the bottom. Abruptly, the juvenile turned and shot for the surface.

Jake watched with mild amusement as Achilles raced upward through the curtain of barracuda, entertained by the way the school scattered like a blizzard. His smile quickly faded when he realized Destiny was still nearby, sitting calmly astride Hercules. The girl's ability to go without breathing for such a lengthy period was a point of continual amazement for him, and he scrutinized her for several more seconds before turning and focusing his attention back on the wreck.

Sunken vessels had always fascinated Jake, and he was itching to gain entry inside the hulk. The sloop lay on its port side, and as he studied it, he discovered an area near the starboard bow where the hull appeared to have been breached. He would have considered squeezing through the hole if not for the heavy concentration of sea anemones congregating around it, knowing how painful their stings could be. As he scanned the wreck, he realized sea anemones were in abundance, their polyp-like arms waving to and fro as they filtered nutrients from the water.

In studying the vessel, Jake was impressed at the transformation that had taken place during the past twenty-two years. Various species of coral and soft sponges crowded the hull, with the ever-present population of anemones clinging anywhere they could gain a foothold. The reef had become an adoptive mother, claiming the vessel as its own.

Moving to the side of the wreck where he could view the deck and superstructure, Jake noted a mound of broken calciferous branches lying below an open hatchway. As he examined the mound, he realized it had been part of a dense stand of black coral that had established itself along the sloop's topside deck. It soon became apparent to him that the sloop's hatchway had been cleared of the obstructing black coral that had overgrown it. Picking up several of the broken fragments, he scrutinized them closely, noting that no algae or other forms of marine growth had taken root where the branches had been fractured. In his estimation, the breaks were recent, hinting that someone had already worked the wreck within the past several weeks. Supporting this assessment was a heap of thick hemp rope and rusted chain lying adjacent to the mound, their surfaces lined with a slick coating of algae. Nudging the heap, he could see two small Danforth anchors attached to the chain. To him, it seemed as if the rope and chain had been recently removed from the sloop's hold.

Jake dropped the fragments and swam for the cleared hatchway, its blackened interior appearing like a dark window. In preparing to enter, he stopped short, noticing that Achilles had returned. Clutched in the dolphin's hand was the end of a rope that trailed toward the surface. This had been prearranged prior to the dive. Grinning at the juvenile's helpfulness, Jake took hold of the rope and tied it off to the sloop's rear starboard railing, then dove down to the hatch opening. Poking his head in, he flicked on the underwater flashlight he carried, aiming the beam in front of him.

With the exception of a few small reef fish and a couple of lone crabs, he so far found the cabin to be unoccupied by any potentially dangerous denizens of the deep, particularly morays. Morays loved confined spaces. With their habitat suddenly invaded, such eels would see the intruder as a threat and possibly attack. Cautiously, he made his way forward. All unsecured objects within the cabin lay haphazardly strewn against the vessel's port side, the side on which it rested. Squirming his way toward the forward compartments, he found more of the same disarray.

Jake knew that Grahm's primary reason for coming here was to find out what had happened to his wife. With that in mind, he searched diligently among the wreckage for human remains, something that might indicate the fate of the passengers. Gradually he worked his way through the galley, reaching the crew's quarters. For the next fifteen minutes he poked around, moving as far forward within the boat as the obstructing debris would allow. Although he found numerous signs of past human habitation, the place was devoid of anything remotely conforming to the skeletal anatomy of a human. Unless the salvaging party that had preceded him had removed any dead, as best he could tell, no one had gone down with the sloop.

Backing up, he turned himself around and made a quick exit from the wreck. Achilles was there to greet him. He looked around for Destiny, but neither the girl nor her mount were anywhere to be seen. Only one other albino was nearby, and from the lateral scar marring its flank, he recognized Natalie. From his perspective, this was a good thing. He needed the remainder of the pod to maintain vigilance. With the possibility of that rogue sub on the loose, he had no desire to have the *Angel's* crew caught napping. He had discussed this with both Zimbola and Destiny before the dive, and the girl had agreed that the dolphins would keep a sharp lookout, fanning out in all directions around the *Angel*. If any of them detected the sub, the girl would alert Zimbola of its approach.

Glancing up at the sloop's railing, Jake reached for the nylon rope and checked his watch. Having been down almost twenty-four minutes, he thought it wise to begin his ascent. As he rose higher, he noticed the immense school of barracuda had moved downstream, leaving the water between him and the *Angel* clear of any other life forms. With

Achilles at his side, he continued upward slowly, careful not to exceed the speed of his vented air bubbles rising toward the atmosphere.

Grahm stood anxiously on the swim platform when Jake poked his head above the surface. "Did…did you find anyone?" he stammered nervously, the question uttered as if the man were afraid of what he might hear.

Jake shook his head before lifting his face mask to his forehead and spitting out the mouthpiece. "I found nothing that would suggest human remains," he clarified softly, keeping his tone sensitive.

The news seemed to elicit both relief and disappointment in the scientist's face. Clearing his throat, Grahm said, "The brass plate Achilles brought up proves it's the Tursiops."

Jake removed his fins and climbed from the water, noticing that everyone else had assembled on the *Angel's* stern, that is, all except one. He looked around sharply. "Where's Destiny?"

Phillipe pointed at the nearby island. "I saw her go in that direction, Jay Jay."

Shedding his tank and weight belt, Jake squinted his eyes and scanned the water in front of the distant cliffs. There was no sign of either the girl or Hercules. Inexplicably, he felt uneasy. Turning, he looked at the juvenile albino floating adjacent to the platform. "Is Destiny okay, Achilles?"

"You should not worry, Jay Jay," Achilles trilled. "Destiny is not in any danger."

Jake nodded, mollified by the answer for the moment, but kept his gaze fixed on the dolphin. "Any sign of that sub?"

"No, Jay Jay."

Zimbola caught Jake's eye. "There be anything for Zimby to pull up?" he asked, indicating the cleated off rope.

"Sorry, big guy, but I didn't see anything worth salvaging."

Jake went on to explain to Grahm what he'd seen, cognizant of Grahm's lingering anguish. "We're tied off to your boat," he said gently. "You want to throw on a tank and have a look at her?"

Grahm nodded, looking glum. "Paying my last respects is only appropriate."

Jake pointed to some scuba equipment on the rear deck. "Phillipe has gear laid out for you and your assistants."

"That's very kind of you," the scientist murmured. He turned to Parker and Henderson. "Are you lads up for a dive?"

Jeffrey Parker smiled exuberantly, giving Grahm a thumbs up. He appeared eager to hit the water. Nick Henderson, who had been uncharacteristically quiet as of late, did not share the same enthusiasm. "If it's alright with you, I'll be staying topside, professor. I'm still not feeling up to speed."

"That's quite all right, Nicolas," Grahm said resignedly, almost as if he had expected this. "Jeffrey and I will go without you."

While both men suited up, Jake scanned the surrounding water with the binoculars. There was still no sign of Destiny or other members of the pod. It wasn't until Grahm and Parker descended on the wreck, however, that he decided to take action. "Hold the fort," he told Zimbola as he began slipping on his mask, fins, and snorkel again.

Zimbola did not look too pleased. "Where you be going?"

Jake stood perched by the rail. "Nowhere in particular." With that said, he launched himself over the side, letting his mind focus on only one thought: Take me to Destiny, Achilles.

As he plunged below the surface, Achilles was right there waiting for him, and within seconds he was being whisked rapidly across the water.

Chapter 4

*A*bout 100 meters from a place called South Point, Achilles stopped flippering. South Point was the name shown on Jake's chart representing the southeast side of Navassa Island. Holding onto the juvenile's dorsal fin, Jake studied the abandoned lighthouse poking above the crown of green vegetation topping the karst.

"Please take this moment to hyperventilate, Jay Jay," Achilles advised. "From here we must go below the surface."

"How deep?" Jake wanted to know.

"We will descend to a maximum depth of sixteen meters below the surface for a brief period."

Jake nodded, then began purging his lungs of excess carbon dioxide. Seeming to know when his passenger was ready, Achilles dipped below the surface, arrowing at a steep angle toward a submerged outcropping overgrown with plangent, lush corals. As the dolphin powered deeper, a narrow recess in the reef suddenly came into view, and an instant later Jake was pulled into the dark opening. All traces of sunlight quickly vanished, and he felt like a man being swallowed by a black pit as the albino raced swiftly along. And although the feeling was strange, he had no fear. He trusted Achilles implicitly, intuitively knowing the albino would not endanger his life.

The ride went on for perhaps another half minute through pitch-blackness before a faint luminosity accosted his eyes, and within seconds the light grew stronger. Moments later, he was back in atmosphere, looking up at an immense subterranean cavern bathed in the soft glow of an eerie green light that seemed to emanate from multiple sources located both above and below the water.

Jake took in several deep breaths before dipping his face below the surface again, staring around in amazement. A strange subaqueous architecture abounded below him, its swirling geometric patterns suggestive of those commonly exhibited by seashells. The structure was vast in size and organic-looking, its smoothly curving free-flowing lines appearing to extend toward the far sides of the cavern. Underwater visibility was very clear, allowing him to see at least thirty dolphins in the immediate vicinity, all of them engaged at various tasks as they used their prehensile appendages to move and manipulate material. But the creatures were not albinos.

Jake lifted his head above the surface again and removed the snorkel from his mouth. "What is this place, Achilles?" he gasped in wonder.

"This is what Jacob likes to call Gaia Two," the juvenile trilled back. "It is both a manufacturing facility and a place of learning. As you can see, it is still under construction."

Jake continued to stare in awe, a multitude of questions dancing through his head. "What do you teach here?"

"We educate others of our kind on the great plan."

"Plan? Are you referring to your pod's idea for a sea mining corporation?"

"I am referring to the world yet to come, Jay Jay."

It was then that Jake became aware of Destiny as she floated toward him astride Hercules' broad back. She was aglow with excitement, and Jake could not dispel the idea that perhaps he had something to do with her current state of mind. "As you'll soon discover, this place holds many wonders," she announced happily.

Jake gestured at the water as the girl joined him. "What are they doing down there?"

"They're erecting a skeletal framework," Destiny effused.

Repositioning his face mask, Jake placed his head back in the water. Studying the dolphins at work, he now realized they were emplacing wire mesh that connected with strands protruding from the bulkier material that formed the organic-looking structure below him. Suddenly remembering what Jacob had told him about the other *thurentra*s, he raised his head above the surface once more. "Is that wire made from magnesium?"

"Mostly," Destiny answered. "But magnesium in its pure form is soluble in sea water and will easily corrode. But alloyed with small amounts of manganese and aluminum, it has a tensile strength comparable with that of structural steel and will not dissolve."

"Manganese, huh. Where do you get it?"

"In this cavern, there are twenty-two *thurentra*. Several of them produce polymetallic nodules primarily comprised of manganese."

"What about the others?" Jake asked. "What do they produce?"

"Mostly magnesium oxide, better known as the mineral periclase, comes from fifteen of the *thurentra*, while four of them produce gold and platinum."

Jake was impressed. "Okay, but how is the wire produced? You're not going to tell me the magnesium wire comes in the extruded form I see below us, are you?"

Destiny appeared amused. "Yes."

Jake felt his jaw dropping again. "You're yanking my chain?"

The girl seemed confused. "I'm not familiar with that term."

"You're kidding, right?"

Destiny looked back at Jake with endless patience showing in her eyes. "Why would I mislead you about a thing like that, Jay Jay?" she said softly, angelically. "There are three other organisms that feed on the polymetallic nodules. The alloyed magnesium that comes from them is in the form of long strands of wire."

Jake nodded in understanding. "Now I get it. So the wire mesh defines the shape of the finished structure, becoming the framework for the heavier material that makes up the shell. I assume these dolphins also install that material, too."

"The shell is grown through electrolytic action. Seawater is saturated with calcium carbonate in the form of positively charged ions. Once precipitated out of solution, it is able to solidify into a kind of sea cement, the same material from which these caverns are made. By applying an electrical current through the wire, the wire becomes a cathode upon which calcium carbonate agglomerates. Because magnesium is a good conductor of electricity, voltage will readily flow through it, allowing the accretion of sea cement to adhere around it. Anodized this way, the magnesium is virtually corrosion-proof."

"What produces the electric current?"

"The *thurentras*!"

Jake thought back to his first glimpse of the *thurentra* back in the cove. Achilles had warned him against touching the hybrid organism. And from what Grahm had told him, Nick Henderson had learned this lesson the hard way. "As far as I know, electric eels are the only creatures capable of building an electric charge of any significance."

"A *thurentra* can produce an electrical potential many times greater," Destiny offered. "Making contact with them can be quite dangerous."

"Can I see them?" Jake asked.

"They all lie at the bottom of this cavern. In order to view them, we must swim through the interior of the structure you see being built."

Jake felt himself growing excited. "I'm game."

Without waiting for a reply, he began hyperventilating again, preparing himself for an extended dive. When he was ready, both Achilles and Hercules jackknifed downward in unison. Growing accustomed to the juvenile's switchback motion, he was learning to hold on with less and less effort. Turning his head, he was able to get an up-close look at the other dolphins as they labored away. These were the gray strain of the new breed, the ones that did not converse in human languages.

Pulled through a series of rounded, smoothly winding corridors that more or less descended around a central hub within the structure, Jake scrutinized the source of illumination within the meandrous passageways. A substance appearing like a glowing green moss periodically lined the interior walls. Towed deeper, he felt his eardrums pop as he swallowed hard to neutralize the growing weight of water pressing in upon them. Rounding a final bend, the bulbous outline of a *thurentra* came into view. But unlike the one in the cove, this one was much larger. Accumulated at its base he could see mounds of chalky white sediment, the substance seeming to ooze from the bottom of the organism. As he looked on, a gray bottlenose swam in to scoop up some of the material, filling a bowl-shaped object clutched in its fully extended hands. The dolphin twisted around briefly to regard Jake just before moving away, and for an instant, Jake had the feeling the dolphin was Thetis, Achilles' mother.

Achilles hovered for the moment, giving Jake the opportunity to study the bloated organism lying before him. Hundreds of tentacles joined with the main body of the thing, all of them pulsing like veins leading to a heart. A steady stream of bubbles flowed from the crown of the creature, rising up into a suspended flared pipe that captured the escaping gas. The pipe appeared to consist of the same agglomerated sea cement as the rest of the dolphin-made edifice, rising vertically to join with an overhang situated above it.

For the next two minutes, Achilles guided Jake past fourteen more *thurentra*, all of them nearly identical to the first and strung out along a huge arc that followed the foundation of the edifice. The sixteenth hybrid was different, however. Scattered around its base was a lush, mounded carpet that sparkled under the pale green light cast upon it.

As if to gauge the reaction of his rider, Achilles held still as Jake pondered the sight. Here were two of the rarest metals on the planet, elements in scarce supply that mankind deemed as exceptionally valuable. And yet a plentiful stockpile lay before Jake's eyes. It was an abundance of wealth that could elevate humanity's poorest into a life of leisure and endless pleasures, something many people would kill for to acquire. It was the stuff investors flocked to in times of political instability and economic crisis, mediums of exchange that provided the backbone to international monetary systems and gave most governments their underlying puissance. From humanity's perspective, this was what made the world go round, true power distilled into its most abstract material form. Gold was potential energy transmogrified into whatever the possessor desired, whether it be land, ships, planes, or food.

Jake eyed the gleaming mounds, vaguely aware just how much the metals had escalated in value in the face of inflating global economies primarily tied to soaring energy costs. Plain and simple, the world seemed to have an unquenchable thirst for oil. Demand for the black liquid continued to climb, with emerging markets like China and India adding considerable pressure on OPEC to produce ever greater quantities of the fossil fuel in recent times. Historically, the price of gold tended to follow what the world market was willing to pay for a barrel of oil. And though he had not stayed current with its latest value, he remembered that it was about five months ago that gold had hovered around $920 an ounce when the price of oil had hit $100 per barrel. By his estimate, the wealth that lay piled before him was staggering.

Flippering forward, Achilles showed Jake three more *thurentra* surrounded by similar glittering masses, altogether tons of it. Here was additional concrete proof of the things Jacob had spoken of the underlying and necessary financial muscle that would allow the plan to proceed further and gain momentum.

Stunned by the sight of such immense riches, Jake found himself analyzing the implications of it all. Destiny and the albinos had at their disposal the means to take down any possible barriers that stood in their way, legal or otherwise. An intermediary like Jacob, having lived apart from the world's mainstream most of his life, might not be the best choice to negotiate those issues in an effective way, or so he assumed. Such a task would require the skills of someone more hardnosed and ruthless, a person used to operating on the edge of legitimacy. He was surprised at the name of one individual that suddenly came to mind. But although Chester Hennington was well suited to fulfill such a role, Jake knew the man could not be trusted. While Hennington was used to dealing with unsavory sorts, the broker's uncontrollable greed would ultimately prove to be a liability.

Jake quickly dismissed these thoughts, scooping up a handful of the precious grains and letting them spill back into the gleaming mounds strewn below him. Gold and platinum could buy widespread cooperation from governments that might otherwise seek to disrupt new and innovative ventures taking place in international waters, even though those ventures might fall outside their jurisdictions. A fertile environment of laissez-faire was essential if the pod's vision of a multinational corporation on the open seas was going to succeed. Precious metal was more potent than actual money in that it didn't really require a banking transaction for it to exchange hands. Used in the modus operandi conforming to the real world, it could be employed as an incentive, greasing the palms of already tarnished officials and bureaucrats wherever they might present a problem. Most likely, international laws would be amended to deal with an autonomous sea colony operating beyond the boundaries of any nation. As such, Jake could easily imagine the United Nations, the most corrupt quasi-legal authority on the planet, getting into the picture. With its image already sullied by a growing resume of egregious behavior and corruption, most notably the infamous oil for food scandal tied to the former Hussein regime in Iraq, the world body might actually be used to the advantage of Tursiops Worldwide.

Jake's awe was quickly superseded by pragmatism as he pondered these things, and he suddenly grew uneasy. Though the gold would provide the needed leverage, such wealth would also leave the plan vulnerable, for he realized a good portion of the yellow metal would have to be sold or exchanged in order to purchase the equipment and machinery required to get the initial colony started. Eventually the metals would leave behind a trail that might inevitably lead back to the cove or even this cavern. The very thing men had fought, plundered, and died for throughout the ages was here for the taking, easily accessible once it was known what lay hidden under the island. As far as he could see, the albinos would not try to defend the precious cache. To them, the metal held no intrinsic value, being viewed as nothing more than a tool to be applied in a manner consistent with how the world operated.

Pivoting his head, Jake espied Destiny looking over at him as she sat astride Hercules. Though optimistic over the plan, the girl had only experienced a small sample of what lay in store for the pod. And while her sense of duty was steadfast and to be admired, her naivety and generosity were sure to become stumbling blocks that got in the way. He had already gotten a firsthand look at an underlying fragility in her makeup. He had seen her tears over the prospect of Thetis dying, and he could not help but wonder if she would be able to bear up to losing any of the pod should the plan go awry.

Jake put these thoughts aside, feeling a need to breathe again. As if knowing this, Achilles abruptly altered his motion and shot for another passageway, following the tubular corridor as it wound its way upward in a steep spiral. More than a few gray dolphins broke from their labors and moved out of the way, allowing the two albinos with their riders an unobstructed path to the surface. Reaching atmosphere, Jake sucked in air, curiously monitoring his dive watch as he did so. He had been down nearly six minutes and yet he had felt little strain.

"I would like to see more," Jake said, addressing Destiny as she floated beside him on her mount, "but I think it would be wise to check up on the *Angel* first."

"There is no sign of the submarine, if that's what you mean," the girl assured him. She spread her arms expressively, describing a semicircle. "Most of the pod is still stationed all around your vessel, patrolling the sea several kilometers from where it sits at anchor. If they see anything considered to be a threat, you'll be immediately notified."

"Even so, I better let Zimby know what's going on. He might get it in his head something's wrong and pull anchor."

Destiny nodded in agreement, then abruptly cocked an ear as if focusing on a sound only she could hear.

"What's going on?" Jake demanded.

"Artemis has detected the approach of a surface vessel heading toward the island from the east."

That was all Jake needed to hear. Pumping up his lungs with several enormous inhalations, he gulped down a final breath before Achilles dove. Leaving the pale green light in his wake, he let himself get hauled back through the blackened cavity that would take him to the world above.

Chapter 5

Walter McPherson felt bored as he sat aboard the *Sea Lion*, though he was glad to leave Port-au-Prince far behind him. The very idea that Frank Jaffey and Ben Loomins had made such a place their base of operations repulsed him. Never before had he seen such squalor, and from what he'd heard, gang violence within the beleaguered city had gotten so out of hand that many businesses and factories were closing shop. Haiti's problems were inveterate and seemingly irreversible, with nothing in sight in the way of viable solutions to raise it out of the muck in which it was mired.

Staring out over the ocean, McPherson hoped his luck would change for the better on this day. One way or the other, he was determined to bring back at least one healthy specimen of this mysterious breed. Already he had taken delivery of the dead gray dolphins with those strange hand-like appendages. Chester Hennington had not been helpful about how the creatures had been captured, keeping the identity of the seller anonymous. Surprisingly, the chubby little broker had appeared distant and preoccupied during their discrete meeting, even after receiving a hefty bundle of cash to complete the transaction. Though the carcasses were currently packed in ice aboard the Casa, it gave him little comfort in knowing these unusual trophies might be all he came away with on this grueling trip.

As if in answer to this thought, Jaffey's voice suddenly blurted over the radio. "Bird of Prey to Predator!"

Standing at the helm, Ben Loomins keyed the mike's transmit button. "Go ahead BP."

"I hadn't expected this, but it seems I'm receiving a signal on that little doodad his majesty gave us."

Though McPherson was fed up with Jaffey's subtle innuendoes, he cast aside his annoyance in light of the other tidbit of information the radio message held.

The inkling of a smirk was evident in Loomins face as he glanced over at the naval captain. "That sounds very interesting BP. What's our next move?"

A short pause ensued before Jaffey responded, his speech erratically garbled by static but understandable. "Bird of Prey advises you to home in on acquired target. Stand by for numbers."

Trying to leash his growing excitement, McPherson watched as Loomins scribbled down a set of coordinates. It had been he, McPherson, who had provided Jaffey with the doodad to which the pilot referred, a piece of hardware that had actually been designed by Nick Henderson. It was a tool used for tracking the movements of dolphins outfitted with something Henderson had called a DBT device. Based on what he was hearing, it sounded as if there were more creatures out there with such a sending unit strapped to their bodies.

McPherson smiled inwardly at the exorbitant price he had paid in order to recruit Henderson's cooperation. He wondered how Dr. Grahm would react if the scientist ever found out how one of his young assistants had been so easily bought off. Turncoats like Henderson, it seemed, were everywhere these days, opportunists who had no scruples about taking a bribe whenever it crossed their path. Manipulating people through bribery and monetary incentive had become a way of life for McPherson. Coming from an exceedingly wealthy family had taught him at a very early age how money could be used to one's advantage, and he had taken the lesson to heart, employing it to invoke a successful military career. It was a game he fully enjoyed playing.

But in this case, it had not been he who had approached the grad student to make him turn traitor. No, it had been the other way around. Henderson had somehow ferreted him out from among an elaborate maze of military channels, making him privy to a new breed of dolphin with extraordinary attributes. It had been Henderson who had offered to give away the secret for money, and McPherson had readily accepted.

But Grahm had refused to cave under the captain's threats to turn over the dolphin, unexpectedly fleeing Miami with the creature in tow a short time later. Just before leaving, however, Henderson had managed to get word to him of Grahm's plans. Mailing him the device Jaffey called a doodad and the manner in which it could be used, the computer whiz had explained how they could stay in contact using the device. When the time was right, Henderson would alert him where to find these magnificent creatures, that is, provided he wired another sizable deposit into a certain offshore bank account.

Letting his thoughts coast along while Loomins repeated back the coordinates over the radio, McPherson was absolutely certain the man who had stolen the two albinos right out from under Loomins' nose was not Nick Henderson. The man Ben Loomins had described was much too muscular and conditioned to match Henderson's scrawny physique. By assuming Henderson's identity, though, the thief must have had some knowledge of what Henderson had been up to. But this time around, things would be different. He would make sure of that.

Loomins keyed the transmit button again. "Have you established the target heading, BP?"

Jaffey's voice came back buzzing with static. "You're gonna love this, P, but it ain't moving at all."

Loomins swiveled his head and looked over at McPherson again, seemingly entertained by what he saw in the captain's face. "What's your ETA, BP?"

"I'm just gaining altitude, P. You should be seeing me in approximately seventeen minutes. I strongly recommend you stay well clear of the target until I'm able to get there and drop the package. Is that understood, P?"

A formidable scowl overcame Loomins' features. "There's no need to remind me, BP," he stammered, his face suddenly reddened with bottled up rage. "I know the procedure."

"Just refreshing your memory, P. I wouldn't want to see you blow this a second time. Bird of Prey out."

McPherson said nothing as Loomins put down the mike in agitation. Still steamed over the remark, Loomins matched the coordinates given him with a spot on a chart laid out before him, circling the location so hard with the point of a pen that he cut through the paper where a small island in the shape of a teardrop was shown.

Studying the location, McPherson found it interesting that this had been their original destination all along. Perhaps the area was where many more of these creatures congregated. The possibility that he might actually be onto the mother lode of this new species brought on a renewed feeling of elation. With such creatures in his custody, he would have a powerful bargaining chip in furthering his career, something that would set the stage for new innovations in naval military tactics, something that would undoubtedly bring him back into the good graces of his superiors and advance him very rapidly to the rank of rear admiral. Having made the decision to stay aboard the *Sea Lion* rather than Jaffey's plane was so far proving to be a wise choice. This way, he would make sure nothing went wrong should they get another chance at snaring one of these amazing animals.

Focusing eager eyes on the balmy horizon off the vessel's bow, he could just make out the hazy white band that was supposed to be Navassa Island, the vicinity where the first two dolphins had been bagged. In order to limit the Casa's time in the air and save fuel, Loomins had sailed for Navassa well in advance of Jaffey. Once the plane caught up with them, it would scoot out ahead and unload the system that would ultimately incapacitate the unique creatures, making them easy to net.

Checking his watch, he estimated when he might gain sight of the plane. By nature, he was not a patient man. For some strange reason though, he wanted to prolong the joy of anticipation he was currently experiencing, savoring the thought that the prizes he sought were almost within his grasp. This was the most excitement he had had in a long time.

Jake left Achilles at the dive platform, climbing up onto the *Angel's* stern where Zimbola, Phillipe and Hector awaited him.

"We be receiving company," the Jamaican said, pulling the binoculars he held from his eyes and handing them over to Jake.

Jake spotted the vessel Zimby had been studying, then lifted the optical device and peered through the lenses. Though the boat was more than a half-mile distant, he recognized its lines immediately. "How long they been sitting there?" he asked.

"Not long. She's a fast lady. Come outta the south like a Mako on the hunt, then cut her engines just as quickly."

Scrutinizing the vessel further, Jake had a clear view of the boat's larboard side as it floated without power. No breeze had sprung up yet and the sea lay flat.

"That's the *Sea Lion*," Jake offered, raising the glasses to the sky overhanging the horizon to the south. "If my guess is right, we'll be seeing a spotter plane joining her very shortly." Handing the binoculars back to the big man, he glanced over at Hector. "We've got a Code One on our hands."

Hector nodded gravely, then scrambled away with Phillipe following.

Jake turned and stared up at the Jamaican. "I take it Grahm and Parker are still on the wreck."

Zimby checked his watch. "They still have fifteen minutes."

Craning his torso over the side, Jake looked down at Achilles and started to open his mouth.

"There is no need to speak, Jay Jay," the young albino twittered. "Destiny and the others have already been informed of the danger. We will take the necessary precautions."

Though Achilles was reading his mind again, Jake was no longer surprised. The juvenile began to submerge when the tendrils of an idea worked its way into Jake's thoughts. "Achilles, wait!"

The albino stopped and looked back up. "I will do as you say, Jay Jay. The probability of success is actually quite high."

Jake felt himself smiling. Achilles was thinking right along with him on this one.

Logging off the laptop computer as he sat in his thatched dwelling, Jacob could not remember feeling so lonely. With the entire pod gone, the place he called Gaia seemed inordinately serene today, as if all the other life forms, both fauna and flora, residing within its midst were aware that Destiny and the dolphins were missing. Even the roar of the falls seemed to have waned, evidenced by a flow of water that lacked the usual potency. The feeling was exacerbated all the more by Emmanuel's prolonged absence. Taking into consideration unforeseen delays so common to incoming flights bound for Port-au-Prince, he knew his cousin should have returned by now. Something was definitely wrong.

The familiar sound of another watercraft suddenly reached his ears, and within moments he was standing on the shore awaiting Jimenez as the fisherman nudged the sand with the bow of his boat.

"Have you gotten any word on Emmanuel?" Jacob asked in Creole, as if expecting the man to alleviate his fears.

Jimenez shook his head gravely as he hopped onto the shore. "Lucette is beside herself with worry. She has not slept in days." He looked past Jacob, setting his eyes on the two dwellings set back from the water. "Do you have bottles for me?"

Jacob nodded, grabbing one end of the first empty cylinder slid over the boat's gunwale. Further conversation between the two men was not necessary. There wasn't much more to say anyway. They were following a set schedule. Jimenez had visited the cove on many previous occasions, each time for the dual purpose of picking up cylinders topped off with hydrogen gas and collecting more of the dolphin paintings. A brooding silence took hold of both men as they began unloading the spent bottles filling the boat, a routine they had carried out twice each week now for almost the last two years. Once the load was replaced with recharged cylinders, Jimenez would deliver the gas to the owners of four cantinas, two in Saint-Marc and two in Gonaives. But first the dolphin art would be dropped off with Amphitrite.

Word of Malique's benevolent mambo had spread far and wide in the last year, sending people in droves to the tiny seaside fishing village in the last several months. What had started out as a trickle was slowly turning into a flood. With a growing influx of sick and injured seeking to be cured, more and more of Amphitrite's time had been taken up, necessitating that she remain as close as possible to where she could do the most good. Both her and Jacob had agreed long ago that Gaia would be off limits to the masses, particularly since a human intrusion of significant number could easily offset the delicate ecosystem that existed within it.

It didn't take Jacob and Jimenez long to complete the task of loading recharged cylinders into the boat, and minutes later Jacob found himself waving a final farewell as Jimenez rounded the bend leading to the rocky inlet. As always, Jacob's mind began to fill with a variety of matters, both large and small, and as he strolled idly along the shore, his thoughts fell back on ways of reversing global warming.

By his estimates, global warming was accelerating, spurred on by increasing demands for oil. In the last two years, Asia had surpassed North America in the consumption of petroleum. Already, China had become the second-largest importer of the liquid fossil fuel next to the United States even though the typical person in China used only ten percent on average what the typical American consumed. Jacob had done enough research on the subject to know that every day, 200 million automobiles in America guzzled roughly eleven percent of the world's daily output of oil. Not surprisingly, the United States was the only industrialized country that was less energy-efficient than it had been two decades earlier. Since 1980, when gasoline was still relatively cheap, Americans had made the switch from smaller cars to gas-guzzling SUVs and minivans, all of which currently accounted for about half of all cars in the United States as opposed to just seven percent in 1990.

Americans, it seemed, lived in a car-driven culture, establishing themselves as the most energy-inefficient consumers on the planet. This inefficiency was exacerbated all the more when many U.S. citizens moved from the cities to the suburbs and exurbs, with seventy-five percent of the population choosing to commute longer distances each day. Only five percent of Americans relied on public transportation to get to work, a far cry from the twenty percent of Europeans who used bus or rail to reach places of employment. At present, two-thirds of America's petroleum consumption went toward transportation. At the present rate of consumption worldwide, about 1.1 billion tons of carbon dioxide was currently being produced annually by road vehicles.

Both Jacob and the pod had done calculations, making logical assumptions based on research about the spiraling tempo of oil consumption worldwide. Starting with the current year, if China and India paralleled the same growth rate South Korea had undergone since 1980, those two countries alone would end up consuming three times as much energy as the U.S. does today seventy-five years from now. Developing and then solving third, fourth, and fifth order differential equations, they had discovered that the amount of carbon dioxide dumped into the atmosphere would reach a critical level long before that took place. Mathematics had given them an advance look at the disasters that would befall the world if such irresponsible actions continued to go on uncurbed much longer. It could not be refuted. Sea levels would rise dramatically. Jacob glanced dismally all about him. Portions of Gaia would become submerged, destroying the dwellings he, Destiny and Amphitrite lived in, though he well knew it would take many more years for that to happen. Malique would also drown in the ensuing floodwaters, as would the entire Haitian coast. The frequency of hurricanes would escalate, with the destructive force and accompanying size of such monster storms becoming greater than anything mankind had previously seen. But even before mankind felt the full brunt of those disasters, Jacob was convinced of another potential calamity that was even more disturbing, and that was the threat of horrific war. Amphitrite had prophesied this many years earlier, foretelling of a conflict that would be triggered by diametrically opposed ideologies fostered by segments of humanity, compounded further as oil-hungry nations fought to control the major petroleum supply lines flowing out of the Middle East. It was a war that had the potential of decimating the human race long before global warming could take its toll.

With the collective pod mind assisting him, Jacob had constructed one mathematical model after another, each leading him to the same conclusion. Change was desperately needed if catastrophe was to be averted. This was not a political issue to be hashed over and endlessly discussed by feckless politicians and inveterate societies. Decisive actions had to be taken, and very soon if the impending cataclysm was to be averted. Based on recent satellite measurements published in one of the scientific journals he had recently read, the second-largest ice cap on the planet, the ice sheet covering Greenland, was melting into the surrounding oceans at a rate three times faster than it did four years earlier. The Greenland sheet accounted for about ten percent of all the ice on earth.

He thought about the last item he had been researching. That item was salps. Salps were low member organisms in the ocean food chain, transparent jellyfish-like creatures about the size of a human thumb. Swarming by the billions in hot spots that have been known to cover immense areas of the seas, salps had the ability to transport tons of carbon each day from surface waters to the ocean depths where it could be kept from re-entering the atmosphere. The oceans absorbed a small percentage of all atmospheric gases, including greenhouse gases like carbon dioxide. Increases in this gas from burning fossil fuels continued to exacerbate global warming, with the planetary hydrosphere absorbing significant amounts of it and becoming more acidic in the process. This increasing acidity was beginning to contribute significantly to the destruction of many coral reefs around the world.

With barrel-shaped bodies, salps propelled themselves through the water by drawing water in the front end and forcing it out the rear in a jetting action. Passing over a mucus membrane within the organism, the water was vacuumed clean of all organic material. Salps consumed all types of microscopic carbonaceous plants from surface waters, including phytoplankton, which used the carbon dioxide to grow. They swam, fed, and produced waste continuously, taking in small packages of carbon and transforming them into bigger packages that sank rapidly in the form of fecal pellets. When salps died, their bodies also had a tendency to sink relatively fast, becoming a dead-end in the food web provided they remained uneaten on the way down.

Jacob had learned that one particular species of salp, Salpa aspera, multiplied quickly in dense swarms that flourished for months, covering as much as 100,000 square kilometers of ocean surface and transporting up to 4,000 tons of carbon to deeper water each day. During daylight hours, they were known to swim deeper to avoid predators and the effects of damaging ultraviolet rays. Ascending back up at night in a vertical migration, they aggregated and reproduced when food was abundant. Because of this behavior, they released fecal pellets in deep water where few animals were able to ingest them. In this way, they allowed the oceans to absorb excess carbon dioxide in a manner that prevented it from re-entering the atmosphere. Jacob well knew that to permanently remove excess buildups of this greenhouse gas from the atmosphere, the carbon had to be removed from the planet's active biocycle.

As of late, Jacob had been exploring more and more possible ways of reversing global warming caused by escalating build-ups of carbon dioxide in the atmosphere, and he had quickly discovered that salps had shown much promise toward that end.

Fertilizing the oceans with iron was another method that also showed great potential, and one that might prove valuable in proliferating phytoplankton blooms in areas where upwelling was absent. A strong biological response occurred when dissolved iron was added to the topmost region of the hydrosphere, causing algae to quickly multiply and absorb excess carbon dioxide in the upper water column. But from the research Jacob had uncovered, algae blooms alone were not enough to be an effective solution to removing greenhouse carbon dioxide from surface waters since the carbon would return to the biosphere in the exhalations or metabolic processes of the animals that fed upon the algae. Applied in combination with phytoplankton-consuming salps, however, he saw that a rapid carbon export to deeper water was quite possible.

Jacob already knew of the existence of one huge phytoplankton bloom, and it was very close to Navassa Island. Years earlier, he and Amphitrite had seeded the water there with three other *thurentra*. Those organisms had been created by splicing the mysterious oblate jellyfish with the largest variety of sea cucumber they could find. And while he had never actually seen them, based on what the dolphins had told him, the resulting hybrids had grown to immense proportions, drawing huge volumes of cold, nutrient-rich water from the oceanic depths where dissolved nitrates and nitrites were plentiful. With their taproot network of tentacles reaching down thousands of feet along the seabed, the water they brought up was forty degrees lower than the 80-degree water at the surface. This he had discovered by using a Fahrenheit thermometer to measure the temperature of the water rising directly above the *thurentras* pumping it. It was this hybrid-induced upwelling that had caused the immediate surface waters adjacent to Navassa to become rife with life, with vast schools of tuna drawing the attention of huge fishing trawlers he had seen near the island as of late.

When mixed with the warm surface water near Navassa, the colder upwelling also provided another benefit to the local environment. It cooled the surrounding water. With average ocean temperatures at the surface rising with global warming, water vapor was being released in linearly increasing amounts, slowly working its way toward a critical runaway greenhouse effect where the release of water in gaseous form into the atmosphere would jump dramatically. Jacob well knew that water vapor was far and away the most powerful of all the known greenhouse gases, able to absorb infrared energy over a much broader spectrum than carbon dioxide.

Jacob thought back to the hydrogen gas he had just helped Jimenez load into his boat. The use of hydrogen as an alternative fuel had no environmental downside provided the resulting water vapor produced from burning it was kept from entering the atmosphere. If the vapor was contained, hydrogen was a clean, renewable source of energy, and one that could be used to lead the way in achieving a scientific revolution that would transform the world.

In the last several weeks, Jacob's mind had been churning with possible projects Tursiops Worldwide would pursue once the first sea colony was established, and he tried to busy himself with such thoughts. But nagging inexorably within the midst of such noble musings was Emmanuel's prolonged absence. It was imperative that Emmanuel return with the necessary paperwork that would launch the corporation the albinos had envisioned. They needed to get started right away in order to avoid a looming catastrophe. The fate of the world depended on it.

Making a decision, he rowed himself out to the pinnace and cranked up the motor. He would go to Malique and see Amphitrite. Perhaps she had had another one of her extraordinary visions. Maybe by now she would know what had become of his cousin.

Frank Jaffey took the Casa in low, swooping over his partner's craft at close to 200 knots. Although the signal had stopped, he still had a fix on its point of origin. The vessel that lay at anchor further ahead caught him by surprise, however, and he toggled the transmit key. "Bird of Prey to Predator, you ever see that boat before?"

"Come on back, BP, you're breaking up."

Jaffey keyed the mike again, altogether forgetting about radio protocol. "The boat off your port side. You recognize it?"

A momentary pause ensued before Loomins answered. "Negative, BP. Why do you ask?"

"Never mind, Predator. What say we bag us some dolphins?"

"Just drop the package, BP, and we'll do the rest."

Jaffey took a good look at the unknown vessel as he overshot it, seeing two divers removing scuba gear on the boat's rear platform. One other person was assisting the divers, and all three looked up sharply to observe the plane as it passed less than 300 feet above them. "No can do until an actual target is spotted, P. Give me a moment to circle."

Coming around hard, Jaffey let his eyes roam over the water, trying to take in every square meter of the ocean surface. He could not recall having ever seen a sea so flat. Conditions were perfect for spotting quarry from the air. Banking hard left, his gaze came to bear on something white amid the surrounding indigo. "Well, well, look what we have here," he said aloud to himself, letting a wide grin spread over his face. Abruptly, he again keyed the transmit button. "I've got a target, Predator. I'm coming around for a drop run," he blurted excitedly. "Stand by to come on in on my command!"

"I read you, BP. Standing by."

Jaffey kept his eyes locked on the target, keeping it off his port wing as he guided the aircraft on a course parallel with the island. He needed to open up some distance with it before swinging back around and setting up his drop vector. Timing was everything if the operation was going to be successful. So far, the prize appeared to be fully cooperative, seemingly unaware of the plane buzzing noisily overhead.

Satisfied with the distance he had opened up, Jaffey dipped his port wing again, taking the Casa into a lazy bank before preparing the aircraft for a final approach. Gradually, the target swung into the center of his windshield, and several hundred meters directly behind it was the boat carrying the divers, its bow facing him.

Cutting back on the throttle, he continued to maintain perfect alignment with the creature floating languidly on the sea below. His preoccupation with the quarry was intruded upon as the vessel behind it suddenly rocked back on its stern, its bow rising ostensibly above the water. Disregarding the distraction, he steered the plane lower, engaging the hydraulics that would open the bay doors situated at the Casa's belly.

Thumbing the intercom button, Jaffey gave an order to the others stationed in the rear. "Stand by for a drop!"

Over his headphones, a voice came back curtly. "Ready when you are."

Jaffey started a backward count in his head as he checked his altimeter and air speed, content that everything was proceeding exactly as it should. Five…four…three…what the devil?

In that instant, a watercraft shot out from behind the anchored vessel, racing rapidly along the boat's starboard side and heading directly at him. Much too seasoned a pilot to let his concentration waver, Jaffey resumed his interrupted mental countdown. Two…one…He triggered the electronic release.

"Package away!" he cried.

Nearly two seconds elapsed before a response blared back loudly. "Package delivered!" the same voice confirmed.

Throwing more power into the engines, Jaffey pulled back on the yoke, lifting the Casa's nose skyward and banking sharply left.

"Predator to BP!" Jaffey was nearly deafened as Loomins voice suddenly cracked from the earphones like gunshot. "You've got a visitor! There's a guy on a waverunner under you!"

Jaffey banked the plane harder, coming around as fast as possible to have a look, but before he could complete the turn, Loomins voice sounded again. "It's him!"

It took Jaffey only a fraction of a second to make the connection. "Calm down, Predator. You're getting yourself all worked up for nothing. There's nothing he can do to stop us now."

By this time, he had opened up enough of an angle to glimpse the waverunner, and with a start, he realized the man driving it was bearing directly at the sounder he had dropped. Nervously, he shifted his gaze further back to locate the white dolphin he had targeted, but the creature was nowhere to be seen. The package had just splashed down and was bobbing violently as it settled into its watery cradle. It required a fairly stable orientation for the sonar emitter to disengage from the floatation bags and sink below the surface, and that would take roughly three more seconds.

With rising panic, Jaffey turned his eyes back to the man racing along below and was immediately dumbstruck. He could only stare helplessly at the trail of whitewater that streaked away from the waverunner, a trail that was reaching for his piece of electronic gadgetry with disconcerting swiftness.

Jake had concealed both himself and the Kawasaki upon which he sat under a tarp, awaiting the right moment to launch the waverunner after the plane had buzzed them. Seeing the aircraft swing wide before taking on a glide path that would bring it straight for Achilles, he gave the order for Hector to deploy the water chute. Sliding down backwards to meet the sea, he noticed the familiar shift in the boat's superstructure as the *Angel* settled back on its haunches.

Turning the ignition switch, Jake felt the Kawasaki purr to life, its engine seemingly ready to take on any challenge. Twisting the throttle to full, he held on tight as the waverunner leapt forward like a greyhound eager for an all-out run. Leaning his weight, he exploded past the *Angel's* starboard side, reaching maximum speed within seconds. With the sea like a sheet of glass, he knew the watercraft under him would have the striking capability of a cobra.

The plane, he could see, had its cargo bay doors fully ajar as it homed in on the juvenile's position, and an instant later something fell from between them. The very scenario Jake had predicted was now taking place before him. In that moment, Achilles' dorsal fin disappeared from view, leaving only a few ripples marring the sea's glossy surface.

Continuing to plow straight ahead, Jake moved aside the swivel guard that blocked the arming switch to the right-side torpedo. A flick of the toggle was all he needed to prepare the 40mm missile for launch. Aligning the waverunner with the plummeting object's projected point of impact, he let his thumb find the launch button that would send the torpedo on its way. With his gaze now focused on the thing accelerating toward the sea, he knew his timing had to be precise.

The geyser that erupted when the object met the water was truly spectacular, but Jake had no time to admire the resulting plume. With a deft thumb, he depressed the launch button and watched the torpedo leap away.

A white spumy rope appeared to spring forth across the water, growing rapidly in length as it raced forward on a vector that was straight and true. Unlike his encounter with Mat's boat, Jake had not tampered with the projectile to reduce its potency. This was a standard 40mm torpedo, packed to the brim with hellacious explosive. Even a glancing strike against the thing currently settling on the water would send out a shock wave of sufficient magnitude to severely damage it, or so he hoped.

Cutting back a quarter turn on the throttle, Jake sheared away from the target, getting clear of the impending explosion and taking on a heading that was ninety degrees to port. Even so, the booming blast of compressed air that caught up with him was more than he had expected as the torpedo detonated. Looking back at the damage, he could see various components of the object still aloft, flung high in all directions from the force of the strike. Within moments, they fell back into the sea, with only the remains of several floatation bags hanging in tattered disarray on the ocean surface.

The possibility that Achilles had failed to escape the ensuing shock wave in time to avoid injury weighed heavily on Jake's mind, and he glanced about anxiously in an attempt to locate him. As if to calm his worry, Achilles suddenly rocketed from the water close to the *Angel*, performing one of his signature quintuple somersaults.

Letting go with a relieved sigh, Jake altered the Kawasaki's heading by several more degrees to face the oncoming vessel, his expression suddenly turning grim. Though he held no particular animosity toward Loomins and his partner, he would do whatever it took to keep them from capturing any more dolphins. With cold deliberation, he armed the sixty, prepared to discourage any retaliatory responses made by the crew of the *Sea Lion* as it bore closer.

Chapter 6

*M*cPherson had trouble believing what he had just witnessed. From a distance, he had watched as Jaffey made the airdrop. No sooner had the sounder splashed down, it had been destroyed, blown to pieces by a person skimming across the sea on a waverunner. Nearly speechless, he turned to stare at Ben Loomins. "You're sure it's the same guy?"

Driving the *Sea Lion* forward with the engines wide open, Loomins was beside himself with rage. "Fuckin' A right it's him." For emphasis, he put the spyglasses to his eyes again, taking another look at the man riding the waverunner. "But this time he's gonna pay," he added, his face contorted in ugliness. He put down the glasses and pulled the magnum pistol from the holster strapped to his thigh, clicking open the barrel to make sure the firearm was fully loaded.

"What are you going to do?" McPherson asked in annoyance, looking at Loomins as if he were insane. The sight of handguns had always made him feel uneasy. This whole situation was rapidly disintegrating, turning into something way beyond his control. Becoming a party to any egregious incidents had not been part of his plan, and he surely had no desire to be implicated in one that might possibly mar his naval career.

"I'm gonna kill that bastard!" Loomins screamed. "I'm gonna blow his god damn brains out!"

Jaffey's voice suddenly blared over the radio. "Stand down, Predator! Do not approach the waverunner!"

Loomins ignored the command, continuing to drive the vessel onward as fast as it would go.

The radio blared again. "What the fuck you doing, Predator?" Jaffey's voice boomed in panic. "I told you to stand down, the guy on the runner has torpedoes! Stay clear of him!"

The words caused the blood in McPherson's veins to freeze. Torpedoes? A vague remembrance of something to do with waverunners and torpedoes unhinged itself from the back of his mind, but he had no time to dwell on it now. Instead, he grabbed Loomins' by the arm, yanking hard to pull him out of his focused rage. "Did you hear him?" he yelled tremulously. "Stand down! You want to get us killed?"

Loomins lifted the pistol, pointing it directly in McPherson's face and cocking the hammer. "Get the hell off my bridge!"

In Loomins' eyes, McPherson could not mistake the cauldrons of murderous hate. Abruptly, he released the man's arm and backed away, certain Loomins would shoot him if he did not comply.

Loomins waved the gun. "Off my bridge!" he bellowed.

McPherson scampered down the ladder, not having any desire to provoke Loomins any further. Reaching the rear deck, he saw Charlie leaning against the port railing with the Haitian crewmen. The whole group was staring around the side of the vessel, following the movements of the distant waverunner. In Charlie's hand was the carbine rifle he had seen before.

"You've got to stop your brother!" McPherson shouted. "He's gonna get us all killed."

Charlie glanced his way momentarily. "Ben knows what he's doing."

"Jaffey said the sounder was destroyed by a torpedo," McPherson explained hurriedly, aware of his own rising panic. "The guy out there might have another one. He can sink us."

The full impact of McPherson's words seemed to awaken Charlie, for Charlie's mouth suddenly came ajar. "Holy shit!" he cried. Bolting for the ladder leading to the bridge, he started to climb the rungs, but the vessel abruptly lurched and he nearly lost his grip on the hand-railings.

McPherson's eyes went wide as a cloud of wavering darkness seemed to loom up from the sea, portions of it swarming all around and then engulfing the *Sea Lion* in frenzied, bludgeoning violence. Like a cresting wave, it heaved up and hammered down upon him. Something slapped wetly against his chest and before he could fully grasp what was happening, his entire body became entrenched in a rush of flapping, slippery chaos. Shielding his face with out-flung arms, he tried to ward off the silvery-gray throng before being knocked from his feet.

Amid the turmoil, he felt the vessel lurch under him again, this time more violently. Horrified, he sensed the *Sea Lion* teeter precariously to one side before righting itself in a sustained list. As if in protest to the way the vessel was being violated, the clamor of the engines rose in a distressed shriek, only to die away a moment later by whatever was smothering the props.

A dead quiet descended as the confusion ended almost as quickly as it had started. Getting hold of his senses, McPherson tried to rise. With great effort, he forced aside the mass of wriggling, slithering bodies bogging him down, barely managing to stand erect. What in god's name?

"Help me!" The voice belonged to Charlie. Mired deep in the squirming throng, he tried to get to his feet, failing miserably in the attempt.

McPherson stared dumbly at the mass of fish overwhelming the deck. Wading through the bodies, he realized he was bleeding as a red trickle worked its way down his arm. Bringing a hand to his cheek, he located the source, flinching when his finger found where the flesh had been lacerated. Heaped high all about him were barracuda, perhaps thousands of them, their cylindrical bodies continuing to shudder convulsively under the hot sun, their teeth appearing like tiny daggers jutting from protruding lower jaws.

Afraid he might get bitten again, McPherson ceased moving, aware that the Haitians were now busy pushing fish over the side.

"Jesus Christ," Charlie hollered, "will somebody get these goddamn fish offa me."

The drone of the Casa slowly grew in pitch, and like a man in a stupor, McPherson looked up to watch the aircraft shoot above him with less than fifty feet to spare. With the *Sea Lion* now dead in the water, he continued to follow the plane as it took on a course that would take it back to the man on the waverunner.

Chapter 7

She had never been able to understand why she was the hub of the pod, the sentience through which all the others focused their mental energies whenever the synergy inherent of a collective mind needed to be achieved. Such comprehension was irrelevant anyway. To Destiny, knowing when to form a mind meld with the others was instinctual, as natural as satisfying one's hunger for food. Like the moon exerting its pull on the oceans to produce the tides, it was a phenomenon that simply was.

She had seen Jay Jay destroy the mechanism dropped from the aircraft, the thing that had enervated Hermes and Aphrodite. And she had seen the watercraft that had previously captured them bearing straight for him, sensing intense anger emanating from the vessel. And yet there was fear, too. Based on what she knew of its crew, there were also innocents aboard the boat, Haitians that worked for Ben Loomins.

A potentially deadly confrontation had quickly arisen, one that had necessitated defusing, for if left unchecked only misery would follow. And misery was something she and the others felt obligated to dispel whenever they came across it.

Inciting the nearby shoal of barracuda into a frenzy aimed at swarming the *Sea Lion* had been far easier than expected. The mental suggestion she and the others had imparted to the horde was something they had never before tried. And though the act had caused the death of numerous fish, she felt no remorse. Unlike a human, the mind of a barracuda was very limited, entirely governed by instinct and incapable of conscious thought. Whatever members of the pack had perished would ultimately become food for other predators in the food chain, their essence continuing to live on.

As Destiny looked across the water at the vessel drifting aimlessly without power, she sensed the outrage lessen, replaced by confusion and frustration. Still linked to the others, she could clearly feel it. The negative emotions pulsing from Ben Loomins had ebbed sufficiently for a shred of rational thought to take hold of the man. But there was something else hanging in the air, something far more puissant than Loomins' ire.

Startled by the strength of it, she stared back at the island. An overpowering iniquity seemed to lurk somewhere to the northwest of her position. It was the same feeling she had experienced during her first sighting of the submarine, but much more pronounced this time. Her mother had taught her long ago never to ignore perceptions that lay beyond the boundaries of her physical senses, for when they occurred, they often portended undesirable events yet to come, events that might be averted. And while such extrasensory attunement was infrequent, tending to come at the oddest moments, Amphitrite had stressed it could be taken as a forewarning from God to be on one's guard.

Bashir, Destiny knew, was currently somewhere on the island, taken there by Jimenez to right a wrong he had abetted. What exactly that wrong was, she had no knowledge, though she did perceive it had something to do with the sub.

Do not try to understand everything going on about you, her mother had emphasized. You have a special purpose to fulfill in this world. All will eventually become clear, but first you must take heed of the inner voice that resides deep within you.

Turning her gaze in another direction, Destiny spotted Jay Jay as he steered the waverunner back up the retractable launching chute extending from his boat's stern. From her vantage point, she could see the *Sea Lion* was far enough away from the *Avenging Angel* to pose no threat. For the time being, the Loomins brothers would be busy trying to repair their vessel.

Satisfied with the outcome, she let her eyes linger on Jay Jay as he climbed off the Kawasaki, now snug within its berth atop the *Angel's* rear superstructure. Here was the man prophesied by the painting on the cave wall, the man she had come to think of as 'The Protector' long before fate had brought them together. She had known only a few men in her life, all of whom she loved dearly. And although Jacob, and to a lesser extent Emmanuel, had become father-figures to her, the feelings she held for them in no way came close to what she felt for Jay Jay, for whenever she was near him her heart beat faster. This was a different kind of love, one that utterly confused her, and yet one she could not deny.

She had gotten insights into such love from the novels Jacob had given her to read, a love that could only exist between a man and a woman. And now she was actually feeling it for what it truly was. Though eternal like the limitless wellspring of pure love flowing forth from infinite dimensionality, there was a physical side to the emotion she was experiencing. It was a deep yearning, an inexplicable hunger akin to the albino matings that occasionally intruded their way into her awareness.

With great difficulty, she tried distancing herself from such thoughts, knowing she should investigate the source of evil originating from somewhere further back on the island. Strangely, she was besieged by a sudden impulse, recognizing that Bashir needed her help.

Just before Hercules submerged, she cast her eyes upon the *Avenging Angel* one more time. Those aboard the vessel still required Jay Jay's protection. The unknown danger she sensed was all too real for him not to remain where he was. One threat had just passed, only to be replaced by the possibility of another, one that might prove to be far worse.

And she realized, too, that the safety of Dr. Grahm was especially important to her. Without knowing why, she felt an unaccountable closeness to him. Oddly, this last thought stayed with her as Hercules dove beneath the surface.

From the bridge, Ben Loomins watched the Casa shrink to an indistinct dot before disappearing over the horizon. The last thing his partner had told him was that he would return with a boat to tow the *Sea Lion* back to Port-au-Prince if the vessel remained inoperable.

He knew Jaffey must be ready to kill somebody by now. A short time earlier, Jaffey had made one mad water-skimming pass at the man on the waverunner, trying to ram him with extended landing gear. Their assailant had easily dodged the maneuver, veering off to one side at the last moment and adding insult to injury by firing on the aircraft with an automatic weapon. After that, Jaffey had immediately backed off, circling at a distance, and remaining clear of both the waverunner and the vessel that had launched it.

Loomins could not recall his partner ever sounding so enraged over the radio. Normally, Jaffey tended to be the most levelheaded between them. "That bastard shot a hole in my wing!" Jaffey had screamed. "I'm losing fuel!" Just before flying away, Jaffey had had the presence of mind to inform him about one little oddity he could clearly see from the air. "There's a really big dolphin down there, a white one with someone riding it."

Disgustedly, Loomins mulled these things as he dropped his gaze to the mass of fish strewn over the rear deck. The Haitians were still busy clearing away hundreds of barracuda swamping the boat, most of them inundating the vessel's port side. Slowly, the *Sea Lion* was coming back on an even keel.

He could tell Charlie was still shaken by what had happened. In all his years at sea, both he and his brother had never experienced anything that had come close to this.

"What now?" McPherson said, staring up at him.

"We try and get this boat up and running again," Loomins said heatedly. "The props won't turn."

"How could something like this happen?" McPherson persisted.

"I don't know!"

McPherson turned his gaze in the direction of the other boat anchored a quarter mile away. Every so often, a white dolphin made an impressive leap close to the vessel. "Maybe these white dolphins are tamer than we think." As he spoke, the creature made another spectacular leap. "That one there seems to be with the people aboard that boat."

Loomins felt his frustration growing. "Nothing I can do about it unless I get the props turning again. They're froze up solid." As an afterthought, he said, "Stay on the lookout for more of those creatures. Frank told me he saw a big one with somebody riding it."

"Maybe it's that girl you let get away the other day," McPherson criticized smugly. "You know, the one your crew calls the white witch."

The sound of barracuda being tossed into the water abruptly ceased, halting the biting retort about to fly from Loomins' tongue. He glanced sharply at the Haitians to see why they had stopped. All three of them stared speechless at McPherson.

"Get back to work!" Loomins snarled.

For the moment, all three men ignored the command, pulling their eyes from McPherson and looking nervously at the surrounding water.

"If you want to keep working for me, you'll do as I say," Loomins threatened.

With great reluctance, the men went back to work, their efforts now considerably slower.

Loomins looked over at his brother. "Charlie! Grab a mask and hop over the side. I need to know what's fouling the shafts."

Charlie pointed to the other vessel. "What if that guy decides to take a run at us while I'm in the water?"

"Are you blind?" Ben decried. He addressed his brother as if speaking to a child. "Can't you see his waverunner's back on that boat? Get your ass in the water!"

Charlie stared up at him defiantly. "No way I'm gonna let myself become chum. Look what these fish did to me." He indicated his wounds. "Their teeth are like razors. If I go in the water, I might get torn to pieces."

Ben turned heated eyes back to McPherson. "What about you? You got any balls?"

The naval captain bridled in annoyance. "You forget who's in charge here. You work for me. Already you seem to have forgotten about the $80,000 I advanced you to deliver me a dolphin, and so far you've screwed up twice."

Ben gawked fixedly down at McPherson for a long moment, his mouth hanging agape. "Goddamn!" he finally bellowed, moving to the ladder and climbing down from the bridge. "Get me the dive gear, Charlie! I'll do this myself!"

It took Ben less than three minutes to shed most of his clothing and don the scuba gear. The magnum pistol was turned over to Charlie's keeping. One by one, he stared contemptuously at the others. "I guess I'm the only one around here with any moxie. The rest of you are nothing but spineless wimps!" With that said, he lowered his dive mask and jumped into the sea.

Destiny had never fully explored all the underwater terrain surrounding Navassa Island. Neither had the other members of the pod. What she was looking for did not require exploration, however. Homing in on Bashir's location was more like following a scent, though the use of her olfactory senses to accomplish this was not needed.

The island was like a huge mesa of honeycombed limestone jutting above the sea, the top of a submerged mountain rising from the oceanic depths abutting the Cayman Trench. Hidden within the upper portions of this geologic structure were a vast maze of interconnected tunnels and vaults, all of them created over the eons by the incessant action of carbonic acid eating away at the remnants of the ancient coral reef comprising the rock. The huge subterranean grotto housing the *thurentras* was only one of numerous caverns that lay concealed beneath the island's surface.

As Hercules skirted the lush coral, Destiny studied the life-encrusted topography intently, knowing they were getting close to Bashir's position. Passing a collapsed section of reef, a sense of deep foreboding suddenly grabbed hold of her, its malevolence springing forth from an inky maw that yawned wide. Here it was again, the raw strength of it nearly disorienting her. The feeling passed quickly as Hercules ignored the opening and continued on for perhaps another hundred meters, eventually finding a darkened crevice amid a thriving forest of elkhorn coral. Intuitively, Destiny knew they had reached the right place as Hercules sent a pulse of biosonar into the cavity to gauge its configuration.

Rising sixty feet to the ocean surface, both Hercules and Destiny recharged their lungs before descending once again, this time entering the opening. With her mount periodically emitting bursts of sonar, Destiny was able to catch vivid mental pictures of what lay before them. Like the tunnel that led to the structure the dolphins were constructing, this one gradually wound its way upward, although it was more constricted in several places. At one particular bend, Hercules was barely able to squeeze through, and Destiny had to hug the dolphin tightly in order to avoid portions of jagged rock protruding down. A short distance beyond this point, they emerged into a small dome-shaped cavern partially filled with water, the chamber inundated with ebony blackness.

With his built-in sonar, Hercules continued to share the images he was receiving, and in spite of the total darkness Destiny was able to perceive a shelf of rock off to one side. Wide enough to accommodate her small frame, the shelf was only slightly submerged. Climbing from the albino's broad back, she stepped onto the ledge, her feet covered by several inches of water. A sense of Bashir's presence suddenly came to her again, now much stronger than before.

Somewhere ahead, a light flickered, and with it the sound of someone talking. Wading through the water, she groped her way through the darkness, guided by the cavern's arched wall where it met the shelf. Following the sound, she was able to hear the voice more clearly. Stealthily, she poked her head around a bend where the light still glimmered.

Standing several meters away were two men in heated discussion, the muted light from a handheld lantern dancing eerily off the face of one of them. Destiny recognized the man immediately. It was Bashir.

Chapter 8

The damage Ben Loomins found was startling. A mass of hemp rope and rusting steel chain had somehow managed to become entangled around both drive shafts, taking them out of alignment. Attached to the chain were small anchors that had gouged the props, severely bending the blades. His vessel was not going anywhere.

How this could have happened seemed impossible. Dubiously, he eyed the void of deep indigo falling away beneath him. Off to one side more than a hundred feet from where he floated, he could see a huge congestion of barracuda filling the sea, but now they were moving away. In open water like this, the calamities that had wreaked havoc on his vessel were not supposed to happen.

Irately, he finned forward under the hull, checking for more damage. As yet, he had refrained from dropping anchor, letting the boat continue to drift slowly along. Whatever current existed was slowly taking the *Sea Lion* further away from the unknown vessel that had launched the waverunner. The farther away he got from the man who had destroyed the sounder, the better, he finally conceded. As best he could tell, his assailant had weaponry far superior to the meager firepower he currently possessed.

The bodies of dead barracuda, some of them shredded and torn beyond recognition, continued to splash down into the sea on both sides of his vessel, attesting to the labors of the Haitians still clearing the deck above him. Torpidly, they drifted along with the boat, littering the water all around him. Sudden movement caught Loomins' eye as something large and torpedo-like darted in, snatching one of the fish in a mouth lined with serrated teeth. Caught off guard by the sight, he felt his heart buck in his chest like a stallion unexpectedly coming upon a rattler. Other large shapes quickly shot in to feast on the carnage, and he realized he was in the midst of a rapidly developing feeding frenzy. Sharks were flitting all about him, some of them three times his size.

With legs pumping, Loomins turned and sped for the boat's rear platform, wanting only to get out of the water. He had been stupid to let the crew keep on dumping fish while he made the dive. One thing after another was going wrong, and he berated himself for not having thought this out better. Reaching for one of the struts supporting the platform, he pulled himself along under the cantilevered overhang. Something rough and abrasive brushed rudely against him from behind, and with a strength born by terror he got a hand on the ladder hanging down into the water.

Just before pulling himself clear of the thrashing mayhem beating the sea all about him, Loomins became aware of one more anomaly, one that he found to be every bit as strange as the chain that had mysteriously fouled his props. With his breath catching in his throat, he suddenly shivered uncontrollably. Inexplicably, he realized the sea had become very cold.

You do not understand," Bashir pleaded. "Bringing misery to others will contaminate your soul forever. There will not be seventy-two virgins waiting to give you pleasure in Paradise. If you continue with this insanity, only the fires of hell await you."

"You have betrayed us!" Kalid spat angrily. "You have betrayed Islam."

"No, my brother, it is you who has betrayed Islam. The killing of innocents is not Allah's way. If you continue on this course of madness, you taint the true Muslim faith, you defile your soul forever."

"Infidels are not innocent. They seek to desecrate Muslim cultures and Muslim lands, polluting them with unholy and obscene decadence. The Great Satan's bombs have killed many of our people. It is our obligation as Muslims to destroy those who are an abomination in the eyes of Allah. The Prophet prescribed this to be the duty of all those who follow the true Word."

"Your mind is twisted by hate."

"Have you forgotten your sworn allegiance to Allah? Under the banner of jihad, you made an oath to vanquish all those who are unclean, vile, and evil."

"I beseech you to rethink what you are doing, Kalid."

"I should kill you," Kalid threatened, "but I am sure Yeslam would be very displeased if I did not leave this task to him. You are no longer one of us."

"Yeslam is not a fit leader. He uses Islam as a pretext to do as he pleases." Bashir studied Kalid's face carefully. "Do you truly wish to follow this man?"

Kalid seemed hesitant to respond, and Bashir could see he had struck a chord of dissent. When Kalid finally answered, the words came out dull, devoid of all emotion. "Osama, himself, entrusted this mission to Yeslam. Our great leader, may he live forever, has ordained it. Do you presume to question his judgement?"

"Bin Laden deludes himself into believing he is fighting some kind of holy war, that he is doing God's work. He has often said that he looks forward to martyrdom in a showdown with the American troops hunting him. Yet he remains hidden among the Pashtun like a coward, imposing himself on their unique hospitality while others carry out his murderous directives. I have given him much thought as of late and find him to be a man without a fiber of moral decency or honor. He is nothing more than a deceiver, a vicious killer who is obsessed with spilling the blood of others. When the war with the Soviets ended in Afghanistan, he looked for other excuses to justify his passion for killing. That was when he decided to prey on the Americans and other Western cultures to satisfy his thirst for blood, hiding behind the veil of Islam and inflaming Muslims to hate anything outside the boundary of our religion." He stopped his diatribe momentarily to gauge the look of horror that was steadily growing on Kalid's face. "Yes, I do presume to question the judgement of such a man, for he places missions like this in the hands of people with the same moral temperament as he, himself, possesses. Godless murderers without any sense of honor or faith."

"You are mad!" Kalid croaked in disbelief. "You have completely lost your sensibilities."

Bashir was truly saddened. Kalid was beyond reason. "No, my Muslim brother," he uttered softly. "It is you who has lost yours. I will pray for you."

"But who will pray for you?"

It was not Kalid who had voiced the question. Bashir spun around to see Raduyev loom up out of the darkness. In the light cast by the lantern, the Chechen's expression was perfidious and cruel, but Bashir was not afraid. He had come back here to do what he could to stop a colossal tragedy from occurring, knowing he might die in the process. Raduyev was a brutal and unforgiving sort, a man who would kill as easily as drawing in a breath of air.

For over a day now, Bashir had poked around in these caverns deciding on a course of action, doing his best to remain hidden from the others. Driven by thirst, he had raided the food stores, making off with some of the limited fresh water and rations, including the lantern. He had thought he had been surreptitious in doing this while most of the Al Qaeda team slept, but now he knew otherwise. Kalid had obviously awoken and spotted him skulking about, eventually following him into the unused passage Bashir had taken to remain out of sight.

As he stared at Bin Laden's lieutenant, Bashir had to assume Raduyev must have tailed Kalid and overheard most of the ensuing confrontation that had just taken place. Opening his mouth, Bashir blurted the only words he could think to utter in that instant. "You deserted me. You left me to die."

Raduyev ignored the accusation. "How did you get back here?" he hissed warily, looking beyond both men to scan the unlit portions of the chamber. "Someone must have helped you."

"Yes," Bashir affirmed proudly. "But it was not just someone. It was the angels of God who saved me. They rescued me from the madness that was slowly consuming me."

The Chechen studied him oddly before projecting a pernicious sneer. "Angels would not waste their time on a pitiful blasphemer like you," he rasped cuttingly. "You have offended Allah and all those who serve him. You are lower than a Jew. You are the filth that comes from the bowels of a Zionist pig."

Bashir let out a disdainful little laugh. Caught up in mind-clouding hate, men like Raduyev never seemed to grow tired of using anti-

Semitic slurs as a form of insult. Ever since having been saved by the strange angelic beings, Bashir's thinking was the sharpest it had ever been, and it suddenly dawned on him that in the Muslim world most political legitimacy was acquired through the bashing of Israelis. With this in mind, he responded with the only logical reply within him. "Then perhaps I will learn how to create rather than destroy."

Raduyev's expression abruptly stiffened, his eyes ablaze with the threat of mayhem as his hand came to rest on the hilt of the Bowie knife strapped to his side. "You think Jews do not destroy?" he said scornfully.

"They only destroy in self-defense. Look at what they have done with just a tiny sliver of desert. Perhaps we can learn from them."

Ashamedly, Bashir could not help but measure the accomplishments of his own Palestinian people against those of the Israelis. In the Arab world, illiteracy, poverty, and disease still reigned supreme while Israel boasted a $100 billion economy with less than one-thousandth of the world's population. During a brief but enlightening discussion he had had on the beach the other night, the man called Jacob had gently pointed out several unavoidable truths that, though disturbing, had opened his eyes. Israel had the highest ratio of university degrees per capita on the planet, possessing some of the world's finest medical, scientific, and technically sophisticated research facilities. By comparison, the record of his own people was sorrowful, with the predominantly Sunni Palestinians achieving next to nothing that could be considered beneficial. Even the network of high-tech greenhouses the Palestinians had inherited from the Jewish settlers upon Israel's withdrawal from Gaza ended up falling into ruin and vandalization. After more than sixty years, the Palestinians of Gaza continued to live off foreign aid, putting their efforts into building rockets and bombs instead of a future, and teaching their children to intensely loathe everything associated with Zionism. The hate of his people was poisoning their minds, preventing them from pursuing anything even remotely constructive. Unfortunately, there seemed to be a bottomless pool of young Palestinians who sought to satisfy the rage instilled in them by radical Muslim clerics incessantly preaching anti-Semitic hatred.

Bashir knew that the recruitment of Muslim men to the call of jihad was escalating. Both Hezbollah and Hamas were steadily growing in numbers these days, gaining more and more political support among the Muslim moderates to wipe Israel off the face of the planet. They never seemed to tire of provoking the Jews through suicide bombings, kidnappings, hijackings, murders, or other forms of mayhem, periodically prodding the Zionist bull into retaliating, then running to the United Nations for protection. Every time this happened, it seemed, the UN tended to openly condemn Israel for its use of disproportionate force, interceding itself into the conflict before the retaliation could escalate to a point that would obliterate the paramilitary infrastructures of either Hezbollah or Hamas.

Based on what he had heard over the last several years, Bashir was convinced that Hezbollah had gained dramatically in strength. Firmly rooted among Lebanon's general population, Hezbollah had no scruples about using civilians as human shields to discourage Israeli bombing strikes. Using Lebanese residential homes as launching sites, they fired Katyusha rockets designed to kill Israeli citizens. Tactics like this worked well in their favor, serving them on the public relations front that molded world opinion. Collateral damage caused by Israeli bombs in taking out a launch site often killed women and children, drawing widespread condemnation from other nations.

Now that his thinking was clear, Bashir could plainly see the escalating fatalities and misery such strategy brought to the people of Lebanon. These things, however, were of little concern to Hezbollah. Lives were unimportant, only results. A state within a state, Hezbollah was a Shia Islamist political party within the Lebanese government. Fortified by members of the Iranian Revolutionary Guard, it received substantial financial backing from the Iranian government, essentially making it Iran's attack dog. And the government of Iran, led by a group of rabid Islamo-fascists, had vowed to exterminate Israel. Iran, he was certain, would never relent on this primary goal, constantly testing the will of the international coalition.

To its credit, Hezbollah had often demonstrated innovative skills in carrying out its objectives, and Bashir wondered about all the good that could be accomplished if this same creativity were ever used toward constructive rather than destruction ends. As had been proven many times, Hezbollah seemed to have an uncanny ability at raising vast sums of money to fund its operations, most of it funneled into terrorism, guerrilla warfare, and media coverage that both justified and glorified their efforts.

The recent alliance between Bin Laden and Hezbollah struck Bashir as odd, however. In the past, Hezbollah and Al Qaeda had pursued different agendas, with Hezbollah focusing primarily on Israel and fomenting sectarian violence in Iraq while the Sunnis of Bin Laden had previously confined themselves mainly to Afghanistan, Pakistan, Yugoslavia, Bosnia, and Chechnya. Hezbollah wanted to eradicate the Zionist state while Al Qaeda wanted to destroy the United States. Al Qaeda's Sunni Wahhabist ideology was largely incompatible with Hezbollah's relatively liberal brand of Shia Islam. Surprisingly, Bin Laden had initially demonstrated a distaste for the Shia suicide bombings and attacks on civilian targets in Iraq, and he had openly condemned Hezbollah for preventing Palestinians from using Lebanon as a staging area for incursions against Israel. Hezbollah, on the other hand, had denounced Al Qaeda for killing innocents, claiming its own resistance toward the Jewish state by whatever means to be justified and legitimate. Despite these differences, something had changed in recent times, though Hezbollah continued to publicly deny any links to Bin Laden's organization.

And Bashir now understood what had united the divergent militant groups. In order to wipe out Israel, Iran needed Israel's closest ally neutralized, and that meant collaborating with Al Qaeda to take down Bin Laden's greatest enemy.

All these things coursed in the back of Bashir's mind as he stared back at Raduyev. He could see his brash retort had the equivalency of a stinging slap. In the feeble light cast by the lantern, the Chechen's face darkened, glowering with malignant hatred.

In a flash, Raduyev drew his blade, positioning the point of it under Bashir's chin. "The words of a Jew-lover are nothing but gibberish to me," he ranted. "Tell me who brought you here or I will send you off to the fires of hell this instant."

"I already told you," Bashir said calmly. "I was helped by angels."

"Liar!" Raduyev screeched. Grabbing Bashir by the throat with his free hand, he pulled the knife back in preparation for a lethal underhand strike that would plunge the shaft deep into the Palestinian's abdomen.

Bashir offered no resistance. He was prepared to die now that he was completely free of the dogma and ignorance that had blinded him from the truth his entire life.

"Stop!" a voice suddenly cried out, the sound ringing through the chamber.

Spoken in English, the outcry had come from somewhere behind Bashir. As Raduyev continued to clutch his throat, Bashir noted the look of shock this sudden intrusion had evoked in the Chechen's expression. With eyes opened wide, Raduyev stared over Bashir's shoulder, trying to discern the presence lurking in the darkness.

Pivoting his head around as far as the Chechen's restraining grip would allow, Bashir tried following Raduyev's gaze.

"Stop!" the voice repeated firmly. "Don't hurt him!"

It was then that Bashir saw Destiny's slender form materialize out of the blackness.

It had never been Destiny's intention to become involved in the disputes between men. Conflict, she knew, was the result of fear, and fear only intensified the perception of separateness that kept people at odds with one another. But then conflict always seemed to leave misery in its wake, and as she watched the scene that was taking place before her, she knew she could not let Bashir die.

"I have seen you before," said the man holding Bashir by the throat. "You were riding an accursed white dolphin."

Destiny moved closer, fully exposing herself in the light spilling from the lantern. She had heard enough of the confrontation to know these were the Islamic extremists Jay Jay had talked about with Jacob. "Please let this man go," she implored. "He means you no harm."

For one seemingly unending moment the man stared back at her as if she was crazy. All at once, he threw his head back and let out a harsh, rabid laugh. "Allah is truly a wondrous and accommodating God. He delivers into my hands the very thing I have been thinking about these last several days." Abruptly, his expression changed into a sneer. "I do not know how you got in here, but you will soon pay a most painful price for meddling in our business."

Up close, Destiny sensed something emanating from the man that was altogether different from the first individual Bashir had been arguing with, and it made her blood run cold. An aura of negative energy seemed to surround him. It was the same iniquity that had invaded her awareness a short time earlier. Here was a man whose soul belonged to the dark side of creation, a sentience she intuitively understood would be immune to the benign effects of the dolphin art.

Bashir struggled against the hand gripping his throat. "There is nothing you can do against an angel," he gasped. "She has the power to heal severe injuries in seconds."

"Silence!" Raduyev snapped. "I forbid you to speak any more." He looked over at the other man. "Grab her, Kalid!"

Destiny remained still as Kalid stepped toward her, keeping her gaze fixed on Raduyev. "Release Bashir at once." She could see a tinge of confusion manifest itself fleetingly in his eyes, knowing immediately that such a man fed off the fear he was able to instill in others. By showing no fear, she was diminishing his command of the situation.

"Did you hear what I said, Kalid?" Raduyev yelled. "I told you to grab her!"

Ignoring Kalid, Destiny stood her ground, continuing to lock eyes with Raduyev. She was not going to leave without Bashir.

Overcoming his hesitation, Kalid reached for her arm. Blue sparks suddenly flared, accompanied by the sound of a sizzling pop as his fingers made contact. Kalid screamed as he was flung back violently, his body slamming against the cavern wall and crumbling to the floor. The acrid smell of ozone hung heavily in the air.

In slack-jawed disbelief, Raduyev stared at Kalid's unconscious form. Shifting his eyes back to Destiny, he said, "What manner of satanic trickery is this?"

Bashir managed to pry Raduyev's fingers from his throat. "Your twisted brain refuses to accept what your eyes have just seen," he admonished disdainfully. "Trying to capture one of Allah's angels has sentenced you to eternal suffering in the next life." Taking advantage of the Chechen's bewilderment, he moved quickly to Destiny's side, bringing the lantern with him.

Destiny looked back at Raduyev. "Do not try to follow us," she said, the hint of a warning firmly implied in the words.

Raduyev did not reply, totally aghast at what he had just witnessed.

Turning, Destiny led Bashir back to the pool of water flooding the adjacent cavern. "You'll have to hold your breath for at least two minutes if I'm going to get you out of here," she told him.

Bashir gave her a venerating nod, his eyes filled with pious awe. "For you, my sweet angel, I will hold my breath for all eternity. Forever will I be your humble servant, to do anything you wish of me."

"Be sure to keep your head low," Destiny instructed as Bashir straddled Hercules' broad back. With that, the albino bull dove.

The sight of Destiny with Bashir sitting behind her as they rode Hercules surprised Jake. He had been keeping to the *Angel's* pilothouse where he had been maintaining an uninterrupted vigilance of the *Sea Lion* as it continued to drift without power nearly a half mile away. Descending to the main deck, he moved quickly to the boat's dive platform where he helped the girl come aboard. Meeting Jake's cold stare, Bashir smiled meekly up at him as he continued to hold fast to the large albino, seemingly unsure if he should follow.

"You have nothing to fear from this man," Destiny assured him after he had taken the girl aside. "Bashir is not the same person that attacked you back at Gaia. He has changed."

Jake studied Destiny's earnest expression. "How did you find him?"

Destiny looked away. "All will be revealed soon enough, but now is not the time."

The girl's comment jarred something loose from Jake's memory. Achilles had made a similar statement the day before, though it was in response to a different question. Such evasiveness puzzled him. "I need answers," he insisted hotly, wondering if Destiny's naivety was impeding her judgement. "Bashir is an Islamic militant. I've had experience with men like him and deception is part of their ideology. How do I know he can be trusted?"

Destiny turned her face up to Jake again, her eyes searching his. "His mind is no longer fettered with irrational fear. Of this he has purged himself. Fear is the underlying cause of all human conflict, the wedge that separates people and brings on hate. In shedding his fear, Bashir has become fully aware of our commonality, the unifying force that connects us all."

Jake turned his head to observe Bashir standing beside Phillipe and Zimby. All three were laughing at something said, possibly a shared joke. Perhaps what the girl was telling him was true, but then again, one could never be completely certain. "All right," he finally conceded. "I'll rely on your judgement for the time being, but if he causes me any problems, I'm holding you responsible."

A mischievous glint suddenly showed in Destiny's eyes, adorned by a mirthful smile. "Oh…and what do you propose to do if it turns out I'm wrong about him?"

Jake took immediate pause. This was the first sign of outright flirtation he had seen in the girl, a quality he had assumed was not in her character. "I, uh…I'll think of something," he stuttered. "Perhaps a good spanking will be in order."

"What's a spanking?"

Staring down at her, Jake realized her innocence was showing again. Now it was his turn to be evasive. He made an effort to give her his best enigmatic grin. "You'll find out if such punishment is ever warranted."

Destiny responded with a mock pout. "Then I guess I'll never get to learn the meaning of the word."

Jake became reflective. "You're quite sure about Bashir, aren't you?"

The smile on Destiny's face turned serious. "Very sure. A change in one person is like a ripple on the water, radiating out to affect everything it touches. If enough people underwent the same positive change that has transformed Bashir, the whole world would become a better place. Strife and war would become a thing of the past."

Jake fell silent, musing over the girl's logic. Obviously, she was seeing things that were alien to him, things he had difficulty understanding. The dream with the rainbow had given him only partial insight to the mysteries Destiny and the dolphins shared, but now his memory of it had all but evaporated, leaving him devoid of most of the things he had previously grasped. Still, some shreds of it continued to stay with him.

Looking in the direction of the *Sea Lion*, Jake said, "I don't think Ben Loomins is very happy right now. I assume you had something to do with what happened."

Destiny nodded demurely. "I only wanted to keep him away from you. Someone might have gotten killed."

Jake frowned, knowing what she really meant. Destiny didn't want anyone aboard the *Sea Lion* dying as a result of his actions. "But you must have known about the chains Achilles tied off to his propeller shafts. Loomins was just sitting there waiting for his partner to show up. The chains would have been enough to stop his vessel."

"I had to be sure," Destiny said softly. "Those chains were old and corroded having sat on the bottom all those years. Achilles wasn't convinced they wouldn't break."

Jake let out a long weary sigh. "And you thought I would've fired upon Loomins if he kept coming?"

"You might not have had any other option. I wanted to prevent such a possibility from happening."

Jake narrowed his eyes, looking for clues in the girl's face that would reveal more. Had she seen something? Using their collective mental capability, had she and the pod made some kind of statistical analysis of all the information available to them and come up with a probable future event? Trying to second-guess what was going on was starting to wear him out.

Deciding to steer clear of the subject, Jake said, "I'm getting ready to pull anchor. Dr. Grahm has seen enough of his boat and would like to be leaving. As for myself, I've got to be in Port-au-Prince tomorrow."

Destiny stared up at him, her demeanor serene. "Will I ever see you again?"

"Only if I'm still welcome back at the place you call Gaia."

"You'll always be welcome there, Jay Jay. The pod has accepted you as one of their own."

"I have one problem, though."

"Yes?"

"What do I do about Bashir?"

Destiny turned around to observe the Palestinian. "Bashir is now my responsibility. I'm sure Jacob can use his help…at least for the time being."

"I just hope you're not being overly optimistic about this change in him. I'd hate to see him revert back to what he was."

"Bashir sees the world through different eyes now. Free from the confusion that had plagued him all his life, he has finally found himself. He no longer has a desire to harm anyone. I sense within him a need to build rather than destroy."

Jake thought about the dolphin art again. Having been exposed to its strange power, he believed what Destiny was telling him to be true. But as he began making preparations to get underway, he suddenly realized there might actually be a potentially bigger threat aboard his vessel than the one Bashir posed. With bells and whistles going off in his head, he became aware of the way Nick Henderson kept staring at the *Sea Lion* floating in the distance.

A jumble of thoughts wended their way through Raduyev's neurotic brain, most of them perverse and ugly. This was the second time he had been thwarted by the dolphin girl. What angered him even more was Bashir's insistence that she was an angel sent by God. But now that he had time to analyze the strange occurrence he had witnessed, he was convinced such a claim was absurd. Bashir was stupid to think Allah would pit one of his angels against followers of the one true religion. Physically, Bashir had been the weakest among his team. It only followed that his mind would exhibit the same shortcomings as his body, easily fooled by another's duplicity. Obviously, the girl had purposely misled the Palestinian into accepting this false belief. Most likely she had been armed with some kind of defensive weapon hidden under the wet suit she wore, perhaps some kind of a taser that produced a powerful but non-lethal electrical shock. It was the only plausible explanation he could come up with to rationalize what he had seen her do to Kalid.

Initially, the event had left Raduyev stunned, and by the time he had regained his wits, both Bashir and the girl had vanished, disappearing beyond a heavy grouping of stalagmites. Using the flashlight he carried, he had followed, ignoring Kalid's inert form sprawled on the cavern floor. He had not traveled far before discerning a faint glow. Drawing the 9mm Browning from his shoulder holster, he had advanced rapidly toward it. The lantern Bashir had taken with him had sat deserted on a rocky ledge, its light reflecting off a pool of darkened water. Movement had caught his eye, and he had turned his light to follow it. A huge white dolphin had dipped below the surface, the girl and Bashir sitting in tandem astride its back. The unexpectedness of the sight had caused him to react too slowly. Nevertheless, he had aimed his pistol and emptied the clip, nearly deafened by the shots echoing hollowly about the low-slung chamber. When nothing had floated to the surface, he could only surmise the bullets had missed their targets. After that, he had scrambled hurriedly to the surface to investigate where they had gone. Obviously, they had escaped through one of the many underwater tunnels that riddled the island and were on their way back to the boat that had brought them here.

He had been right. From a concealed position that overlooked the sea, he had watched Bashir and the girl ride the huge white dolphin out to the vessel he had failed to destroy two days earlier, and as he studied the boat through the spyglasses, his rage continued to mount. Once again, his chance at retribution had been foiled.

Silently he cursed the girl, vowing to get revenge. If not for the repairs that were currently taking place on Allah's Sword, he might have been able to take the sub out to where the boat lay at anchor and ram it into a mass of splintered wood. But now all he could do was observe the people aboard it, powerless to do anything. Magnified through the optics of the spyglasses he was looking through, he had a clear view of the man he had failed to kill, and his hatred abruptly soared to a new height.

Seething with rage, he swung the binoculars by seventy degrees to the west to observe the other vessel he had noticed a short time earlier, this one further out to sea. Through the lens, he could make out several members of its crew working hard to clear the rear deck of fish. Another crew member was shedding scuba gear, and by the manner in which the man was gesticulating, Raduyev could see he was clearly angry.

Disregarding the sight for the moment, he brought the glasses to bear on the first vessel once again, realizing its anchor was being hoisted. With intensified frustration, he continued to watch as the boat swung around to take on an eastern heading, the lettering on its stern taunting him all the more.

Watching the vessel depart, a sudden realization closed in on him with the power of a hydraulic vise. His hidden base had now been compromised. Bashir knew enough about the mission to bring it to a screeching halt should that information fall into the wrong hands. And with the Palestinian traitor currently aboard Javolyn's vessel, he could only assume such a possibility to be inevitable. That left the Chechen with only two options. Either he would have to eliminate Javolyn and those of his crew very quickly, or he would have to accelerate his original timetable. He already had one Rodong rocket in readiness, and that he could fire any time he chose.

As the departing vessel gradually grew smaller in size, only one thing provided Raduyev with a modicum of appeasement, and that was the information he had supplied to Ortega. We shall soon see who is the true avenger, he consoled himself.

It was just after sunset when the *San Carlo* crept close to the tiny seaside village. Setting its anchor, it floated no more than 500 meters offshore, awaiting its intended cargo. Standing on the walkway outside the unlit bridge, Sebastian Ortega aimed a powerful spotlight shoreward, blinking it on and off three times. Several seconds elapsed before he was answered in kind, though the signal coming from the village consisted of only two short flashes followed by two more after a brief interval.

Satisfied, Ortega glanced at the luminous dial on his watch before turning to Pedro. "We have fallen behind schedule," he announced acidly. The odor of something in the air made him look at the man a little more closely. In spite of the stench of rotting fish hanging over the ship, the smell of liquor on Pedro's breath was almost as pungent. Cardoza's nephew, it seemed, continued to offend him on a daily basis. "I want these villagers brought aboard as quickly as possible. Any more delays and I will hold you personally responsible."

Pedro shrugged as if such a threat were inconsequential. "I have no control over how fast these Haitians can climb a ladder."

"Just do it!" Ortega growled.

Pedro shrugged again, saying nothing as he moved to the stairs that would take him to the lower deck.

Watching him go, Ortega could not help but think how easy it would be to put a bullet in the back of the man's head. But doing that, he knew, would bring the wrath of Cardoza down on him, the only thing that had always kept his desire to do away with Pedro in check. He had seen firsthand what Cardoza's pet tiger had done to others, and he had no wish to suffer the same fate.

Ortega was in a particularly bad mood, having taken the trawler to the coordinates given him by Omar before coming here. Lowering one of the newly acquired motorboats over the side, he had sent five of his men ahead while he and Fernando had taken the helicopter in a coordinated raid designed to catch by surprise all those residing in the hidden cove. Unfortunately, the place had been deserted. Both the man who had attacked him back at Navassa and his boat were missing. Being denied the baleful things he envisioned doing to the man continued to grate on him as though he were being dragged over jagged coral, and now more than ever he needed some form of satisfaction.

Even more disappointing was the absence of the girl and those incredible white dolphins seen with her. The thought of this only served to increase his irritable mood, and as he watched the loading of human cargo, he entertained himself with the various ways he might go about finding them. Remembering the other vessel he had spotted from the air during his flight to Saint-Marc, he made himself a promise to seek the boat out at the first opportunity. But right now, he had a delivery to make.

And following the delivery, the *San Carlo* was committed to assisting Omar with something else. Even after the trawler got underway, Ortega continued to muse over what that something else entailed.

It was late evening by the time the *Avenging Angel* pulled abreast of the cliffs concealing the cove entrance. Out of the darkness, another boat arrived at the same time, its size much smaller than the North Sea trawler.

"It's Jimenez," Destiny informed Jake. "Let him come alongside." The dolphins had detected the watercraft's approach long before it materialized out of the gloom, and now the girl sensed something to be very wrong.

As the boat came alongside, Destiny recognized another man in the boat with Jimenez. It was Ronaldo Trebek.

"Everyone in Malique is missing," Jimenez told Destiny, his voice crackling like dry twigs caught in a flame. "I came here looking for Jacob, but he is not in the cove. I found it strange that his boat was tied to the main pier in the village, but he was nowhere to be found."

Destiny listened with Jake and Grahm at her sides. Something nudged her consciousness, and she became aware of the other creatures that had always stayed close to her mother. Hearing their whispers, she immediately went rigid.

Though foretold several years earlier by Amphitrite, Destiny had never thought it would come to pass. Erzulie had once again come to Malique leading a band of men.

Acknowledging Jimenez's searching eyes, she found it difficult to utter the words aloud. "They have all been taken away."

In the glare of the *Angel's* deck lights, Jimenez appeared to shrink back in horror. And while Trebek seemed downcast, Destiny could see her words had not impacted him in the same manner.

"Who took them away?" Jake demanded.

Destiny was momentarily confused. Fighting through the disorientation, she was able to perceive occasional glimpses of what had taken place. Glancing about her, she looked in the direction where urgency was most needed. "Both mother and Jacob are prisoners of Erzulie. They have been taken south."

"Who is Erzulie?" Jake asked.

Destiny turned to stare up at him. "A witch of the voudun. Her son is a ranking member of the Tonton Makout."

Jake shifted his gaze to Zimbola who hovered close. "Zimby, that name mean anything to you?"

Zimby stiffened with graveness. "They are the worst type of scum. It is rumored that a man by the name of Ternier is their leader. He runs the prison in Port-au-Prince."

The mention of the name elicited something residing deep inside Jake, causing him to stare sharply at the Jamaican giant. "Henri Ternier?"

Zimby nodded grimly.

"How long have you known this?" Jake asked in surprise. The name had remained lodged in his memory ever since Myers had told him a man called Henri Ternier had murdered his grandfather.

Not a trace of guilt showed in Zimbola's face. "Long enough to know that revenge will not bring back Mercades."

The first twinges of anger boiled up from the pit of Jake's stomach, but he quickly gained control of himself. "You should've told me this before."

"Would it have made a difference?" the Jamaican replied.

"It might have," Jake retorted, becoming aware of the perplexity this sudden turn in the conversation had invoked in the faces of Grahm and his assistants.

Jake brought his attention back to Destiny, his manner pressing. "What about the others? What happened to them?"

"North," Destiny answered dully. "Most have been put aboard a ship that is heading north. It's the same ship you fought against."

"You mean the fishing trawler?"

"Yes."

Jake watched Destiny's face anxiously. "Jacob and your mother…do you sense them?"

Destiny nodded. Her mother's presence was very strong now though she knew she was many miles away.

"Can you take me to them?"

"I think so."

Grahm spoke up for the first time, looking completely bewildered as he stared at Jake. "What do you intend on doing?"

Jake thrust out his jaw, his face a mask of determination. "I'm going to rescue a friend."

You want me to do what?" The speaker's tone indicated incredulous disbelief.

Jake faced the man he had come to see with a calm air. On his way back to Port-au-Prince he had made a brief satellite call, arranging this impromptu rendezvous on the fly. The face-to-face meeting just beyond the harbor limits was necessary. He could not afford the risk of having this discussion overheard in a monitored phone conversation.

"I'm asking for your help, Mat," Jake said. "This job will require a true professional."

"But breaking into Haiti's National Penitentiary. You're joking, right?"

"No, Mat, this is no joke. You ever hear of the Tonton Makout?"

Mat fell silent for several seconds. "Yeah. They were a paramilitary group here in Haiti. The Duvalier's used them to keep the population in check when they ruled the country. The Makout were disbanded years ago."

"Wrong," Jake shot back, looking to see how Mat reacted to what he said next. "They're still around and they work for a guy named Henri Ternier who runs the prison. You remember the name, don't you? He was the one who tortured and killed Myers' grandfather, Mercades Myers."

"How do you know this is the same man?"

"I don't, but whether or not he is, I still have to spring some people from the prison he runs."

"And you think we'll just be able to saunter in there and break them out."

"Goddammit, Mat, don't make me call in my marker."

"I know I owe you, buddy, but what you're asking is nothing short of nuts, something that could easily mushroom into an international incident. If word ever got out that a member of the DHS abetted a prison break in a sovereign nation, the media would never let it go, not to mention the mess it would put Uncle Sam in."

Jake hesitated before letting out a remorseful sigh. "You're right, Mat. Only an asshole would make such a stupid request. Forget I ever asked. I've got to go."

"Wait a second, Jake, tell me you're not going to be so dumb as to go this alone."

"There are some things in life that cannot be ignored, and this is one of them."

"But why?"

"Because some friends need help and the people holding them will torture them if I don't get them out of there. I'm talking about people whose only crime is trying to make the world a better place."

Mat did not immediately reply, lapsing into a deep and prolonged silence. Finally, in a changed voice that was soft and conciliatory, he said, "All right, Jake, count me in. Tell me how you'd like to do this."

With brooding eyes, Chester Hennington stared pensively at the man looking back at him. Though the reflection remained the same as it always had, he knew that inwardly he had changed. Why then, he continued to ask himself, had he arranged for Ortega to rendezvous with Ternier at Malique. Hadn't he betrayed the woman?

But deep down he knew the answer. The white mambo had intended for it to happen. With unrestrained willingness she had given him the amulet, knowing it would be handed over to Ternier. Then she had done something to him. Using some strange miraculous power, she had opened him up, giving him the means to transcend both his mind and body to connect with his soul. And in so doing she had rid him of an immense burden, cleansing him of all the rot that had built up inside. But in the process, he had become a party to something that would defy reason under normal circumstances. He had continued to do what he had always done, following the same path for which his talents were best suited. This confused him all the more. Now free of the guilt that had always nagged away at him, he had nevertheless provided aid to three of the vilest men he had ever known.

Yes, it was the only explanation he could come up with. The white mambo had wanted this to happen even though it would bring harm to the entire village, including herself. None of this made any sense.

Nonetheless, he felt no compulsion to interfere with the web that was rapidly forming, though those ensnared in its strands would surely meet their doom. Falling into Erzulie's clutches would be a fate worse than death, of that he was certain. And yet all he could do was look on like a man awed by the sight of a huge spider about to sink its deadly fangs into a helpless victim, too horrified to do anything to stop it. Without understanding why, he felt no remorse over his own feckless behavior, realizing he was willing to let events unfold regardless of how hopeless they appeared.

With deep resignation, Hennington dropped this thought, focusing on another matter. Another of his clients had finally contacted him and a package needed to be delivered. It was important he notify Javolyn right away.

As he reached for his wireless phone, the device unexpectedly rang. "Who is calling?" he asked in French. But from the number displayed on the phone's small screen, he already knew.

The voice that answered was cold and impatient. "Come to my office at once!"

Wearily, Hennington got up and reached for his white jacket, mildly surprised that Ternier had arrived back so soon from Malique.

With Mat providing suggestions, Jake began putting together a plan. Ronaldo Trebek proved to be an invaluable asset as they hashed out the obstacles they were sure to encounter. Trebek had insisted on accompanying Jake back to Port-au-Prince once he had learned where Amphitrite and Jacob had been taken. Standing over a chart table aboard the *Angel*, all three men studied the layout of the prison compound Trebek had sketched out.

Trebek tapped a finger on the drawing, emphasizing one particular area. "It is here where you will find them," he proclaimed emphatically.

Jake raised an eyebrow. "How can you be sure?"

Trebek lowered his eyes and fidgeted slightly, suddenly appearing self-conscious. "Long ago, I was a member of the Tonton Makout. Having to admit this is a source of personal shame for me. I used to work with Ternier and know the way his mind works." He placed a finger on the sketch again. "There are holding cells in this area that were used for interrogation and the torture of political dissidents. Ternier has always had a penchant for torturing his enemies. It gives him pleasure. I can assure you he still uses those cells for this purpose."

Jake's expression hardened, and Trebek found it necessary to look away. Placing a finger on the paper again, he added, "At the end of this hallway is a steel door that leads to Erzulie's chamber. To gain entrance to this area, you must first get past the guards posted at the door blocking the opposite end of the hallway."

Mat shook his head. "That's the least of our problems. Just getting into the compound is what concerns me. I've seen that penitentiary. It's like a fortress."

"There is a way in," Trebek intoned enigmatically. "One where you will not meet any resistance."

"Where?"

"Here!" Trebek indicated a place further back from the north side of the prison. "This is your way in, an entrance to an underground tunnel." He drew a line that terminated inside the prison close to the interrogation area. "This tunnel dates back to the days when Haiti was a French colony."

Mat still looked skeptical. "And you think it'll be unguarded, or at the very least unsecured."

"Yes."

"Explain!"

"Only Erzulie and her spawn use this tunnel. Ternier is Erzulie's spawn. The locals who know of this tunnel keep clear of it, believing a terrible curse will befall them should they ever wander into it."

"You can take us to this tunnel?"

Trebek hesitated, his expression turning grim. "I will lead you into the prison."

"I assume you know the danger you'll be putting yourself in if you do that," Jake offered.

A small wistful smile came to Trebek's face. "It is but a small price to pay. Think of it as a form of atonement for past sins. I can never truly repay the white mambo for saving me from a former life ill spent."

"I will also go with you," Zimbola said, crowding in close to stand beside Jake.

Jake opened his mouth to object, but before he could voice his disapproval, Destiny stepped forward to join the discussion. "I'll be coming as well." Up to this point the girl had been standing off to one side, her manner subdued and distant.

"That's not a good idea," Jake said, bristling at the suggestion. "Way too risky. I'd rather you stay aboard the *Angel* until this business is finished."

Upon learning what had happened back near Malique, he had insisted Destiny remain with him in order to keep her safe. Putting her back in the path of danger was something he would not allow.

Destiny locked eyes with him, and within them Jake could see a massive unwillingness to go along with what he wanted. "There is more to this than you can see," she said in that soft mellifluous voice of hers. "People I dearly love are being held captive in that prison. I must go."

"No way." Jake was adamant.

"This is not a matter of choice. I must go to clear the way for the future."

Zimbola placed a gentle hand on Jake's shoulder, stilling the protest about to be launched from his lips. "Going without the girl is not a good idea."

Jake spun, turning a sulky glare on the Jamaican towering over him. "Are you out of your mind, Zimby? You want to get her killed?"

Frustration showed in the giant's expression. "The girl will bring balance to the plan. She will provide the light against the darkness that will block our way."

"Say it in terms that have meaning to me," Jake snapped irritably, his tone scalding.

"Without Destiny's help, Erzulie will defeat us. A witch of the voudun is very powerful and can only be countered by one strong in white magic."

Jake's face soured even more. "You're wasting your time if you expect me to buy into that voodoo crap. I've told you before, black magic doesn't exist. This Erzulie is just a woman who can be stopped with a bullet like anyone else."

Zimbola looked ridiculously helpless under Jake's cold stare. Here was the subject that had caused them to butt heads whenever it arose, an irritating source of disagreement that had often come between them in the past.

Destiny came to Zimbola's defense. "You have to trust what your friend is telling you, Jay Jay." Her tone continued to remain dulcet and disarming, but Jake could not mistake the underlying conviction her words conveyed. "A gun barrel will not be enough to stop Erzulie," she stressed.

Jake was momentarily taken back. He had not even considered the girl to be capable of believing in such nonsense. To accept voodoo was to believe in the supernatural, an acceptance of phenomena at variance with the world he was able to grasp.

Abruptly, Jake shrank back within himself. Hadn't the girl already demonstrated her ability to invoke events that were discordant with the physical universe he had come to know? Having to confront such a quandary flustered him, and he suddenly found himself at a crossroad. And then it hit home. With unsettling clarity, he knew he had to let Destiny have her way. All his instincts were now clamoring for him to withdraw an obstinacy he could no longer justify.

Discharging a reluctant sigh, Jake found himself caving. "You'll stay behind me! You won't leave my side!"

"I will not hinder you," Destiny agreed.

Mat, whose head had been swiveling back and forth in confusion over the interplay, looked alarmed. "Jake, are you nuts?" Though Mat was a close friend, he had never liked calling him Jay Jay. Dismayed, he turned to stare at Destiny uneasily, then swung back to face Jake. "You'll be putting this whole mission in jeopardy if you let her come."

"There's no time to explain, Mat. You wouldn't believe it if I told you anyway." Jake kept his eyes on Destiny as he said this. "All I can tell you is that we'll be worse off if we don't take her. You'll have to trust me on this one."

Mat shook his head, glancing sideways at Destiny in perplexity. "Voodoo and witches. Now I've heard it all."

Chapter 9

Suspended upside down by a rusty chain looped severely about his ankles, the man whimpered weakly. The chain had cut deeply into the flesh, causing a dark brown mass of congealing fluid to form about the links. Scattered all over the man's naked body, red and purple clusters of burns and welts puckered grotesquely. As if in supplication to the harsh discolorings, the contents of the man's bowels had dribbled shamelessly down his back.

Sniffing the rank air, Ternier licked the drool collecting on his lips as he took in the sight. The combined smell of blood, urine and feces had always excited him. By keeping the man alive a little longer, he had prolonged his own pleasure.

Apprehending Emmanuel Baptiste had provided Ternier with far more than he would ever have expected. The legal papers found in Baptiste's possession had initially surprised him, but then after careful scrutiny, the documents had raised some compelling questions. First and foremost, a business venture of the magnitude described by Tursiops Worldwide would require considerable financing. And it was the source of this financing that had interested the Colonel the most.

Ternier stepped closer to Baptiste's inverted form and turned to one of the men beside him. "Remove the hood!" he ordered.

The man nodded gravely, then stooped low to untie the hood covering Baptiste's head.

The Colonel immediately assumed the mien of a maestro pleased with the results of his work. Baptiste's face was swollen and pasty almost beyond recognition. It was the look of a man close to death.

Prodding Baptiste's head with the tip of his boot, Ternier watched the man swing back and forth several times before speaking. "I ask you again, how were you going to finance this operation?"

Though Emmanuel's eyes were reduced to mere slits by the distended flesh surrounding them, his gaze seemed to focus on the man standing above him. Somehow finding the strength, he spit forth a wad of bloody saliva that fell short of Ternier's boots.

"Go ahead and kill me already!" he moaned between labored gasps. "I will never tell you!"

The Colonel shook his head ever so slightly, eliciting a small sadistic laugh. "Such stubbornness will do more harm than you ever imagined." Pivoting his head, he looked over at the other man in the room. "Bring in the woman!"

Through eyes horribly swollen, Emmanuel had trouble recognizing the female being supported between two burly guards, her legs dragging limply behind her. Slowly the fuzzy image coalesced, and Emmanuel's straining heart pounded so hard it seemed his chest might burst. A dizzying moment passed before he became cognizant of the deafening animal wail that filled the room. It was the sound of incredible despair, a cry that had surged up from the depths of his being to echo hopelessly off the cell walls.

The woman that had been brought into the room was his wife, Lucette.

Amphitrite lay without complaint in the darkened chamber, her ankles and wrists shackled in such a way as to leave her spread-eagled horizontally on a raised slab of concrete. Adjacent to her on an identical slab, Jacob was similarly pinioned.

From a nearby table, Erzulie cackled raucously as she played with the amulet dangling between her gnarled fingers. "You were wise to relinquish this little trinket," she rasped, the words sounding as if rising through a throat filled with gravel. "The whisperings of the rada cannot be ignored. It was only a matter of time before they realized one such as you would be unworthy to possess it. You had no choice but to give it up. The amulet would have become a danger to you had you insisted on keeping it." Once again she cackled triumphantly. "Is this not so?"

Amphitrite did not reply, twisting her head around just enough to see the amulet glow with the ominous redness of a burning coal within Erzulie's claw-like hands.

"Is this not so?" Erzulie repeated, this time screeching out the question in a shrill, hideous shout.

"The wisdom of the rada is not for me to question," Amphitrite offered appeasingly. "Their motives are often hidden and rarely understood. The fact that you are now the amulet's possessor reveals their intentions."

The answer seemed to satisfy the crone. "Yes, yes," she readily agreed. "It was their wish that I should have it."

Erzulie suddenly rose and drifted closer. With her hood lowered, the room's gloomy interior did little to conceal the woman's frightful ugliness. "But now it is my wish that you pay for the humiliation you had put me through so many years ago."

Amphitrite could only watch as the witch of the voudun leaned over Jacob.

Upon being escorted to the prison by the four policemen Ternier had assigned to Hennington, the broker was immediately taken to the interrogation area he had been shown before. Led to one of the cells abutting the corridor, he was appalled by the sight of the man and woman within the room.

"Do you know this man?" Ternier asked, his hypnotic eyes studying Hennington closely.

Overcoming his initial shock, Hennington shook his head slowly. "He is unfamiliar to me." He managed to keep his face neutral despite seeing the results of Ternier's depravity.

The Colonel continued to scrutinize him carefully, his gaze bearing down on him like sharpened spikes. "You do not remember him from your trip to Malique?" With his hands clasped stiffly behind him and his gaze never leaving Hennington's face, he began pacing off a leisure circuit of the two dangling forms. "I find that rather strange since Malique is but a tiny hamlet. Surely you must have seen this man."

Hennington could only shrug. "My stay there was very brief. Perhaps this man was out fishing. All the men there are fishermen."

Ternier nodded. Seemingly satisfied with the explanation, the intensity of his gaze abated a notch. Saying nothing for the moment, he turned his back to the broker, stepping slowly back around the two people hanging inverted. "The condition of these people does not upset you?" he said at last.

Hennington fought down the impulse rapidly taking hold of him, and it was not fear. Something flashed in the back of his brain as he looked upon the two parties ravaged by torture, and he was suddenly reminded of the inhuman abuses inflicted upon his Tainos progenitors.

Ternier's manner took on an added measure of sternness when Hennington failed to answer. "You seem to have lost your tongue?"

Hennington could feel the rage building within him, and he had great difficulty masking his emotions. Ternier's cruelty was without limit, on a par with the conquistadors that had decimated his ancestors. With a boldness he hadn't known was possible, he looked deep into the mesmeric orbs that had terrified him not so long ago, and within them he sensed a growing trace of confusion. He now understood why he had been summoned here. Ternier had deemed it necessary to perpetuate the fear that kept him under his thumb.

Encouraged by the comprehension quickly enfolding him, Hennington probed deeper. Instilling fear in others was the only thing that gave Ternier his power. Like the insatiable demon he was, the Colonel fed ravenously from it, but without such sustenance he would rapidly weaken and become nothing.

In that instant Hennington saw the Colonel's regal bearing begin to unravel. In that instant he saw the Colonel not as a man but as a vile thing to be eradicated the way one might crush a disgusting cockroach beneath one's heel. And in that fleeting interval of time, he came to realize his transformation was now complete. The nexus his entire existence had been inexorably aimed at had finally been reached. The greed and cowardice had now been erased forever, replaced by something he could never be ashamed of, something absolute and good.

Drawing strength from it, he sprang with a swiftness he never thought possible, and as he rose up to clutch Ternier's throat, the sound of gunfire did little to deter him from the thing he sought.

With Trebek leading the way, the group of five moved along a maze of seedy alleyways bordering on the waterfront. Exhibiting the cunning silence of jackals on the hunt, they traveled swiftly under the cover of darkness. The hour was late, with the streets of Port-au-Prince mostly deserted. Terror always lurked in the shadows following sunset, and because of it the city belonged to the ever-present gangs prowling the night.

As if to confirm this, a large band of zenglendoes brandishing machetes and knives suddenly skulked out of the gloom to surround the group. But at the metallic sound of rounds being chambered with obvious intent, the thugs scattered like gazelles, and within seconds the alleyway was once again left deserted.

Clutching the MK-23 Stoner at high-guard, Jake carried the most firepower among the group. The MP-5 submachine gun wielded by Mat provided ample backup to the Stoner, as did the infantry-version M-60 held by Zimbola. Earlier, Jake had taken the time to instruct Trebek in the use of the 9mm Colt submachine pistol he had acquired from Bashir, and from the way the Haitian handled the weapon he could see the use of firearms was nothing new to the man.

And although he knew it would have been absurd, Jake had offered his USP-9 semi-automatic pistol to Destiny as an added measure of protection. As he had anticipated, the girl had readily declined the invitation, appearing repulsed by what the gun represented.

Jake kept his senses on full alert as he followed Trebek, wanting only to reach the prison compound as quickly as possible. With the prospect of torture awaiting those taken by Erzulie, he knew every second counted.

It was another five minutes following the encounter with the zenglendoes that Jake was able to perceive an abrupt rise in a narrow alleyway strewn with garbage and debris. Straining his eyes against the darkness, he could just make out a place where the trash was heaped high. It was here that Trebek brought the group to a halt.

Trebek motioned Jake to his side and pointed above the mound of garbage. "The prison is located up there along higher ground," he said, keeping his tone low. Directing his gaze at the trash heap, Trebek pointed again before moving behind the mound.

Jake followed on his heels and flicked on the combat light he had taped to his Stoner. Pointing the weapon, he probed the darkness. Completely hidden behind the piled-up garbage was the mouth of a small culvert set back in an earthen slope, its entrance yawning darker than the surrounding night.

"This is the way in," Trebek whispered. "We must be very careful from here on."

Jake noted the nervousness in Trebek's voice. "You don't have to take us any further if you're having second thoughts about doing this," he proposed, offering the Haitian a way out. "We can take it from here."

Trebek expelled breath like a slowly deflating balloon, as if tempted to take the offer. Seeming to make a decision, he looked back at Destiny. "No!" he affirmed with finality. "I have a debt to pay."

"It's your call."

Trebek took a deep breath, then turned quickly and entered the dark opening. The rest of the team formed up in single file, advancing on his heels. Jake was second, with Destiny and then Mat following closely behind. Zimbola carried up the rear toting the sixty and more than a thousand rounds of belted ammunition draped loosely around his massive shoulders.

Once inside, Jake had Trebek and Destiny flick on the flashlights he had given them. Almost at once the dual beams caught the skeletal remains of a decomposed corpse. It hung limply by the neck from a hook embedded in the tunnel's brick-lined ceiling, tatters of withered flesh continuing to adhere to the bones in various places. An amused grin adorned the skull, its empty eye sockets staring back at the group as if daring them to venture into the black void that lay beyond. The smell of rot and decay hung heavily in the air like an oppressive invisible vapor.

Trebek halted at the sight, standing frozen for several seconds before retching convulsively. Gaining control of himself, he swung around to address Jake, his voice racked with the strain of gagging. "There will be more of this, but you will soon get used to it."

Jake fought down the bile rising in his throat. He had seen the aftermath of similar death and had never gotten used to it. He turned abruptly to see how Destiny was responding, but the girl gave no visible signs of gagging though her eyes were moist with emotion. "Are you all right?" he asked.

"I'll be okay."

Jake looked back at Trebek. "Let's keep moving."

Sidestepping the suspended cadaver, Trebek pushed on with everyone falling into step behind him. As they penetrated further into the tunnel, a potpourri of human and animal bones littered the passageway, either dangling obtrusively from the arched ceiling or scattered about the mud-encrusted floor.

Along the way a wooden bench blocked their path, its surface supporting a row of human skulls smiling ominously up at them. Glistening with wetness, the skulls sat snugly rooted in a base of hardened wax that kept them affixed to the wood. Directly above, water dripped oppressively from a fissure in the ancient brick that formed the culvert's flattened oval construction. The droplets plunked down heavily upon the skulls in a steady cadence, the sound imparting a chilling resonance to the unnerving sight.

A cacophony of hushed squeals startled everyone as several things went skittering underfoot, and Jake could have sworn he saw several rats the size of a fully-grown alley cat brushing past his legs.

A succession of other benches blocked their path as they made their way deeper into the culvert, each bench lined with human skulls in the same manner as the first, and as the team pressed on, they eventually came upon a sheet of cloth draped across the passageway, the fabric smeared with grime. Trebek halted in his tracks, playing the beam from his flashlight over the material. Drawn crudely in blood in the center of the cloth was a skull and crossbones. Cautiously, he prodded the barrier with the barrel of his Colt. Satisfied it was not rigged with any surprises, he went to push past it.

"Stop!" Destiny cried. A cold chill had begun accosting her seconds earlier, and in her it had now taken definitive form. Her mother and Jacob had been taken into the prison via this route, and she was hearing the warning one of their captors had voiced when they had passed this way.

Trebek immediately froze, pivoting his head around slowly to see what the girl meant.

"A trap awaits you just beyond the cloth," Destiny clarified gravely. "Do not go another step!"

"How do you know that?" asked Jake.

Before Destiny could answer, Zimbola sidled his looming bulk past Mat and interceded. "A white witch can see things others cannot."

Jake let his eyes linger on the big man momentarily, the giant's face inscrutable in the dim light reflected off the cloth barrier. Swinging back around, he scrutinized the girl once again. "What kind of trap are you seeing?"

"A pit with sharpened wooden stakes lies just behind the sheet."

Jake stepped past Trebek and pushed the cloth aside, shining his light on the earthen ground on the opposite side.

"The pit lies hidden under a false floor," Destiny advised grimly.

Jake swung back around to face the girl. "Is this the only thing we have to be concerned with right now?"

"For right now, yes."

Jake tugged hard on the sheet, tearing it loose from its overhead fasteners, then looked back at Mat. "Help me with one of those benches back there!"

With each of them hefting a side, the two men moved a skull-laden bench into position and heaved it into the area Destiny had indicated. Abruptly, the ground gave way and the bench disappeared into the concealed sunken pit with a dull thud. Directing his beam down into the hole, Jake could see the fate Trebek had narrowly escaped. The bench lay at an odd angle ten feet below him, hung up on a dense cluster of pointed spikes. One of the skulls had torn loose from its waxen base, its left eye socket penetrated fiendishly by one of the pointed shafts.

"Please be careful," Destiny warned. "Those stakes are tipped with a lethal poison."

Jake studied the width of the pit. Only a narrow ledge remained along the tunnel's right side with sufficient breadth to allow passage. "Everyone watch your step," he cautioned. "There may be more booby traps."

Further on the team was welcomed by several more suspended cadavers in various stages of sickening putrefaction, each one seeming to beckon the group onward. One after the other, the gruesome sights left no doubt as to what the group would be facing. All the while Jake kept his senses on full alert, prepared for the unexpected but also trusting in Destiny's uncanny ability to forecast the presence of danger.

It wasn't long before the team came upon a fork in the tunnel, and Trebek came to a halt, suddenly appearing unsure of himself.

"Which way?" Jake asked.

Trebek scratched his head, looking truly confounded. "I do not remember this."

Jake turned to Destiny. "Any suggestions?"

The girl studied the twin passageways for several moments, her expression mired in concentration. "The tunnel to the right will take us where we need to go."

"And the left?"

"Only danger lies in that direction."

"Right it is then," Jake concurred, confident that Destiny had chosen correctly.

Guardedly, Trebek ventured right with the rest of the group following. He had not gone more than ten paces before the passage began to slope downward. Gradually it took on a moderate grade, and it wasn't long before the illumination from the light he held showed the decline before him plunging beneath a pool of stagnant water, the surface slick with a coating of organic slime and giving off the foul stink of raw sewage.

Trebek looked back at Jake. "They have flooded the tunnel!" His tone was dismal and he appeared spooked. "It was never like this in the old days."

Stopping at the water's edge, the Haitian seemed to stare at something lurking further out in the pool. Within seconds he backed away and spun around. "Do…do you see it?" he stammered in horror. He had the manner of a man suddenly besieged with terror, glancing back over his shoulder as if afraid the thing he had seen would emerge from the pool to pounce on him from behind.

Jake moved Trebek out of the way and played his light searchingly over the water. "I don't see anything. What did you see?"

Trebek had difficulty speaking, continuing to remain wide-eyed. "It…it-" He had only gotten a fleeting glimpse of it, a hideous thing with jagged teeth. And now it was lurking somewhere below the slime, waiting to rise up and sink those puncturing fangs into anyone foolish enough to get close.

"Do not let your eyes deceive you," Destiny interposed, her voice placid and calming. "What you saw is an illusion created by Erzulie. There is nothing there to harm you." Reaching up, she placed a hand on Trebek's temple. "If you look hard, you will see through the illusion."

The Haitian's panic slowly abated, his wild-eyed stare changing over to one of embarrassment. He pulled his gaze from the fetid water, turning to Destiny's calming influence. "You are right," he acknowledged. "The monster I saw was one of the mind. I-" The sudden alteration in the girl's expression made him stiffen again.

Destiny was rigid, shuddering. Something icy cold and terrible was closing in. Sensing the approach, she spun around and gasped, staring back the way they had come.

Jake turned quickly to follow her gaze, his eyes stabbing into the darkness. He was able to discern something resembling coal tar, a growing splotch within the tunnel's black void. It flowed down the slope of the passageway, oozing slowly forward like heavy crude dumped from a barrel.

The warning sprang from Jake's mouth before he realized he had yelled it. "Zimby, behind you!"

Zimbola whirled, piercing the darkness with his light, and his breath hitched tight in his throat. The lead forms drew back, throwing up skeletal arms to block off the light, and Zimbola saw eyes that burned red with the raging embers of hell. Stacked behind them in the darkness were similar forms, a compressed horde of emaciated inhuman things composed of hideous rotting flesh and fungus-encrusted bone. The mass of things hung back momentarily under the sudden illumination, seeming to coalesce even more as they crammed the passageway. And then in unison the horde surged forward as though intent on destroying the very light clinging to them.

Trebek's eyes enlarged to the size of engorged dotted grapes, and he wailed aloud, his previous fright regenerated by the mob of vile things closing in. "It is Erzulie's walking dead!" he screamed. "We are all doomed!"

The lead forms pressed forward, letting loose with a horrifying mix of hissing and screeching. Hobbling and limping on decayed limbs, they moved like old decrepit men suffering from some disabling malady, and Zimbola could not pull his eyes away from the claw-like hands that reached toward him.

"We are doomed!" Trebek repeated shrilly, shrinking back toward the pool of slime at his back.

With both Mat and Zimbola in his way, Jake could not use his Stoner. He sprang forward, brushing past a dumbstruck Mat and reaching Zimbola's side. Zimby stood frozen, his belief in witchcraft crippling him with terror and nearly seizing up his convulsing heart as it jumped in his chest.

The lead forms were almost upon them, their putrid breath leaking from between broken and splintered teeth blackened by rot, and Jake felt the sickening oiliness of it climbing up into his nostrils and coating his throat. Almost retching, he lifted the Stoner's barrel, pulling back on the trigger just as claws caked with offal raked out.

The front rank disintegrated. Bits of grizzle and decayed bone flew backward as though spat from a meat grinder, spattering other bodies coming up from behind. The carnage suddenly worsened as Mat opened up from Zimbola's opposite side, and within the tight quarters the din of both weapons was shockingly loud. All at once the giant Jamaican stirred, the thunder of the guns jarring him from his bout of paralysis. He blinked just once before the sixty in his enormous hands came alive, and in moments the horrible things clogging the tunnel were quickly torn apart as all three men hosed the corridor.

Jake ceased firing, grabbing Zimbola by the arm and yanking him hard as the sixty continued to bark. "Save your ammo, big guy!" He had to shout to be heard.

Reluctantly, Zimbola let up on the trigger, staring wide-eyed and shaken.

Though incomprehension filled Mat's face, he was able to overcome his initial shock. "Tell me that didn't happen!" he suddenly vented, breathing heavily.

Something tumbled dully down the slope of the tunnel as he said this, and his eyes came to rest on the maimed skull as it rolled to a stop at his feet. One of the sockets was empty where a bullet had gouged it, but the remaining eye was bloodshot and scalding, fastened on him and continuing to burn fiercely as though aware of his presence.

With his stomach beginning to churn, Mat kicked the vile thing away. "Man, that's disgusting."

Jake had no time to mull over what had just happened. He was growing impatient, knowing any more delays could result in a failed mission. Based on what he'd seen so far, it was a foregone conclusion that the longer Destiny's mother and Jacob remained imprisoned, the more likely they would suffer a cruel ending. Consulting his wristwatch, he noted the time. "We've got to keep moving, even if it means wading up to our necks through this filth."

Trebek nodded penitently, the shadow of fear still heavy in his eyes. He needed to get away from this part of the tunnel. "I will not fail you again."

Jake tossed him the light. "Go then and take point!"

"Keep to the exact center of the tunnel," Destiny instructed. "You will find a narrow walkway concealed less than a centimeter below the water's surface. The water is much deeper to either side."

To Jake it made sense. If what the girl said were true, it would be the means by which Erzulie could get through the tunnel. It was also one more reason why the culvert had been left unguarded. Even if the locals were bold enough to overcome their fear of Erzulie's grisly artwork and get past the hidden death trap and those vile things to make it this far, a seemingly impassable pool of raw sewage would provide a final psychological barrier of revulsion to discourage them from venturing any further.

As the team treaded tentatively out onto the water, no one commented on the girl's incredible foresight until it became evident her prediction was correct.

Treading his way carefully atop the disgusting liquid waste, Mat leaned close to Destiny. Keeping his voice low, he asked, "Are you sure you were never in this place before?"

"Never."

"If you ever want a job with the DHS, please let me know. You'd save us a lot of trouble."

With the tunnel continuing to descend deeper, the waterline rose higher, causing the male members of the team to duck their heads lower and lower to avoid the sloped ceiling. It wasn't until the team had covered another thirty meters before the gradient finally leveled off and began to rise again. This was a relief to Zimbola who had been forced to negotiate the lowest level of freeboard in a near squat. When at last the giant stepped clear of the offending pool, his immense exhalation did not go unnoticed by the rest of the group. It was evident that the potential for falling into the decaying offal had repulsed him far more than anyone else on the team.

Continuing to lead the way, Trebek soon located the tunnel's terminus where a set of concrete steps rose before him. "This I remember," he said, shining his light up at the rusted underside of a recessed trapdoor at the top of the stairway.

Jake stared up at the entrance that would provide them access into the prison. Trebek had briefed him thoroughly on the layout of the area immediately above the trapdoor, at least what the Haitian could remember. Although there was no way of knowing how security protocol had changed within the prison in the past twenty-two years, Trebek had said that even the guards refrained from going near the passageways Erzulie regularly used.

Destiny moved to Jake's side, glancing up at the corroded metal hatch above them. "You will find the door unlocked," she said, seeming to read his mind. "The room above is empty."

Jake elicited a grim-faced nod. "I hope so, otherwise this little ordeal will have been a complete waste of time." He turned to acknowledge the rest of the team, finding it necessary to reiterate only a few items of the battle plan he had previously laid out. "Everyone check your weapon and keep to the plan. I'll go first. No one is to follow me until I do a recon. I don't want anyone poking their head above that trapdoor until I give the 'all-clear.' Let's all avoid getting our heads blown off, shall we." His eyes roamed from face to face. "Are we all on the same page?"

Mat smiled back at him, a knowing gleam in his eyes. "You just look after your own hide. And for once in your life try not to do anything stupid like putting yourself in the line of fire."

Jake ignored the words, turning to Destiny one more time and studying her face. In her eyes he could see fear, but the fear he read was entirely selfless, set aside only for the people around her and those they had come to rescue.

"Stay behind Mat and Zimby!" Jake told her. "You can count on them to protect you."

Wearing the same face that had taken him through many a horrendous battle in the past, Jake bounded up the stairs with the agility of a cat, moving into position just below the trapdoor. Bracing himself, he applied upward pressure on the corroded metal plate until it pivoted on its hinges. Surprisingly it offered little resistance. Cautiously, he raised it higher, cringing at the squeal of rust impeding the pivots. Bringing his eyes level with the upper floor, he quickly swung his head to both sides to insure no one was lurking nearby. A small concrete room surrounded him, its stark interior dimly lit by light streaming in through a grimy glass window reinforced with wire mesh. Noting that the trapdoor was positioned close to the back wall, he could see the room was unoccupied. This was one of the holding cells Trebek said was used for interrogation, and the light making its way in came from the adjacent corridor.

Jake lifted the lid higher, keeping a firm grip on it as he clambered up through the opening with the Stoner at the ready. Careful not to let it come clanging down, he lowered the lid to the opposite side until it came to rest against the concrete wall behind him. Strangely, he began to reassess Zimbola's notion that Destiny was a white witch. Everything the girl had so far predicted had proved to be true.

Striding silently to the glass window, he surveyed the abutting corridor from his darkened position. Off to his left he saw the heavy metal door that, according to Trebek, was Erzulie's quarters. When he had first been told this, he found it rather odd that a woman would choose to live within one of the most deplorable prison strongholds in the Western Hemisphere, a place that reeked of human suffering and decay. But now having seen examples of the woman's fascination with death, he was beginning to understand why.

As if to epitomize this newfound thought, a muffled cry of agony suddenly breached his ears. Following the sound, he perceived the scream to originate from somewhere off to his right in the adjacent corridor, possibly in the holding cell next to the one he was in. Shrill enough to penetrate the concrete wall separating the two rooms, the cry hung in the air for several more seconds before dying away.

Stepping back along the glass, Jake increased his field of vision, now looking in the opposite direction. The grating screech of a door opening on rusted hinges followed by ringing footsteps caught his ear. Several people were coming down the hallway. Listening intently, he heard the door let out another protest before clanging shut with abrupt finality. It was then that he caught a glimpse of four men striding into view before they entered the adjacent cell.

Recognition hit him like a sledgehammer, and with a start he realized one of the men was Hennington. *What the hell is he doing here?*

Moving quickly, Jake sidled up to the holding cell's door and tried the handle. The door was locked. This was a point Trebek had failed to mention, and one in which Jake should have paid more attention. It was only reasonable to assume the door of a holding cell would only open from the outside. Silently, he let out a curse in spite of knowing it would only present a minor inconvenience.

The alarm that had been sounding in Jake's head was ringing more shrilly now, fueling his need to act. In two bounding strides he shot across the room, suddenly aware of the darker blotches staining the cell's walls and floor and the chains hanging idly from the ceiling. A history of depraved violence entrapped him, reaching out from all quarters like the sinister hands of a demon. But Jake was not to be deterred from his goal, completely immune to the residues of terror.

Mat was perched just below the trapdoor opening, waiting eagerly for Jake to give the "all-clear." Handing Jake his weapon, he pulled himself through the entrance in a flash. In less than fifteen seconds, the rest of the team followed, with Trebek the last to emerge.

Using a combination of whispers and hand gestures, Jake let the others know of his improvised plan. Zimbola nodded, then aimed the M-60 at the cell door as the others in the group huddled farther back. The discharge of the weapon was deafening within the confined space as a short burst disintegrated the door lock.

Leaping forward, Jake threw all his body weight behind a kick that sent the door crashing open. Dashing into the corridor, he bolted immediately to his right in anticipation of the resistance that would surely come from the far end of the hallway. Already the massive steel door that separated the interrogation area from the rest of the prison was beginning to swing open. It was obvious the guards stationed on the other side were eager to investigate the cause of the disturbance.

The Stoner bucked harshly as Jake let go with a burst of discouragement. A shower of sparks exploded against the heavy metal barrier, and abruptly the door slammed shut. And although the hallway before him was now empty, the adjacent interrogation cell was not.

Chapter 10

*A*t a glance, Jake took in the scene of horror, noting the man and woman hanging upside down by the ankles and bleeding profusely. Five Haitian men stared back at him, shocked by the threat of the smoking weapon in his hands.

Jake was even more shocked. The sight of Chester Hennington struggling with a seventh man was something Jake would never have expected. Little more than an insignificant flea to his much bigger adversary, Hennington was shoved violently away, his small pudgy frame sent slamming into a nearby wall.

With Mat backing him up, Jake poked the barrel of the Stoner into the room. Hennington's opponent brought smoldering eyes to bear on the sudden intrusion, his orbs burning into Jake with sizzling hatred.

"Colonel Ternier I presume?" Jake growled coldly. "I've heard a lot about you, and none of it at all flattering."

Ternier straightened to his full height, throwing all the dignity and authority he could muster into his bearing. "Who are you and what do you want?"

"I'm your worst nightmare," Jake rasped, "a man who will have no qualms about sending you and your cohorts to the farthest reaches of hell if you don't disengage these two people from those chains this instant."

Ternier fidgeted slightly, still laboring to present the regal posture that defined him. "You are insane," he hissed brazenly, his eyes rebellious and boring into Jake with hypnotic intensity. "Only a madman would attempt to come in here by force. I do not think you have the slightest idea what you are up against."

Jake felt the heat of his own ire growing rapidly in temperature. "You see this weapon I'm holding. It can fire 750 rounds a minute. Try my patience anymore and I'm turning your miserable hide into dog chow." For emphasis, he aimed the Stoner directly at Ternier's head, caressing the trigger with an eager finger. "Don't make me ask you again to get those people down."

Ternier wrung his hands, his attempt at haughtiness beginning to unravel like strands of a rope under too much strain. Turning his head slightly, he barked an order to several of the men standing behind him. "Do as he says!"

Within moments, both the man and woman were lowered to the floor, their ankles free of the chains.

"I know these people." The words came from Trebek who was stationed to Jake's rear. "It is Emmanuel and Lucette Baptiste."

A look of genuine surprise shot across Ternier's face as his eyes fell on Trebek for the first time. "You!" he hissed contemptuously. A string of guttural invectives abruptly left his lips as he lapsed into Creole.

"Speak English!" Jake snapped, giving the Colonel a deadly stare. "Otherwise, I might be tempted to pull this trigger." Though he understood some of the local dialect, he wasn't quite sure what had just been said.

"He calls me a traitor," Trebek translated scornfully. "He says I have betrayed the trust of the Tonton Makout."

Trebek returned the Colonel's skewering glare with a scowl of his own. "But I never had the same appetite for torture and murder as this man," he uttered gruffly.

A vicious sneer suddenly descended on Ternier's face. "Such words are unbefitting of you, Ronaldo," he said, keeping the conversation in the language Jake could comprehend. "As I remember it, you used to take great pleasure in punishing others."

"I am no longer the same person you once knew."

Ternier let out a condescending laugh, but before he could reply Jake silenced him by pointing the Stoner menacingly. "Does the name Mercades Myers stir anything in that memory of yours, Colonel?"

The question seemed to throw Ternier off balance for one microsecond before he managed a look of supreme innocence. "I am unfamiliar with that name."

"You killed him, you murdering bastard!" The screaming accusation did not come from Trebek.

The Colonel's expression turned baleful again as he swiveled his head to locate the new speaker.

"You killed him the same way you killed so many others," the speaker went on. The voice belonged to Hennington. "Only a monster would do the things you do to other people."

Out of the corner of his eye, Jake noticed the broker rising from the floor. "I don't know what you're doing here, Chester, but I think it would be wise if you moved behind me," he advised, speaking out the side of his mouth.

Hennington complied, moving to stand behind Jake.

"Now I want everyone's hands raised real high where I can see them," Jake ordered, addressing Ternier and the others. He leveraged the command by waving the Stoner threateningly again. "All of you! Up against the wall!"

From further down the hall, Zimbola called out to Jake in a booming voice. "All secure, Jay Jay. The other holding cells are empty."

Satisfied for the moment, Jake focused his attention back on Ternier again. "Where are the others?"

A smug little smile flashed briefly on Ternier's face. "Whatever do you mean?"

"A man called Jacob and a woman called Amphitrite," Jake shot back angrily. "Where are they?"

"Forcing your way into the prison of a sovereign nation is a violation of international law."

"So is the inhumane treatment and torture of innocent people."

Ternier appeared to regain some of his former arrogance. "The man and woman you seek are dissidents of Haiti. They threaten the political stability of this island nation."

Mat moved forward to stand at Jake's side. "This guy's stalling. A friendly little chat with him is a waste of time."

Emmanuel suddenly stirred, letting out a prolonged moan.

"Get Destiny in here!" Jake barked at no one in particular, wondering why the girl had not entered the room to attend the victims of Ternier's sadism.

"Destiny is not here," Trebek blurted out in dismay.

"Where is she?"

"She was standing in the hallway a minute ago, but now she is gone."

Jake could not believe what he was hearing. Facing Mat, he said, "If any one of these assholes so much as twitches, blow his head off."

Mat's expression turned fiendish. "It'll be my pleasure."

Shoving past Hennington and Trebek, Jake glanced anxiously up and down the hallway.

As Trebek had stated, Destiny had vanished.

Erzulie had been too busy to notice the heavy steel door barring the way into her chamber swing silently open, nor did she see the petite silhouette framed in the entrance a split second later. Then, just as noiselessly, the door swung closed, with the bolt sliding back into place with little more than a whisper.

The nature of the psychic link Destiny felt was on a level she had never before experienced, a guiding power that inexorably drew her forth like a moth drawn to the flame. As if she were a wisp of air, she slipped into the gloomy lair with wraith-like stealth, now fully aware of what she must do. A minute earlier she had been able to distort the curvature of space-time just enough to cushion the din of gunfire so that the sound of it did not alert the witch of the voudun. Evoking this had been a simple mental exercise, one she was able to bring about with the combined help of her mother and the albino dolphins currently awaiting her in the harbor. Opening the door to the chamber should have been impossible to a normal human being, but this had also been accomplished without the girl ever having to make physical contact with the seemingly impenetrable barrier.

In a far corner of the chamber, Erzulie leaned over a small black cauldron. "You are going to love my little potion, my darlings," the witch sibilated gleefully. "Filling this pot with rainwater that fell on the sixth day of the sixth month and heating it to a boil works best."

Erzulie stepped back, holding out the amulet. A red light suddenly pulsed from it, brought to bear on the water in the cauldron and bringing it to a sizzling boil almost instantly. Reaching behind her, she began dumping one after the other the contents of several small bowls into the pot. "Six hairs from a pig…six feathers from an owl…six scales from a snake…extract from the bark of a 66-year-old mapou tree."

Happily the hag stirred the mixture before pulling a jar from a shelf and dropping whatever it contained into the pot. "And six teeth from a six-day old cadaver."

Without emotion, Destiny watched Erzulie go through the strange ritual, cognizant of her mother and Jacob pinioned to the concrete slabs. And although Amphitrite appeared to be physically restrained, she knew the appearance was a false one. For it was really the mind that mattered, and the thoughts and mental images pulsing from her mother's mind were enormously powerful, merging in harmonic resonance with her own.

"And last but not least," chortled Erzulie, "six hairs from each of you." Having said the words, she sprinkled something held between fingers resembling talons into the steaming brew.

A sense of agonizing pain suddenly invaded Destiny's being as she continued to stand unobserved by Erzulie. It was Emmanuel's and Lucette's torment she was feeling. And while their suffering had been a necessary placation in the midst of the immense evil engulfing her, their pain would soon culminate, replaced by the healing that would soon come. With arrant certainty, she knew they would survive, with both of them living in a state of discovery rather than recovery. She understood the role pain would play in their lives. They would remember their trauma not as an enemy without purpose, but as something transforming to the spirit. They would absorb and process it before making it a part of a more vigorous and adaptive consciousness. And in the end, they would become stronger and wiser for it.

Years earlier, Destiny's mother had described the vision that had come to her in a dream. The iniquity gripping Haiti had festered far too long, and like all wickedness, would ultimately come around full circle to feed on and then destroy itself. Erzulie and her spawn were the embodiment of absolute evil, doing the only thing evil was capable of doing, and that was doling out more misery. By nature, they were predatory creatures, desiring only the means to bring about human suffering. Possession of Esmerelda's amulet provided them with such means, or so they believed. And according to the dream, their obsession with destruction and death might one day come to an end, but only at great risk to those bold enough to oppose them.

Destiny knew not hatred, for within her the concept held no meaning. It was an emotion she had never experienced, and therefore, one that could not sully the purpose she had been born to fulfill. As Jacob had explained to her many times in the past, the world was much too full of destructive emotions and actions that defied reason, all of which posed a detriment to the planet. Sometimes people could make things so difficult that plain old logic escaped them. National swoons, just as national hysterias, had a way of obliterating rational thought. Anger and hatred, it seemed, were rapidly approaching a critical level that was taking humanity to the very brink of extermination. If his refined view of the Gaia theory was correct, perhaps there was some super intelligence at work that had engendered beings such as herself and the albinos to remediate the harm that was being done.

"I have heard of that marvelous mind of yours, Jacob," Erzulie said aloud, looking over at her male captive as he lay restrained atop the stone. "You are a man of great intellect I am told, a pundit who thinks it is possible to pull Haiti from the squalor that has plagued it for centuries." The witch let out a shrill laugh. "You think this corporate venture you have designed will make your vision a reality."

From where Destiny stood, she could see Jacob move his head to heed the witch's rantings, though he said nothing.

"Such an enterprise would require vast sums of money, would it not?" Erzulie went on. "Now where do you suppose a lowly fisherman like yourself would be able to find so much wealth?"

When Jacob failed to respond, the witch grew angry. "There are many ways to loosen a man's tongue, most of them very painful and usually fatal." Erzulie cocked her head, her manner suddenly calm again. "But to destroy such extraordinary intelligence would be foolish when it can be put to better use."

Dipping a ladle into the cauldron, Erzulie removed a small portion of the heated liquid. "Yes," she said as she walked toward Jacob. "While killing you would give me great pleasure, I have decided to let you live to serve my son, Henri."

Moving to within inches of Jacob, the witch cackled harshly. "With your help, Henri will become the undisputed king of the Caribbean, a man other leaders will bow to. Cuba's Castro, Venezuela's Chavez, they will be nothing compared to Henri once he is able to pluck the fruits of your vision."

"I will never help your son!" Jacob spat. "You and your offspring are a pox on Haiti. Kill me already and be done with it!"

"Oh, but you will help him," Erzulie disagreed, seemingly amused by Jacob's vitriolic outburst. "No one has ever been able to resist the effects of this potion. It will shackle your mind. It will make an obedient slave of you. Pleasing your king and his mother will be your only desire. You will be unable to recall your former self, who you once were. Only your magnificent intellect will remain intact, subservient to Henri's will."

"I reject this black mysticism of yours. You will never take possession of my mind."

In the dim light, Destiny saw the hideous grin that took hold of Erzulie's ugly features. "Your Haitian heritage is your vulnerability. It resides at the center of your being and will prove to be your enemy. Scientific beliefs and logical leanings are merely superficial layers of who you think you are. Ingrained deep down inside you is the very thing that will cause you to surrender to my magic. You cannot escape it. Has not our little encounter many years ago already demonstrated this to be true?"

"I am not the same man you fought against back then."

"You are Esmerelda's grandson. That is enough."

Jacob suddenly gagged, his jaw clenching in an effort to keep his lips sealed. He appeared to struggle briefly before his mouth jerked wide as if being pried by invisible hands.

Erzulie cackled shrilly. "See how easily I am able to manipulate you. You are like a puppet, powerless to fight the strings that control you."

Extending the ladle above Jacob's open mouth, the witch began to pour the liquid, but before it could reach its target Destiny intervened. Diverted by some unseen power, the hot fluid reversed its flow and splashed up into Erzulie's face with explosive force. The witch immediately stiffened, appearing frozen solid by the unexpected assault, and time seemed to hang still for one brief moment before a high-pitched squeal strong enough to shatter glass left the old hag's lips. As if in protest, various jars within the chamber burst into fragments simultaneously, and the stack of human skulls lining one of the walls abruptly collapsed.

Now free of the restraints that had bound her to the concrete slab, Amphitrite suddenly arose to face the maddened witch of the voudun. A second later, the shackles holding Jacob fell away, and he immediately sprang to his feet.

Amphitrite spoke for the first time, her voice calm and without emotion. "We are leaving this place, Erzulie. If you still have the courage to come after us, Navassa Island is where we will be."

It was then that the witch noticed Destiny for the first time. Her mouth hung open as she transferred a shocked gaze from mother to daughter, alternating her eyes between the two. "I should have known a cheval would have spawned another," she hissed. "But now I will kill both of you."

"Your powers have been weakened," Amphitrite said. "That cocktail you brewed has sapped your strength. You of all people should know the negative consequence of getting mapou extract on you instead of its intended victim. It will take hours for you to regain your strength."

Erzulie raised the amulet to test Amphitrite's supposition, but when the charm barely produced a few feeble sparks, the witch let out a frustrated scream. "I will follow the three of you to the ends of the earth. You will never escape me."

Amphitrite stared back without fear. "As I have already said, you have only to go to Navassa Island to find us. But I warn you, you will place yourself in great peril should you be foolish enough to go there."

Amphitrite turned and raised an arm. Forty feet from where she stood the latch securing the doorway slid sideways and the heavy steel barrier swung open. Ignoring the string of profanity railed by Erzulie, she walked calmly toward the exit with Destiny and Jacob beside her.

Jake remained immobile, ready to meet any opposition coming forth from behind the door as it opened. A deep sigh of relief escaped his lips when Jacob appeared, and the tightness in his gut relaxed a notch when Destiny and another woman stepped from the gloom a second later. The door slammed shut behind them with booming finality, and Jake felt the floor beneath him shudder as the sound echoed down the hallway like cannonade.

Jacob gave him a grim nod that seemed to conflict with the small smile Destiny displayed. "Jay Jay, this is my mother, Amphitrite."

Jake stared in disbelief, finding it difficult to accept this, for the woman with Destiny appeared to be not much older than her daughter.

Chapter 11

Sitting in the *Avenging Angel's* salon, Nick Henderson turned his head to glimpse the painting propped against a wall. Almost immediately his face soured. Try as he might, he saw nothing to indicate anything exceptional within the pattern of lines and colors.

"Do you see it, Jeffrey?" Bashir effused excitedly.

"I think so, but for me it's more of a feeling than a visual perception. What about you, Professor?" Parker asked Grahm. "Does it spark anything within you?"

"Yes indeed," Grahm said, nodding absently. "I must admit, I have never been moved by art, but there is a certain mesmeric quality to the work that automatically draws me in. If I could sum up with one word what I'm feeling, I'd say that one word is hope."

Henderson stifled his growing irritability. The dolphin painting was no different from any of the abstract art he had seen in museums. It instilled nothing within him when he looked at it. As a matter of fact, it gave him a splitting headache if he stared at it too long as he was doing now.

Averting his eyes, Henderson massaged his temples. He was bored out of his mind. Those around him were just killing time awaiting the return of Javolyn and the people that had accompanied him. Their unending obsession with Bashir's painting was beginning to grate on him. On top of that he didn't like the camaraderie that had developed between Grahm and Javolyn. The professor had been much too accommodating in agreeing to stay aboard the *Angel* while Javolyn and the others had gone off to rescue Jacob and the girl's mother.

Served the Haitian right for being abducted, Henderson thought. Though Jacob seemed inordinately intelligent and learned, there was some arcane quality about the man that rubbed him the wrong way. Most likely it was Jacob's doomsday forecasts concerning the fate of the planet and those absurd theories of his that were the cause of this. In any event, he disliked the man intensely.

He hated Javolyn even more. He had run into a few others like him at one time or another in his life. Strong athletic types had always offended him, mainly because they always seemed willing to stick their necks out under the banner of some noble cause, prepared to risk life and limb to perform what they deemed to be a good deed. Yes, he truly loathed the way they tended to attract the prettiest girls, usually luring the damsels with their superior muscles rather than their inferior minds. A deluge of resentment and jealousy suddenly swept over him as he pictured the way Destiny had taken to the *Angel's* skipper. While he had hungered for the girl from the first moment he had set eyes on her, the girl had hardly given him a second glance. And from what he had noticed lately, it was obvious she was in love with Javolyn.

The man Javolyn had met up with just outside the harbor seemed to be cut out of the same mold. Obviously an old friend, he thought it odd that Javolyn had purposely kept Bashir out of the man's sight until the rescue team had left the vessel.

A sense of impending helplessness gripped Henderson as he contemplated the constantly shifting events that had recently occurred. Surprises were at every bend, keeping him off balance. The final payoff he had sought had so far eluded him. To assuage his disappointment, he let his mind revert back to the possibility of gold, certain he had spotted gleaming mounds of it at the base of the *thurentra* when they had first entered the dolphin hideaway. But then strangely it had all disappeared. Refusing to believe his eyes had been playing tricks on him, he had snorkeled around the *thurentra* at every opportunity, feigning scientific curiosity as an excuse for his actions. In short order he had managed to pick what amounted to a handful of shiny grains from the cove's sandy floor, confirming that his eyes hadn't deceived him after all. As far as he could tell, the little he had found gave the appearance of gold. Maybe even platinum. And if that were true, it meant there was a sizable cache of precious metals hidden somewhere within the verdant hideaway

Jacob called Gaia. Yes, the more he replayed it over in his mind, the more he was convinced that Jacob had instructed the dolphins to hide the gold before those aboard the *Angel* became aware of it.

Henderson felt imprisoned being stuck aboard the *Angel*, and something akin to claustrophobia suddenly closed in on him as he continued to dwell on all the things that had happened over the last several days. McPherson must be steaming by now, and rightly so. Capturing the albino specimens should have been a relatively simple operation. He had done his part, providing the naval captain with the hardware that would show the location of a dolphin wearing a DBT. The plan had worked just as he had envisioned it, at least initially, but then Javolyn had stuck his nose in and screwed everything up. The man had a proclivity for danger, always spoiling for a fight. If not for Javolyn's interference, McPherson would have the dolphins by now, and in the process would have dished out the remainder of the money he had agreed to pay. That was the deal. Secretly activating the spare DBT aboard the *Angel* during their second visit to Navassa had given McPherson and his associates another signal to home in on. But once again Javolyn had butted in, keeping the captain from paying up.

"Are you feeling all right, Nicolas?"

Henderson realized Grahm was scrutinizing him. "Huh?"

"Are you ill, lad?"

"I just need some air. It's stuffy in here."

Rising, Henderson went out on deck and leaned over the railing. In the moonlight he could make out the dorsal fins of several albinos as they floated near the stern. Idly, he watched them for several minutes, the thought of the gold continuing to nag away at him like the promising aroma of ambrosia. As far as he knew, he was the only person outside Jacob's small circle that had any knowledge of the other thing the *thurentra* was able to produce. Maybe if he took in McPherson as a partner, the two of them could come up with a way to take control of the little hideaway the girl and Jacob called home. And even if they never found the hidden cache of gold, they'd still be able to collect all future outputs of the yellow metal discharged by the strange organism. Better yet, perhaps one of the dolphins could be captured and ransomed in exchange for all the gold that had previously been produced.

Damn! He was having trouble thinking. Looking at the dolphin art had made him dizzy, and his head felt like it was going to burst. Bringing both hands to his forehead, he began to rub his temples furiously.

Another thought suddenly loomed up. What if Javolyn's little foray failed and everyone in his party were either captured or killed? With both the girl and Jacob out of the way, he'd be able take over the dolphin hideaway and harvest the *thurentra*'s produce. It would take some resources to carry this through, most likely hiring a boat and some people to help him, but once all the albinos went back to the cove, he would be able to block off the entrance with a net. Then he'd be able to enrich himself further by selling each specimen to the highest bidder.

Plagued by these musings Henderson began to grow feverishly energized. Here was the chance for him to become rich beyond his wildest dreams. Deviously, he began to plot other possibilities. As he sifted through various options, one idea stood out from the rest. Perhaps sabotaging the *Angel's* engine would give him the assurance he needed. Even if Javolyn's rescue mission were successful, he could not possibly escape the harbor with an inoperable vessel. Then maybe Haitian authorities would be able catch up with him. In any event, such a delay might at least prevent Javolyn from escorting the girl back to the cove just long enough for McPherson and his associates to regroup and kidnap the girl right here in the harbor. Jacob would surely reveal where the gold could be found in order to get Destiny back. Of course, he'd need to send a message to McPherson in order to initiate such a plan. But once McPherson learned of the gold, he'd be a fool not to go along with such a scheme.

Convincing himself that it could work, Henderson moved to the hatchway that led to the engine compartment and began to lift the cover. In his excitement he failed to hear the footsteps that plodded the deck behind him.

"Is there something I can help you with?"

Henderson spun, startled by the intrusion. Hector stood before him, his expression grim in the moonlight.

Groping for words, Henderson barely managed to stutter them out. "Oh, uh…North Sea trawlers have always fascinated me. I…uh…wanted to see your engine."

Hector shifted his stance, bringing his face to within inches of Henderson's. "The engine room is off limits to anyone other than ship's crew."

"Is that the captain's policy?"

Hector pivoted his head sideways and spat, then turned back to stare coldly at Henderson. "Nope, it's my policy."

Henderson felt rattled, his cheeks beginning to burn under Hector's steady gaze. "My apologies," he blurted, finding it necessary to back away from the shorter man's fireplug frame. Quickly, he changed the subject. "Do you think it's wise to let Bashir have the run of this vessel? I mean, isn't he some kind of terrorist?"

Hector's manner remained unchanged. "Destiny feels the man is no longer dangerous and Jay Jay believes her."

"What if the girl is wrong and Bashir waits for the right moment to strike?" Henderson countered, putting a full measure of sarcasm into his tone. "He could sabotage this boat very easily with everyone's guard let down. He could kill us all in our sleep. Must I remind you that his people tried to destroy this vessel?"

"He no longer thinks as he once did."

Henderson's irritability returned with a vengeance. "How do you know that? No one changes so quickly. Tell me you don't actually believe that stupid painting in there caused him to change his behavior?"

Hector studied Henderson for a long moment, raising his eyebrows before responding. "The painting does not affect you?"

"Oh, I'm affected by it, all right," Henderson said, unable to keep the anger he was feeling from showing in his voice. "Looking at it for too long makes me ill."

"I am sorry to hear that," Hector said evenly. "The painting seems to give the rest of us great pleasure when we stare at it."

Henderson felt like he was talking to an idiot. With growing impatience, he tried another tact. "You realize your boss is risking all our skins by attempting this little raid of his. If he's caught by Haitian authorities, we could all go to jail. I understand the jails in this country are among the worst in the world."

"Jay Jay will not fail."

"What makes you so certain?"

"Jay Jay used to be a Navy Seal."

"And you think an ex-Navy Seal is invincible?"

"Jay Jay is not like other men."

Seeing the look on Hector's face, Henderson was convinced his words were falling on deaf ears. Having worked with computers most of his life, he had grown used to the orderliness such hardware had given him. But here in Haiti, there was no order to anything, and as of late, nothing seemed to make sense anymore.

Staring over Hector's shoulder without meaning to, Henderson once again glimpsed the painting through one of the salon windows. Abruptly the pounding in his head resumed. Turning to avoid the sight, he set his eyes shoreward and shuddered involuntarily, wondering why a man like Javolyn would choose to stay in a place like this, operating out of a land that offered only squalor. When he had first arrived in Port-au-Prince, he had been horrified at the fetid trash lining the streets and the untreated human waste flowing freely in the drainage canals. On the way from the airport, he had seen the head of a man lying in the road, the decapitated body sprawled obscenely a few feet away. The man that had driven them from the airport had said ransoms were now commonplace in Haiti and that an old woman walking her dog earlier that morning had been swept up for ransom. When her unarmed husband had come to her defense, the man had been literally beheaded by the kidnappers abducting her. The slum-ridden city was a dangerous place. Everyday hundreds of extremely violent thugs held it hostage. Law and order were practically nonexistent here, almost completely overshadowed by anarchy.

The thought of Javolyn and the others trying to play hero annoyed Henderson to no end. Javolyn was nuts to venture into the city at night, an urban wasteland where most of the 7,000 UN peacekeeping force spent the bulk of its time simply protecting foreign service staff against the roaming gangs.

As he continued to stare shoreward, Henderson's knees nearly buckled as his eyes suddenly focused on something hovering high over the city, a thing pulsing with a strange assortment of lights. No, that's not possible, he told himself. Convincing himself he was merely hallucinating, he tore his gaze from the glowing object. Strangely, the thing's essence made him envision the hand of an avenging deity.

"I think I'll get some sleep," Henderson said tiredly, noticing the way Hector kept staring at him. Obviously, the man had not seen the thing floating in the sky.

Henderson abruptly winced in reaction to the stabbing pain that shot through his brain. The throbbing in his skull was almost unbearable now. If he didn't lie down in the next minute, he just might collapse.

"Yes, you look like you could use some rest," Hector agreed, though his voice held no sympathy. "You do not appear very well."

Henderson went below deck to the small bunk Javolyn had assigned him, the nausea he was feeling bringing him to the brink of retching. Just before reclining, however, he had the presence of mind to reactivate the spare DBT he had kept in the case stowed under the bunk. Maybe he could still attract McPherson's attention yet again, bringing him and his cohorts here to this place in the harbor. Maybe by now the *Sea Lion* was up and running again. Then he could present his plan to the Navy captain. And if McPherson failed to show, he could always send him a coded electronic message describing that there was considerably more to be gained than just the new breed of dolphin. In any event, he had to rest, for at this moment he felt as if he was going to die.

Chapter 12

*C*ruelty and injustice were two of the things Javolyn hated most, so when Amphitrite insisted all prisoners be freed within the adjacent holding block, he had no objections against doing this.

"Tell your goons to drop their weapons and open the door!" Jake ordered.

The Colonel hesitated, his eyes flicking in expectation toward his mother's quarters at the far end of the corridor.

"Do it!" Jake barked. "Do it or so help me, I'll kill you where you stand."

Ternier brought hateful eyes back to Jake, briefly studying the anger emblazoned on his face before turning and sliding open the portal on the steel door that separated him from the next cell block over. Cautiously, he kept his face off to one side as he spoke through the opening. "This is Colonel Ternier," he said, speaking in Creole. "This prison has come under attack by insurgents who are currently holding me hostage. I want all of you to place your weapons on the floor and open this door."

A moment passed before the door swung slowly open, squeaking gratingly as it did so. Standing behind Ternier's large frame, Jake prodded him through the doorway with the Stoner's muzzle. Eight guards stood in frozen puzzlement on the other side, all of them glancing nervously at the weapon Jake wielded.

The sight of human misery overcrowding the nearest cell caused Jake to stare back in utter disgust at Ternier. "Tell your men to open all these cells!" he growled, finding it difficult to control his trigger-finger.

"You realize you will be creating an international incident if I do this," the Colonel warned.

"No, I won't," Jake snapped. "A piece of scum like you will keep this whole thing real quiet, knowing that once the World Court got wind of what's been going on in here, you'd be brought up on charges for crimes against humanity."

Ternier's eyes flashed as if a flare had been ignited behind them. "The men in these cells are dangerous. Releasing them will only bring more crime to the streets of Port-au-Prince. You cannot-"

Something ethereal began to take form in the air, causing the Colonel to stop in mid-sentence and stare.

Dumbstruck, Jake studied the thing that hung before him, recognizing it immediately. A three-dimensional image of the dolphin painting that had been brought aboard the *Angel* suddenly came into sharp focus. But unlike the static painting depicted on the canvas, the replication that shimmered before him was dynamic, surges of energy rolling along the oddly snaking geometric lines that gave the art its unique definition. A sense of utter happiness splashed over him as he drank in the thing's intoxication, unable to tear his eyes away.

Ternier jerked spasmodically, suddenly falling to both knees. Grimacing, he let out a thunderous roar, clasping his cranium between quivering hands. A split second later, several of the guards emitted piercing screams and collapsed, writhing uncontrollably on the floor, and holding their temples as if stricken by some unseen enemy battering the inside of their skulls.

Riding the wave of euphoria washing over him, Jake became vaguely aware of Destiny and her mother stepping past him and throwing their arms wide. Instantly, the pulsing hologram slid down the hallway. Incredibly, the door to each jail cell swung wide open as the glowing thing swept past. A mixed chorus of joyful cries and agonizing shrieks echoed incoherently within the corridor, the rapturous outbursts at odds with the screams of physical distress. Slowly, many of the inmates began to rise and stream past the bars that had imprisoned them, appearing to be caught up in something blissful and incongruous with their befouled and oppressive surroundings.

Jake felt a hand close on his wrist and, dumbly, he turned.

"We must go, Jay Jay!" Destiny urged softly. Her face was angelic and filled with joy. "We have done all that was meant for us to do here."

Jake had to rouse himself as if awakening from a deep sleep. Pivoting around, he faced the others in his party, noticing the jubilance etched on each face. "Let's move, everyone!" he managed to croak. Stepping back the way he had come, he felt Destiny grab his wrist again.

Destiny pointed in the opposite direction, looking down the length of the hallway that was rapidly flooding with the prisoners that had crammed the cells. "This way!"

Jake started to protest, but Trebek gave voice to the same thing he was thinking. "Going that way is too dangerous. It will take us through the main gates of the prison."

"It's alright," Destiny said. "No harm will come to us if we move quickly."

Jake shifted his eyes to Amphitrite, seeing the same elation reflected in her manner as that of her daughter, a look that conveyed assurance. Behind those eyes, destructive thoughts were not possible.

Spinning around, Jake saw that Ternier and his acolytes currently posed no threat, all but two of them still clutching their heads as if being pelted by stones. Only a few of the inmates still remaining in the closest cell displayed the same throes of agony, squirming wildly on the cell's grungy floor. Of those inmates able to walk, however, he could see the afterglow of rapture lighting their faces. With the exception of Emmanuel and Lucette, all those in his party exhibited similar fugues. Even Hennington appeared spellbound. Still incapacitated from his recent ordeal, Emmanuel Baptiste hung listlessly over one of Zimbola's enormous shoulders while his wife was being borne along by Mat in a comparable carry.

"We'll do as Destiny says!" Jake barked. "Let's move, people!"

Working their way through the gathering throng, Jake led the others as fast as the mob would allow, moving along with the flood of inmates flowing down the hallway.

It was nearly sunup by the time Jake and the others met up with Phillipe. The lad had been awaiting their return just offshore at one the dilapidated docks situated along the waterfront. Jake's party had now doubled in size by those he had rescued, and it had taken two trips in the skiff to get everyone safely aboard the *Angel*. Everyone, that is, except the girl and her mother. Because several of the albinos had also been there to meet them, Destiny and Amphitrite had chosen to ride the dolphins out to the vessel. Upon Jake's insistence, even Hennington had been urged to accompany them in order to avoid Ternier's wrath once the Colonel recovered from the strange debilitation that had struck him and his henchmen.

Getting out of the prison had been surprisingly easy, though Jake had found it strange that every door that should have barred their way had been left wide open. With no guards to obstruct them, they had trudged unthreatened through the dingy corridors of the detention center, pushed along by the exodus of shabby detainees seeking freedom. Eventually they had found their way out into the streets. Amazingly, no one had tried to stop them, not even the gangs that normally roamed the back alleyways within the capital city. But as the group raced on, the sight of people writhing on the ground or stooped over in sickness continued to stay with them, their shrieks of pain filling the air like the cries of demons rising up from hell. In stark contrast to this, many more of the locals stood outside their hovels with faces glazed and blissful, their rapturous gazes riveted skyward as though caught in the grip of an evangelistic revival.

It was only when Jake looked up that he understood the reason for what he was witnessing. Struck by the surge of euphoria that descended to engulf him, he nearly stopped in his tracks to take in the beautiful sight. There, high above the city, something glowed with the vibrant luminosity of a multicolored neon sign hanging against the stars. Here it was again, the same phenomenon he had witnessed back in the prison. Like the benevolent hand of some omnipotent god, an enormous hologram of the dolphin painting floated majestically in the heavens, its three-dimensional imagery of pulsing lights intertwining soothingly before shooting to infinity.

Chapter 13

Once aboard the *Angel*, Mat took Jake aside. "Where can we speak privately?"

Jake immediately led him up to the boat's pilothouse. "What's on your mind, buddy?"

"What do you plan on doing now?" Mat asked.

Jake felt the adrenalin that had carried him through the night beginning to ebb away. "I've got other business to take care of," he said.

"Yeah…like what?"

Jake was at an impasse. He had already committed himself to the gig Hennington had arranged for him, but then again, he hadn't forgotten about the villagers that had been abducted from Malique and taken away aboard the *San Carlo*. For what purpose they had been kidnapped, he could only guess. Although his first impulse was to head north in the hopes of intercepting the tuna trawler, he was now desperately low on cash, and without it he would not be able to buy the fuel that would replenish his badly depleted tanks. Without sufficient fuel, he could not even consider trying to hunt down the trawler.

Letting out a big sigh, Jake gave voice to the only thing that made sense to him right now. "For starters, I'm going to bring the people we saved back to their homes."

Mat did not appear very pleased. "And then I suppose you'll be picking up where you left off, engaging in those illegal smuggling runs you've grown so fond of lately."

Jake looked away. "A man's got to eat."

Mat's displeasure soured further. "I just don't get you anymore. Making a piss hole like this your base of operations doesn't fit the Jake I know."

"Some people change."

"Yeah," Mat nodded in agreement, "some people. But you're not one of 'em. I watched you closely tonight. You're still the same guy I used to sweat and bleed with. You haven't changed one little bit. What gives that you're not telling your old Uncle Mat?"

Jake stood mute for a long moment, cognizant of the way Mat was scrutinizing him. Perhaps it was time for him to come clean with his old friend. "You remember our little stint in Tora Bora?"

"I'd have to suffer amnesia to ever forget it."

"Well, I made a promise to Myers back then, one I aim to keep."

Mat kept staring. "Go on."

"He made me promise I'd find his kid, the one he told us about."

"Uh, huh!"

"Phillipe is Myers' kid."

Mat's jaw dropped. "You mean the boy that works for you?"

"Yep."

"Now that you mention it, I thought I saw something in him that reminded me of Myers. How'd you ever find him?"

Jake shrugged. "Just lucky, I guess."

"Well, it seems to me you fulfilled your promise. Yet you continue to stay in these waters. Why?"

"I still have another promise to keep," Jake confided.

A look of genuine intrigue suddenly transcended Mat's countenance, but he said nothing, waiting for Jake to offer more.

"You remember the treasure Myers told us about?"

"Yeah. All of it was seized by Haitian authorities."

Jake felt it difficult to extinguish the smile wanting to creep onto his face. "Wrong!" he corrected. "They only got half of it."

Mat absorbed this tidbit of information for several seconds. "Are you telling me Mercades managed to hide half the booty?"

"Yes."

"So where is it?"

"It's hidden in the waters north of here…at least that's where I think it is."

"But you're not sure?"

"To tell you the truth, I've been so busy lately, I haven't been able to confirm if I've actually located it."

"So what happens if you find it?"

"Phillipe will get most of it."

Mat's eyebrows rose. "Really."

"Yeah. That was the other half of the promise I made, that I'd recover what was left of the treasure and make sure Phillipe was the primary recipient."

Mat stared at Jake, unable to conceal the admiration he was feeling for his friend. "I see," he said. "Does the boy know this?"

"Not yet."

Mat looked around him, studying the layout of the pilothouse before shifting his eyes to the deck below. "This was Mercades boat, wasn't it?"

Jake nodded.

"And Zimbola was Mercades' loyal friend that Myers had told us about?"

"Right again."

"So I take it this vessel also belongs to Phillipe."

Jake shook his head. "The *Angel* has two owners, each with an equal share…Zimbola and me."

Mat let all of this sink in, seeming to analyze what Jake had revealed. Finally he said, "So what happens if you recover the treasure?"

Jake expelled a long hearty sigh. "I really haven't given it much thought."

"You'll at least stop running illicit contraband, won't you?"

Jake could not help but produce an enigmatic grin. "Well, I just don't know. There's something about those running gun battles at sea that gets a fella's blood going. It's a habit that's gonna be hard to break."

Mat grinned back. "Always the wise ass."

"I've learned from the best."

Mat's expression suddenly mellowed into one of deep reflection. "Now tell me, buddy, what the hell's going on with the girl and her mother? Am I going crazy, or are those women actually psychic?"

Jake sighed again. "I wish I knew the answer, and no, you're not going crazy."

"So how did you get mixed up with them?"

For the next ten minutes, Jake gave Mat a rundown of the events that had led him to the girl near Navassa Island and the ensuing trip to the cove, including his fight with the crew of the Colombian tuna trawler. When Jake told him all about the strange white dolphins Destiny communed with and the other unusual powers she possessed, his friend stared back as if Jake had lost his mind.

"I wish you'd stop putting me on, old buddy," Mat said, his tone holding no humor. "You must think I was hatched out of an Easter egg to buy into a whopper like that."

Jake noted the look of disbelief in his friend's eyes. "I know it's a hard story to swallow. Even though I've seen what I'm telling you with my own eyes, I have trouble believing it myself. But tonight, you had a front row seat in witnessing what Destiny is capable of, things that would normally seem impossible to most people."

Pointing to the barely distinguishable scar on the back of his upper arm, Jake said, "See this. About four days ago I took a bullet through the triceps, compliments of the Colombians I fought against. Destiny was able to heal the wound completely in a matter of seconds just by touching it. From what I've been told, she inherited this ability from her mother who has the same power."

Mat shook his head skeptically. "I don't know…this whole story seems far too weird. I mean, come on, voodoo and white witches of the vau…what do you call it?"

"Vaudun."

"Whatever!" Mat was beginning to look annoyed. "It's all just too much to accept, especially the part about dolphins with hands and how they're able to carry on a conversation in human languages."

"These dolphins are fairly new to the planet," Jake explained. "My guess is they're the result of some kind of evolutionary jump. From what I've seen, they seem to have an intellect way above human intelligence. Somehow Destiny is able to establish a communal mind link with them that, at least in part, is responsible for the unique powers she displays."

Jake assessed the doubt still clouding Mat's face and sighed. "I can see I'm still beating a dead horse here." Turning, he grabbed a flashlight hanging from the bulkhead and began to exit the pilothouse. "Follow me! I've got something to show you that might change your mind."

Leading Mat down to the vessel's rear deck, Jake leaned over the port side. He was about to call to Achilles when the albino poked his head above the water.

Shining the flashlight down into the dolphin's face, Jake said, "Mat, I'd like you to meet Achilles."

"Hello, Mat," Achilles trilled. "You must trust the things Jay Jay tells you."

Mat appeared stunned. "Are my ears deceiving me, or did that dolphin just speak to me?"

"Achilles, please show Mat your hands!" Jake requested.

Using his tail for leverage, Achilles rose higher out of the water to display the abnormal appendages he possessed.

"Catch!" Jake blurted, tossing the flashlight down to the young dolphin.

Exhibiting precise dexterity, Achilles caught the flashlight in his left hand, then tossed it back up to Jake.

"Now do you believe me?" Jake asked, turning to look at Mat.

Utter astonishment manifested itself on Mat's face. "Holy shit!"

"Here's something else for you to chew on," Jake intoned. "Achilles, tell Mat what the pi ratio of a circle represents and give him the actual number out to the eighth decimal place."

"Pi is the circumference of a circle divided by its diameter. It is both a universal mathematical constant and an irrational number, having an infinite string of digits with no discernable pattern emerging from its numbers. The first time the sequence one through nine is encountered, it is over five hundred million digits into the ratio. The pi ratio calculated out to eight decimal places approximately equals three point one, four, one, five, nine, two, six, five."

Mat continued to look flabbergasted. "Jesus Christ, how does he know that?"

"Let me show you something else," Jake said, ignoring the question. As he led Mat into the *Angel*'s salon, only Grahm, Parker, Trebek, Hennington and Jacob currently occupied the cabin.

"Does that painting look familiar?" Jake queried Mat, pointing to the dolphin art leaning up against the wall.

As Mat cast his eyes upon the canvas, Jake could see the effect it had on his friend, a profound nurturing of the spirit.

Mat stared, silently transfixed as if in a stupor, seeming to forget about Jake's presence for the moment. "I…I saw something very much like this during our escape from the prison. I thought I was hallucinating at the time."

"Looking at it makes you feel good inside, doesn't it?"

Mat nodded distractedly, unwilling to pull his gaze away from the masterpiece. "Where…where did you get this?"

"Achilles produced this painting," Jake stated. "Members of his pod have produced a lot of paintings like this. Even though each work of art is different, they all seem to have one thing in common, and that's the remarkable effect they have on people."

The painting continued to dominate Mat's attention. "How can a painting do this?" he asked, his tone indicating awe. His eyes seemed to rove over every facet within the artistic expression.

"I have no explanation," Jake said, "though Jacob, here, believes it triggers some kind of neurological mechanism in the lesser used side of the human brain."

Finally managing to withdraw his gaze, Mat looked at his watch. "Well, good buddy, I'd like to stick around and continue chatting, but I have other business to take care of. If my boys are as punctual as they've shown me in the past, they should be pulling alongside at any moment."

No sooner had Mat uttered the words, something bumped lightly against the *Angel*. Moving back out on deck, Jake saw the hulking silhouette of *Relentless* abutting the North Sea trawler's starboard side. Two members of Mat's team stood near the boat's stern, lending a hand as Mat climbed aboard.

Just before the DHS vessel pulled away, Mat smiled back at Jake. "If it's not too much of an imposition, I'd sure like to have one of those paintings."

"I'll see what I can do about getting you one," Jake said.

"Don't be a stranger, buddy. Stay in touch." And then Mat was gone, his boat purring off into the twilight of dawn like a phantom drifting across the water.

As Jake watched his friend depart, he suddenly realized he hadn't seen Destiny or her mother in some time now. As if responding to his concern, Achilles suddenly surfaced close by, and before the question lurking at the back of Jake's mind could be vocalized, the adolescent albino gave him an answer totally unexpected.

"Destiny and Amphitrite have gone, Jay Jay," Achilles warbled.

"Gone?" Jake blurted. "Gone where?"

"I cannot tell you at this time."

The comment left Jake almost speechless. "Why can't you tell me?"

"Do not be mad, Jay Jay. Destiny has made me promise not to reveal her whereabouts until three hours from now."

"What's wrong with telling me right now?" Jake fumed.

"I am bound by a promise."

Jake scanned the water all around the *Angel*. There was no sign of any other dolphin. "Excluding yourself, Achilles, are any other members of the pod still here?" he asked.

"Two others still remain," Achilles said.

"Who?"

"You and Jacob remain."

Jake began to grow frustrated. "Achilles, please…I must-"

The hand placed on Jake's shoulder made him spin around. Hennington stood before him.

Jake studied the blend of humbleness and anxiety written on the broker's face. "What were you doing in the prison, Chester?"

"For many years now I have been Ternier's pawn, a man possessed by both selfishness and fear," Hennington confessed. "But it was the white mambo who turned me away from my own insatiable greed and the coward I had become."

It took Jake several seconds to deduce what was being said. Apparently, Colonel Ternier had used the broker as his personal agent, capitalizing on Hennington's unique talents for shady dealings in order to enrich himself. Like Bashir, however, Hennington had undergone some inner transformation for the better, a cleansing of the spirit brought about at the hands of Destiny's mother. Perhaps Hennington was going to walk the straight and narrow from here on out.

Jake nodded in understanding. "You realize Ternier will kill you if he ever finds you."

"I can no longer allow myself to live in fear."

"What about our little business arrangement?" Jake found it necessary to ask. Though the idea of running illegal contraband did not sit well with him, he desperately needed cash to refuel the *Angel*. Deep down he knew this would be his last smuggling run.

Shame flashed briefly across Hennington's face. "Do you know what supernotes are?"

Jake stared blankly.

"Supernotes are extremely high-quality copies of foreign currency."

"You mean counterfeits?"

"Yes."

"You're telling me that was to be the shipment?"

"Yes."

"Which currency and how much?"

"United States greenbacks in one-hundred-dollar bill denominations. About $140 million in all."

Jake was dumbstruck by the amount. "Where was it coming from?"

"Pyongyang, North Korea via Kingston."

Something stirred in the back of Jake's mind. While in the Seals he had learned of North Korea's state-supervised currency printing plants that churned out high-grade counterfeit currency, primarily in the form of American greenbacks but also in Japanese yen, Thai baht, and in recent years, euros. These were high-speed banknote presses like those used by the U.S. Bureau of Engraving and Printing.

"And who was to be the recipient?"

Hennington leaned against the railing and looked down at Achilles, staring briefly at the dolphin before turning back to Jake. "The man you recently made an enemy of was to be the recipient."

"Henri Ternier?"

Hennington produced an affirmative nod. "The Colonel is an ambitious man and is waiting for the right moment to take control of Haiti."

"Coups are nothing new to this country," Jake said, unperturbed by the news. "Keeping a secure grip on the reins of power is generally short-lived. I don't think Ternier would have any more success than his predecessors, especially with U.N. troops stationed here to counter a government takeover. Even if he initially succeeded, the U.S. wouldn't stand for it. Uncle Sam would march right in and kick him out."

The broker frowned gravely. "Ternier knows this. That is why he has aligned himself with some powerful allies. He has been planning his move for a long time now, and when conditions are in his favor, he will strike."

"He's told you this plan?"

"No, but I have acted enough on his behalf to figure out the things he has set in motion."

Something shifted heavily along the fringes of Jake's consciousness, and his mind was suddenly forging ahead like a tugboat abruptly cut loose from the towline it had been straining against. "So North Korea is one of his allies."

"I think so."

"What makes you believe that?"

"Counterfeit bills are normally purchased with bona fide money at anywhere from thirty to seventy percent of their face value, but the Colonel was to receive the counterfeits without having to pay anything in exchange."

"Sounds like Pyongyang's intent on funding something free of charge. What was Ternier gonna use the phony money for?"

"To buy weapons and the cooperation of U.N. troops and other factions within Haiti. He has already bribed several U.N. commanders not to interfere in his activities. And because of it, he has managed to stockpile an impressive arsenal of weapons for a military coup. A continuance of this type of corruption would be child's play for him."

Jake tightened his eyes sullenly. "Yeah, but how would he prevent the U.S. from coming in here and ousting him?"

Hennington played a brooding gaze over Jake's face, drawing a deep breath before replying. "By introducing turmoil in your own government through some catastrophic event. An incident even greater than what you Americans refer to as nine-eleven would strain Washington's resources enough to divert its attention completely away from Haiti, possibly forestalling indefinitely, maybe even permanently, any military response aimed at restoring order to this insignificant country."

The hazy picture lingering at the back of Jake's mind suddenly became a little clearer, and an image of the rogue sub sprang to the forefront of his thoughts. "You mentioned other allies of the Colonel. Did he make any deals with Islamic extremists?"

"I was his go-between in arranging a meeting between a Colombian and a man representing an Asian heroin cartel. The cartel man went by the name Omar. Whether or not he was a Muslim I cannot say. What I can tell you is Ternier has strong ties with a powerful Colombian drug lord called Cardoza. One of Cardoza's lieutenants, a man called Sebastian Ortega, met with Omar for the meeting."

"What was the purpose of this meeting?"

"I do not know because I was not present when it took place. I simply arranged for it to happen. But some kind of a deal had been struck involving the delivery of at least twenty able-bodied Haitians to Omar."

"What were these people needed for?"

"Again, I do not know, but it was Ternier who actually provided Ortega with the people Omar requested. They were abducted from the village of Malique early last night."

To Jake, the picture was now beginning to come into sharp focus. "Where and when was this meeting held?"

"At Navassa Island almost five days ago. That is where the people were taken."

This bit of information put Jake's thoughts in a tizzy. The Colombian-Jihadist connection he had theorized was now being confirmed, and instinctively he knew where Destiny and her mother had gone.

"I have a problem, Chester," Jake found himself saying, "one I'm hoping you'll help me with.

Hennington held Jake's gaze, the expression on his face open and unguarded, and Jake saw a new quality to the man he hadn't seen before. "I'll help you any way I can, Jake," the broker offered.

Jake had never liked asking anybody for anything unless a problem involved people other than himself. "The *Angel* needs fuel, and at this moment I lack the cash to pay for it."

Hennington did not bat an eye, reaching into his pocket and stuffing a thick wad of bills into Jake's hands.

Jake nearly choked with gratitude, but before he could offer any thanks, Trebek came out on deck to join the conversation.

"Did you tell him?" Trebek asked Hennington.

Jake alternated his gaze anxiously between the two men. "Tell me what?"

The broker met Jake's questioning eyes and sighed tiredly. "We have reason to believe Ternier knows the location of a hydrogen bomb lost by the United States military many years ago."

Even though the early morning air was warm, something akin to frostbite raced wildly through Jake's bones, and he berated himself unmercifully for having neglected the thing bubbling like fermenting ale in the recesses of his brain, a thing he had failed to follow up on ever since capturing Bashir. Why he hadn't pressed the man for more information he could not explain to himself, though he suspected it had something to do with his trust in Destiny. The fact that Ternier was somehow linked up with Islamic terrorists was proof enough that something cataclysmic was about to happen.

With growing apprehension, Jake listened carefully to the story related to him by both Hennington and Trebek. When they had finished, Jake knew he needed additional facts, and he rushed to locate Bashir who he assumed was still aboard the *Angel*.

"We cannot find him anywhere," Zimbola eventually informed Jake following a thorough search of the vessel.

Staring back over the side, Jake was about to question Achilles on the matter, but the juvenile spoke up before Jake could utter a word.

"Bashir has left with Destiny, Jay Jay," Achilles twittered. "But I still must keep my promise."

Jake looked back in frustration, knowing how binding a promise could be. Abruptly, he called out to his First Mate. When Zimbola appeared, he said, "Pull anchor!"

"Where we going?" the big man asked.

Jake fingered the wad of money in his hand. "First we top off our tanks, then we head back up the coast."

Racing into the *Angel's* salon, Jake found Grahm and Parker talking quietly with Jacob. "Leaving you here to catch an outgoing flight would put you and your assistants in too much danger, Professor," Jake stated gruffly. "For the time being I'm going to leave the three of you with Jacob back at the cove. Later on I'll come pick you up and drop you off in Kingston where it's a lot safer."

Grahm's expression turned to one of deep concern. "Where are you going, my lad?"

Jake hesitated, unsure if he should disclose his plans, but not seeing any need for secrecy, he came right to the point. "I'm going back to Navassa."

Chapter 14

Carried along by Hercules, Destiny glanced over at her mother, strangely moved by the sight. The technique used by Amphitrite to ride a dolphin was entirely different from her own, mainly because the creature that most often bore her was considerably smaller and anatomically different than Hercules. Nevertheless, Athena still had the ability to plow through the sea with a remarkable degree of efficiency despite the load she carried. And if Athena somehow tired, there was always one of her progeny to take over the task of towing Amphitrite.

Surrounded by an entourage of other pod members, Destiny tried to grasp the full magnitude of what lay before them. But contrary to the occurrences she had been able to foresee at the prison, any gleanings into future events now seemed to be blocked by a blanket of mist. The familiar harmonious resonance that had always preceded precognition was completely absent, leaving a disconcerting uncertainty hanging in its place. The communal conjoining of minds did little to penetrate the fog, and the notion that she might actually be the cause of the problem clung to her perceptions like annoying cobwebs in a dusty room. As she contemplated this, the sensation transformed into something more potent, intruding its way into her thinking like some clumsy beast entering a chamber filled with fragile glass, and begrudgingly, she suddenly knew it could not be denied or ignored. She had compromised herself. She had fallen in love, and in so doing she had contaminated the purity of the vinculum she held with the others. Bias now took away her selflessness, putting the pod at risk. Try as she might, she could not rid herself of the thing she felt. In loving Jay Jay, she had sought to protect him rather than allow him to provide the support she and the others would require in their quest to meet head-on the danger that was fast approaching. They were nearing a critical nexus in the time-space continuum, and the battle that had to be fought could not be avoided. To a large degree, she was failing the purpose she had been created to fulfill by keeping Jay Jay out of the fight. And yet she was powerless to do otherwise.

Tormented by these thoughts, Destiny pressed on, vaguely aware of how her mother and the others regarded her. As always, there was not a shred of condemnation or accusation directed at her. By nature, they were all inherently gentle creatures, and it was not within them to judge. They were simply following a course of action guided by something on a subliminal level.

Destiny noticed Bashir weakening as he sat directly behind her. Once again, they were sharing the same mount. With his arms clasped securely about her waist, she had felt the man's strength gradually ebbing over the last few kilometers. But Bashir would be needed, of that much she was sure, and the respite he required would be forthcoming very shortly. Having been summoned earlier on, Jimenez was not far off and would soon meet up with them. Then Bashir as well as she and her mother would climb aboard the fisherman's pinnace and sail the remaining distance to Navassa Island with the dolphins leading the way.

A sense of impending disaster suddenly seized Destiny in a crushing grip, causing Hercules to flinch spasmodically as he continued to push west. The feeling spread quickly to the other dolphins ringing her, and all at once they let out a high-pitched squeal of distress.

The winch screeched in protest under the strain, then abruptly quieted as the unknown load finally came to rest on the *San Carlo's* stern deck. Holding back the grin he felt, Raduyev kept his emotions in check, looking instead to the questioning frown coming to bear on Sebastian Ortega's face. The Cardoza lieutenant was staring fixedly at the canvas tarp wrapped tightly about the thing pulled from the depths. And from what Raduyev could see, it was obvious Ortega was more than just a little curious about the object salvaged from the sea floor.

"When will this ship of yours arrive?" Ortega asked indifferently.

The Chechen studied Ortega's mien carefully before answering. The man's eyes betrayed the boredom he was trying so hard to exude. The Colombian desperately wanted to see the thing hidden under the tarp. But the deal between them had already been struck, and Ortega had no need to know the tarp's secret.

"We will make the transfer just after nightfall," Raduyev said, shifting his attention to the two divers climbing from the sea. He was quite pleased with the way they had conducted themselves during the recovery operation that had just taken place in 140 feet of water. The mujahidin fighters Gullu Sherkhan had brought with him were showing skills he had not expected. Even though the task required nothing more than locating the load and attaching a shackle to it, he was still impressed with how quickly they had carried it out.

Raduyev stared back at the thing brought up from the ocean floor. In the sunlight, the canvas tarp shrouding it glistened green with a budding growth of algae. This was to be expected given that the tarp had been left submerged during the last three weeks. After all, it was he who had done most of the work in preparing the thing for recovery, risking the bends during more than a dozen separate dives executed from the sub over a span of nearly two weeks to complete the task. The coordinates provided by Henri Ternier had proved surprisingly accurate, making it fairly easy for him to locate the military aircraft that had carried the object. Much of the plane had been buried in sand that had accumulated around the airframe, pushed up against and almost covering it as a result of passing storms over the last several decades. Getting to the object had not been easy, requiring him to use a cutting torch in removing part of the fuselage so that the thing could be lifted out. Airlifting the sand smothering it had proved less difficult, and in the end, he had managed to expose its bulk. Girthing the thing with chains had proved much more problematic, however, and he replayed in his mind the arduous task of having had to dig out more sand covering the frame supporting the twelve-foot-long bomb in order to get the links around it in two places. Then it had required eight large air bags, each with a lifting capacity of roughly 460 kilograms to nudge the 3,500-kilogram bomb off its cradle just enough to allow him to wrap the weapon in the tarp that now kept it hidden from prying eyes. Entwining the tarp with additional chain had not been as time consuming, and after that he had deflated the lift bags and let the load fall gently back into its cradle, certain that the chance of accidental detonation was extremely remote.

Based on what he knew of the bomb, it was a Mark-15 with an explosive yield somewhere between 1.9 and 3.6 megatons. Beneath its metal shell was eighty kilograms of conventional high explosives, a removable capsule housing the plutonium trigger, a mass of highly enriched uranium, and the lithium-6 deuteride compound, the actual fusion material which comprised most of the bomb's volume. Constituents of Bin Laden had researched military records on the lost bomb, discovering that it was one of eleven nuclear bombs lost by the Americans during air and sea accidents, what the Pentagon referred to as "Broken Arrows." And although the U.S. Air Force had long insisted the plutonium capsule needed to trigger the weapon had been removed from it before the ill-fated flight, his examination of the bomb showed it to be entirely intact. Supporting this was a pentagon memo from 1966, which seemed to indicate that the bomb was a complete weapon.

As Raduyev mulled this, Ortega drew in a deep breath, his nostrils flaring to analyze the muggy air wafting over the sea. Staring off into the distance, the Colombian set his eyes on the dark mass of clouds building off to the east.

"We may be getting some weather, my friend," Ortega stated. "Nightfall may come earlier than expected with those clouds headed this way."

Raduyev had noticed the darkening sky earlier, though he didn't think it would amount to much.

Ortega shifted his gaze in another direction. About a quarter mile away a large school of whales had congregated, various behemoths within the group spouting as they breached. "Those are humpbacks, my friend. You do not normally see many whales in these waters, but the feeding must be good to attract so many."

Raduyev barely nodded, not really caring.

Ortega swung around to face him, his manner turning icy. "I checked out the location you gave me. The place was empty."

Though there was only the slightest hint of challenge in Ortega's tone, the Chechen was rather glad the man's attention had shifted away from the bomb. Producing a lazy shrug, Raduyev shifted his gaze to the island not too far from their present position. "I fulfilled my end of the bargain. The coordinates I gave you were accurate. That is where those people had gone."

Ortega nodded stoically, his eyes flitting over the Chechen's face like those of a poker player deciding if he should raise the bet. "There was a cove a short distance back from the cliffs, just as your message had indicated. It was very well hidden, a natural sanctuary."

"Did you find any signs of occupation?"

"Si…I discovered living quarters, two small cottages. One of them contained a laptop computer and was filled with books."

Raduyev fought down the bile suddenly rising in his throat. Having to discuss the place where he had failed to crush Javolyn was just one more ugly reminder of how he had been bested by the former Seal. Despite his annoyance, he felt it was time to bring to light the thing chaffing away at the back of his mind. "Did you learn what those men were doing in these waters?" He made a show of letting his eyes fall on the boat tied up alongside the trawler to indicate what he meant. Apparently, the *San Carlo* had come across the vessel while heading out to meet him.

"What makes you think anyone was aboard her?"

"I saw this boat drifting without power near the island yesterday. Six men could be seen on her deck."

A nefarious smirk came to Ortega's face. "Several of my crew are interrogating them as we speak. They claim to be dolphin hunters. I saw this boat a few days ago heading toward the harbor in Port-au-Prince. It was towing the same waverunner used to attack us."

Several seconds passed as Raduyev studied the Colombian's expression. "You will not find the man you are looking for among those you have captured."

Ortega's smugness vanished immediately. "How do you know that?"

Raduyev felt something clench deep down in his gut. "The person you seek was a Navy Seal at one time, a man called Jake Javolyn."

A dark frown sprang onto Ortega's face. "You know this man?"

"I have a vendetta to settle with him. He and that accursed girl we saw with him were out here yesterday, but they sailed away."

Ortega reined in his anger. "What were they doing?"

"I do not know." Raduyev brought his eyes back on the tethered vessel. "But I think they may be the reason why this boat became inoperable."

Ortega's face darkened further. "Maybe these dolphin hunters know something about him?" Contemplating his own question a moment longer, his expression changed into a sneer. "Follow me below deck, my friend. Perhaps they can provide us with some answers."

Destiny was amazed at the size of the creature rising up from the depths to trail behind them. It was immense, the largest shark she had ever seen, and from the mental feedback she was getting from the others, it appeared to be a tiger. And as she well knew, the teeth of a tiger were the most dangerous of all sharks. Even without biting down on prey, they were capable of causing extensive damage to flesh with as little as a raking strike during a slack-jawed attack.

But as she sensed the animal's approach, she felt a familiar presence driving the creature on. Erzulie was following them.

Through some arcane ritual of the black arts, the sorceress of the voudun had found a way of pouring her essence into the predator pursuing them. And while the witch was seeing them through the shark's eyes, it was Erzulie's will that was controlling the monster, compelling it to attack.

Normally the albinos should have been able to easily outpace it. Compared to the new breed, tigers were relatively slow swimmers, only capable of reaching a maximum speed of thirty-two kilometers per hour, with short bursts of higher speeds lasting no more than a few seconds. But Erzulie was forcing the 30-foot monster forward at an incredible rate, making it drive its 6-ton bulk through the sea at a speed that at least equaled their own.

With the threat rapidly closing in on them, the group went into a defensive posture. Every member of the pod suddenly altered their formation, flaring out to both sides in flanking maneuvers to surround the beast. It only took Destiny a moment to realize where the shark's attention was directed. The monster had targeted her mother, or at least the dolphin she was riding. Being the slowest member of the pack, Athena was the most vulnerable.

Discovering the shark's intent, the pod quickly adjusted its movements. Hermes and Aphrodite darted in to intercept it as it closed the gap on Amphitrite. At the same instant, Apollo and Artemis circled around, rushing up on the shark's rear as Coral and Reef raced to Destiny's side. With Destiny having no time to give Bashir a full explanation as to what was happening, she simply asked him to release his hold on her. No sooner did he comply, Coral extended her powerful forelimbs to pluck him from Hercules' back. A look of surprise came over the Palestinian's face as he was carried off to one side out of harm's way.

The tiger's jaws parted wide, displaying flattened triangular teeth with notched and serrated edges. Waving its wedge-shaped head from side to side, it lashed out with frenzied vigor, eager to have its razor-sharp weaponry come in contact with dolphin flesh. And while the albinos nearest the jaws were successful in remaining clear of the slashing strikes, they were ineffective in discouraging the beast from its targeted prey, that being Amphitrite and her mount.

Destiny held on tight as Hercules dove deep, responding to the imminent threat. She felt his heart pound thunderously within his powerful body as he rapidly gained speed. Flattening herself against the dolphin's back, she reduced the drag on the albino as much as possible, knowing what Hercules had in mind. The giant levelled off and began to rise, increasing his momentum further, and as Destiny looked up, the tiger's bulk blotted out the sun hanging above the ocean. It was then that she realized how close those snapping jaws were to Athena.

Hercules flicked his tail with a final explosive snap, slamming beak-first into the beast's belly with such force that Destiny was nearly flung free. Stunned from the impact, the albino bull fell away slowly, dropping languidly into the abyss beneath him.

Destiny focused, channeling most of her life energy into her mount, desperately trying to revive him. Apollo and Artemis swooped down to help, keeping Hercules from falling any deeper by supporting his body with their own. Reef, Hermes, and Aphrodite quickly joined in the rescue, and conjoining their minds with Destiny's, concentrated on bringing Hercules back to full consciousness. Within moments, the giant albino responded, and with renewed purpose, prepared for another assault against the colossal shark.

But another assault was unnecessary. Already the enormous tiger was plummeting into the depths as if in slow motion, its heart completely ruptured by a combination of overstress from the impossible demands Erzulie had forced upon it and the crushing impact of Hercules' charge.

A flood of relief washed over Destiny as she glanced up toward the surface, noting that her mother and Athena remained unscathed. Riding Hercules back to the surface, she waited for Coral to restore Bashir to his former perch behind her. With the others forming up around her and Amphitrite, they once again resumed her northerly heading.

Another half hour passed without further incident, after which time Jimenez finally chugged his pinnace into their midst. Few words were exchanged as Bashir and the women climbed aboard, and a moment later the entire group set out for the place where an unavoidable but necessary showdown had been prophesied long ago.

Chapter 15

*E*rzulie let out an agonized scream. She had felt the trauma inflicted on the tiger shark as if the pain were her own, and she clutched her chest protectively as if the heart beating within were on the verge of bursting. The paroxysm passed quickly, however, and she exhaled sharply as though a knife had been pulled from her lungs.

Henri placed a hand on her shoulder. "What is wrong, mother?"

Erzulie gasped, drawing breath hungrily. "They…they have beaten me again." She stared in bewilderment at the quartz crystal at the center of the amulet, no longer able to view the pod they were pursuing. Once again, the chevals had escaped her.

Ternier's face contorted into a mask of blistering rage. These chevals were causing him nothing but problems. "It does not matter," he consoled her. "Once we reach Navassa Island, we will join forces with our allies. Our combined strength will be more than adequate to defeat these chevals once and for all." All at once his anger changed over into a malicious grin. "Sebastian Ortega will be especially pleased to know the girl and dolphins will practically fall right into his waiting hands."

Erzulie nodded absently, continuing to eye the ancient charm as if doubting its potency for the first time ever. "Perhaps that is the reason the rada are urging them to Navassa."

The Colonel took a moment to espy the sea sliding past one of the boat's starboard windows. The rumble of the engines was somehow reassuring to him as they pushed the craft toward the island. The sound only tended to reassert his sense of power. He had grown rich over the past several years despite the vast fortune the hurricane had taken from him many years ago, affording him the luxury of the modern yacht he now possessed. It was a sleek vessel, far too good for the men he had chosen to crew her. He had commissioned its construction in Miami two years earlier, and it was only three weeks ago he had finally taken delivery of it.

"We will destroy them completely this time," Ternier reiterated. "And once Omar launches his missile, Haiti will finally be ours for the taking."

Erzulie released the amulet, letting it fall back into place between her withered breasts. "When will that be, my son?"

"Very soon, mother. Very soon."

Sitting at his computer console in Toulouse, France, the telemetry specialist noted the location of the pulsing signal. Enlarging the magnification further, he was momentarily surprised to find that it did not originate from one of those strange white dolphins he had seen several days earlier. This time the signal was coming from a boat, and from the look of the watercraft, he sensed her to be exceptionally seaworthy. Yawning, and without giving it much thought, he relayed the information to the anonymous client. On this occasion, however, the transmission would be broadcast automatically every three minutes. For all practical purposes, he was finished doing what he had been paid to do.

The hour was late and boredom was creeping up on him. Sipping some of the steaming coffee from the mug he held, he decided to take another look at the thing that had grabbed his attention once before. With his free hand, he punched several computer keys, and almost immediately the color coded imagery of sea temperatures surrounding Navassa Island filled the screen.

Surprised by what he saw, he almost spilled his coffee. Thinking his eyes might be playing tricks on him, he accessed the history file, retrieving the latest stored frame and comparing it against the current image. There was no mistaking it. The algae bloom had grown, its size broadening significantly without any reduction in concentration. That meant the amount of upwelling near the island had increased.

Acknowledging the irregularity as something of passing interest, he changed screens, pulling up real-time satellite visual imagery of the waters where the upwelling was occurring. With the exception of a ship sitting stationary several hundred meters from the pocket of cold water that delineated the sector of upwelling, nothing else was visible. Lowering the magnification, he broadened the picture. Off to the east, a heavy patch of cloud cover blocked a view of the ocean. More than likely a storm was brewing, and from the look of it, the water just south of the island was going to be subjected to a heavy blow.

Finding nothing else of interest to arouse his curiosity, the specialist saved the latest images, storing them away in the system's data banks. Propping his feet up on the desk, he leaned back in his chair, and within seconds fell off into a light sleep.

Jake stared first at Jacob, then at the others. Firmly rooted in all four faces was a look of conviction. Nevertheless, he felt it necessary to convince them otherwise. "There is no telling what we'll be facing at Navassa," he advised. "All I can say is each of you will be putting yourself in danger if you insist on coming along. You might even get yourselves killed."

Jacob appeared unruffled. "I am not afraid of dying."

"The same goes for me," Hennington insisted.

"You will have to physically eject me from this vessel to keep me from going," Trebek growled.

Jake turned to Grahm. "What about you, Professor?"

The scientist sighed wearily. "Count me in!"

"What about your assistants?"

"Nicolas is still ill. We can drop him off in the cove. Jeffrey will tend to him."

Jake nodded in agreement. "Makes sense." He shifted his eyes to Jacob. "Provided Jacob doesn't mind."

"I do not mind."

"Phillipe will accompany them," Jake said. "We'll drop them off with provisions to tide them over." He had considered leaving Emmanuel and Lucette with them as well, but it was Jacob who had insisted they would be better off aboard the *Angel* where he could tend to them. Though Amphitrite and Destiny had healed their injuries, they still had not fully recovered from their ordeal.

The boat's intercom suddenly buzzed, and Jake answered the bridge. "What's up, Zimby?"

The Jamaican's deep voice boomed from the speaker. "Kingston has issued a weather advisory, Jay Jay. There may be a storm headed for Navassa. Do we hole up at the cove, or do we keep going?"

"We'll be dropping Phillipe off with Jeff Parker and Nick Henderson. After that, we sail for Navassa, storm or no storm."

Ortega felt only contempt for the man tied to the chair before him. The one admitting to the name of Walter McPherson had so far shown a total lack of courage, practically blubbering like a baby. While the Loomins brothers had proved much tougher, it had taken very little persuasion to get McPherson to open up. Pedro had barely begun to administer the type of beating he was so fond of doling out, and McPherson had spilled information like a media newscaster, spewing much more than expected.

Fingering the device recently retrieved from the *Sea Lion*, Ortega motioned Pedro away from McPherson. Pedro scowled savagely, backing away begrudgingly. He did not like being denied his pleasure. He was just getting started.

"So, what exactly does this little thing do?" Ortega asked, ignoring the look Cardoza's nephew was giving him.

McPherson grimaced, his right cheekbone now swollen and taking on a bright purple sheen. "It's a telemetry device. It transmits the location of whatever it's tied to."

"And this was taken from one of the two white dolphins captured a few days ago?"

McPherson answered with a frenzied nod, his eyes filled with fear.

Out of curiosity, Ortega turned to observe the scornful expression etched on Omar's face, judging the Islamist to be equally revolted by

McPherson's shameful display of gutlessness. "If this device transmits a signal, where do you keep the receiver?"

"We don't have one aboard the boat," McPherson whined.

"Then how are you able to determine the signal's location?"

"The tracking unit is kept aboard a spotter plane which guides the *Sea Lion* into position."

"And then what do you do?"

"The boat's crew stands by while the plane drops a sounder to incapacitate the dolphins." McPherson was speaking very quickly now. "After that the crew moves in to drug them with sedation darts just before netting them."

"By what means does this sounder you speak of incapacitate them?"

"It sends out a blast of sonar just strong enough to stun them."

"You said two white dolphins were captured. Did they by any chance show any unusual appendages?"

The panic that had been showing in McPherson's face instantly changed over to astonishment before subsiding into perplexity. "I…I'm not sure I understand what you mean?"

Ortega studied his expression a moment longer, then looked over at Pedro and gave him a subtle nod.

Pedro's mouth displayed a sadistic grin, and he pounced on McPherson with renewed eagerness, balling a fist and throwing a punch.

By moving his head at the last moment, McPherson was able to avoid the brunt of the strike, his jaw taking only a glancing blow. "Okay… okay," he yelled, tucking his chin down against his chest to protect it from further harm and straining wildly against his bonds. "They had these strange foldout forelimbs with hands."

With a stern look, Ortega warned Pedro off again. "So how did they manage to get away?"

McPherson glanced timidly over at Pedro to make sure he was not about to launch another blow. "Two people sabotaged the capture. They pretended to be stranded on a waverunner. Loomins picked them up, a man and a woman…they freed the creatures."

"Describe these people."

"I wasn't there when it happened," McPherson groaned. "You'll have to ask Ben Loomins."

Tied to another chair, Ben Loomins was out cold, his face showing Pedro's nasty work. Slumped in a chair next to him, his brother, Charlie, was in similar condition.

Ortega looked to another of the *San Carlo's* crewmen standing close to the unconscious man. "Wake him up!" he ordered.

The crewman lifted a bucket of water and splashed its contents over Loomins' drooped head. Coming awake and sputtering weakly, Loomins stared groggily about him.

Squatting down to look into his eyes, Ortega said, "Describe the people who freed the dolphins you caught."

Loomins blinked dumbly for several seconds, the question seeming to be beyond his understanding.

"The people who freed the dolphins you captured," Ortega repeated in an ugly snarl. "Describe them!"

Intense rage suddenly took hold of Loomins. "A man and a woman freed them," he bellowed, as if the memory of the incident angered him far more than what Ortega was doing to him. "The woman was about five feet tall and very pretty…she had long black hair and looked to be about eighteen years old at most." Loomins face glowered still hotter. "The guy was about six feet and looked like a weightlifter…I think he had green eyes and a trident tattooed on his left forearm."

Ortega lifted his eyes to glimpse the hatred emblazoned on Omar's countenance. "Does that sound like Javolyn?"

Before Omar could reply, another crewman entered the room. "A vessel is approaching from the west, Sebastian."

Ortega mulled this. According to his sources, the nearby island was not scheduled for any military surveillance or scientific expeditions in the immediate future. Skewering Pedro with a vicious glare, he said, "I am going topside for the moment. You will refrain from hurting these men anymore until I come back. Is that understood?" He needed to know more about these strange white creatures, and the men tied to the chairs might have a lot more to tell him. The last thing he wanted was Pedro beating the life out of them before they could provide him with additional information.

Pedro barely acknowledged the order, exhibiting the manner of a carnivore denied a chunk of bloodied meat laid before it.

With that said, Ortega left the room, somewhat mystified that Omar was still accompanying him. By the time he made his way back up on deck, the unknown vessel was within hailing distance under a sky that had darkened considerably, its bow working hard against a restless sea. He could see the weather was rapidly deteriorating.

"They request permission to come alongside," the same crewman informed Ortega. Using a handheld radio, the crewman continued to stay in contact with the *San Carlo's* bridge.

Ortega studied the vessel as it drew closer. She was a rusting hulk with the lines of an ocean tug that had spent too many years at sea without ever seeing dry dock. "Ask them what they want?"

The crewman did as he was told, bringing the radio to his mouth again and carrying on a short discourse with the bridge. "They say they are here to tow the other boat back to Port-au-Prince."

Ortega sneered wickedly. Things were getting better and better. "Tell them to pull up to our port side and throw us some lines."

Chapter 16

With the *Avenging Angel* finally holding to a steady course, Jake wondered if he had made the right decision. As expected, Phillipe had not liked being left behind. Even Parker had objected to being put ashore, much rather preferring to accompany Grahm. But once Jake had explained the perils they were sure to encounter, Parker had eventually given in, seeing the wisdom in keeping out of harm's way. Not surprisingly, however, was Henderson's desire to get his feet back on dry land. As a matter of fact, the electronics whiz had seemed all too eager to revisit the cove.

Hector had told Jake how Henderson had fallen ill after looking at Achilles' painting, and it was this that made him continue to dwell on the decision he had made. While in the prison he had seen the way the painting had adversely affected Ternier and most of the men that served him. People with inherently vile natures, it seemed, were apt to become sick, at least temporarily, when exposed to the dolphin art, forever removed from the boundaries of redemption. And it was this observation that only had served to further increase both his dislike and distrust of Henderson.

As the coast receded farther behind him, a feeling of deep-seated uneasiness began to take hold of Jake, gradually mounting with each passing minute as if to match the growing sea. Already the *Angel* was beginning to pound its way through quartering swells as the storm approached from the east. The sky had darkened considerably, exacerbated all the more by the approach of nightfall.

Ever since Hennington had informed him about the nuclear warhead, Jake had tried to contact Daniels, putting in a satellite call to his friend every few minutes to warn him about the bomb. But each time he had done this, the call would not go through.

Checking his current GPS coordinates, Jake could see they were now less than ten minutes from Navassa, even taking into account the reduced headway they were making under the deteriorating conditions. Already the island's southern shore was showing up on his radar screen, and some distance back from it was a sizable blip that told him all he needed to know.

Jake turned to note Zimbola eyeing the screen from his position at the helm. "If that's the *San Carlo*, she's not moving."

"She be sitting at anchor, I suppose," the Jamaican offered. His gaze came to bear on another blip just beginning to impinge on the screen as he said this. "And she be having company."

Jake scrutinized the screen again, studying the object making its way slowly toward the first vessel. "If we can see them, I have to assume they can see us."

"What shall we do?"

Several ideas flashed quickly in Jake's mind, but only one held any merit, though even that seemed pretty foolhardy. Nevertheless, he had to give it a try. "I want you to bring us to within a half-mile of those ships and then hold your position. Don't go any closer! If any vessels come in this direction, I want you to back away."

Zimby looked confused. "So we just be sittin' here?"

"For the time being, yes, but I want everyone at the ready, all weapons locked and loaded like before."

Suspicion crept onto the big man's face as he stared at Jake. "What you be doing?" he asked, emphasizing the you.

"I'm going over the side for a closer look."

Zimby gazed back as if Jake were nuts. "The sea, she be gettin' angrier by the minute. How will you make it back?"

"Let me worry about that, okay. Navy Seals trained in weather like this all the time. Mercades' grandson would have considered it nothing more than a stroll on the beach."

Zimbola looked doubtful as the *Angel* suddenly rolled, then pitched hard under him.

"Besides, Achilles will be with me."

"Are you sure that dolphin still be with us?"

"Oh, he's still with us alright." Jake could feel the juvenile on the fringes of his awareness, an all too familiar presence that had continued to grow stronger during the last several hours. It was a sensation that would not go away.

With a utility belt holding six spare ammo clips wrapped snugly about his waist, his USP-9 submachine pistol riding his right thigh, and his K-bar strapped firmly to his right calf, a feeling of invincibility began to consume Jake as he held on tight to Achilles' compact form. Even so, he knew such a state of mind could be counterproductive, perhaps reckless, and Mat's chastening stare loomed briefly in his thoughts, a sober reminder that many lives were depending on him. At least try to be a little cautious, he chastised himself.

Jake suddenly shivered involuntarily, aware that the water temperature had dropped markedly. Achilles was only breaching the surface whenever Jake needed air, otherwise avoiding the heavy surge where avalanching whitecaps made the going more difficult. Somehow the dolphin could sense whenever Jake's lungs were in need of recharging, and it was only at these times the young albino would also take the opportunity to breathe. For some inexplicable reason, though, Jake's ability to remain submerged had improved significantly in the last several days, and he wondered if it had something to do with the bond he shared with the juvenile.

Keeping his dive gear to a minimum, Jake had foregone the use of his swim fins, only strapping on his dive mask with snorkel and wearing the same shorty wetsuit he normally utilized in these waters. With Achilles doing all the work, he didn't require swim fins anyway. But now he was freezing, and he could feel the first signs of hypothermia creeping up on him. Why was the sea so damned cold he couldn't help but ask himself?

We will pass beyond the boundary of the upwelling shortly, Jay Jay, Achilles informed him, apparently reading Jake's thoughts again. *You are experiencing the water pulled from the oceanic abyss by the largest of the thurentra that are below us.*

Jake now understood why the area immediately adjacent to the island abounded with huge schools of fish, and no sooner had the thought crossed his mind than he sensed an abrupt upward shift in the ambient water temperature just as Achilles had said. Already he was beginning to warm up again.

Another minute passed before the juvenile broke the surface, and it was then that Jake glimpsed the two ships, taking in the scene with a critical eye before focusing his thoughts. *Bring me to where those boats are tied alongside the smaller of the two ships, Achilles.* It had become quite clear to him that speech vocalizations were no longer necessary for him to communicate with the albino.

Earlier in the day the juvenile had finally owned up to where Destiny and Amphitrite had gone, confirming what Jake had assumed all along. Regardless of this, their safety continued to weigh heavily on his mind.

Your concern is my concern, Jay Jay.

Then they are still okay?

At this moment, no danger befalls them. They are currently on Navassa Island.

Achilles sounded again, eventually surfacing within twenty meters of the tethered boats. Though it was now very dark, light cast from the few deck lights turned on aboard the tending ship provided just enough illumination for Jake to identify the watercraft used by Ben Loomins. The *Sea Lion* was straining hard against her mooring lines as she rode the heaving sea alongside the *San Carlo*.

Take me to the stern of the Sea Lion, Achilles!

Doing as Jake requested, the albino dove, following a parabolic course that brought Jake just beneath the *Sea Lion*'s swim platform. Grabbing hold of one of the struts supporting the swim platform, Jake held on as the vessel above him pitched heavily with the surge.

See if you can detect anyone aboard her, Achilles!

The juvenile immediately shot deep in a bid to gather momentum that would take him into atmosphere, and a moment later Jake caught a glimpse of the dolphin's sleek form as Achilles leapt from the sea. Less than two seconds elapsed before the answer Jake sought rang clearly in his thoughts. *The watercraft appears to be abandoned, Jay Jay.*

Stay close, Achilles! I'll call you if I need you.

Pulling himself along the platform's undercarriage, Jake found the edge, gripping it firmly as the *Sea Lion* plunged into the trough of a passing wave. Timing his move, he used the boat's ensuing upswing to pull his body completely from the water. A wash of foaming turbulence surged over the platform as he landed on hands and knees, and he was nearly swept back into the sea as the vessel began to drop again.

Scrambling quickly, he fought for balance, making his way up onto the vessel's rear deck as it reeled violently underfoot. With a free hand, he pulled his dive mask down around his neck to improve his field of vision. Holding onto the railing, he looked upward, checking to see if anyone was currently stationed along the side of the ship above him. Satisfied that he had gone unobserved, he slipped into the *Sea Lion's* main cabin, prepared to take down anybody that might be lurking there. But upon conducting a rapid surveillance of all the compartments below deck, he soon discovered Achilles' assessment to be accurate.

The Seal rule of never leaving a room or place of concealment unsecured behind you before proceeding on ahead was too thoroughly ingrained in him not to have carried out a complete search of all the spaces below decks, and as he turned to move away from the most forward compartment, he spied something familiar. The webshot he had used on Charlie Loomins had been placed back in storage, a cartridge taped snugly to its stock.

Reaching for the device, Jake tore the cartridge loose and chambered it into the barrel. Checking to see that it was still in working order, he made sure the safety was on before slinging it over his shoulder and making his way back up on deck.

A driving downpour had begun sometime while he had been inside the vessel, and the sting of raindrops against his face pelted him unmercifully as he squinted through eyes reduced to mere slits. A caving ladder had been left hanging down the *San Carlo's* side, the end of it reachable only when the *Sea Lion* was above mid-rise as it rose and fell along the ship's hull.

Waiting for the right moment, Jake was able to grasp the third rung from the bottom before the deck of the *Sea Lion* fell away beneath him. With arms straining, he quickly pulled himself higher, his feet finding the first rung, and in a matter of seconds he climbed the remaining distance to the deck above.

Luck was still with him, for the inclement weather seemed to be discouraging any members of the ship's crew from venturing outside. Stealthily, he hastened along the deck before finding a companionway leading to the superstructure above. Another stairway took him yet higher, and from what he remembered of the ship's layout, he knew the helipad was located just aft of the bridge. From such a vantage point he might be able to see much more.

Jake froze, the sound of voices suddenly drifting back at him above the rush of wind and rain for one fleeting instant. Remaining still, he perked up his ears and listened. Several seconds passed before another burst of conversation reached him, but the words were too garbled to garner their meaning.

Leaning over the railing, Jake latched onto one of the tubular joists supporting the helipad, swinging his body outward and working his way hand over hand along the framework. The driving rain had made the support slippery, and at one point he nearly lost his grip. Moving more cautiously, he pulled himself along, grabbing a succession of other structural members until he reached the opposite end of the platform's underside.

A bolt of jagged lightning suddenly flashed close to the island, briefly connecting the maddened sky with the roiling sea, and seconds later a thunderous boom came rolling over the water. In that instant, Jake caught a glimpse of the other ship, its dark mass momentarily illuminated within the cloak of tumultuous darkness surrounding it. And though the sight was fleeting at most, he knew he was looking at a freighter. The vessel was holding to a position about 300 meters from the *San Carlo's* port side, and as best as he could tell, she had not dropped her anchor, apparently standing by as she rode out the gale. But for what purpose, he wondered? Usually when ships rendezvoused in such a clandestine manner, a transfer of cargo was almost inevitable. And if something was going to be transferred, he had to assume the storm was delaying the operation.

As the lightning faded, Jake managed to get a hand over the edge of the platform, pulling himself up until his eyes were just above the level of the helipad. The Bell Ranger that had attacked him almost a week earlier sat perched, its main rotor fastened down to its tail boom and quivering under the assault of wind. Two men were at work with their backs to him, one of them holding a flashlight steady while the other turned a wretch. Unprotected from the elements, both men appeared to be soaked to the bone.

Jake lingered in his current position a moment longer, trying to ascertain what the men were doing. And all at once recognition hit home with brutal clarity. He was very familiar with the type of armaments typically retrofitted to rotary-wing aircraft, and there was no mistaking the electronic Gatling gun jutting obtrusively from the helicopter's port side. With such a weapon, the Bell Ranger would have a firepower capability greatly superior and far more lethal than anything Jake could throw back at it. Once airborne, the aircraft could be used to destroy the *Angel* with a single strafing run.

As Jake studied the scene before him, the man with the wrench looked up at his partner and said something, but his words were incoherent, drowned out by a blaring clap of thunder. Another burst of lightning erupted, and Jake ducked down below the blinding glare suddenly flaring over the helipad. Thunder crackled again, and then the sea was plunged into darkness once more.

No longer intent on caution, Jake removed the webshot and placed it on the deck, then heaved his body over the edge of the platform. One of the crewmen had disappeared, and a flicker of light at the far end of the helipad told him where the man had gone. The beam of the flashlight continued to bob as the man descended the steps leading to the next level down.

With the stealth of a jungle cat on the verge of a kill, Jake sprung to his feet, gliding like a ghost as he slipped up behind the other crewman. The cry of dismay that left the man's mouth was immediately cut off as Jake clamped a forearm snugly against his throat in a rear-naked choke. Applying pressure, he held on tenaciously until the man began to slump. It was only then that he released the hold.

Laying the man on his back, Jake knelt down on one knee and pulled the K-bar from its sheath, keeping the point positioned near the man's Adam's apple. He could see the man was barely conscious, gasping to suck in air.

"If you cry out or struggle, I'll kill you!" Jake snarled, keeping his face just close enough to be heard above the storm's din. "Nod if you understand me!"

The man lay rigid under the knife as another bolt of lightning flashed, his eyes focusing on the wet steel as light from the electrical discharge glinted off the blade. Abruptly, the man nodded.

Jake glanced behind him to make sure his six was still clear before resuming the conversation. "I have some questions and you will cooperate by answering them! Are we on the same page?"

The man nodded again.

"People from the village of Malique were kidnapped and put aboard this ship yesterday. Where are they?"

"They're not here," the man croaked. "They were taken to the nearby island."

"Where on the island?"

"I don't know."

"How were they transferred?"

"By boat. They were moved there this morning before dawn."

"For what purpose?"

"If I knew I would tell you. I'm just a pilot, not privy to the deals Ortega makes."

Jake thought back to the information Hennington had provided him. "Sebastian Ortega?"

"Yeah."

An assortment of thoughts began to race through Jake's mind. "The person Ortega has been consorting with out here, a man called Omar… where is he?"

"As far as I know, he's still aboard this ship."

Jake let that sink in before pumping the man further. "What about the boats tied up alongside this vessel? Why are they here?"

"The one boat was picked up earlier today. It was floating without power. From what I've been told, the other boat was sent to tow the first boat back to Port-au-Prince. Ortega has taken the crews from both boats down into the hold of this ship for questioning."

Shifting his gaze to the darkened sea, Jake indicated the unknown freighter, its dark bulk barely visible as it maintained position. "What's that ship doing here? I have to assume she's waiting for something to be transferred over to her?"

"Something was pulled from the sea floor and brought up on deck several hours ago. I don't know what it is, but as soon as this storm lets up, Ortega's gonna have it moved to the Aden."

The name evoked something Grahm had told Jake, and he looked back toward the freighter. "What else can you tell me about that ship?"

"She's called the *Spirit of Aden*. She flies a Yemeni flag." The man stared up earnestly. "That's all I know."

It was becoming increasingly evident that the man lying before Jake was being more cooperative than he had anticipated. "What branch of the U.S. military did you serve in?" Jake continued to grill.

"U.S. Army. How'd you know?"

Jake placed his free hand on one of the Gatling gun barrels. "Only a person with extensive military training in aircraft maintenance would possess the know-how to mount one of these to a helicopter."

"It's not something I wanted to do," the man said ashamedly. "I'm not proud of being a party to the things Ortega does. He and most of his crew are nasty sonsofbitches. He'd feed me to the sharks if I didn't follow his orders."

"Then why do you work for him?"

"Because I was too stupid to know what I was getting myself into when he hired me to fly this bird. But now it's too late for me to get out. Ortega would have me killed if I ever tried to quit the organization."

The sky lit up with still another eruption of lightning, leaving the pilot's face fully exposed in the dazzling, evanescent glare. He was not a young man, perhaps in his late fifties or early sixties, possibly of Latino descent. Before the light faded completely, Jake was able to discern something in the man's eyes that suggested he was telling the truth.

Another bout of intense electrical activity lit up the night, the crash of thunder so severe that it drowned out all possibility of further dialogue for the moment. Pelted harshly by the driving downpour, Jake felt the helipad quiver under the onslaught. A rapid succession of earth-shattering thunderclaps seemed to explode directly overhead, hammering down on the *San Carlo* as he waited anxiously for the disturbance to subside. The possibility that he risked getting fried out here in the midst of all this metal weighed only briefly on his mind, knowing it was a risk that had to be taken. More than two minutes passed as he hovered over the man, but finally the din abated.

Before Jake opened his mouth to resume the interrogation, the pilot spoke. "You've come to free the people Ortega kidnapped, haven't you?" Not waiting for an answer, he added, "I'll help you any way I can."

"How do I know you can be trusted?" Jake rasped.

The pilot hesitated as thunder rolled overhead again with deafening pandemonium. A procession of receding strobe-like flashes ignited within the curtain of cloud scudding low over the water. "I guess I'd ask the same question if our roles were reversed," he managed to say above the sound. Though he shouted to be heard, the words were barely perceptible. "But you're gonna need help and I'm the only option you have right now. So, you can either trust me or not. Take your pick."

Before Jake had time to mull this over, the pilot spoke again, more quickly this time. "Somebody's coming back up here. You better hide before you're seen."

Jake shot a quick look toward the stairs. Someone was shining a light, the beam stabbing the darkness from below. Swiveling his head back, he talked rapidly. "I'll be watching you closely. If you give me away, I won't have any problem shooting both you and whoever is climbing those stairs."

"Hurry!" the pilot urged.

Having no choice but to heed the warning, Jake sheathed the K-bar and scurried back to where the webshot lay, sliding his body back over the edge of the platform until only his head poked above it. The worst part of the storm seemed to have passed now, with the rain starting to taper off and the roar of thunder beginning to fade off toward the west like the dull thumping of a distant battery sending artillery rounds off into the night.

Jake watched as the glow of a flashlight reached the top of the stairs, his right hand reaching out onto the helipad deck and resting on the stock of the webshot should he need it. The light danced along jerkily as its holder moved to join the pilot. Jake's heart pounded heavily, all his senses on full alert for any signs of betrayal by the man offering to help him.

"Con quien estas, Fernando?" the interloper said, the beam from the flashlight playing briefly over the pilot's face. "Yo escuche voces!" Jake couldn't tell if it was the same man as before, but he understood the words. Who were you talking to, Fernando? I heard voices.

Fernando was back on his feet, appearing to be working on the Gatling gun once again. "I'm surprised you were able to hear me at all above the thunder," Fernando said loud enough for Jake to hear. "I was reminding you not to come back up here unless you had the coffee I asked for."

The other man handed something over to Fernando. "Why are you talking in English?"

"Old habits die hard, Antonio. Don't forget, I spent more than twenty years working for the U.S. Army."

Fernando paused, and Jake saw him bring something to his lips.

"That's good!" Fernando said, continuing to keep the conversation in English, his voice sounding light and jubilant. "Colombian coffee is the best in the world."

Jake remained at the ready, keeping his finger poised on the webshot trigger should he have to use it. For the most part, the snaring device was his current weapon of choice. Though it would not be nearly as effective as the USP-9, it would be non-lethal and far less noisy, and the last thing he wanted was to alert the others aboard the *San Carlo* that their vessel had been infiltrated by an unfriendly.

"Do you think this weapon will fire?" Antonio asked.

"If it doesn't, Ortega will have my hide."

The wind had now died down considerably, and Jake did not have to strain his ears to discern everything being said. From his place of concealment downwind of the two men, the sound of the conversation drifted directly at him. And although the helipad was still shrouded in darkness, he was able to perceive Antonio run a hand along one of the Gatling gun barrels.

"Ortega will become even more dangerous with such a weapon," Antonio stated. "He will probably use it along with those grenades he likes to toss down on dolphins whenever he sees them."

"Killing dolphins is an obsession with him," Fernando agreed, his voice reflecting disgust. "But I don't think he would attempt to destroy any of those white dolphins we saw when this ship came under attack by the man on the waverunner. Ortega wants to capture them alive."

Jake felt his blood begin to boil. As long as he had breath in his body, he would make sure no one nabbed or harmed any member of the pod ever again. Nevertheless, he kept still, listening intently as he watched Antonio's dark form squat down next to the newly installed weaponry system.

"He is even more interested in getting his hands on the girl we saw riding one of them," Antonio said. His tone held sadness, almost as if he knew that sooner or later Ortega would succeed in doing this.

"You don't want to see the girl get harmed, do you?"

"Of course not." Antonio sounded indignant. "Is your memory beginning to slip, old man? Have…have you forgotten the story already?" he stammered in annoyance.

"Tell me what happened again," Fernando said calmly, almost fatherly. "The story fascinates me."

As Jake listened, he had the impression Fernando was purposely guiding the conversation along solely for his benefit.

"She owed me nothing. I was dying and she saved me." Antonio's voice took on a slight quaver. "Something ruptured inside me when the torpedo struck our boat and flung me into the sea. I could feel my life slipping away. The girl could have left me to die, but she chose to come back, even with her own life still in danger. I know it sounds impossible, but her touch stopped the bleeding and I felt whole again." He paused at the memory. "There are no words to describe what I felt when she did that to me."

"Yes…she did the same thing to everyone in your boat," Fernando said. "But unlike you, the others continue to hate her. I believe they would try to hurt her at the first opportunity."

"They are all ungrateful scum!" Antonio spat bitterly. "It is unfortunate we are forced to work alongside these animals."

"What about the man who fired the torpedo? If you had a chance to kill him, would you do it?"

"I cannot blame him for protecting the girl. Pedro wanted to keep her from escaping the net and we were trying to stop her from doing that. His courage is something to be admired."

"What if Ortega ordered you to kill him?"

Antonio did not immediately answer. Rising to his feet, he moved over to the top of the steps, directing the beam from his flashlight below as if checking to see if anyone was lurking there. Coming back to where Fernando stood, he said, "If Ortega ordered me, I would not do it."

Fernando posed another scenario. "What if the man needed help? Would you help him?"

"Why do you ask such questions?"

"Curiosity, I suppose. I have always been a student of human nature. There is nothing more noble than putting one's own life at risk to aid another in need. Life-threatening situations have a way of molding most men, making some much nobler than others. In Vietnam I saw how danger brought out the best and worst in people."

"What about you? If Ortega told you to use this weapon on the same man, would you do it?"

Even from his position, Jake could not mistake the heavy sigh that escaped the pilot.

"I hope I'm never faced with such a situation," Fernando said.

"But if you were?" Antonio pressed.

"I could never pull the trigger on such an honorable man," Fernando admitted. "If I did, I wouldn't be able to live with myself."

"But then you would be a dead man for not following Ortega's order," Antonio pointed out.

"Yes," Fernando agreed. "And so would you."

Both men remained quiet for a protracted moment, each seeming to ponder that possibility. In the midst of this, Jake's uneasiness escalated further, and he glanced quickly in the direction of the island. Somewhere on that desolate hunk of craggy rock was Omar's base of operations. Everything he had so far learned in the past several days pointed to that one conclusion. If large enough submerged tunnels and hidden subterranean caverns existed beneath the island that could be entered from the sea, it was possible the Islamists had discovered a place to hide a submarine. And because Bashir had been an integral part of that operation, the former terrorist would know exactly where the base was located, including its precise layout. That, and that alone, had to be the reason why mother and daughter had taken Bashir with them. Bashir would lead them to where the villagers had been taken. Omar needed those people for something, otherwise why bring them there? Keeping them alive and under control would become burdensome, a task that would require constant supervision by his small force of men and place an enormous strain on the limited supplies he had on hand.

Jacob's description of the way the conquistadors had enslaved the Tainos for the purpose of working the mines abruptly entered Jake's thoughts. The Spaniards of old had been brutal, slowly starving their captives into a state of emaciation as they worked them to death. A vision of such carnage began to fill his mind with stunning clarity, and now he understood what Omar had in mind. The Islamic radical would use the Haitians to enlarge the chambers and passageways comprising his submarine base until they could no longer serve him. Feeding them would not even be a consideration. They would be used like subhuman chattel the way the conquistadors had used the Tainos.

As Jake thought this out, he couldn't understand why Destiny hadn't asked for his help. Ever since meeting the girl, helping her had become a routine undertaking, something she had readily accepted. It didn't make sense that she would suddenly avoid using his skills in attempting to free the abducted villagers. Certainly, that was her main objective in going back to the island in the first place, to free them.

The sound of Fernando's voice pulled Jake from these musings. "What's to become of the men Ortega questions?"

"Knowing Ortega, he will probably kill them. He has already sent the three Haitians found aboard the first boat off to the island along with the people taken from Malique. I'm told they had been successful in catching two of the white dolphins."

"What did they do with them?"

"They lost them."

"How?"

"Two people tricked their way onto their boat and cut the dolphins free. Omar thinks one of them was the same man who attacked us. The dolphin girl was with him when it happened."

As Jake clung to the edge of the helipad, he felt it begin to vibrate, and almost at once the sound of heavy machinery being activated cut the air. Turning his head, he blinked as several floodlights abruptly came alive further back along the ship's stern. A cable was being attached to the lifting rig used for deploying the ship's small tug. It was the same boat he had seen towing the *San Carlo's* seine, and on its deck was a large object, its bulk wrapped in a tarp. And although the sea had not moderated enough for the crew to pick the tug from its cradle and sling it over the side, Jake had the impression those responsible for launching it were anxious to send it on its way at the first opportunity. As the boat was being readied, Jake saw several deckhands lock their gazes on the freighter as it continued to hold station off their port side. He held no doubts as to where the tug was going.

Spying half a dozen crew members moving under the lights, Jake thought it best he leave his present position. If any one of them happened to look up in his direction, there was the possibility he might be spotted.

Re-shouldering the webshot, he pulled himself back along the supports in an effort to reach the stairs but held up immediately as another light flickered below him. Quickly, he scrambled back amongst the framework, managing to stay hidden in the shadows as another crew member ascended to the platform above. With the ship continuing to sway in the face of buffeting waves and gusting winds, the crewman staggered awkwardly up the steps as he fought for balance, his arms holding two wooden boxes. After the man had passed, Jake scrambled back to the stairway and moved lower.

Part of the conversation he had just overheard bothered him, and in spite of the danger Ben Loomins and his brother were in, he knew he could not let them die. He had not forgotten Destiny's perspective on the ripples of causation, and inwardly he saw her beautiful face staring up at him, a face full of kindness and compassion. If the brothers were murdered, their deaths would be on his head because he had been directly responsible for their boat breaking down.

Stacked one atop the other at the base of the steps, Jake noticed two more boxes similar to the ones the crewman had been carrying. Lifting the hinged lid on the top box, he discovered a dozen concussion grenades. He was intimately familiar with the type. These were MK3s, tarred cardboard canisters filled with TNT. Such grenades did not throw out shrapnel, relying instead on their shear explosive power for killing.

Plucking two grenades from the container, he hooked the spoons over his utility belt of spare ammunition clips, then closed the lid and moved forward. Seeking entrance inside the ship, he had to jump back into shadow once again as two men suddenly emerged out on deck.

"-cannot wait much longer," one of the men complained. "The cargo must be sent over now."

"Too dangerous," the second man said. "We risk losing the tug if we try to launch her now. Your precious cargo is way too heavy. Without calmer conditions, the tug will swamp or capsize."

"The Aden's captain grows impatient. He has a schedule to maintain."

"So do I," the second man growled. "But I cannot ignore the weather."

Jake was only able to discern their dark forms as they filed past, but something in the voice of the first man held a ring of familiarity, though he had trouble placing it. By contrast, the accent of the second speaker was far different, heavy with a distinct Spanish inflection.

"Where is the rest of that shipment?" the Spaniard demanded. "So far you have only given me half of what you had promised. Have you forgotten our deal?"

"You will get it," the first man hissed back. "I already told you, it is aboard the other ship. But first the bomb-" The speaker abruptly went silent.

The Spaniard immediately halted, seemingly very interested in what had just been said. "A bomb you say. Is that what sits on my ship? A bomb?"

When the first speaker failed to answer, Jake realized a slip of the tongue had just occurred.

"What kind of bomb?" the Spaniard pressed.

"You have no need to know."

"Oh, but I do," the Spaniard blurted heatedly. "Judging from the size of it, it is a very large bomb. An accidental detonation could sink this ship. Lowering it into the sea under these conditions might set it off. Perhaps I should take a look at this bomb."

"We made a deal!" the other man snarled.

The Spaniard began walking again, and the other man followed. Jake listened as their bickering continued, the sound of the argument gradually ebbing away as the men distanced themselves from his place of concealment.

Something seemed to flutter in the back of Jake's mind, and he realized Achilles was speaking to him.

Another vessel approaches, Jay Jay!

What kind of vessel?

It is what those of your kind refer to as a cruiser. It has an overall length of nearly twenty-five meters.

Jake did a quick mental calculation. *An 80-foot yacht was nearing the San Carlo. Keep me posted on what that vessel is up to, Achilles!*

Slipping into the passageway the arguing men had exited, Jake became aware of the overpowering stench within the ship. Outside the vessel, the smell had not been nearly as offensive, most of it carried off by the gusting winds. But without the movement of air, the odor of rot clung to everything like a thick blanket, making him think back to the prison in Port-au-Prince.

Finding no one to challenge him, he found a companionway as the ship lurched lazily under him. A clamor came faintly to his ears, and as he began to follow the sound it quickly died.

Several doors lined the short hallway Jake found himself in, and just as he was coming abreast of the last door, it suddenly opened. In that instant he came face to face with a swarthy Colombian. Like a deer suddenly caught in the headlights of an oncoming vehicle, the Colombian just stared, a surge of confusion consuming his features as he looked Jake straight in the eyes. Nearly a half-second elapsed before bewilderment turned to shock, but by then it was too late as the point of Jake's right elbow shot up and caught the man directly in the throat. A choking gasp barely left the man's lips as Jake followed the blow up with a crushing uppercut that landed cleanly under the man's chin. The Colombian's head snapped back, and before he could slump, Jake pushed him back through the doorway, stepping into the room the man had been vacating and closing the door behind him.

A tiny bunk adorned one end of the enclosure, and as Jake looked around, he could see it was a tiny stateroom, not much bigger than a large closet. Scanning the compartment for items he could use, he spotted a roll of duct-tape lying in one corner, and just above it a filthy rag was draped over a hook protruding from the wall. Grabbing both items, he stuffed the rag into the man's mouth, making sure it stayed in place by placing several wraps of the heavy adhesive around the man's face. The Colombian was out cold and offered no resistance, so it was relatively easy for Jake to finish the job by binding his ankles and wrists and trussing them together behind his back.

Leaving the man on the floor, Jake cracked the door to the room slightly ajar and peeked out, making sure the hallway was empty before venturing out again. Finding another companionway at the end of the hallway, he descended deeper into the ship's hold. No sooner did he reach the bottom of the stairs, the sound of yelling resumed. An intermittent chorus of shouts and screams grew louder as he made his way down another hallway. The corridor turned by ninety degrees, and he found himself facing a steel door with a small glass window smudged with oil and grime.

On the other side of the door, someone hollered angrily. Sidling up to the door, Jake risked a peek through the glass. Six men were strapped to chairs, with one of them currently taking a beating from a pugnacious individual standing over him. Three others of the *San Carlo's* crew hovered nearby, each of them wearing a cruel grin as they watched what was being done.

Jake recognized the man doling out the beating almost immediately. It was Pedro, the Colombian Zimbola had hammered unconscious back in Port-au-Prince. With his face and neck still discolored by splotches of heavy bruising, Pedro's expression was hideous, a mask of insane rage as he struck the man tied to the chair before him.

Pedro drew a bunched fist back again, and his victim yelled before the blow landed. "Up yours!"

A dull smack could be heard as Pedro's fist struck, and even with the welts swelling the victim's face, Jake thought he recognized Frank Jaffey.

"Tell him already!" one of the other men screamed. "Give him what he wants!"

Jake swung his eyes along the glass and was momentarily shocked to discover an old acquaintance. Walter McPherson was the last person he would have ever expected to see.

"For god's sake, tell him!" McPherson screamed again.

From what Jake could ascertain, the Colombians were much too engrossed in the punishment being meted out to notice him peering from the other side of the glass, and he did not let the opportunity go unheeded. Deciding that the grenades he had appropriated might get in the way, he removed them from his belt and placed them on the floor. He then unslung the webshot from his shoulder and took a deep breath. Grabbing the doorknob, he flung the door open, and in one smooth motion he leveled the webshot at Pedro and fired.

Even as the net mushroomed open, Jake was across the room in a flash, catching the closest crewman on the temple with the butt of the snaring device before his foe even realized what was happening. Jake slid past as the man fell, and in a single stride he was on a second man with blinding quickness. The crewman was slow to react, and Jake was able to snap a crunching front-kick between the man's legs. Lifted off the floor from the force of the kick, the man was immediately rendered unconscious by a jarring right that had all of Jake's weight behind it.

The last man was more alert, and before Jake could move in on him, the glint of a blade lashing out made him pull up short. Parrying the slash with the barrel of the webshot, he executed a lightning riposte by lunging, jamming the muzzle of the device up into the man's nose. He then pulled back as blood spurted. His adversary bellowed out in pain, lifting an empty hand to a face now appearing like a blood-gutted mask. Startled by the amount of gore smearing his fingers, the man turned flaming eyes on Jake, impaling him with the uncontrolled fury burning deep within them.

Jake recognized the all-consuming insanity, clearly aware of how dangerous the man had become. His opponent reversed his grip on the knife, preparing to rush at him in a foolhardy lunge, all sense of self-preservation completely evaporated by an animalistic need to destroy. The man had a squat, powerful build, making Jake feel like a matador awaiting the charge of an enraged bull.

Calmly, Jake stood his ground as the Colombian lowered his head and let out a horrendous roar before charging. Waiting for the right moment, Jake timed his move perfectly as the man came straight at him. With a natural fluidity, he simultaneously sidestepped and leaned back to avoid the point of the blade as it arced down at his head in an overhand strike. As his foe thundered past, he swung the webshot by its barrel, slamming the stock into the Colombian's head with all the force he could muster. The man dropped like a boulder, all 250-plus pounds of him, falling to the floor facedown and staying there.

It was only then that Jake took stock of how his first victim was faring. Pedro was struggling madly, effectively entangled in the webshot's tenacious netting.

"We've got to stop meeting like this," Jake said, his tone holding a trace of humor as he stepped unhurriedly towards the entrapped man.

Pedro squirmed even harder, answering Jake with a torrent of profane vitriol issued in Spanish. The invective was abruptly silenced as

Jake spun the webshot around and casually drove the stock against the back of Pedro's head.

With all four opponents laid out cold, Jake brought his gaze to McPherson. "Now why would a captain in the U.S. navy be out here hunting dolphins?"

For several seconds, McPherson could only stare, his face swollen and bleeding in various places from the beating Pedro had given him. "You…look familiar," he finally stammered.

"I should," Jake remarked bitterly. "Think really hard and maybe you'll remember my name. But right now my main concern is getting all of you off this ship. After that, you're on your own."

"It's him!" someone else said. "He's the sonofabitch I told you about."

Jake gazed over at Ben Loomins, ignoring the comment. The man looked none too pleased to see him despite what he had just done.

Drawing his K-bar, Jake moved first to Jaffey, cutting him loose from his bonds. Groggily, Jaffey looked up at him, one eye swollen shut. "Try getting your wits about you and help me free the others." He pointed to the bull-like Colombian he had felled. "Use his knife to cut them loose!"

With all the battered men still hurting, little was said as everyone was finally set free. Looking through the glass window to the corridor beyond, Jake could see it was still empty. "Sit tight a moment!" he said to Jaffey." With a push on the door, he moved out into the hallway and retrieved the two grenades he had left there, hooking them back onto his belt.

Opening the door again, Jake looked back at the others. "Follow me!"

Moving back the way he had come, Jake kept his pace slow enough for the others to keep up. Upon reaching the main deck, he poked his head out into the night air. Feeling the wind on his face, he could tell it had died down even further, now no more than a moderate breeze.

An analog of Achilles' voice suddenly reverberated in the back of Jake's mind. *Jay Jay, the cruiser is headed for Navassa Island.*

I hear you, Achilles. Thanks for telling me.

Turning to face Frank Jaffey, Jake said, "I'm going to create a diversion. As soon as you hear a ruckus, you and your men get back aboard the tug and get the hell away from here as quick as you can."

Jaffey nodded gravely. "If I ever come out of this with my hide intact, I'll consider the slate wiped clean between you and me. You've cost me a lot of money, fella, but I'm willing to let that slide under the present circumstances."

"Maybe you are, but I'm not," Ben Loomins chastised, glowering at Jake contemptuously. "When this is over, you and me have some unfinished business to settle. I wouldn't be in this mess if it weren't for you."

Jake spoke calmly. "Maybe I'll take you up on it, pal, but right now I'd get ready to move if I were you." With that said, he scurried toward the ship's stern, knowing what had to be done.

Chapter 17

With Bashir leading the way, Destiny and her mother moved furtively among the maze of subterranean caverns, illuminating the way before them with the hand-held underwater lights Jimenez had given them. It had been late afternoon by the time Jimenez had finally taken them to within ten kilometers of Navassa, dropping them off unseen while the sea was beginning to take on a hefty chop. From there they had covered the remaining distance to the island, leaving Jimenez to sail off alone beyond the reach of the approaching storm. Prior to using the hidden subaqueous passageway that led to the *thurentra* grotto, they had spied the tuna trawler from a distance, and it was then that Hermes and Aphrodite had broken away from the pod to investigate.

Awaiting a report from the albino siblings, the two women had made a cursory inspection of the latest progress carried out on the submerged habitat still under construction, scrutinizing only the upper portion of the structure. At seeing the strange edifice being built by the team of gray dolphins, Bashir's eyes had widened with wonder as he stared through the dive mask Jimenez had lent him.

They had not stayed long, however. Upon receiving observations made by Hermes and his sister, they had moved on again, riding their mounts back out to sea through a noticeable surge that had worked its way into the hidden tunnel. Bashir had trouble holding his breath for even relatively short stretches beneath the surface, and with the full brunt of the storm now upon them, they were forced to keep close to atmosphere where the turbulence was the most brutal. Nevertheless, their mounts easily fought their way through the sweeping waves, eventually locating the same submerged tunnel Destiny had used when she had rescued the Palestinian.

"I must be careful where I step, my beautiful angels," Bashir warned in a low voice. He directed his light at the cavern floor before him, searching the immediate vicinity meticulously before taking a few more steps. "It is possible Yeslam has prepared a few surprises now that he knows his base can be reached from another underwater route."

"What kind of surprises?" Amphitrite asked.

"Yeslam may have placed explosives with a trip-wire. Being angels, you cannot be harmed by such a device. But if I am killed, I will not be able to help you unless I also become an angel."

"We are not angels, Bashir," Destiny corrected softly. "We're as mortal as you are."

Bashir stopped short and turned to face the girl. "Surely you jest with me," he said, refusing to accept what had just been uttered.

"I'm sorry if I have misled you. I would never think to jest over such a matter."

"But…you have the power to heal…the mind as well as the body. I saw you render Kalid unconscious without lifting a hand. Only an angel has such power." In the semi-darkness, Bashir sounded dismally disappointed.

"Yes, you did." Destiny concurred. "But this ability is not entirely mine. I had help."

Bashir's disappointment quickly turned effusive again. "If you had help, then it is only the Almighty Allah who bestows you with such miraculous power. Either way, he both favors and blesses you. Even if you are not an angel as you claim, he treats you as though you truly are one."

Destiny produced a helpless smile. Trying to convince Bashir otherwise was going to be a losing battle. She thought of an appropriate reply, but before she could utter a word, the sound of voices reverberated among the cavern walls.

Bashir turned off his light, and Destiny and Amphitrite did the same. "We must be very cautious from this point on," he said quietly. Just as he finished saying this, a soft glow could be seen emanating from somewhere up ahead. "The main chamber is very close."

The threesome crept silently forward, with Bashir periodically lighting the way to check for booby traps. Another half-minute passed before Amphitrite let out a curt warning. "Do not take another step, Bashir!" She paused. The sudden intuitive flash allowed her to sense the danger that blocked their way. "Shine your light on the ground before you!" She could see it clearly in her mind, directly in front of Bashir.

Bashir stooped low, flicking his light on again. Less than a meter from where he stood, a thin wire was stretched tautly less than twelve centimeters above the floor. Moving forward, he traced the wire and located an object lodged tightly into a crevice off to one side. With great care, he worked it free, then moved it carefully away from the rock wall to put slack in the wire attached to it. Holding the thing, he regarded Amphitrite with increased awe. "Allah allows you to see through divine eyes," he whispered reverently. "Yeslam has seen fit to place a Claymore mine in this tunnel. He has six such devices. Hopefully this will be the only one barring our way."

Amphitrite said nothing as Bashir gave the trip-wire a soft tug, removing the detonation cap from the mine. Gently, he placed the Claymore off to one side where it would no longer pose a threat. Turning off his light, he crept forward once more. The glow from up ahead had grown stronger and seeing the way before them was becoming easier.

Destiny felt concern. Unlike her mother, she had failed to sense the threat, though she suspected the reason why. Her mind had become too clouded with other matters. Achilles had relayed recent events to the others, and through them she knew that Jay Jay had come back to Navassa to find her. The very thing she had wanted to avoid was now rearing its ugly head, a thing that put the man she loved in great danger. No, it was more than just danger. Jay Jay would die.

The future had been clearly shown, memorialized on the chamber ceiling behind the waterfall, painted long ago by an unknown but clairvoyant Tainos artist. Clutched within the jaws of a fierce Bengal tiger, a man was depicted being torn apart. When she had first discovered it at a much younger age, the sight had depressed her, and later she had found it necessary to fabricate a makeshift ladder so that she could climb up to the overhead mural and cover it with mud. But at the time, little did she know she would fall in love with the stranger shown there.

Deep in her heart, however, she knew that such an act would do little to change what had been prophesied long ago. Whether or not that future could be altered as Jacob and her mother had often contended, she did not know, but now more than ever she would use every fiber of her being to forestall the event she feared most.

Jake used the cover of darkness to his advantage, keeping to the shadows and slipping unseen to the ship's larboard side. Moving swiftly, he came across a cluster of 55-gallon drums strapped securely to the deck. Intermingled with the rank odor of rotting fish was the unmistakable smell of diesel. Using his K-bar, he pried the cap from one of the drums, then cut the straps holding it in place. Tipping the drum on its side, he let the fuel splash out onto the deck.

Under the spotlights further back toward the stern, he could see the tug still sitting in its cradle, a small group of men standing next to it. With the possibility of a hydrogen bomb resting within the small vessel, Jake felt the full burden of what he was up against, and it pressed down upon him like a thousand tons of earth. One way or another, he had to keep the tug from being launched.

With overwhelming purpose, he pulled one of the grenades from his belt and pulled the pin. Letting the grenade slip from his fingers, he turned and raced forward toward the ship's prow, making a mental count in his head as he did so. Just before reaching four, he ducked down behind a crate of heavy hawser.

The ensuing blast sent a shock wave through the air, and a split second later several oil drums erupted in a titanic explosion of heat and light. A wall of flames abruptly engulfed the side of the *San Carlo*, further enhanced by a succession of secondary blasts as other drums flared. Amid the expanding inferno, shouts could be heard as men rushed to see what was happening.

Satisfied, Jake sped to the other side of the ship to observe the men he had freed taking advantage of the confusion. One by one, they climbed down the caving ladder leading to Jaffey's towing vessel. All too slowly another minute passed before the boat got underway, and with a lumbering motion far too subdued for Jake's taste, it began to veer off to the south.

Remaining hidden in shadow, Jake turned to study the havoc he had caused. Crewmen were scurrying like ants to get the inferno under control. The flames had spread and were licking high, engulfing a sizable portion of the ship's superstructure and effectively blocking access to the flight deck. And even though a margin of safety separated him from the firestorm, the heat from it was rapidly becoming unbearable.

With several options open to him, Jake chose the one that seemed most sensible under the present situation. Doing something to sabotage the transfer of the bomb could wait. The fire was delaying that transfer, and if the Colombians failed to bring it under control, it was probable such a transfer would not take place at all. Helping Destiny was now his main priority, and if he could help her free the people abducted, he would refocus his efforts on making sure the bomb did not fall into the wrong hands. Right now, it was crucial that he join up with her as quickly as possible. She was much too naïve to understand the type of men she would be facing. And if he did not get to her at once, she and her mother would surely get themselves killed.

Slipping from his place of concealment with the stealth of an eidolon, he strode rapidly to the starboard railing, nearly colliding headlong into two crewmen looking to get clear of the flames. Both men came to an immediate halt, staring in stunned silence at Jake's presence. Fully exposed under the harsh glare of the inferno, their expressions turned to alarm.

Jake was the first to react, automatically resorting to the physical assets that had made him a standout athlete, those being speed and quickness. Snapping a front kick to the genitals of the man on his left, he shifted his body weight a millisecond later to flatten the man on his right with a left hook that struck like lightning. Not taking the time to appraise his work, he pulled the dive mask that had been hanging around his neck up onto his forehead.

Someone shouted. Almost immediately, something pinged off a metal support adjacent to Jake's head, making him duck back into shadow. A hail of bullets followed, caroming off a cluster of steel members directly in front of him and sending a shower of sparks flying. Snatching the USP-9 from the holster riding his thigh, he tore the watertight plastic wrap from the submachine pistol. Normally, the weapon would have fired even during immersion, but using a protective seal gave him an added degree of assurance it would still operate in spite of its previous submergence.

From the direction of the ship's bow, two more members of the crew were moving toward him. Illuminated by the flames, their faces glowered with rancor, one of them wielding an axe, the other an AK-47.

Cocking his weapon, Jake opened up with a short burst. One of the rounds caught the man holding the axe, spinning him around and knocking him to the deck. Abruptly, the man's partner dove for cover.

More shouts reached Jake's ears, and he turned to see two more assailants making their way along the gangway behind him. Letting loose with another burst, he stopped them in their tracks, scoring a hit on one of them.

With deft quickness, he removed the spent clip and inserted another from his utility belt. Pivoting back around, he spotted the man with the AK poking his head out from behind a bulkhead. Jake brought his weapon to bear and squeezed the trigger, spewing half a dozen rounds. The man managed to retract his head just in time to avoid being hit. For good measure, Jake spun around and sent a spray behind him again. Jamming the weapon back into its holster and pushing down the Velcro flap that secured it, he pulled his dive mask into place. Calmly, he pulled the remaining MK3 from his belt and pulled the pin. Almost delicately, he placed the grenade at his feet just before vaulting over the railing.

Keeping the dive mask pressed firmly against his face, he dropped twenty feet into the sea's cooling embrace, happy to escape the inferno's searing heat. Ten feet below the surface, Achilles was right there waiting for him.

A cascade of bullets ripped the water above. Jake felt a mild sting on one of his buttocks, but didn't think the skin had been penetrated. Slowed by the denser medium of water, several rounds zipped dangerously close before losing velocity. Languidly, they fell away.

The machine gun fire abruptly stopped as a weak shock wave whipped past, and Jake knew the grenade had detonated, the force of the blast carrying down from the ship's deck and rippling out into the surrounding water.

Take me to Destiny, Achilles!

The young dolphin did not move, appearing not to have read the request hanging in Jake's thoughts.

Still submerged, Jake petitioned Achilles again, surprised that the juvenile had not heeded him. Keeping the appeal at the center of his mind, he focused on a parallel thought. *Achilles, I-*

I am very sorry, Jay Jay… but I…I cannot do that.

Jake was astounded at the intensity of sorrow resounding in the dolphin's response. If dolphins were capable of crying, he could have sworn he was sensing a monumental amount of emotional pain emanating from the albino.

What's the matter, Achilles?

Achilles did not immediately answer, and Jake suddenly became aware of the mental barrier being erected, something analogous to a wall of solid steel through which nothing could penetrate. The depth of emotion Jake had been touched with was now gone, and an aura of sterility seemed to surround the newly evolved cetacean. The bond that had connected them was beginning to break.

I have been instructed to take you back to your vessel, Jay Jay. The thought was delivered like a blast of polar air, cold and devoid of all warmth.

Tell me what's troubling you, Jake pressed, grabbing hold of Achilles' dorsal.

Achilles turned and gathered speed. He did not respond to the question.

Can you hear me, Achilles? What's wrong?

Achilles would not answer, and Jake could only hold on as he was pulled through the sea with disconcerting swiftness.

Chapter 18

The inexplicable illness had eventually passed, and Nick Henderson felt restless. Unable to sleep, he arose from the sleeping bag he had laid out on the sand and walked to the water's edge. Almost an hour had elapsed since nightfall had descended, and with an intermittent cloud cover obstructing most of the starlight, the cove was very dark.

Wading out into the water until the wavelets washed up around his knees, he looked to where he thought the *thurentra* lay submerged, his mind continually churning over the treasure the organism produced. He had purposely kept to himself ever since Javolyn had put him and the others ashore, and with Parker and Phillipe currently holed up in Destiny's tiny, thatched cottage, Henderson could now conduct the search he had yearned to undertake, this time unobserved and without interference. With all those annoying white dolphins gone, he was free to investigate the places where the gold would most likely be hidden.

Glancing behind him, he eyed the soft glow emanating from the doorway of the small abode. More than likely, Jeffrey and Phillipe were engaged in a game of chess, something Phillipe seemed to enjoy playing. Regardless, with more of that migraine-inducing dolphin art hanging obtrusively along the cottage's interior walls, there was no way he was going inside to see what they were up to.

Leaving the water, Henderson walked back to where his sleeping bag lay, pulling his mask, fins and snorkel from the duffel bag situated next to it. Rummaging further, he groped for the dive light amid other personal items, finally locating it near the bottom of the bag. The dive light was fully charged and would last him a little over an hour.

With the dive gear in hand, he made his way down the beach, following the sound of the waterfall. The roar of plunging water gradually grew louder, eventually drowning out the softer sounds of nocturnal animals foraging among the lush foliage that dominated the cove walls.

He had given it a lot of thought, and through a process of elimination, he had come up with the best place to hide a cache of gold within the cove's confines. For one, it would be the dolphins that did the hiding, not Jacob. The gold had been hidden fairly quickly, and with Jacob occupied with his guests, the Haitian could not possibly have moved it. That meant the cache had to be submerged. And if that were actually the case, what better place than the base of the falls where eddies of aerated turbulence would obscure underwater visibility.

With his dive booties already on, Henderson made his way close to the base of the falls and attempted to slip his swim fins on in the manner he had seen Javolyn use. Hopping on one leg, he stumbled off balance and fell down, skinning his knee on a rock as he did so. Cursing in anger, he struggled some more, finally succeeding in donning the rest of the gear. Tentatively, he stepped clumsily into the water. He had always hated having to walk erect with ungainly fins strapped to his feet, and with the rocky shore before him, the task was made all the more difficult. Unable to see the curtain of falling water within the backdrop of night, he was suddenly unnerved by the sound. It thundered ominously like the rumble of some enormous lurking beast.

The dive light did not immediately come on when he flicked the switch, and he had to smack it with his palm several times before it came to life. Lowering his face into the water, he directed the beam against the rocky bottom and pushed himself further out, his excitement over what he might find overcoming his fear of the ebony blackness that lay beyond.

Henderson had been disappointed when McPherson had failed to show back at Port-au-Prince. Surely the signal emitted by the DBT had been strong enough to follow. But Henderson had a more direct way of contacting the naval captain, and hopefully the message he had sent had been received by now. Unbeknownst to Javolyn and the others, he had managed to send off an electronic communiqué just before the *Avenging Angel* had sailed from Port-au-Prince. The unit he had provided McPherson had an additional feature he had thought prudent to install, and that was an electronic text receiver, one that automatically translated the communique's encryption.

He had still been nauseous when he had transmitted a second message via the wireless laptop he always kept close at hand. That was right after Javolyn had dumped him off. And while Parker had glanced his way at the time, Parker had no way of knowing what he had been up to. The special program he had developed did the encoding. He knew he had been taking a risk in sending it, but then again it was a risk he had felt worth taking. Surely the naval captain would not try anything underhanded and grab the entire booty for himself, especially since there would be plenty to go around. Now all McPherson had to do was home in on the DBT signal. Out of sight within his duffel bag, the DBT was still transmitting.

Cautiously, Henderson swam toward the thundering falls, now keeping his head above the surface. Shining his light out in front of him, he spotted the curtain of aerated water, making sure to stay well clear of it. Finning to his left, he skirted the gravity-driven deluge. Eddies tugged at him with surprising force, and he had to work hard to avoid being sucked under. The far end of the waterfall was suddenly before him, and he kicked with all his strength to gain the backside. There was still a good amount of turbulence here, and he hugged the rock wall to escape being pulled toward where the flow was heaviest.

The rock behind the waterfall was relatively smooth, and he had trouble locating a finger hold where he could rest. A small projection was suddenly before him, and gratefully he grasped it. For the next two minutes he breathed heavily, regaining his strength. Fully rested, he began to make exploratory dives along the face of the rock, periodically dropping to the bottom and looking for anything unusual. The water was not very deep, and the base of the rock was strewn with sand and pebbles. Hampered by poor underwater visibility, however, he had no success at finding anything that remotely resembled grains of gold.

At one point during his search, he stumbled across an opening in the cliff face, a rift wide enough to easily accommodate him. Ebony blackness surrounded him as he made his way between the rock, and even the beam of his light failed to penetrate the turbidity below him by more than a few feet. Fighting back his fear, he continued on into the confined space, discovering there to be no flow at his present location.

The fissure began to narrow as he penetrated deeper, and as he finned on, it changed direction. Rounding a bend, he distanced himself further from the base of the falls. As he studied the layout before him, he suddenly became excited, for he knew this would make a perfect place to hide treasure.

Aiming the light above him, he gauged the overhead clearance, daunted by the tight space. A succession of rocky crags overhung the water, providing air pockets that afforded little room for maneuvering. Willing himself forward, perhaps another thirty feet, he saw where the crevice appeared to end. A short distance out in front of him, the rock met the water.

Filling his lungs, he jackknifed his body awkwardly, his legs flailing spastically above him. The attempt caused him to bash one of his legs against the rock, and skinning a shin, he cried out in pain. Abruptly, he pulled up and massaged the stricken area. Being in such cramped quarters made him nervous. He was suddenly not so eager to do this, and he almost decided then and there to abort the dive. But with the promise of riches beckoning him on, he overcame his fear, but just barely.

He jackknifed again, this time succeeding in getting his fins below the water. Kicking himself downward, he maintained contact with the rock wall using his free hand. He had only descended a few feet when something glinted below him. With his heart pounding, he stabbed his dive light deeper. He could not believe what he was seeing. A glittering mass inundated the bottom. At this location, the water was not very deep, maybe just over his head.

Overcome with joy, he plunged his fingers into the material, pulling up a heaping handful and bringing it close to his face. Shiny grains spilled loosely from his palm. Jamming his hand back into the mass, he had trouble digging down. The granular substance was very heavy and resisted him.

Needing air, he rose back to the surface and lifted the dive mask from his face. Holding the light to the grains held in his hand, he stared in wonder. He was utterly amazed at his good fortune. It was gold all right.

And if he were not mistaken, there were lesser quantities of platinum mixed in.

Unable to contain himself, he took another deep breath and dropped down again. For the next ten minutes he busied himself with gauging the total size of the treasure. It filled the bottom of the cavity for almost twenty-five feet. In his estimation there had to be tons of it below him. He was going to be rich beyond his wildest dreams.

Filled with an elation he had never before experienced, Henderson spat out his snorkel and let out a triumphant cry. He was going to be rich! Far richer than anything he had ever imagined!

Swept away with emotion, he barely heard himself above the rumble of the falls. In his excitement, he accidentally slammed the dive light against one of the outcroppings. Euphoria quickly turned to panic when the light flickered briefly before going out altogether.

Frantically, he struck the light with his palm. When it failed to come on, he tried the switch, jiggling it on and off like a frenzied madman. The dive light would not cooperate. Screaming out in frustration, he thrashed around, abruptly smacking the top of his skull into an overhead projection. Clutching his head with both hands, he applied pressure against the injury, groaning in agony and nearly blacking out. The pain gradually ebbed into a dull throb, and it was only then that he realized he had let go of the light.

Groping around with renewed violence, he tried to find it. Being slightly buoyant, the light had to be floating close to him, but try as he might, he failed to locate it. Completely disoriented, he didn't know which way to go to get out of the fissure. With a strength born of shear panic, he clawed his way along one of the walls, and in moments he banged his head again. Shit! He was going in the wrong direction. With his mind in a tizzy, he reversed direction, losing contact with the wall. In desperation, he kicked hard with his fins, only to slam up against the rock again. Abruptly, he stopped, panting hard and frozen with fear.

Cut off from all light, the bass rumble of the falls dominated his senses, and his mind began to career in disarray. Something seemed to brush up against his body, making him flinch. The realization that he was not alone struck home with frightening force, and he kicked his legs insanely to fend it off. Within seconds he grabbed hold of himself, wondering if his imagination was playing tricks on him. No! He had definitely felt something touch him. The thought sent an immense shiver coursing through his body, and the illness he had experienced hours earlier suddenly returned with a vengeance.

He tensed again. Whatever had touched him was back. Treading water, he moved quickly to get away from it. There was a presence close at hand.

Unable to elude it, he was suddenly besieged by a strange image that sprang to the forefront of his thoughts. Instinctively he took refuge in it, instantly understanding there was another means of escape. The thing he had seen shimmering in the night sky high above Port-au-Prince was there before him again. All at once he was moving, flowing along one of those lines that seemed to connect with infinity. Yes, he would travel at the speed of light to get away.

But something was hindering him. It had caught up and latched on, squeezing with a pressure that was incomprehensible. Dizzily, he grabbed his temples and fought for breath. His head was going to explode.

Bearded men wearing steel armor and crude metal hats were storming past. Armed with lances, swords, and blunderbusses, they charged through a pristine tropical forest, some of them with large canines on leashes. They were after something, their faces rancorous with brutality.

Bowled over by their passage, he could see what they were chasing. Scantily clad men and women, small in stature, were scrambling for their lives. Body parts were scattered across the forest floor, and those unfortunate enough to be run down were being hacked to pieces, their screams filling the air. A massacre quickly unfolded before him, and as he looked on, he found himself oddly stirring to the gruesome slaughter, much too fascinated to avert his gaze.

A young girl lay sprawled on the ground next to him. She was gasping for breath, unable to go another step. Something in one of her hands caught his attention, and he saw at once that it was a small idol made of solid gold. Transfixed by the sight, he rose to his feet and stared down, drawing the sword he carried. Confronted with two choices, he chose the one most satisfying. A single tear trickled down one of the girl's cheeks as her eyes met his, but he felt only pleasure as his arm swung the blade in a killing stroke. He would have his gold. The girl's life was of no importance.

The scene faded, and once again he became aware of the pressure inside his skull. It had intensified. The presence was causing it, something unseen yet nevertheless there. Looming all around him, it swarmed in upon his senses, a sentience immeasurably vast. In the blink of an eye, he was able to grasp its fundamental nature, and with startling clarity he suddenly came to accept the things Jacob had hypothesized. Strangely, the presence was not vengeful. He was not even certain it was aware of itself. Nevertheless, it had a purpose, and that purpose was to survive. In fulfilling that purpose, it would bring into balance those entities threatening its existence. And if the imbalance could not be corrected, then the offending entities would simply be destroyed.

It began to dawn on him that the presence was speaking. It had always spoken to him, though he had never noticed. It had a voice. The rumble of the falls was its voice. No, that was only partly right. There was so much more to it than that, something all-encompassing in its profundity. He was beginning to see it clearly now, and he could not discount the rustling of the trees nor the whisper of the wind. Though soft and lilting, was the serenade of a songbird any less important than the roar of the surf? And yet these were only some of the things that gave it voice.

With his mind now reeling in the midst of such comprehension, Henderson began to tremble with renewed intensity. Only then did the possibility that he might never again see the light of day enter his thoughts.

Chapter 19

*J*ake was totally caught off guard. Upon climbing back aboard the *Avenging Angel* he found his vessel to be completely abandoned. A feeling of total dismay gripped him as he conducted a frantic search of every compartment, only to discover there was no one aboard. The North Sea trawler had been left adrift, completely deserted.

Crestfallen, he sat down, his mind trying to piece together what might have happened. Adding to the mystery was Achilles' recent behavior. The young albino had broken off all communication with him, remaining silent in the face of all Jake's queries.

The return trip to the *Angel* had taken much longer than expected, mainly because the vessel had drifted a significant distance from where Jake had left it. With the clarity of hindsight, he realized Achilles had been searching for the *Angel*, apparently trying to locate it by reaching out with his biosonar in all directions. Upon finding it, the dolphin had simply dropped him off at the stern end and then swum away.

Jake climbed up to the pilothouse and got a fix on the boat's current position. He could see that the wind and waves had driven it nearly eleven kilometers from where he had left it. Making a few educated assumptions about the vessel's rate of drift during and after the storm, he calculated that the helm had to have been deserted for at least ninety minutes for the *Angel* to drift that distance. A glance at his watch told him the boat had been abandoned somewhere between ten and fifteen minutes after he had left it. Without anyone to steer the vessel into the oncoming sea, it was a wonder the *Angel* had not swamped or capsized during the gale.

With this in mind, he could only surmise that hostile forces had managed to storm the *Angel* and take captive all those on board. But how? Zimbola and Hector had been armed to the teeth, prepared to defend the boat at the slightest sign of trouble. At the very least, Zimby would have spotted the approach of another vessel on radar and taken evasive action.

Jake was dismal. None of it made any sense.

Combing the vessel, he could find nothing that would indicate a skirmish had taken place. Everything was pretty much in order, everything except for the missing crew. No bullet holes, no overt damage, and no signs of blood. And Zimbola would never leave his beloved boat under any circumstances. No matter what, he would have held position, standing by for Jake to return.

With these things overwhelming his thoughts, he stared off into the distance. The flicker of a lazy glow emanated from the direction of Navassa. The fire he had started on the *San Carlo* was still ablaze, though from the intensity of the light, he judged that it would soon burn itself out.

Bringing his eyes to the instrument panel, he noticed that the engine was still idling. Dully, he stared at the gauge, contemplating his next move.

The radio suddenly hissed, interrupting his thoughts. A garble of static blared from the speaker. "…you listening…Avenging..gel."

Jake reached for the microphone, prepared to answer if someone was actually hailing him. A good ten seconds of unbearable silence followed before the radio hissed again. "…advise you respond…ing *Angel* if you ever want ……your comrades alive."

Eagerly, Jake depressed the transmit button. "This is the Avenging *Angel*. Please identify yourself, whoever you are?"

Another burst of words flowed from the speaker, this time coming in crisp and clear. "Intruding into the affairs of a sovereign nation is not a wise thing to do, *Avenging Angel*." The voice sounded content, self-assured, and Jake realized he had heard that same voice before.

Jake waited for more, but the person behind the voice fell silent.

"What do you want?"

The reply came back quickly. "The same thing we all want. Satisfaction."

Another pause ensued, and Jake fought down his growing irritability. "Just state your business."

"You will come ashore at the nearby island. You will come to the base of the old lighthouse on the eastern side. And most importantly, you will come alone."

"And if I don't?"

A heavy pause hung in the air. "Then your friends will pay the price of your obstinacy," the voice said smugly. "All ten of them."

Jake's mind was sent spinning. What was going on here? There had only been eight people aboard the *Angel* when he had left it. Zimby, Hector, Grahm, Jacob, Hennington, Trebek, Emmanuel, and Lucette. But the voice on the radio had said there were ten. Was it possible Destiny and her mother had been captured as well?

He brought his gaze back to the glow many miles away. It was now very faint. Lifting the microphone back to his mouth, he said. "I'll do as you say. But harm a hair on their heads, and you'll wish you'd never been born."

Not waiting for a reply, Jake turned off the radio. He couldn't help berate himself for having left Zimby and the others to fend for themselves while he had gone off to play hero. And now they were going to pay with their lives for his stupidity.

Filled with self-loathing, he engaged the prop and turned the *Angel* around, bringing it on a new heading.

The sound of suffering reached Destiny's ears long before the misery could be seen. The men in the adjacent cavern were as cruel as those depicted in the cave murals back at Gaia. The cry of pain had come from Samuel. He had only sought to protect Louwanda and had been struck down.

Bashir was the first to intervene, leaping on ahead of Destiny and her mother. "Stop this insanity at once," Bashir yelled. Striding boldly from the darkened passageway, he stared reproachfully at Kalid. "You will invoke Allah's wrath if you do not release these people immediately."

Kalid turned, his mouth hanging agape at seeing Bashir again. His eyes widened further at the sight of the two women entering the chamber behind him.

Destiny took in her surroundings at a glance. The subterranean grotto was very large and well-lit in those areas where human occupation existed. A series of electric bulbs were strung out at intervals along a portion of the perimeter. Closest to her, other lights were positioned along the lowest stalactites hanging from the cavern roof. Further back along one of the walls, rows of wooden crates were stacked high, and adjacent to the crates was a makeshift eating area, outfitted with cooking grill, two tables and foldout chairs. Beyond that, an array of sleeping cots took up more space. Droning dully in the background, the low hum of a generator could be heard. The light revealed a nearby pool of water, its surface perfectly flat and giving off a silvery sheen under the electric glow. The pool appeared to be substantial in width, extending off into a void of inky blackness where the light could not reach.

Three other bearded men also turned to witness this sudden intrusion, each of them holding a rifle. Samuel lay at the feet of one of them, moaning in pain.

Herded amid a grouping of stalactites were twelve Haitians. Several of them were struggling under the weight of a wooden crate each had been forced to carry. At seeing Destiny and Amphitrite, their anguish abruptly turned hopeful. Destiny could see that most of them were from Malique, but not all. Standing among the villagers were the three crewmen she had seen aboard Ben Loomins' boat.

Overcoming his initial shock, one of Kalid's constituents stepped forward, his eyes flitting pensively between Bashir and the two women. Destiny studied his face, profoundly moved by the man's drooping, lugubrious eyes that resembled those of a bloodhound.

The man brought his gaze back to Kalid, who continued to stare speechless at Destiny. "Do my eyes deceive me or has Bashir arisen from the dead?"

The question had been spoken in Arabic, and though Destiny did not speak such a language, she was able to translate the question through her mental link with the albinos. The albinos were currently keyed into her senses and those of her mother, observing and listening to what was taking place. With the capacity to converse in numerous human languages, they continued to interpret what was being said.

The man with the bloodhound eyes spoke again when Kalid did not reply. "Has Satin grabbed your tongue that you cannot speak, Kalid?"

Kalid finally found voice, and his words were sodden with fear. "Keep your distance from the girl, Gullu. I do not advise touching her. To do so is very dangerous." He pivoted his head slightly, staring at Amphitrite with wary eyes. "The other woman may be equally dangerous."

"They are only dangerous to those who oppose them," Bashir said, his tone simmering with haughtiness. "What you see standing before you are two of Allah's messengers." He riveted Kalid with reproachful eyes. "Do you still refuse to accept the power Allah imparts to his angels?"

Gullu looked back at Destiny, studying her intently before transferring his gaze to Amphitrite. "Do you profess these women to be angels, Bashir, servants of the Almighty?"

Destiny detected mockery in his tone, though confusion filled his face.

"Yes," Bashir said, his manner softening. "They will show you the way as they did me."

Gullu turned back to Kalid. "Tell me what he speaks of?"

"Bashir has deluded himself into believing these women are angels. He claims they have the power to heal mortal wounds in seconds."

"Only Allah has such power," Gullu said scornfully.

Gullu stepped closer to Kalid, peering into his eyes. "Why do these women frighten you, Kalid?" He posed the question as if amused.

A flood of shame washed over Kalid's face. "Over a day ago the younger one knocked me unconscious when Yeslam ordered me to grab her. She was with Bashir in these caverns. Yeslam believes she is armed with a concealed taser capable of delivering a severe electrical shock."

Gullu's expression immediately clouded. "Yeslam told me none of this. Up to now, he led me to believe Bashir was killed during your little escapade along the Haitian coast."

Bashir laughed heartily. "Yeslam has shown himself to be the liar he truly is. He seeks to hide the truth from those willing to follow him. Angels of Allah have no need of concealed weapons. In their hands lies the power behind all of Paradise."

Bashir spun around to regard both women. "Perhaps it is time to demonstrate Allah's power to these non-believers."

Destiny had no desire to deny Bashir his delusion. Both she and her mother were perfectly content to let him act as their spokesman. Some inner, yet inexplicable sense told them Bashir had to perpetuate such a falsehood if they were going to free the villagers.

Destiny felt the full synergy of all the albino minds come together in something akin to a controlled explosion, the force of it reaching out to her and Amphitrite. Without understanding the actual mechanism that caused it, a hologram of the dolphin art materialized out over the subterranean pool, pulsations of multicolored light dancing swiftly along the twisting and intertwined curvature of the three-dimensional geometry.

Bashir pointed, drawing all eyes to the breathtaking image. "Search your feelings as you look upon the power of God."

Gullu and Kalid stared, suddenly mesmerized.

A howl of pain broke the air, and Destiny saw two of the bearded men closest to the villagers drop their weapons and sink to their knees, each clutching his head as if struck by an invisible demon.

"Search your feelings!" Bashir repeated imploringly, his voice rising further and quavering with emotion. "Ask yourself if it is truly Allah's way to destroy and kill."

The hologram continued to hang in the air, holding the attention of everyone except the two fallen men. Amphitrite stepped forward, coming to stand before the one called Gullu. Gullu seemed not to notice, spellbound by the thing floating over the water. Placing a hand on his forehead, she said, "Let go of your hate. Hate is an illness that prevents you from being whole." She was about to say, "Holding onto it will impair your ability to think clearly and will destroy your soul forever," but she sensed something within the man before she could convert the thought into words.

The essence Amphitrite was feeling was laid bare, easily read much like an open book. And in reading the man, she was suddenly reminded of Chester Hennington, for here was another victim caught up in the web of circumstance. The threat of violence against Gullu's family back in Afghanistan was a tangible thing, and it was this threat that had forced him into abetting the people he served. But the shadow of tragedy was also evident, for Gullu's son had been murdered by these same people.

Removing her hand, Amphitrite stepped over to Kalid and performed the same ritual, quickly sensing the man would no longer present a danger.

Destiny remained immobile, watching her mother move to the last standing man. The two fallen men were beyond help. Tormented by something unseen, they continued to writhe convulsively on the cavern floor.

Bashir grabbed Kalid by the arm. "Where are the others?" he demanded.

Kalid stared enraptured, his gaze still clinging to the hologram of lights, and Bashir had to shake him hard to get a mumbled response. "Azzum and several others have taken the submarine. The rest of the team is in the passageway that leads to the surface."

Bashir turned quickly to Destiny. "Our work is not yet complete."

Yes, Destiny thought, our work is far from over. Even from down here she could feel Erzulie's iniquity pressing still closer. Erzulie and her son were now on the island, and there were others nearby who pulsed with the same intensity of evil. In unison they presented an incredibly powerful force, an alliance that might actually defeat the pod's combined strength. And if that were to happen, millions of people were going to be killed. Forged from the dark side of creation, the entities they were pitted against could never be turned.

And with the pod's latest member purposely kept from the impending fight, she wondered if they had any chance of winning at all. She knew she was being selfish, knowing her actions were jeopardizing everything they had worked so hard to achieve. But she could not bear the thought of Jay Jay dying.

Expelling a long breath, Destiny let the albinos channel another surge of energy through her. It was then that the hologram floated past everyone, disappearing into the tunnel that would take them to the surface above.

Bashir ran over to where Samuel lay and helped him to his feet. He started to move in the direction the hologram had taken, but suddenly stopped. Stooping, he picked up the two firearms dropped by the fallen men. Although both men had stopped writhing, they were breathing hard, their hands still pressed tightly against their skulls as though attempting to subdue the demons trapped within them. Bashir stared down contemptuously at one of them. "It does not surprise me that you feel only pain, Mahmood. Those who are truly evil cannot be saved." Walking over to the edge of the pool, he flung the weapons into the water.

An odd feeling descended on Destiny as she watched the guns sink from view. Almost at once she realized Jay Jay was still in danger. Yes, she clearly felt it now. Jay Jay was being lured to the island, and that was the last place she wanted him to be. The thought caused her to break her focus, and she suddenly realized she was failing the others, failing the purpose she had been destined to fulfill.

The entire planet may be lost if you try to help him. It was her mother speaking. What has already been implanted in the fabric of true reality may very well be unchangeable, my daughter. The thought Amphitrite was conveying was not meant to chasten, though it did hold immense emotional distress.

Destiny could not help herself. Strangely she was filled with feelings she was unable to suppress. Forgive me, mother, but I must go to him.

Sprinting to the water's edge, Destiny dove just as Hercules broke the surface. Molding herself to the albino's back, she held on as the dolphin powered into the depths.

Chapter 20

*J*ake brought the *Avenging Angel* around to the east on the darkened ocean, holding to a wide arc that kept the vessel well clear of the *San Carlo*. It was important he stay beyond the range of the tuna trawler's radar, especially since Ortega had at his disposal a helicopter armed with an electronic Gatling gun. He thought it prudent to assume the fire he had started had not engulfed the ship's helipad. And he could never be sure the pilot would actually defy Ortega's order to use the weapon against him.

Even if he were spotted on radar, Jake reasoned, the Colombians had no way of knowing the identity of his vessel or who was aboard it. The *Angel* would be seen as a blip on the screen, just another boat making its way through the Windward Passage in the middle of the night.

It was understandable that the *San Carlo's* captain would be enraged over the fact his vessel had been infiltrated and sabotaged. But while some of his crew had come into direct contact with the man responsible for damaging his ship and freeing the dolphin hunters, they had also seen that same man leap over the side. With no other boats close to the *San Carlo*, they might assume the man had either drowned or been forced to swim to the nearby island.

Steering the *Angel* to the eastern side of Navassa, he turned the bow towards the west. With a portion of the island now between him and the tuna trawler, he would remain hidden from the *San Carlo's* radar.

As he brought the *Angel* still closer to the shoreline, his own radar picked up another vessel in close proximity to the island's southeast side near Lulu Bay. Continuing on in, he closed to within 100 meters of the shore before dropping anchor.

His vessel rocked stiffly in the swells as the Danforth bit, and he heard the surf hissing against the nearby bluffs, every so often drowned out by the boom of a crashing breaker. The sea had calmed down considerably since the storm, but it was still fairly rough.

Jake stared in the direction of the sound. With no moonlight available, a veil of complete blackness hid the shore. And whoever was baiting him ashore remained hidden in that blackness. He was at a complete disadvantage. No matter what, he would have to venture into the trap that awaited him if he was to have any chance at all of freeing those taken hostage. Used as bait, ten lives lay in the balance.

Faced with such an internecine dilemma, Jake set about preparing himself for what lay ahead.

With the surf hissing at his back, Jake made his way up the escarpment with the aid of NV goggles. He had tried giving Mat one more call on his satellite phone before leaving the *Angel*, but he could not even get a signal. After that he had swum ashore, towing the things he would need on a small inflatable float trailing well behind him on 200 feet of nylon rope. The surf had been quite nasty, and he had been tumbled around in the breakers. But he had purposely moored the *Angel* near this particular spot because it was the only place on this side of the island where there was a narrow break in the low-slung limestone cliffs, a fissure just wide enough to provide a way up. He remembered it well, having climbed it once before when he had made a brief exploratory stopover at the island a year earlier.

Already he was limping, having been slammed up against some rocks in the turbulence. Still, he had managed to pull the float up on the rocks with him, and climbing higher to get clear of the billowing spray, he had removed those items he had sealed in plastic wraps. Toweling himself off, he had slipped on coveralls and a pair of sneakers. With great care, he had sewn one particular item into the inside collar of his coveralls, mindful of the threat it posed. After that, he had strapped on other equipment, including the night vision lenses, before beginning the sharp ascent.

Climbing as fast as he dared, he doubted a trap awaited him at this particular location. In the veil of darkness, the escarpment was exceptionally dangerous here, unstable in many places, and it would have presented as much of a hindrance to an enemy as it did him. The karst could be treacherous, concealing a multitude of small but deep crevices where cacti and razor-sharp thorn brush often grew. The recent rains had left the ground slippery, and he had to be careful where he stepped to keep from destabilizing the loose rocks and rubble that lay before him. Regardless of this, he was unable to prevent a small avalanche of stones from skittering down the escarpment every so often, but the hiss of the surf at his back was loud enough to mask the sound.

During the climb, he made it a habit to periodically scan the lay of the land above him through the NV lenses, when at last he was able to glimpse the pinnacle of the old lighthouse. The island's lower terrace was now behind him and the escarpment had become less steep, ascending to the plateau upon which the lighthouse stood. Even so, the route he found himself taking meandered its way erratically in the rising karst, mainly to avoid the worst areas of dogtooth coral, and he realized he still had a distance to go to reach the lighthouse. The wind had subsided even more since he had come ashore, and with the limestone cliffs now far below him and hushing the occasional boom of a breaker, a grim stillness descended over the island.

Readjusting one of the straps on his rucksack, he was automatically reminded of the thing it held, and once again he lifted his gaze to the lighthouse. The feel of the Stoner in his hands did little to lighten his mood as he studied the structure that used to keep shipping at a distance. Hampered by a rugged landscape studded with jagged limestone and dense thickets of underbrush, the going would still be slow. The vegetation had thickened, and as he climbed higher his muscles tensed like coiled springs in readiness for an unexpected attack. In the terrain that now lay before him, he knew that an ambush or booby trap would be easy for someone to set up. In spite of this, he took a deep breath and forged on, foregoing any measures of Seal-like stealth, for they were expecting him.

Drawing closer to the lighthouse, something rustled nearby, making him go rigid. Through the night scope, he was able to catch sight of a bird launching itself toward the tower, but the startled creature quickly disappeared from sight.

With the walk-around observation deck of the lighthouse beginning to loom high overhead like the brim of a jaunty derby, Jake knew he would be meeting opposition at any moment. He was glad he had brought the night vision glasses. In the darkness it would have been nearly impossible to wend his way through such treacherous terrain without stumbling into something injurious. Taking inventory of the tall structure, movement suddenly caught his eyes. There were people up there on the lower turret.

Before he had a chance to assess the situation, a sibilating whoosh cut the night air. A moment later, a flare lit up the landscape, and Jake was nearly blinded by the intense glare. Immediately, he lifted the NV lenses from his eyes, blinking back the spots dancing before them.

Something blared loudly, and he realized someone was speaking through a megaphone. "Do not be shy, Mr. Javolyn. Your presence is required if we are to begin this little party." The speaker paused, eliciting a little chuckle of delight. "After all, you are the guest of honor."

Jake ducked down, glancing all about him as the flare wafted slowly down on its tiny parachute. Carried by the wind, it drifted off to the west.

The megaphone blared again. "If you please, Mr. Javolyn. There is no need for caution. Otherwise, you will force me to resort to harsher measures." The speaker was practically laughing now.

Another whoosh reached Jake's ears as a second flare streaked skyward. Someone yelled, the sound coming from above. With the flare igniting, he could see a person being dangled from the lower turret. The person was being hung upside down by a rope tied to his ankles.

Jake realized it was Trebek.

"I advise you to show yourself, Mr. Javolyn. Ronaldo never did like heights. We can drop him right now if that is your wish."

Jake held back a moment longer, caught in the throes of indecision.

"From the things I have learned about you, I am sure you will not want his death on your hands." The speaker's tone had taken on an edge.

Jake lowered the Stoner to the ground, pushing it off to one side near the base of a small tree rising from a depression. Quickly, he removed the holster carrying the USP-9 from his thigh and placed it next to the Stoner. He did the same thing with his K-bar and NV glasses, making sure the items were effectively shielded by the side of the depression. Scooting forward to where the foliage thinned, he glimpsed a group of armed men. They stood in a small clearing abutting the base of the lighthouse, their gazes searching the underbrush in which Jake lay hidden. With a critical eye, he gauged his current position with respect to the base of the lighthouse, knowing that anything beyond twenty meters would doom him to failure. He realized it was going to be close as he slipped his arms from the rucksack. Too damn close!

Careful not to snap any twigs, Jake looped one of the rucksack's shoulder straps over a tree branch at the height of his head, mindful of how he oriented it. He then took a deep breath, and before the descending flare had a chance to fade completely, he strode boldly out into the small clearing with his hands raised high.

Another flare rose skyward and ignited. "A most wise decision, Mr. Javolyn," the speaker lauded imperiously. "I am sure your friends will be very grateful for what you are doing for them."

Several men converged from opposite sides as Jake separated himself from the underbrush. Unceremoniously, they prodded him forward with Kalashnikovs until he was within twenty feet of the tower.

A sickening scream suddenly erupted, followed by a heavy thud a moment later as Trebek's body impacted harshly with the ground.

A deep sigh arose from the loudspeaker. "Such a pity Ronaldo had to die. But then again, it is a fate all traitors deserve."

Like phantoms in the flare's fading light, the dark forms of more men emerged from behind the lighthouse. One figure glided silently forward and something analogous to a blazing gush of crimson flame shot out, leaping from the figure to a pile of tree branches stacked high. In spite of the recent rains that had drenched everything on the island, the flame quickly overcame the resistance of the wet wood, taking root and sprouting rapidly into a sizable bonfire. In moments, dense clouds of billowing black smoke and steam belched upward as the pyre sizzled and blazed.

"As I told you, Mr. Javolyn, meddling in the affairs of a sovereign nation was not a very wise thing to do." This time the words were spoken without the aid of the megaphone.

Jake turned in the direction of the speaker. Light cast from the bonfire revealed the man's face as he walked close to where Jake stood. The man was Henri Ternier.

"I've come here just as you asked," Jake said, keeping his temper at bay. "Now let the others go."

The Colonel let out a small laugh. "I see you have come unarmed, Mr. Javolyn. No knife, no guns." As the Colonel said this, the silent figure that had lit the fire skulked forward to join him. The figure wore a cowl and cloak, seeming to float rather than walk as it approached.

Jake's eyes were immediately drawn to the pendant hanging from the figure's neck. It burned with an ominous intensity, giving off the color of molten steel.

"Let the others go!" Jake repeated, aware that his words had come out in a snarl. He could not help himself. Diplomacy was not an option here. Men like Ternier offended him to the very core.

One of the men surrounding Jake jabbed the stock of his Kalashnikov hard into the small of his back, sending a wave of pain rippling through his body. Jake regained control of his buckling legs and spun around. In that instant he was willing to die if given a moment's gratification at killing his attacker with his bare hands.

The man's sneer abruptly wavered at seeing the look on Jake's face, and he backed up a few paces in spite of the weapon he held.

Jake turned back around to face Ternier. The Colonel grinned loftily, the light from the flames exposing teeth that made Jake think of a nocturnal predator toying with cornered prey. In the end, though, the predator would indulge in tearing the prey apart. "Are you a gambling man, Mr. Javolyn?"

Jake did not answer, choosing instead to glare back defiantly at the predator that was preparing to sink deadly fangs into him. Ternier was the type of individual he would love to have a go at one on one.

Ternier answered for him. "Of course you are. But you are obviously a fool as well, for only a fool would be stupid enough to break into Haiti's

National Penitentiary and come away thinking there would be no price to pay."

"Do what you will with me, but let the others go," Jake snapped irritably. He looked past Ternier, hoping to see one of the others the Colonel had kidnapped, but all he saw was Trebek's crumpled body.

"I might consider letting the others go if you provide me with some information," said Ternier, unruffled. "It is but a simple request."

"And what might that be?"

"The whereabouts of gold, Mr. Javolyn."

Jake stared back, keeping the glare in place. "I would think a two-bit counterfeiter like yourself would have no need of gold."

A trace of somberness worked its way into the Colonel's grin. "You have a sharp tongue, Mr. Javolyn. I have a special way of dealing with people who show impertinence, one you will find to be very unpleasant."

Jake needled Ternier more by producing a sneer. "You forget, I've already gotten a firsthand look at this special way of yours. Sooner or later, a whole gang of human rights groups will be screaming for your hide once word reaches enough ears about what you've been doing to people. Once the Hague investigates you, you'll be toast."

The gibes had the desired effect, and Jake saw some of the Colonel's smugness fall away. He readily understood that the man before him was unused to people not showing fear with the threat of torture and death imminent. Instilling fear was Ternier's source of strength.

Ternier stared for a long moment, his eyes stabbing into Jake like crazed, hypnotic daggers. "We seem to be getting away from the main point of discussion, Mr. Javolyn. Jacob's cousin informs me they have amassed a substantial cache of gold and platinum. They had planned on using it to launch a global enterprise, one that might prove to be highly profitable when one considers these intelligent dolphins that will play a large part in the operation."

"If such a cache exists, what makes you think I would know about it?"

Ternier searched Jake's face with a penetrating gaze for a long moment. When he finally spoke, his tone was filled with culture and refinement. "I was hoping I would be talking to a reasonable man, but your stubbornness leaves me no choice. You have no idea what you are dealing with, Mr. Javolyn." He turned and looked down at the cloaked figure standing next to him. "This woman is a voudun priestess. She has powers that many people outside of Haiti would find to be, shall we say, unimaginable, what some might even call impossible. It was her magic that allowed us to board your boat unopposed."

The Colonel turned to address one of his men. "Bring out the large one."

The man disappeared into the shadows. Moments later, a hulking form surrounded by several men was escorted from the darkness, and Jake realized it was Zimbola.

Jake brought his eyes back to Ternier, attempting to get a read on what the Colonel had in mind.

Ternier addressed Jake again, his cultured voice seemingly at odds with the crazed look dominating his expression. "Your friend, here, informs me you are a highly skilled fighter, Mr. Javolyn. A warrior of sorts." Glancing sideways, the Colonel let his eyes linger on Zimbola for several seconds. Though Ternier was a big man, the Jamaican was even bigger.

Ternier continued, his tone turning sardonic. "I have often wondered which is the better combination of assets, physical size and strength, as opposed to skill and quickness."

Jake studied his friend, noticing that Zimby didn't look right. It seemed to him as though the Jamaican's eyes were staring right through him.

"Therefore, I propose a contest, Mr. Javolyn," Ternier said. "Yes…a contest between you and your friend, one in which there can only be one survivor." With his face warped into a nauseating grin, the Colonel turned to the giant and pointed a finger at Jake. "Heed the words of your master, Zimbola. At the third beat of the drums, you will kill the man standing before you."

The Colonel swung around and nodded to a man sitting on the ground behind him, and Jake could see the man's legs were wrapped around a set of bongo drums. The man tapped the left drum, then the right a second later. On the third beat, the cowled figure at Ternier's side suddenly whirled, casting a handful of powder into the fire. A burst of red light immediately flared, and the flames leapt up wildly, nearly blinding Jake.

And in that moment Zimbola lunged. The attack came with such swiftness that Jake barely had time to react. Quickly sidestepping, he moved just beyond Zimbola's outstretched arms.

"Zimby…what are you doing?" Jake yelled in disbelief over the rising tempo of the drumbeats. "It's me, buddy. It's Jay Jay."

The giant came at him again, this time swinging a fist the size of a cannonball that would have taken Jake's head off had he not ducked under the massive paw.

"What have you done to him?" Jake gasped incredulously, espying Ternier out of the corner of one eye.

The Colonel let out a fiendish laugh that modulated eerily with the rhythmic drumming. "Your friend has been turned against you, Mr. Javolyn. He is now your enemy."

The group of soldiers encompassing Jake and his attacker moved in closer to tighten the circle, and Jake found himself with less room to maneuver.

"If you wish it, I can stop this little contest," Ternier offered magnanimously, raising his voice to be heard above the sound of the drums. "Just tell me where the gold is."

"Screw you!" Jake bellowed, dodging Zimby for the second time. He was well familiar with the Jamaican's immense strength and had no desire to be caught in the grip of those pulverizing hands. He had once seen Zimby lift the front end of a Ford pickup completely off the ground. Zimby was undoubtedly the strongest man he had ever known.

Zimbola lunged again, and Jake barely eluded those massive arms. The circle of men closed in further as the drums pounded faster, heavier.

"Zimby!" Jake yelled again. "What's wrong with you, buddy? It's me, Jay Jay!"

Doggedly, the black giant stalked him, cutting him off in the shrinking ring. Light from the bonfire glinted briefly off Zimby's eyes, and Jake was startled to see they were as glazed as black ceramic. There was no emotion in his friend's face. None at all!

Jake winced, his legs nearly failing him as something poked him hard in the back. Glancing behind him, he saw one of the soldiers withdraw the muzzle of his assault rifle. Spinning around, Jake managed to move just in time to avoid another swiping blow.

Jake yelled at the top of his lungs. "Wake up, Zimby! You've been drugged." In the background he heard Ternier's malicious laugh. It blended ominously with the flurry of the drums, now a wild frenzy of irritating noise that reached into Jake's head.

"He cannot hear you, Mr. Javolyn," the Colonel chortled mockingly, shouting to be heard. "He will only do what I tell him. It is only a matter of time before he catches you."

Bobbing and weaving, Jake used what little space he had left to keep away from his oversized friend. Zimbola was relentless, continuing to pursue him with tenacious intent.

Jake abruptly stopped and held his ground, the drums pounding furiously, the cadence growing steadily louder. Stubbornly, Zimbola lumbered in at him, a huge unstoppable juggernaut bearing an expression as vacant as wind-carved stone. Timing his move, Jake leaned away from another windmill punch capable of crushing most men. Countering, he landed a hard right to the giant's jaw.

Jake's knuckles abruptly throbbed, his brain racked by the clamor of the drums. He had hoped the blow would jar his friend from the strange trance consuming him, but he realized it had about as much effect as a fly slamming up against a concrete wall.

"Snap out of it, Zimby!" Jake roared. "They've got you drugged."

Zimbola pivoted his body and swung with the other arm, forcing Jake to duck yet again. Vaguely, he became aware of the men jeering him as he scrambled back to the center of the circle.

One voice rose up above the jeers, above the drums. "The gold, Mr. Javolyn…tell me where the gold is hidden and I will put a stop to this."

Jake ignored Ternier, noting the impatience gripping his tone. He waited as Zimby lurched toward him, sliding under an outstretched arm and coming up behind the giant's bulk. Leaping onto Zimby's back, Jake placed his left forearm across the giant's windpipe in one smooth motion. Locking his left hand in the crotch of his right arm, he placed his other hand at the back of the Jamaican's head and squeezed. The use of a rear-naked choke was his only option.

Zimbola whirled, and Jake hung on. The drums were at a fever pitch now, and Jake caught sight of the drummer as the giant spun, the drummer's hands blurs of motion as they pounded out the tormenting, insane din. Tightening the hold further, he wrapped both legs around Zimby's massive body. Zimbola struggled fiercely as Jake applied pressure. The giant staggered one way, then another as the encircling men continued to taunt.

Reaching up with both hands, Zimbola attempted to break the hold by prying his banana-sized fingers under Jake's forearm. Obstinately, Jake held on, squeezing with all his might. He now had the hold firmly in place.

Zimby reeled wildly to one side, colliding with several of Ternier's men and knocking them to the ground. The drums were screaming now, almost as though crying out in sympathy with the Jamaican's pain, and Jake barely heard him above the dizzy crescendo. Zimbola was wheezing, fighting to draw breath. The wheezing grew in both pitch and desperation, at odds with the overriding thunder of the bongos, and it turned into a gasping whistle as the giant's throat was gradually compressed. Starved for air, the Jamaican sank to one knee.

Jake's head throbbed, the insanity of the drums undermining his will, a staccato of crazy enervating sound hammering within his brain, and it was all he could do to keep his focus from being disrupted. His only intent was to take the fight out of his friend, and with a sudden spurt of awareness, he realized his concentration was in danger of slipping away if he did not clear his mind of this overpowering distraction. Continuing to maintain the pressure, he kept himself plastered up against Zimby's back like a leech, afraid to let go too soon.

Zimby tried to rise back up, then abruptly fell to both knees. Gradually, he lowered his head, and Jake felt the man's powerful body begin to sag. The next ten seconds seemed like an eternity as the Jamaican slowly slumped forward, his face finally coming to rest on the hard ground.

Jake immediately released the hold, and as he did, the fever pitch of the drums suddenly cut out, leaving a disconcerting silence in their wake. The stranglehold that had been slowly tightening on his brain immediately eased and he found himself clearheaded once again. Looking down, he was regretful at what he had just done, but he had not had any choice. A rear-naked choke could kill if applied too long, and the last thing he wanted was to put his friend's life in jeopardy. Forcing Zimby onto his back, he pushed hard on the giant's chest to get him breathing again.

Jake felt himself winded and sweating profusely. It had taken everything he had to bring down Zimbola, and now he felt himself paying the price. As he sucked in breath, he became aware of the hushed atmosphere within the clearing. Ternier's men stood quiet, staring as though they had just witnessed the impossible.

Ternier's voice broke the silence. "Very well done, Mr. Javolyn. I have to admit I am rather impressed. It would appear that physical size and brute strength was no match for skill and quickness in this particular case."

The Colonel paused, then sighed, and Jake saw another malicious grin break out on the man's face. "Perhaps I have not challenged you enough. Perhaps I should pit you against a man with abilities more on a par with your own." Turning, Ternier looked at one of his cronies and barked an order. "Bring out the other one."

As the soldier left, Ternier stared back at Jake. The Colonel seemed to be enjoying himself. "One way or another, Mr. Javolyn, I will eventually learn where the gold can be found."

Jake scowled scornfully. Ternier was obviously toying with him. He wondered how the Colonel had been able to sense his presence before he had reached the lighthouse. His eyes settled briefly on the cowled figure standing beside Ternier. The pendant continued to glow eerily red, appearing like an angry bloodshot eye.

Led by several men, another figure emerged from the darkness. The bonfire crackled harshly, sending out a cascade of flickering light that quickly revealed the man's face.

Jake was momentarily shocked, and he had difficulty believing what he was seeing.

Ternier's tone was gloating. "No, Mr. Javolyn, your eyes are not deceiving you. I can tell from the look on your face that you had not anticipated this."

Jake continued to stare dumbfounded, wondering how Ternier had ever managed to capture Mat Daniels.

Jake stared speechless at his friend. Mat wore the same blank expression as did Zimbola.

"I will let you in on a little secret," Ternier said, enjoying Jake's bewilderment. "It was Mr. Daniels who allowed us to get aboard your boat."

Jake said nothing as he studied Mat, numbed by what he was seeing.

"Voudun can be a powerful weapon, Mr. Javolyn. It is an ancient art few people outside the Caribbean truly understand. Applied in the right manner, it can be used to subjugate people and influence the course of human history."

Jake found his voice, strangely recalling one of Jacob's little lectures. "You're a dreamer, Ternier. You see yourself as some emerging dictator who will gain control of Haiti. History books are replete with brutal madmen like you, deranged lunatics who used people to suit their own demented fantasies. Fact is, the misery they created was generally short-lived because the world always has a way of ridding itself of deluded Hitler-types."

Ternier stiffened, his eyes bulging savagely, utterly taken back by Jake's tirade. "My plan is infallible," he said angrily, his comportment momentarily unraveling. "I am not like other men. I have things at my disposal that will ensure complete success."

"You mean like a hydrogen bomb?!"

The Colonel showed surprise. "So you know about that." Nodding, he said, "I have to assume Trebek told you."

"You're truly a stupid man, Ternier," Jake continued to antagonize. "Only an idiot would provide Islamic radicals with such a catastrophic weapon."

Ternier's mien seemed to implode at the insult, and his rebuke came out in a deep guttural hiss. "They will prove to be a powerful ally."

"Temporarily, maybe. But if they ever manage to use this bomb on American soil, then what? They have ambitions just like you, one of them being to take over the world."

"Once I am in power, any attempts to usurp me will fail."

"Oh, really. What makes you so sure?"

Ternier's growing anger suddenly tapered off and a smirk took hold of his face. "Because like you, they will have no idea what they are up against. Think about it, Mr. Javolyn. If I am able to turn your friends against you through the power of voudun, I will surely be able to disrupt any plans to overthrow me in the future, no matter how well thought out."

"You assume too much."

Ternier's smugness dissolved. "Enough of your meaningless prattle. You are about to learn what happens to people who meddle in my affairs." The Colonel turned to several of his men. "Bring out the one called Polanski."

Another man was soon led from the darkness, and Jake recognized him to be one the three agents he had seen assisting Mat Daniels.

"Let us see how well you fare against two combatants, Mr. Javolyn." Upon saying this, Ternier lifted his eyes to the turreted observation deck near the top of the lighthouse, nodding and motioning with a hand.

Jake followed Ternier's gaze. A terrified scream broke the air as something was being dangled in the same manner as before. It was the cry of a woman.

Ternier looked back at Jake, a surly smirk plastering his face. "Your efforts to save this woman will have all been for nothing if you should lose this little contest, Mr. Javolyn."

Jake's dismal failure at keeping another female alive suddenly came back to haunt him as he stared up at the woman. Even though she hung partially hidden in shadow at a height of 130 feet above him, he somehow had the feeling the woman was Lucette.

Struggling for words in the midst of his helplessness, Jake said, "Before you have your fun, Ternier, I'm curious about something?"

Ternier continued to smirk expansively. "Yes?"

Jake looked over at Mat and the other DHS agent. Both men continued to stare dumbly off into space. "I'd like to know how you managed to capture these men."

"As I told you, Mr. Javolyn." The Colonel glanced briefly at the cloaked woman standing at his side. His manner seemed to reach a new level of pomposity as he spoke. "Voudun exercised by a powerful priestess can be highly effective." He paused again, as if to give his explanation more meaning. "But initially, it was not voudun that led to the capture of your friend."

"If not your black witchcraft, what then?" Jake needed to know.

"The very thing that tends to corrupt most men," Ternier said smugly. "A thing called greed."

Jake stared over at Mat in disbelief. "I'm not-"

Ternier's curt laugh cut off Jake's confused reply. "No, Mr. Javolyn. It was not your friend who became greedy, but the man standing next to him. Men in key places can be very valuable, particularly a representative of your country's Department of Homeland Security. I thought it prudent to keep this man on my payroll. I find it rather gratifying that so many people within your government are so easily bought off by those who have the means to purchase their cooperation."

Jake glared contemptuously at the DHS agent. "This man is an informant?"

The Colonel nodded slowly, smiling viciously as he did so. "This surprises you?" Letting out another laugh, he said, "Unfortunately, Mr. Daniels happened to be in the wrong place at the worst possible time. He and his crew were in the process of boarding a vessel on the open sea when I came upon him. The vessel he boarded was carrying some very special contraband meant for me."

Jake thought back to the smuggling run he had failed to undertake for Hennington. "Let me guess," he said sarcastically. "Over a hundred million dollars in United States greenbacks shipped from North Korea, all of them counterfeit."

Ternier's hauteur turned frosty. "Your knowledge of my business arrangements is becoming irksome, Mr. Javolyn. No doubt it was the fat little broker who provided you with this information."

"Yeah, I was the stooge originally designated to make the pick-up for you."

Ternier cocked an eyebrow. "Most interesting. I take it you are the same smuggler Mr. Hennington had used to make other deliveries on my behalf."

Jake's retort was flippant. "Guilty as charged. But I've wised up since then. I'm no longer in the business of smuggling, especially for people having delusions of grandeur. But I'm still curious about how you managed to capture Mat Daniels."

Ternier presented Jake with another sick grin, seeming to take great pleasure in telling more. "Ah, yes…it seems Mr. Polanski, here, killed the other two agents working for Mr. Daniels. He apparently had no problem shooting them in the back during the boarding process. Mr. Daniels was more fortunate, only receiving a slight concussion for his unsuspecting ignorance. Money has a most peculiar way of changing a person's loyalties."

"So, once you were able to take him prisoner, you drugged him," Jake said bitterly. "After that you used him and his vessel to come within striking distance of the *Angel* and capture everyone aboard her."

"You are most perceptive, Mr. Javolyn. But it was so much more than a drug that was used to control these men. Drugs generally have a limited effect on influencing the behavior of a person. Ancient voudun potions are much better. They strip away a person's will, leaving a puppet in place to do a master's bidding."

A deep groan sounded at Jake's feet, letting him know that Zimbola was regaining consciousness. Judiciously, he took it upon himself to step beyond the giant's reach.

Ternier's demeanor suddenly hardened. He no longer seemed amused. "I have wasted enough time on you with idle chatter. Now it is time to pay the price of your meddling."

Jake thought quickly. "What if I gave you the location of the gold?"

Smugness returned to Ternier's face. "So, you do know where it is hidden, after all."

"Yes. But first you must order your men to pull the woman back into the lighthouse if you want me to tell you."

Ternier hesitated, mulling the offer. "As you wish, Mr. Javolyn. It costs me nothing to spare the woman's life a little longer." The Colonel looked above him and shouted an order, and Jake watched as Lucette was pulled back into the tower.

Ternier brought his gaze back to Jake, staring expectantly. "No more games, Mr. Javolyn. Now tell me."

"You're standing over it."

Ternier eyed the ground under his feet. "Am I to believe it is buried right here?"

"This island has a subterranean cavern close to where we're standing. In it you'll find the gold, tons of it."

The Colonel's eyes bulged greedily. "Tons of it, you say?"

"Yes, tons of it. Maybe more than three hundred million dollars, I'd say."

The Colonel's face abruptly clouded with skepticism. "You better be telling the truth, Mr. Javolyn. I can make your inevitable death an eternity of agony should you be lying to me."

"I'm telling you it's right here under us," Jake said flatly.

"Show me the way to this cavern!"

"It's only reachable by water. There's a submerged tunnel on the southeast side of this island that connects with the cavern."

"That does me little good," Ternier snapped. "I am not a diver, nor are any of my men. Is there no other way into this cavern?"

"Possibly. Based on what I've seen, the bedrock comprising this island is riddled with a labyrinth of caves. But trying to find another way in might take months."

Ternier began to rub his jaw idly, seemingly frozen with indecision.

"Maybe you should consult with your Islamic buddies," Jake recommended snidely. "Most of them are trained frogmen. They even have a submarine at their disposal."

The Colonel stopped rubbing his jaw, gaping back at Jake with a strange look in his eyes. "A submarine?"

"You didn't know that?" Jake shook his head disdainfully. "You supply men like that with abducted Haitian citizens to be used as human slaves and you're in the dark on what they've been doing out here? I'm rather surprised that you don't know more about the people you're dealing with, Ternier."

The Colonel produced a caustic frown. "I shall not warn you again to curb that sharp tongue of yours, Mr. Javolyn."

As Ternier said this, two of his thugs moved in close to Jake, prepared to bash him with their Kalashnikovs. Both looked to the Colonel, awaiting his acquiescence, but Ternier stopped them by holding up a hand. "Not knowing everything about the activities of my affiliates does not concern me, only the end results. It is simply their primary objective that holds any importance." The broad grin that suddenly supplanted his expression appeared all the more perfidious by the crazed look in his eyes. "And that objective is nearly upon us."

Jake answered with a gruff chiding smile. "It'll take months for them to get that bomb in working order. It's been submerged far too long to have any chance of working. Before they're able to make use of the nuclear material it contains, this island will be swarming with U.S. troops."

Ternier appeared unperturbed. "Before this day ends, that bomb will be well on its way to Iran. Their scientists will have the know-how to prepare it for a nuclear strike in short order. But long before its ready, a nuclear missile of lesser yield will be launched from this very island. The missile will be capable of reaching the nearest American city."

Stunned by what he was hearing, Jake felt the smile drop from his face like a lead ingot. The ease with which Ternier had uttered the statement left him little room for doubt. "Miami is the closest American city!" he gasped. "You're telling me they're gonna nuke Miami?"

Jake's appall seemed to energize Ternier. "Your government will be crippled by even a small nuclear strike." The Colonel's words were saturated with a bluster meant to sting. "The devastation it will cause will wreak havoc. Your government showed the world how inept it was at handling the damage caused by a hurricane hitting New Orleans. Think how much more impotent it will be in the face of anarchy resulting from a nuclear catastrophe."

Jake felt like he was being crushed by the onus coming to bear down on him. The burden of saving nine lives had just escalated, for it was now the fate of millions that suddenly came to rest squarely upon his shoulders.

From the sea, Destiny had seen the flares lighting up the night sky and exposing the pinnacle of the old lighthouse overlooking the Windward Passage. It was an area of the island that lay directly above the subterranean grotto containing the dolphin refuge.

Climbing aboard the *Avenging Angel* as it rose and fell in the swells, she had found the vessel to be abandoned. As she watched the last of the flares fade, she instinctively knew that Jay Jay had gone to the lighthouse.

She was somewhat familiar with the terrain governing the island's surface, and she knew that even in broad daylight it would be difficult to wend one's way through the jagged bedrock and dense thickets hugging the landscape. But with these same obstacles hidden in darkness, traversing the land would be outright treacherous.

With this in mind, she dove back into the sea and mounted Hercules. There was another way of reaching the lighthouse. A passageway existed that ran from the dolphin refuge to the surface. And it exited roughly eighty meters to the north side of the tower's base, a naturally concealed cleft in the rock situated in a cluster of trees. On several occasions in the past, she had used the passageway to reach the surface. Clinging to the rock walls was the same living matter that provided bioluminescence to the dolphin refuge under construction. Moving through the passage had not been difficult. Each time she had emerged from its entrance, she had made her way over to the lighthouse and climbed the stairs leading to the top of the structure. And although the scene that always awaited her was breathtaking, the awe she felt seemed to be offset by some inexplicable force that lay just beyond her senses.

As Hercules swam for the south side of the island, Destiny knew she was failing the others. And with that failure, something had changed. A new sensation seemed to emanate from the other minds, its epicenter originating from one consciousness in particular. Yes, she felt it more fully now, suddenly cognizant of what was taking place.

Almost immediately, her sense of purpose deserted her, causing her to flounder in the midst of uncertainty. Whatever clairvoyance she possessed was now gone. The collective pod mind had been compromised. Having bonded with Jay Jay, the youngest of the albinos had taken on some of the traits that made Jay Jay what he was. And now it had spread to the others.

At Yeslam's orders, Azzum had assumed command of Allah's Sword, keeping the sub at a depth of three meters below the surface as it cruised close to the island. Originally, he had been instructed to hold the sub in a standby position between the two ships, keeping to a depth well below the ocean turbulence brought on by the passing storm. With a communications buoy fully deployed, he had left a radio channel open, awaiting a message from his team leader. Over an hour earlier, a message had finally come, and Yeslam had been livid with rage. The *San Carlo* had been attacked. Someone had managed to get aboard, setting off a raging fire that had further delayed the transfer of cargo. The man who had caused the fire had killed several of the ship's crew and jumped overboard. Azzum was to conduct an immediate search of the water bordering on Navassa's south side. He was to be on the lookout for anything unusual.

Azzum frowned as he studied the sonar blip on the sub's monitor. The object he was viewing might actually be a small whale, but he could not be sure. Earlier in the day, a school of humpback whales had been sighted near the island. But then again, maybe it was one of those accursed white dolphins his entire commando team had come to hate. He knew that Yeslam was very interested in capturing the girl seen with those dolphins.

Azzum's mind drifted as he considered this. If he could capture the girl himself, he might regain favor with Yeslam. His leader had been extremely displeased with him ever since he had been knocked unconscious during their foray along the Haitian coast. The man who had bashed him in the head was obviously a warrior like himself.

"Shall I continue on this heading?"

The question caused the other two crew members to look pensively at Azzum when he failed to answer. They were spread thin by current circumstances, and the sub's normal contingent of crew had been honed down by necessity for this particular operation.

"Azzum!"

Azzum looked sharply at the man piloting the sub. "Do not yell!"

Nabu lowered his voice. "The object has disappeared. Do you want me to continue on this heading?"

Azzum stared at the monitor, his reverie now broken. The blip had vanished. "All stop!" he barked. With eyes locked expectantly on the screen, he waited for the blip to reappear. When it did not, he said, "Give me bearing and range on the last known position of that object, Nabu."

Nabu did as instructed. "Compass bearing is fifteen degrees. Range is three hundred and twelve meters."

Azzum mulled this information for several seconds before making a decision. "Nabu, you will bring us to within fifty meters of where the object vanished and hold that position."

Nabu followed the order. His expression soured when he realized Azzum was stripping off his jumpsuit. "Azzum, what are you doing?"

"What does it look like, you fool?" Azzum said gruffly. Nabu was beginning to get on his nerves. "I am suiting up. Prepare the airlock. I will make an exploratory dive to see where the object might have gone."

Alarm showed on Nabu's face. "What if Yeslam needs us?"

"I will not be gone long," Azzum said. "Something strange is going on out there. I can feel it."

Azzum moved quickly to where the dive equipment was stored further back toward the stern. Eyeing the three DPVs resting in their holding racks, he decided to take the one Yeslam always used. The headlight on that one provided more illumination than the others, plus it had a built-in sonar device, which the other two lacked. It was perfectly suited for an exploratory dive. Exploratory dives excited him. They sometimes led to unusual finds. It was only a month ago that he and Yeslam had come across a sunken sloop close to where the sub now hovered. Apparently Allah had decided to reward them, for the treasure they had retrieved from the sloop's hold had been immense, and the feel of gold doubloons had been intoxicating. There had been thousands of them. And within the cache of ancient treasure, they had also discovered sealed containers containing 23-year-old bearer bonds issued by a bank in Zurich worth millions. The find had been brought back to their submarine base and stored there.

As Azzum struggled clumsily into his gear, the possibility that Allah might reward him yet again tickled his thoughts. He paid particular attention to the weapons he would carry, making sure to secure them firmly to his anatomy. He was one of Allah's true warriors and he would act as one. The thought that he had already lost one weapon weighed briefly on his mind, but he shrugged it off, certain that he would soon atone for his previous failure.

Chapter 21

Ortega locked heated eyes with Omar. He did not trust the man, but then again, he trusted no one. The two men had been bickering almost incessantly ever since Omar's slip of the tongue about the bomb. "You disappoint me, my Muslim friend," he said irritably. "You should have been more open with me. Our arrangement appears to be one-sided." He flung his hands wide to indicate the heavy damage inflicted on his ship. "Your indiscretion is going to cost me plenty. Three of my men are dead. Three others are either so badly burned or wounded that they are of no use to me."

Raduyev parried with a fierce scowl of his own, his hand hovering near the haft of his Bowie knife. He had also incurred a loss. One of his mujahidin fighters had been killed by a bullet to the head. "Do not try to hold me accountable for your lack of security," he fumed. "The fuel oil you promised me is completely destroyed because you failed to have lookouts posted. I needed that fuel."

Ortega was tempted to pull his handgun at that moment, but the thought of all that white heroin stopped him. There was a lot of money at stake, money that could easily be skimmed from Cardoza. Perhaps his relationship with Omar could still be salvaged. In a calmer voice, he said, "You are certain the man responsible for this is Javolyn?"

The scowl on Raduyev's face darkened further. "Few men would have been capable of getting aboard this ship in that storm. Javolyn is one such man. He fits the description your men gave of the attacker." He spat out the words as though they left a foul taste in his mouth, and his eyes darted in the direction of the island. "He is somewhere out there."

"If he is, we will find him," Ortega said, fighting to keep his tone under control. He had seen the flares over the island. "Perhaps the Haitian colonel will capture him."

Raduyev snarled savagely. "If he is captured, he is mine."

At the moment, Ortega had no desire to argue this point. He could not risk any more delays. In a tone meant to pacify, he said, "If I find him, I will give him to you as a gesture of good will, my friend."

Raduyev did not reply, and Ortega could see the intense hatred continuing to burn fervently in his eyes.

Ortega shifted his gaze, barely able to discern the *San Carlo's* tug making its way slowly toward the freighter. Once the fire had been brought under control, they had finally been able to launch it.

The *Spirit of Aden* was still holding position off their port. If not for a tiny sliver of moon suddenly poking through an opening in the clouds, he doubted the vessel would have been visible at all. He was glad to be rid of the bomb. He was eager to have it hoisted aboard the Yemeni ship so that it could be exchanged for the remainder of heroin they had agreed upon.

And once he had the heroin, he would go after the dolphin hunters Javolyn had helped escape. The one called Jaffey had offered a cache of gold as a bargaining chip in exchange for their lives. But unfortunately, Javolyn had interrupted Pedro's persuasive measures before Cardoza's nephew could extract its exact location from the man.

Ortega wrestled anxiously with this one particular thought, and all at once a flash of insight entered his thinking. Could it be that his prosperity was about to take another new turn for the better?

On impulse, he left Raduyev standing where he was and made his way down to his private stateroom within the ship. The item he sought still lay on the bed where he had left it. Hefting the object, Ortega studied it more closely this time, pressing a few buttons on the device before the same digital readout was displayed.

Ortega was unaware of the indulgent smile that transcended his face as he read the numbers. Yes, he was now certain what those numbers represented. After the device had been discovered, he hadn't had time to fully scan through the limited menu exhibited on its tiny screen, but now he realized it also had a text messaging capability.

He was now convinced of what the unit was used for, noting that it was about twice the size of the sender they had found aboard the broken-down *Sea Lion*. This was the receiver McPherson had claimed to be aboard the spotter plane used for tracking the dolphins. But then again, perhaps the naval captain had not lied at all. Perhaps McPherson hadn't known the receiver had been brought aboard the salvage tug that Jaffey had come in.

A sense of elation took hold of Ortega as he pondered this, knowing he had been right all along to follow his gut instincts. This was indeed a stroke of good fortune. Having one of his men perform a final search of the salvage tug one more time had proved worthwhile, because it had been shortly after the receiver was found that Javolyn had allowed the dolphin hunters to escape in that same vessel.

Pulling up the latest text message, his eyes widened in awe at what he read. Just to be certain he wasn't misinterpreting it, he reread it several more times before placing the device back on the bed. Just before leaving the room, however, he drew up sharply. Pedro was a sneaky bastard, and the last thing he wanted was Cardoza's irksome nephew snooping around his quarters and finding the unit. He had always suspected Pedro of being an informant to his uncle, and he certainly did not want this newfound information leaking out to the powerful drug lord. But then again, the brutish Pedro was rather stupid and wouldn't give the unit a second glance anyway. Nevertheless, he felt it prudent to at least hide the thing from plain sight by placing it under his pillow.

Somewhat satisfied, Ortega locked the door to his quarters before making his way up to the main deck.

Emerging from the cave north of the lighthouse, Destiny groped her way through the heavy underbrush before locating the narrow path she remembered so well. The path would take her to the ruins of two small houses adjacent to the base of the lighthouse. These, she knew, were the old keeper's quarters, at least what remained of them. Bathed in a soft glow of light emanating from some unknown source on the opposite side of the lighthouse, the towering structure presented an imposing silhouette overlooking the landscape. With a waning moon now peeking intermittently from behind an umbrella of low-slung clouds, she had just enough illumination to follow the tiny trail without stumbling into any unseen obstacles. Something stirred briefly in the overhead branches of the thicket she was in, and she attributed it to be the sound of a startled bird fluttering its wings. The sound quickly died, and all was still again.

Upon reaching the dilapidated keeper's quarters, she stopped. Something moved, appearing inky against the pervading darkness. More movement caught her eyes, and she ducked down to keep from being seen.

A voice suddenly rang out, ominous and sibilating. "Do not try to hide from me, cheval. It is a waste of time."

Destiny stared frozen as a shadowy figure emerged, a tiny orb giving off a blood-red emission as though it were the eye of an angry cyclops slowly coming for her. Almost at once, she knew what she was seeing.

"I have been waiting for you," Erzulie hissed, the words pouring from her mouth like grains of salt sliding along a coal chute.

Destiny rose to her feet, looking beyond the witch for anyone accompanying her. For the first time in her life, a sense of complete helplessness accosted her. The omnipotence of the group mind was now gone, leaving only the specter of something vague and uncertain in its place.

"As it turns out," Erzulie went on, "your pathetic rescue ultimately proved fruitless. The only thing you have accomplished is to increase the power you have relinquished to me."

The cackle that suddenly escaped the crone's lips was the harshest sound Destiny had ever heard.

Chapter 22

With the DPV's powerful headlight illuminating the way before him, Azzum had followed the azimuth given him by Nabu. The azimuth had taken him to the place where the unknown object had disappeared. It was there he had discovered a dark opening in the reef.

Hovering only briefly outside the opening, he had decided to investigate what lay inside. Steering the DPV along the tunnel that awaited him, he soon came upon a subterranean grotto. Its immensity awed him. The cavern was far greater in size than the chamber that housed Allah's Sword, and as he glanced about, he became aware of the pale light that seemed to bath everything in a soft greenish glow.

His eyes were quickly drawn to the swirling geometric patterns that lay just below the water's surface. Amazed by the sight, he re-engaged the DPV's propeller, tipping the unit so that it would take him deeper. Overcome by curiosity, he followed one of the curving surfaces. Whatever he was seeing had an oddly familiar texture, and the geometric whorls of a conch shell suddenly came to mind. Nevertheless, the structure did not look natural. Extruded wire mesh protruded along one area where the surface appeared to terminate. Frowning, he glided to a halt, running a gloved hand over the wire. His fingers tingled strangely with the touch.

What is this place? he asked himself, suddenly glancing around in all directions. He had the feeling he was being watched, but as his eyes penetrated the limpid water, he saw nothing that might indicate danger.

Re-powering the propulsion unit, he aimed it deeper. He would learn what was going on here. Following a corridor that appeared to spiral its way down, he eventually located an area where the walls flared outward.

His gaze immediately fell on lengths of rope, intertwined about one another and pulsing rhythmically. Under the DPV headlight, the rope-like strands appeared multicolored and segmented, and as he followed the strands, he saw that they joined a huge, bloated organism. He could see similar organisms strung out at intervals behind the first one, each one seeming to roost upon a bed consisting of a thick, milky slurry.

Azzum followed the line of organisms, puzzled by the sight of gas bubbles discharging from the crown of each creature. The bubbles disappeared into inverted funnel-like tubes situated directly above the rising gas. Something glittered further ahead, and as the DPV pulled him closer, his eyes bulged under his dive mask. Almost immediately, he knew he was looking at gold. Mounds and mounds of gold with the consistency of coarse granular sand. His recent participation in the recovery of treasure from the sunken sloop had left a lasting impression of what real gold looked like, and he was certain he could not be mistaken.

Just to be sure, he began scooping up handfuls of the stuff. The grains were metallic, all right, and weighty, too. Feeling it filled him with joy and he knew in that instant he would not share this find with the others. Though he was a holy warrior, he had never acquired the same level of zealousness held by his peers. He had always refrained from believing himself to hold the same religious conviction as his comrades. He would have been lying to himself had he done that. Born into dismal poverty, he had pursued a life of robbery and murder before joining Al Qaeda. He liked killing; it gave him pleasure. Nevertheless, Allah, in his infinite wisdom, had sought to reward him, probably because he was now devoted to only killing infidels.

Azzum eyed the bloated creature squatting in the midst of the gold, aware that the organism might actually be responsible for producing the valuable metal. If that were true, then the amount of metal would continue to accrue at a steady rate. Stricken with wonder, he turned the DPV so that its beam shone on the unsightly thing. More fully illuminated, he could see its pulsing surface was awash in bright colors. What are you that you are able to produce such riches?

The same weird feeling as before suddenly accosted him, seeming to clutch at his heart this time. Cautiously, he looked all about him again. He could not help it. He had the distinct sensation he was being observed.

Convincing himself he was letting his mind play tricks on him, he brought his eyes back to the organism in front of him. Reaching out, he placed a hand on the thing.

The jolt he felt lasted only a millisecond. Then there was only an all-consuming blackness from which there was no return.

The radio squawked harshly on Raduyev's belt, making him step away from the others so as not to be overheard. As he lifted the radio to his ear, his eyes continued to follow the unloading of the shipment sent over from the freighter. The exchange of cargoes was nearly complete. Ortega would have the quantity of white heroin originally promised him. And with the hydrogen bomb now safely aboard the other ship, a critical phase of the mission he had been assigned had finally come to an end.

"Have you spotted anything?" Raduyev grunted, speaking in English. He had instructed his crew that call signs were not to be used and that radio protocol was to be avoided. Though the broadcasting range of the radios they were using was very limited, one never knew if the transmissions might be intercepted, and the last thing he needed was for the wrong people to overhear someone speaking Arabic in these waters. They would speak in generalities that offered little to an eavesdropper.

Nabu's voice shot back in urgency. "Azzum left us to investigate something that was picked up on sonar. He has been gone more than an hour and has not returned."

The statement caused Raduyev's temper to flare. He could not afford the loss of another man. "Come home!" he growled. The prearranged command meant for Nabu to bring Allah's Sword back to base.

"What about Azzum?" Nabu persisted.

"Forget about him!" Raduyev snapped, livid with rage. "You will wait for me at home!"

A reply came back after a short pause. "We will wait for you there."

Raduyev's mood continued to deteriorate. He now realized his mistake in letting Azzum assume command of the sub during his absence. Perhaps it would have been far wiser to have left Kalid in charge. Kalid was not a diver and would have been unable to venture outside the sub.

As Raduyev put the radio back on his belt, he noticed Ortega striding toward him. "It seems we are both busy with radio calls, my Muslim friend," the Colombian boss said coldly. "I have just received a call from the Haitian colonel. He claims to have captured Javolyn."

The Chechen gaped in disbelief, unsure if he was hearing correctly. "I hope you are not joking with me."

"I am not in a joking mood," Ortega said gruffly. "Ternier requests you go ashore immediately. He will meet you at the lighthouse."

Raduyev glanced up at the ship's helipad. During the fire, he had seen the flames lick their way up close to the flight deck. "Is your helicopter still operable?"

Ortega nodded, his eyes still icy. The explosion Javolyn had caused had left a lasting strain on their relationship. "Yes. I will fly you there. I want to look into the eyes of the man who has caused me so much trouble."

Raduyev stared closely at Ortega's face. From the Colombian's tone, it sounded as if Ortega was having second thoughts about his earlier offer of appeasement. "Javolyn is still mine. You will not interfere with what I have in mind for him."

Ortega shrugged, still appearing annoyed. "Perhaps the Colonel has ideas of his own. From what I hear, he is a man very creative in the way of revenge."

The Chechen stiffened, not liking what Ortega was insinuating.

Jake heard the blades of the Bell Ranger beating the air as it approached. With its searchlight probing the terrain beneath it, the helicopter quickly found the small rectangle of open space near the base of the tower before setting down. Some of Ternier's men had recently fed the bonfire, and the light from it flickered with renewed vitality, providing a sinister aura to the two men who emerged from the copter's cabin.

As the men drew closer, recognition of the one on the right caused Jake to go rigid. Something leapt from the depths of his soul with such savagery that several of the Colonel's men had to prod him back with their Kalashnikovs. The vehemence he felt toward Raduyev was overpowering and he had great difficulty restraining it. Like a reawakening beast that had been locked away in a cage far too long, it surged up with ferocious hunger. And now the beast had to be fed.

Raduyev walked to within ten feet of Javolyn, his face twisted in hatred. "I knew that someday we would meet again," he rasped, ominously fingering the hilt of his sheathed Bowie knife.

Ortega moved to Raduyev's side, sizing Jake up with a grim appraisal. "So this is the man who attacked us."

Colonel Ternier stepped close to the two men. "It appears we all have a score to settle with Mr. Javolyn, here."

Jake stared back in silence as he regained control of his emotions. It was crucial the beast be held at bay for the time being, otherwise it would perish within its cage without any chance at retribution.

Raduyev turned, skewering Ternier with the same scalding gaze. "Whatever you have planned for this man must be put aside. I have plans of my own for him."

The Colonel met Raduyev's gaze with a calculating grin. "For the time being I suggest that no injury be inflicted on Mr. Javolyn. He is currently much too valuable to be harmed."

Ortega scowled murderously. "The only thing of value will be this man's death."

"Do not rush to judgement so quickly, gentlemen," the Colonel said. "It seems Mr. Javolyn knows something I am sure will slake your need for vengeance." Ternier paused, continuing to grin as he studied both men. "At least temporarily."

Raduyev stared back at Jake, his eyes savage and filled with extreme menace. "I have no time for riddles, Ternier."

Jake noticed a slight waver in the Colonel's smile at the Chechen's lack of respect, but Ternier remained diplomatic. "Then perhaps I was mistaken in assuming you would be interested in a worthwhile venture, Omar, one that might very well help finance your objectives." Ternier paused again, waiting for a response, but Raduyev showed no interest as he continued to glare belligerently at his old nemesis.

Annoyance flared briefly in the Colonel's eyes. "I am offering you a share of something that can make you exceedingly wealthy should you choose to take it."

Ortega turned sharply to face Ternier, his cruel demeanor suddenly easing with the prospect of further enrichment. "A share of what?" he demanded.

"I have learned of a substantial hoard of gold that exists somewhere on this island. According to Mr. Javolyn, it is in a subterranean vault directly below us. Unfortunately, the only way into that vault is through a submerged tunnel located off the island's southern shore. Divers will be needed to access that tunnel."

Ternier eyed the Islamist. "You possess the necessary equipment and training to reach this gold."

Raduyev said nothing for several seconds, continuing to glare at Jake as though he might spring upon him at any moment. Finally, he said, "And if I help you recover it, you will turn Javolyn over to me?"

The Colonel gave him a chilling smile. "You have my word."

"I assume we will all get an equal share of this prize," Ortega grunted.

The Colonel's voice was placating. "Are the three of us not partners? Sharing the gold equally goes without saying."

The Chechen threw hate-filled eyes back at Javolyn. "What makes you think this man will show us the way to the gold?"

Ternier appeared to swell with smugness. "It seems Mr. Javolyn is a man who is foolishly ruled by loyalty. He will do anything to keep his friends alive."

Ortega nodded in agreement. "I have seen one of them… a girl who rides a dolphin. Not too long ago Javolyn risked his life to save her."

"Yes," Ternier said, his smile broadening. "The girl's life is a powerful motivator."

Ortega's interest escalated. "You have this girl?"

The Colonel gave Jake a cryptic grin before gesturing to one of his thugs. "Show these men the girl!"

The statement rocked Jake to his heels. He had not even considered that Destiny might be among those held by Ternier. Ten minutes earlier he had accounted for all ten of the captives Ternier had claimed during their radio conversation, having seen the remaining six led from the lighthouse. Jacob, Grahm, Hennington, Hector, Emmanuel and Lucette had all been taken away before the arrival of Raduyev and Ortega. Mat, the traitorous Polanski, and Zimbola had also disappeared, with the black giant taking Trebek's broken body with him. Apparently, the Colonel enjoyed doling out psychological torture as much as he did physical. Ternier was like a crafty poker player, showing his cards only when necessary.

Apprehension filled Jake as Destiny was led around the side of the lighthouse by two soldiers. Floating behind her was the cowled priestess he had seen earlier, the strange ornament around her neck still glowing a choleric red.

At seeing Jake, Destiny squirmed free of the hands constraining her. "Jay Jay!" she squealed.

The soldiers moved quickly to regain control of their charge, but Ternier raised a hand. "Let the cheval go!" The order was barked in a bored monotone, almost as if he had expected such a scene.

No one interceded as Destiny bolted for Jake's protective embrace, hugging him fiercely. "They didn't hurt you?" she cried.

"I'm okay," Jake said.

Destiny looked up into his face, her eyes misty. "They have Jacob and the others."

"I know," Jake replied bleakly.

"Enough of this pitiful prattle!" Ternier scolded impatiently. The Colonel looked sharply at several of his men. "Separate them!" he bellowed.

The soldiers moved in to pry the girl from Jake's arms. As she was pulled violently away, he lashed out with the swiftness of a viper, slamming a fist into an exposed jaw. The man he hit was sent sprawling to the ground, knocked cold.

Jake fell to his knees as something blunt slammed into a kidney, but Ternier stopped his henchmen before they could retaliate further.

The Colonel's eyes bulged grotesquely, his composure now worn thin. "Any more attacks on my men will result in severe punishment to the cheval, Mr. Javolyn," he warned mordantly. "The same thing will happen to her each time you fail to cooperate."

"We are wasting time!" Raduyev snarled.

Ternier studied Jake closely as if to assess his compliance with the warning. "I do not think Mr. Javolyn will give us any further problems," he chortled.

Destiny felt terribly vulnerable and alone as she was led to a place away from the others. And although she knew what must be done, she no longer comprehended how to do it. Something empty resided in her chest, a void around which the fire of her living body existed. She sensed the futility of the paradox, for the fire held no flame. She was floating over unknown ground and held within her cupped ethereal hands was the tender organ of her own beating heart. Confronting insidious forces was something far more difficult than she had ever imagined.

And those same forces were responsible for all the obstacles standing in her way, crude malicious barriers that took all happiness away from life.

Something Jacob had once told her came flooding back. Happiness was a concept within the mind, nothing more. There was no road that led to such a place, for happiness was merely the voyage, not the destination.

Her mother's face suddenly flashed before her. You will become stronger and wiser for your pain. The thought made her feel lost, for she wasn't sure if Amphitrite was speaking to her at this moment. Fearful of what would happen to Jay Jay, her sense of the others had gradually faded. It was she who was responsible for what was happening, for if Jay Jay were to die, his death would be on her hands.

She suddenly became aware of a new emotion surfacing within her, and it rose with such potency that it blocked out all sense of the hurt and guilt she had been feeling. It was something new to her, something that up until now she had never before experienced.

Consumed by this surging state of mind, she realized Jay Jay had been right all along. Gentle persuasion and passive restraint would not be enough to counter the vile natures of the people seeking to do them harm. It was now time to fight back!

With a guard on each side of her, Destiny stared back in defiance at the old crone. She had been taken back to the old keeper's quarters on the far side of the lighthouse.

"A powerful mambo once tried to defy me, cheval," Erzulie gloated in a reptilian voice that was somewhere between a hiss and a cackle. "But your fate will be the same as hers."

"What have you done with the others?" Destiny asked, her revulsion of the hag continuing to build within her.

The crone ignored the question as though she had not heard it. "You are probably wondering how I was able to sense your presence when you arrived here." The witch held the amulet in front of the girl's face, dangling it smugly. "I have always had the power to possess a creature's mind, seeing through its eyes and controlling its movements. But this little trinket amplifies this power even more. There are many birds on this island-"

Erzulie suddenly tensed. The amulet's steady glow abruptly wavered, beginning to blink erratically, its emission of crimson light now turning a deep green. Without warning, the earth heaved beneath her feet, followed by an ear-shattering boom a split second later. In that instant, she knew that something had gone terribly wrong.

Chapter 23

*J*ake had had enough. He had stalled for time as much as he dared, but now he knew it was time to act. Ternier, Ortega, and Raduyev had gotten aboard the Bell Ranger and flown off, leaving him guarded by a contingent of fifteen men, including one stationed on the lighthouse's turreted observation deck above him. With Destiny and the others having been taken away, he was now free to put his plan into motion.

The light from the bonfire had gradually dimmed into a feeble glow and the men closest to him were keeping a respectful distance, though they made him kneel on the ground with his hands clasped stiffly behind his head. Jake had anticipated something like this, and he casually probed with his fingers for the tiny device he had sewn in the lining of his collar. The device was a remote entry key, the kind used to unlock the door or trunk of an automobile from a distance. It was part of an accessory kit he had purchased for remotely deploying the *Angel's* waverunner launching ramp when berthing the Kawasaki. Luckily, he had not gotten a chance to install it, for now it would serve a far better purpose. The radio signal it would send was designed to activate its counterpart, a torsion spring that normally acted as a car trunk release, but he had rigged the electronic release to something else. He had been especially lucky he hadn't triggered it during his struggle with Zimbola, for a jury-rigged remote detonator could be quite unpredictable. From where he knelt, he estimated he was right on the edge of its transmitting range. And that was twenty meters.

Taking a deep breath to steady his nerves, he prayed he was within range as he located the triggering button through the cloth. Twisting around so that the remote aligned with the target, he suddenly flopped forward and pushed down on the button, pressing his face flat against the ground and shielding the back of his head with both hands.

One of Ternier's men began to shout, but the protest of anger never left his tongue as an invisible battering ram seemed to catch the man from behind and send him flying like a leaf caught in a gale. The shock wave rending the air was thunderous, the force of it scattering Ternier's thugs like piffling windblown debris. The rucksack Jake had left concealed at the edge of the clearing had held a homemade bomb. He had been able to construct it using the explosives contained in two of the waverunner torpedoes he kept aboard the *Angel*.

With ears ringing, Jake wobbled dazedly to his feet. Grabbing a Kalashnikov dropped by one of the fallen men, he sprang into action. As soldiers staggered to their feet, he hosed them, cutting them down before they even knew what was happening. In seconds, he emptied the weapon. Flinging it aside, he picked up another, spraying several more men as they tried to get to their feet.

Reflexively, he ducked down at the hammering clatter of return gunfire. Dirt was kicking up all around him. He glanced up to espy muzzle flashes coming from the observation deck above. Pulling the AK to his shoulder and taking careful aim, he stood rock-steady and squeezed down on the trigger, intent on emptying the clip. The firearm bucked, cooperating just long enough to send out a short volley before jamming, and Jake knew his marksmanship had not failed him as a bloodcurdling scream filled the air. The moment was dramatized all the more as one of the logs within the bonfire shifted and flared, suddenly illuminating the object accelerating down from the heights with a spiking burst of light, and Jake followed the flight of the falling man, unable to look away. The man continued to shriek in terror, twisting, twitching, and clawing at the air until he met the ground with a heavy thump, and then all was quiet again.

Jake threw down the Kalashnikov and bolted like a jackrabbit for the thicket off to his right, expecting another storm of return fire to follow him. When none came, he risked a glimpse over his shoulder, seeing more of Ternier's thugs struggling to their feet like drunken sailors.

Grimly, he found his way into the underbrush, and in moments he was able to locate the weapons he had left behind. With resolute purpose, he strapped on his K-bar and USP-9, finally snapping his ammo belt into place before snatching up the Stoner.

Gripped by the same coldness he had felt back in Tora Bora, he moved back to the edge of the clearing. The Stoner shuddered like a jackhammer as he fired from the hip, cutting down four more men clustered together. With a total disregard for his own safety, he ambled calmly out into the clearing, looking to kill anything that moved with the awesome firepower held in his hands. The body count quickly escalated, and it did not take him long to account for fifteen dead men, all of them strewn about the clearing like torn and twisted rag dolls.

No matter what it took, he would get Raduyev for what he had done to Myers. But right now he had Destiny and the others to think about.

Destiny saw the fear etched on the faces of the men guarding her. The stillness hanging in the air seemed to have unnerved them even more than the sporadic bursts of gunfire that had erupted moments earlier.

Shifting her attention back to the hag, the girl watched as Erzulie gazed intently into the amulet's crystal. The light ensuing from the trinket had now changed back to a deep blood red.

The hag turned to the soldiers. "Stay here and keep guarding the cheval," Erzulie ordered in that halting reptilian tone. "If she gives you any problems, kill her."

Within seconds, the witch was gone, seeming to float off into the night.

A disconcerting silence ensued, and Destiny sensed the growing uneasiness of the two guards. Both men fidgeted nervously as they awaited Erzulie's return.

Something clunked dully, making the men whirl around in fright. The sound had come from behind them. From the other side of the lighthouse, the bonfire continued to burn, though it had dimmed considerably. Eclipsed by the tower's dark looming bulk, the fire cast a soft glow to each side of it.

The silence was broken again, this time by multiple clacks coming from one of the back walls comprising the keeper's quarters. Both men turned and fired at the sound, taking their attention away from the girl.

Destiny caught sight of a dark shadow rising up, and in that instant an eruption of gunfire exploded at close to point blank range. Brrrup, brrrup. A lance of stabbing flames shot out, the sound of it drowning out the staccato fire of the guards.

The shadow reached out and grabbed her arm, and she knew at once the shadow was Jay Jay.

Jake stared down at the two men he had just shot, making sure their crumpled bodies did not move. "Where are the others?" he asked.

Destiny eyed the dead men. Though she felt a detached empathy, their deaths did not revolt her. She suddenly realized that some people would have to die if the pod was going to survive and continue fostering their objective.

Getting her wits about her, Destiny stared up into Jake's face. "I don't know. I saw them earlier, but they were led away."

Jake opened his mouth to say something, but stopped short, and Destiny noticed his eyes impinging on something over her shoulder. With his free arm, he moved her slowly aside and leveled his weapon.

Destiny spun as Erzulie's voice rasped out from the gloom. "Your weapon will be useless against me."

Jake was not about to take any more chances. He had seen what this seemingly innocuous old crone had done to Zimbola and Mat, and so he fired, the muzzle of his Stoner flaring a bright orange as it spat a lethal hail designed to destroy. A shower of sparks erupted in front of the witch, the storm of bullets unable to penetrate whatever was shielding her from the deadly barrage.

Jake stopped firing and lowered the Stoner, stunned that Erzulie was still standing. The pendant she wore pulsed savagely, radiating ebbing doses of flaming crimson as though shedding an excess of stored energy. The pulsing quickly died and steadied.

"You cannot hurt me," Erzulie rasped hoarsely. "Protected by the charm of my ancestors, I am invincible."

"Perhaps you assume too much!"

Erzulie froze. The words had come from behind her. Whirling, the crone faced the intruder.

Both Jake and Destiny watched as another dark form materialized out of the gloom. With stolid calmness, Amphitrite stood before the witch.

"So…the mother cheval dares to come here," Erzulie hissed. "You make this easier than I had thought."

"The amulet's empowerment is an illusion, witch," Amphitrite said. "The power contained within it will ultimately destroy all those who seek to use it wrongly. Your obsession in using it for evil and self-gain offends the forces behind it."

Erzulie floated off to one side so that she could observe all three people. "No," the crone countered angrily. "The rada have bestowed this power to me because I am the rightful owner. They saw you as unworthy and forced you to give it up. Deep down you knew it would have been too dangerous to keep it for yourself."

"Giving the amulet up was only a ploy," Amphitrite said without emotion. "Without it, you would have been too cowardly to come here."

Erzulie cackled in amusement, but Destiny detected a waiver of confidence in her tone. "You delude yourself, cheval. I have come here to carry out the wishes of the rada. This amulet gives me the power to destroy all those who oppose my son. The rada wish to see Henri rule, for he is the only one capable of restoring Haiti to its former glory. With Henri as king, Haiti will become one of the world's great powers. In a strange way, the people you are aligned with will contribute immeasurably to making this possible. Henri is fully aware of the business venture Jacob and Emmanuel have concocted and will take control of their plan, using them as pawns to increase his wealth and power."

Destiny sensed the smile that formed on her mother's face, though it was partially obscured in shadow. "If you truly believe this, then destroy me now," Amphitrite challenged. "As I recall, you tried to do this many years ago. You failed then, just as you are about to fail now."

Erzulie hesitated, suddenly seeming unsure of herself. "I have had enough of your interference," she sibilated bitterly, her words coming out in a hateful rush. "You will not only die, but you will also die in unbearable agony."

As if in response to the witch's declaration, a swirling mist rose up around her cloak-shrouded form. The amulet began to glow more fervently, the pent-up energy within it building rapidly.

"You will feel the fires of hell burning within you," Erzulie hissed brusquely. "You will bear the torments of a thousand suffering souls. You will-"

The amulet's choleric red abruptly changed over to a greenish emission, pulsing with such blinding speed that it dazzled the eyes. The fabric of Erzulie's cloak began to smolder where the amulet hung against the cloth, and the pungent smell of scorched flesh began to fill the air. The witch screamed, flapping her hands wildly against her chest as though trying to squash an unseen insect alighting there. The scream grew in pitch, escalating into a horrible screech as the hag's cowl burst into flame.

Amphitrite stood immobile as the fire spread rapidly to consume the hag, her features impassive and sedate under the light cast by the flames. Driven into an agonizing frenzy, Erzulie lunged, intent on engulfing Amphitrite in those same flames, but Amphitrite stepped aside and the witch flew past. The crone managed five more steps before falling to the ground, the fire sizzling flesh as it burned savagely.

Erzulie continued to scream for another ten seconds before her cries began to wane, eventually stopping altogether. When the flames finally died, only a charred corpse remained.

"Come," Amphitrite said, turning to look at both Jake and Destiny. "We must hurry. There is still danger."

Colonel Ternier's eyes blazed in anger as he examined the contents of the final metal chest. "You disappoint me, Omar. There appears to be a discrepancy here."

Raduyev's face clouded as he scanned the stack of cases under the beam of his own flashlight. Ternier was right. By his own count, he was five cases short. "If there is a shortfall, it is because all the cases have not been delivered as yet," he replied, suppressing his bewilderment. Silently he cursed Kalid for not completing the task. The man had more than enough laborers at his disposal to have gotten the job done by now.

Ortega paced impatiently off to one side, appearing like a shadow in the pall of night. Farther back from him, the Bell Ranger's dark silhouette sat quietly. "I am not a shuttle service, Colonel," he said testily. "My time is very valuable and I have business of my own that cannot wait."

The three men had landed in the middle of the small clearing adjacent to the topside entrance leading to Raduyev's hidden submarine base. Debts had to be settled and additional business discussed before they could pursue seeking out the gold with Javolyn's forced cooperation.

Ternier turned to the Colombian and sighed in annoyance. "Has no one ever told you that patience is a virtue, Mr. Ortega? You will be amply remunerated for the use of your aircraft…unless, of course, you feel the girl is not a fair exchange."

Ortega stopped his pacing but said nothing.

The Colonel swiveled his head back to the man he knew as Omar. "When can I expect the rest of the merchandise?"

"Give me a minute to converse with my people," Raduyev said stiffly. "I am sure a reasonable explanation exists for the delay."

"Of course," Ternier agreed coldly. "But if it turns out you are unable to make good on the remainder, I will expect payment in full in United States greenbacks equal in value to that portion missing. By my estimation, you are still short by twenty-five million dollars."

Raduyev was puzzled by what was happening here. Even before they had left the lighthouse, he had radioed his base, but Kalid had not answered. They had first flown out to the *San Carlo* to make sure the remainder of white heroin had been sent over from the freighter. Once aboard Ortega's ship, he had tried contacting Kalid again, but to no avail. To make matters worse, something had gotten caught up in the tug's props while the small vessel was on its way back to the *Aden* to receive the final load, further delaying the operation. Rather than wait for the final shipment, they had gotten back aboard the copter and flown to where he now stood.

To Raduyev it seemed all these infidels had their hands out. The extent of their greed seemed to have no bounds. The Chechen felt the anxiety building within him as he stepped out of earshot of both men. His business with Ternier needed to be concluded very shortly. Once he got the Colonel out of his hair, he would launch the rocket the North Koreans had provided. His base antenna was situated only ten meters from his current position, well hidden in a cluster of trees. Certainly he would be able to reach Kalid from here.

Raduyev lifted the small radio to his mouth, his finger resting on the transmit button, but before he could utter a word, the radio squawked gratingly. Someone was jabbering excitedly. From the sound of the speaker, he knew Nabu was hailing him.

Raduyev had difficulty keeping his voice calm and it came out in an angry whisper. "What is going on? Why has Kalid not brought up all the cases? We are eight short!"

"There is a problem!" Nabu cried. His tone was hysterical. "Our base has been breached. The Haitians have taken control…Bashir-" The transmission suddenly cut out.

Raduyev felt an icy hand reach out to close on his innards, but before the Chechen could find his tongue, the radio came alive again, this time with the voice of a new speaker. The voice was Bashir's. "Your mission is finished, Yeslam! I will not let you kill innocent people."

The radio abruptly cut out again, leaving Raduyev staring at the device in stunned silence.

"You seem perturbed, Omar."

Raduyev looked up. Ternier hovered close, gazing at him expectantly.

"I assume there will be nothing to mar our relationship," the Colonel said. There was an ominous edge in his manner. "I would hate to think you will not honor your end of our bargain when I have already honored mine."

Ternier was reminding him of their arrangement. The Colonel had given him the precise coordinates of the lost hydrogen bomb in exchange for items recovered from the hold of a sunken sloop. Ternier also had provided him with the coordinates of the sloop's location, and Raduyev had done the rest.

It had always puzzled the Colonel why the cheval had scrawled those numbers in the sand where she had left him unconscious so many years ago, a place known to the locals as the Devil's Horn. Upon regaining consciousness, he had given those numbers to memory, having a boding sense of their meaning. After much rumination, he had eventually consulted a navigational chart, and sure enough those numbers had conformed to the latitude and longitude of a location very close to Navassa Island. He had remembered seeing the island in the distance shortly before they had ditched the seaplane in the ocean. With the wind blowing hard in that direction, it was only logical that the sloop would have been pushed close to the island before sinking. But what had amazed him even more was the proximity of the sloop to the lost hydrogen bomb. Both had been less than 500 meters from one another. This he had taken as a positive omen, one that foretold of the glorious destiny that awaited him. And he had been further rewarded when Omar had gotten word to him that the sloop had been found and its contents recovered. With the exception of the bearer bonds that were still missing, the ancient Spanish treasure he had taken from Mercades Myers so long ago was now back in his possession once again. So be it if it had laid in wait for him at the bottom of the sea all these years rather than the Cayman bank vaults where he had originally planned to store it. Twenty-two years earlier, Baby Doc had entrusted him with the delivery of several cases of bearer bonds worth millions to a discreet bank account in the Caymans. At the time, Duvalier had known his reign was almost at an end and had decided to loot the Haitian national treasury. In carrying out Duvalier's orders, Ternier had simply added his own booty to the stolen bonds, arranging transport of the goods via a seaplane taking off from Saint-Marc. Baby Doc had been furious with rage when he had learned the assets he had absconded with had gone down in the sea, but Duvalier's fear of Erzulie had kept him from seeking retribution on her one and only son, and Ternier had escaped with his life.

The Colonel mulled the current situation. The stockpile of weapons Omar had promised were in secured locations in Port-au-Prince, ready to be distributed on his command. He also had in his possession the counterfeit dollars coming from North Korea. His plan had now ripened sufficiently to initiate. But now the bonds were still missing, and he was not going to be satisfied until Omar delivered them into his hands.

"You will get everything agreed upon," Raduyev rasped, throwing venom into his words. He was growing weary of these greedy infidels. "But a problem currently exists, and I will require the use of your soldiers to rectify it."

Ternier grimaced, drawing back in horror as if Raduyev had just doused him with a bucket of scalding water. "What kind of problem?"

Raduyev felt a rush of heat rise to his cheeks, taking momentary comfort that it was still nighttime, otherwise the Colonel would have noted the red flush spreading across his face. "It seems the Haitians you provided me have overwhelmed my people and taken over my base."

Ternier stood frozen, remaining speechless for several seconds. "You had assured me the missile would launch before daybreak," he sputtered in outrage, all his former aloofness seeming to dissolve into a heated meltdown. The Colonel looked at his watch. "Dawn will be upon us in less than ninety minutes."

"The Rodong will go off as planned!" Raduyev assured him. "But I will need your assistance."

Ortega moved closer, looking from one man to the other. "What is this I am hearing about a missile?"

Standing on the bridge, the *Spirit of Aden's* captain stared nervously at his wristwatch. It was crucial he set sail before first light. "What is the holdup now?" he asked his first mate in exasperation.

"The tug from the *San Carlo* has broken down again," the first mate stated.

"I thought they had removed the netting fouling its props."

The first mate shrugged. "They did, but it seems they have picked up more."

The captain gazed across the water at the tuna trawler's dark outline. "Hail the *San Carlo* and inform them they have exactly fifty minutes to pick up the remainder of the cargo," he ordered. "After that we will depart these waters with whatever they have failed to off-load."

The first mate nodded before carrying out the order.

The captain looked at his watch again, his uneasiness continuing to mount. As a devout Shiite Muslim and operative of Iran's Revolutionary Guard, he knew he should be smiling but somehow he could not bring himself to do so just yet. Aboard his ship was the very thing he had come for, a weapon capable of unspeakable destruction once Iranian scientists loyal to the mullahs restored the device to its full potential. With such a weapon in their possession, Iran's nuclear ambitions would be greatly accelerated. With such a weapon, they would bring America's dominance in world affairs to an abrupt end.

Yes, he assured himself, he would allow himself a smile only when his ship was safely underway.

Chapter 24

$\mathcal{M}$at Daniels broke from his stupor with a start, bewildered by his surroundings. He was currently sitting in semi-darkness among a small group of people on the back deck of a large modern yacht. Three men bearing Kalashnikov assault rifles stood nearby, none of them paying him any attention. The men were leaning over the vessel's gunwale, looking intently at something in the water. The sound of distant surf told him a shoreline was not too far away.

Taking inventory of the faces nearest him, he recognized most of the people he had last seen aboard the *Avenging Angel* - Chester Hennington, Zimbola, Franklin Grahm, Hector, Jacob, Lucette and Emmanuel Baptiste. One other person sat to the right of Emmanuel, and as he leaned over to get a glimpse of the person's face, his pulse quickened.

All at once, a flood of lost memory washed over him. He thought it had all been a dream, but now he knew for sure that one of his men had betrayed him. Joe Polanski was a murderous traitor.

A terrified shout caused Mat to stare back at his captors. One of the men appeared horrified. The man gesticulated wildly at the larboard water and cried out in panic. The deck abruptly lurched as something crashed into the hull with jolting force.

Knocked to his side, Mat noticed a dark form loom up from the sea. Huge and monstrous against the backdrop of night, it rose still higher until it towered above him. Reaching an apex, it hung suspended for one brief instant before pitching forward, ever so slowly at first as it gained momentum. Too late to escape the descending mass, the gun-toting men screamed out in terror as a 100 tons of whale flesh crashed down upon them.

Mat felt the vessel's deck disintegrate underfoot as fiberglass and wood splintered. Another huge body rose up and fell, followed by two more as the vessel's stern end was quickly transformed into wreckage by successive hammer blows.

Staggering to his feet, Mat stared in amazement as the deck leaned back, the boat's aft section now tilted below the waterline. The vessel was sinking rapidly.

With water rising up around his legs, Mat saw the others around him responding to the situation. Zimbola was already reaching for several life rings hanging nearby. Without hesitation, the black giant handed one off to Lucette before tossing another to Emmanuel. Spotting two more life rings, Mat followed suit, doling one out to Grahm and another to Jacob.

Vaguely, Mat perceived Hennington share a float with Hector as the deck began to disappear beneath them. Somehow, his eyes found Joe Polanski in the midst of the turmoil, noticing that the DHS agent had climbed a nearby stairway to get clear of the rising water.

Mat's breath caught in his throat. In Polanski's hands was a Kalashnikov, the barrel leveled directly at Mat's head. Even in the dim light, Mat was able to discern the sneer where the stock of the weapon abutted Polanski's face. The vessel suddenly lurched just as Polanski pulled the trigger, and water kicked up five feet away from where Mat floated.

Polanski regained his balance and aimed again, but before he could get off a second shot, another gargantuan shadow surged up from the sea. Throwing up his arms in a futile bid to shield his face, Polanski let out a horrific scream. His cry was immediately cut off as the whale's bulk mashed down with the destructive force of a massive wrecking ball. In moments, the vessel disappeared from sight, leaving a bubbling froth behind.

Mat stared all about him as he treaded water. He could discern seven bobbing heads floating nearby. Using a breaststroke, he swam over to the nearest one, finding Grahm. "Are you okay?" he asked.

"I believe so," Grahm sputtered, spitting out water.

Another person floated over, and Mat could see it was the Haitian he had helped Jake rescue.

"Do you hear the sound of waves?" Jacob said. His tone held encouragement. "I think we should swim toward the sound."

"What happened?" It was Hennington asking the question as he shared his float with Hector.

"I think we just witnessed an attack by humpback whales," Grahm replied. "I would never have believed such gentle creatures were capable of such destruction unless I saw it with my own eyes."

Zimbola's large head moved into their midst, each of his hands grasping a life ring as he towed Emmanuel and Lucette. Moving to within arm's reach of Mat, he stared closely at Mat's face. "Erzulie no longer controls us with her black magic, my friend. We are free of her power."

"It is because Erzulie is dead," Lucette blurted.

"How do you know this to be true?" Zimbola asked.

"Only the death of a voudun mambo can erase the spells she has invoked," Lucette assured him. "Erzulie must be dead."

Mat spun in the water as something splashed behind him. Upon the dark sea he could make out the profile of a fin knifing along the surface.

As if to alleviate Mat's sudden apprehension, Jacob spoke up. "The pod is here to help us."

Upon saying this, the heads of several dolphins poked above the water two feet away from where Mat floated.

A sense of fear gripped Ternier as the Bell Ranger set down next to the lighthouse for the second time. It was an emotion he had rarely experienced over the course of his life, one that made him feel utterly weak and not in control.

"What is going on here, Colonel?" Raduyev snarled belligerently, eyeing the dead soldiers scattered about the clearing. Twenty meters behind him, the Bell Ranger's rotors continued to swish the air at low RPM.

Ternier stared dully at the fallen men, their bodies revealed by what remained of the bonfire he had started earlier. This was too much for him to bear. His boat destroyed and now this. In flying back to the lighthouse, they had flown over the area where his vessel had been anchored. Under the helicopter's spotlight, only debris had littered the water. The sight had sent a chill racing through his bones. And now the chill had deepened.

"Your stupidity has allowed Javolyn and the girl to escape," Raduyev accused in a feral growl.

Ternier had difficulty speaking. His eyes continued to rove dully over the dead men, afraid of what else he might find if he searched further. His mother was a powerful voudun priestess. Armed with the ancient amulet bestowed upon her by the rada, she should have been invincible. All his life he had relied on Erzulie. She was the underlying source behind the power he wielded. Without her he would be little more than a low-ranking official within the Haitian hierarchy. With his mind churning in confusion, he wondered how something like this could have happened.

The escalating pitch of the helicopter cranking its blades made Ternier spin around in alarm. Ortega had been right behind them a moment ago, but now he was back aboard the aircraft.

Raduyev shouted at the top of his lungs, waving his arms frantically. "What are you doing? Stop!"

The Bell Ranger lifted off before the Chechen bolted forward, and both men could only stare as it headed out to sea.

The thought that he might actually be dealing with idiots had come to Ortega only after he had learned about the missile. He had fallen victim to a scheme far bigger than he had ever imagined. Both Ternier and Omar had made him a party to something he would have avoided had he known their primary objective. Social and economic stability in the United States was important to the drug trade. Stability insured open borders and a continuation of the profits his organization enjoyed. Stability meant reduced vigilance by the U.S. Coast Guard. There was an inherent predictability in stability. But a catastrophic upheaval of any kind had the potential of disrupting that trade, and he liked things just the way they were.

But now he was being cheated. Just before landing at the lighthouse, he had received a radio call from the *San Carlo* that had infuriated him. He had controlled his temper, however, giving his passengers no indication of what had been said. He was not in the habit of supplying headphones to those who sat in the rear seats, and without them his passengers had no way of knowing the contents of the communiqué.

As Fernando piloted the helicopter beyond the *San Carlo*, Ortega spotted the tug. The vessel was still adrift without power. The cloud cover had all but dissipated, allowing the moon to cast a rich golden glow upon the water below.

"Bring us to a hover above them and shine the searchlight at their stern," Ortega instructed.

Three Colombians looked up as Fernando brought the aircraft lower. Under the chopper's beam, Ortega caught a glimpse of a fourth man rising to the surface near the aft end of the vessel, one of the divers Omar had brought along to raise the bomb. The water was clear, and Ortega could see some of the netting the diver had just cut free.

Ortega continued to watch as the diver climbed back aboard the small vessel. The diver pulled up his mask and nodded to the other men, and a moment later the tug's operator re-engaged the engine to send the vessel sliding smoothly across the water. The operator looked up and gave the okay sign, letting his boss know that the problem had been corrected.

Ortega looked at his watch, still fuming over the radio message. Five minutes still remained before the *Spirit of Aden* would sail away. How dare the Aden's captain give him an ultimatum after he had carried out his end of the deal! He dismissed the thought, knowing what he would do if the threat was carried out.

Under the searchlight, something in the water caught Ortega's eye just as Fernando was about to take the aircraft out of its hover. Within the circle of light, several objects darted.

Ortega pointed. "Did you see that, Fernando?"

"See what?"

Ortega pointed again, this time angrily. "Down there!"

"I see nothing but water."

A livid scowl came to Ortega's face as he lifted his gaze to bear on the pilot. "Are you blind?" Reaching under his seat, he grabbed hold of an MK3 stored there. Pulling the pin, he hurled it at the water below, the rage within him giving it an extra boost.

"Keep the light trained on the water and hold this position," Ortega growled. "There are dolphins down there! Dolphins with hands! They are the reason the tug keeps breaking down. They foul the props with netting."

Ortega watched as the grenade detonated, the force of it whipping the water beneath them into a frothing mushroom. When the water settled, he saw nothing to give him satisfaction.

"Take us over the tug again!" Ortega yelled. He would be damned if dolphins were going to stop him from getting the remainder of the heroin. Groping under the seat, he grabbed another grenade.

"I thought you wanted live specimens," Fernando said quickly, eyeing his boss as he dipped the Ranger's nose.

Ortega looked over at the freighter, his expression murderous. "That shipment is more important."

The Ranger began to gather speed in an effort to catch the tug.

"Why are we moving so slow?" Ortega complained.

"We'll overshoot the tug if I go any faster," Fernando explained.

"Perhaps I should let Pedro do the flying," snarled Ortega, keeping his eyes trained on the water. "Shine the light out in front of the tug!"

Fernando did as he was told.

On the water below, the tug had lost speed, its driver throwing up his hands in frustration and directing a look of dejection at the aircraft above.

"They fouled her again!" Ortega raged in disbelief, his manner now making Fernando cringe. The searchlight revealed two dolphins below the waterline. Viciously, Ortega yanked the pin on another grenade, flinging it with all his might down into the ring of light. A string of ranting profanity left his lips as he awaited the four-second delay.

The sea abruptly bulged off the tug's bow, lifting the boat's keel at a rakish angle and throwing up a plume of spray. The four men aboard her went sprawling to the deck to keep from being tossed into the water. A moment passed before all four looked up in alarm at the chopper hovering overhead. Under the searchlight's glare, there was no mistaking the panic in their eyes.

"Play the light all around the tug!" Ortega bellowed.

Swinging the light to and fro, Fernando carried out the order.

Ortega's fit of rage escalated further when nothing showed under the beam. His tantrum was interrupted as the radio suddenly came alive with another call from the *San Carlo*.

"What is it?" Ortega screamed, disregarding radio protocol of any kind.

A short pause ensued before the voice coming through his headphones erupted frantically. "The *Aden* is leaving! The captain refuses to wait any longer!"

Ortega turned in his seat, ferreting out the freighter's dark bulk on the moonlit sea. Cursing vilely, he felt his anger soar to yet a new level.

Chapter 25

*R*aduyev moved as quickly as he dared, following the trail that would take him to his objective. Armed with a Kalashnikov he had taken from one of the dead soldiers, he was prepared to take on any resistance encountered. Having familiarized himself with the lay of the land during the past several months, he followed the moonlit footpath that wound its way through the treacherous karst, moving quickly and eventually reaching his destination without any major impediments or mishaps. He had left Ternier back at the lighthouse, unmoved by the man's shameful lamentations over the losses he had sustained.

Launching the Rodong was currently his only concern. Now that the H-bomb had been recovered and delivered, he was free to carry out the second phase of the mission. That had been the plan all along anyway, firing off the Rodong shortly after the high-yield nuclear weapon had been safely stowed aboard the *Spirit of Aden*. It had taken him and his men two months of backbreaking labor to chisel out another of the tunnels near the island's surface in order to make it large enough to accommodate the entire missile delivery system. With an overall length of nearly twelve meters and a diameter of 0.50 meters, the rocket also required a launching carriage that had been difficult to erect in the tunnel's limited space. Provided to Iran by way of Pyongyang, North Korea, the rocket was a smaller version of a standard Rodong missile, having been specially modified so that field assembly was possible. Nevertheless, hauling the various parts up from the submarine pen and putting the thing together had required endless hours of gut-wrenching toil.

Moving into an area of dense underbrush, Raduyev lifted several stones to reveal a metal box. He was the only person among his team who had knowledge of the device's location and operation. Inserting a key, he raised the lid on the box to reveal a small console with keypad, each of the keys glowing a soft red. The launch control was wireless, using a microwave pulse to engage the rocket engine and release the locking mechanism on the launching carriage. All that need be done was for him to punch in the 9-digit launch code to send the missile on its way. This particular Rodong had been specifically designed to carry a nuclear warhead with a destructive yield comparable to that used on Hiroshima. The missile would follow a flight path that had been hard-wired into its circuitry, flying a low-level trajectory over the ocean that would give it a limited profile on radar. Only when it neared Miami would it gain altitude to achieve an air burst for optimal effect.

Raduyev spun at the sound of movement behind him, grabbing for the Kalashnikov he had placed on the ground next to him.

"Do not attempt to fire the missile!" a voice scolded harshly.

Raduyev squinted his eyes, staring at the dark figure standing less than three meters away. It was Bashir.

"You are a pox on our people," Raduyev griped bitterly, "but you will foil me no more, for I am sending you to hell where you belong." With those words, he pulled the Kalashnikov's trigger to be rid of Bashir once and for all.

Raduyev's eyes widened when the weapon failed to fire. Cursing, he threw it down and rose to his feet, drawing the Bowie knife he carried rather than the Browning holstered at his side. "I have had enough of you," he hissed hatefully, preparing to leap at his former teammate. But before he could do so, several more figures joined Bashir's steadfast form.

The first tendrils of dawn were beginning to break, and within the gathering light Raduyev perceived a face he had not seen before, though it was similar to that of the accursed dolphin girl who also stood next to Bashir.

"These angels suppress the firing of your weapon, just as they will keep the Rodong from launching," Bashir said calmly.

Raduyev shifted his eyes to the last person to join the trio, and his expression turned even more hateful. "I enjoyed killing your friend, the little Zionist pig," Raduyev taunted, managing to fill his voice with a smugness he did not feel as he stared at the firearm trained on him.

Jake Javolyn stared back with the look of a predator, his eyes the harbingers of death as his finger rested coldly on the Stoner's trigger.

Raduyev gazed down the barrel of the weapon, his expression turning scornful. "You disappoint me, Javolyn. I had always thought you to be a warrior, but now I see you for the coward you truly are."

Javolyn met the challenge, crouching down to pull his K-bar from its scabbard as he set the Stoner aside. "Let's forego the small talk, Yeslam, and get to the thing we both want. Only this time you won't have the opportunity of resorting to your most noteworthy talent, going for your opponent's back when he least expects it."

"No, Jay Jay!" Destiny pleaded. "Don't do this!"

Amphitrite placed a hand on Destiny's shoulder. "The quarrel between these men cannot be avoided, my daughter. To interfere may have disastrous consequences."

Raduyev let go with a mocking laugh. "Yes, do not try to save this man. To do so will only bring Allah's wrath upon you."

Jake stepped in front of Destiny, careful to keep his eyes locked on the Chechen. "Please take your daughter away from here," he said, directing the request at Amphitrite.

Raduyev continued to mock, his voice taking on a crazed lilt. "What happens here will not matter. Allah has given his true believers a weapon forged by the very hands of his greatest enemy." He laughed insanely. "I find it humorous that the Great Satan will ultimately be smitten by his own creation."

Something buzzed sharply in the distance, making Raduyev whirl to follow the sound. The noise rose and fell like that of a chainsaw working its way through tough oak. He stared aghast as his eyes fell on the source in the dawn twilight. Two miles out to sea a broken laser beam of red light lanced down on the Aden. He knew what he was seeing, and a feeling of utter failure suddenly took hold of him. The Yemeni freighter was being pelted unmercifully, a hail of deadly rounds raining down upon it. Even from where he stood, he could see a portion of the lethal enfilade caroming off the ship's deck and superstructure with incredible ferocity.

The tracers abruptly stopped, and in the sky just above the freighter he saw Ortega's chopper turn, coming around for another strafing run.

"This cannot be happening," Raduyev screamed incredulously, but he gathered himself in quickly, placing glowering eyes back on Jake.

An expansive grin spread across Jake's face; he was truly enjoying the Chechen's alarm and he could not resist goading him further. "I see you and your Colombian buddy are having a little lover's spat."

The buzzing started up again. In the distance, the chopper recommenced its attack, sending another stream of tracers angling down on the freighter. The aircraft appeared like a tiny gnat buzzing angrily over a potential host as it poured the full power of its Gatling gun into the target below. The broken laser remained focused on the ship for a good four seconds before the gun stopped firing. A flash of bright light suddenly lit up the sea as the Aden's aft section flared with the intensity of an exploding nova.

Jake threw another barb at Raduyev. "Could it be your Allah does not approve of your plan?"

Raduyev turned back to his sworn enemy with savage loathing. "You are a dead man!" Screaming out the words, he lunged, thrusting the Bowie forward with deadly intent.

The explosion knocked the Aden's captain off his feet as though he had been back-kicked by a mule. Stunned though he was, he vaguely sensed the deck of the bridge begin to tilt, and he knew at once that at least one of the rounds had found the concealed explosives contained aboard his ship.

He had picked up the explosives in Kingston, loading them onto the freighter's back deck in three large shipping containers. Each container had been crammed with two hundred packing crates labeled Jamaican rum, half of which were filled with dynamite and aluminum powder. The explosives had been destined for various Iranian-sponsored insurgents operating in Iraq and were to be used in building IEDs, improvised explosive devices aimed at killing American troops.

Dazedly, the captain struggled to his feet, aware that his ship was going down. Lying next to him was the decapitated body of the ship's steersman, pulsing spurts of blood continuing to gush from where the man's neck had been severed. This made it difficult to move along the angled deck, for he kept slipping in the gore as it flowed down the sloped surface. Abruptly, his eyes fell upon another ghastly sight. The shredded corpse of his first mate lay near the rear of the bridge, his body torn apart beyond recognition by shattered Plexiglas.

On all sides of him the windows along the bridge had been blown out, and as he grabbed one of the frames for support, he saw several survivors of his crew leap overboard to get clear of the ship. He nearly lost his balance as the freighter began to lean more acutely, and as he glanced astern, he could now see the ship's aft section slipping below the waves.

Drowning at sea had always been his greatest fear, and he wondered why Allah had allowed him to survive both the machine gun fire and the force of the ensuing blast if he was ultimately going to submerge with his ship. Perhaps he was not meant to drown after all. Perhaps God wanted him to live to continue fighting the infidels. Maybe he should make an effort not to perish.

The inane little grin that began to form on his face immediately turned to shock as he reached out to pull himself clear of the doorway. His left arm was gone. Dully, he stared at the bloody stump, a short, jagged section of upper humerus protruding meekly from his shoulder.

Using what little strength remained within him, he managed to get through the doorway as the deck canted further. The ship was sinking rapidly now, and he did not want it to become his final resting place. As water rose up around his knees, he looked back at the nearby island and stared entranced, somehow finding beauty in what he saw. The dawn sun had just cleared the ocean and was bathing the plateau of the nearby island in an unearthly golden light, provoking the moisture from the recent rains into a rising mist of silent splendor.

And then something truly glorious caught his eyes. A spectacular rainbow was gathering rapidly within the mist, forming a breathtaking tapestry of vivid hues that bridged the karst jutting from the sea. With his legs beginning to buckle beneath him, he knew he was now too weak to jump clear of the ship. In an effort to comfort himself, he kept his gaze locked on the beautiful image as his head slipped below the water.

Jake was surprised at how fast Yeslam moved. He had never been impressed with the Chechen's speed, having had numerous occasions during Seal training to get a firsthand look at the man's mediocre quickness. But as his nemesis came at him, he saw no hint of the former clumsiness his opponent had once exhibited.

Raduyev slashed out, nearly catching Jake's shoulder with the edge of the blade. Jake sidestepped the frontal attack, circling to his right and opening up some distance between them. With the ease of a juggler, the Chechen tossed the Bowie to his left hand and lunged again, his arm fully extended like that of a graceful fencer. Jake leaned back, parrying the blade away before the tip could rip into his face.

Backing away, Jake noted the demented expression Raduyev wore. The Bowie flashed once more as the Chechen shifted it smoothly back to his right hand. A break in the thicket behind Raduyev gave Jake a clear view of the ocean, and he could now see that the freighter had completely vanished from sight. Here was the distraction he needed that would provide an opening to his enemy's most vulnerable area, that being his ego.

"Your mission has fallen apart," Jake chided. "Your crew neutralized, your ship sinking." He let out a chortle designed to needle. "A befitting end to a terrible leader, wouldn't you say?"

Raduyev's eyes blazed with pent up rage. "An infidel is no match for a true servant of Allah," he hissed, spittle flying from his lips, "one the Almighty sees as his most cherished warrior."

Jake snickered again. "Maybe…" He circled to his left. "And then again, maybe not. But unfortunately, all I see is a coward standing before me, a man without a shred of honor."

Raduyev's glare deepened into one of the cruelest caricatures Jake had ever seen, and he began flicking the Bowie rapidly between hands. The blade he wielded was longer than the K-bar by a good four inches.

"After I kill you, these women will become my slaves to do with as I please," the Chechen blustered. Intent on antagonizing Javolyn further, he let his eyes rove obscenely over Destiny and Amphitrite, producing a grin charged with lasciviousness. "I am sure they will give me many nights of pleasure." He feinted to his left at this last provocation, only to leap back to his right to execute a backhanded swipe with the blade's cutting edge. The knife grazed Jake's jumpsuit along the chest, tearing open the fabric.

Raduyev's maneuver provided Jake with the opening he had been looking for. In a flash, he slipped in close to his opponent, digging the K-bar deep into the Chechen's left bicep. Raduyev let out a howl, leaping back in startled amazement at how quickly Jake had been able to penetrate his guard.

"That one's compliments of Tesha," Jake harried in an even tone. "You remember Tesha, don't you?"

The Chechen glanced at his bicep, surprised at the blood. When he looked back at Jake, his eyes revealed a dampening bravado. With his confidence now compromised, he was not so eager to take the offensive.

Jake danced to his right. "And I'm sure you haven't forgotten-" Suddenly lunging forward, he jabbed the K-bar high with blinding speed, only to go low in a blur of motion. He withdrew before the Chechen had a chance to counter, completing the sentence as he did so. "-Captain Sheridan."

Stunned by the swiftness of movement, it took Raduyev a moment to comprehend his right thigh had been stabbed. He howled again as the pain caught up with his surprise.

Jake narrowed his eyes gravely, preparing to inflict more punishment, but the sound of the Bell Ranger's Minigun stopped him. Seeing that Raduyev was temporarily hobbled, he risked a peek out to sea. Ortega's chopper was flying low over the water less than a thousand meters away, its weapon blazing furiously as it raked the ocean beneath it.

Standing further back from where Jake stood, Destiny let out a shrill cry. "No!"

Jake winced, bringing his free hand to his head. A sharp sting echoed at the back of his mind as though his brain had been ripped asunder.

Gripped by a sudden bout of nausea, his legs wobbled unsteadily under him.

Ortega looked down at the water in a peeved manner. "I think you could have done a better job," he said angrily, his eyes suddenly shifting to the man sitting in the seat next to him.

"At its highest rate, this type of weapon will automatically kick out of firing mode after a four second burst," Fernando tried explaining. "It's a built-in safety feature to prevent the barrels from melting."

Ortega kept his gaze riveted on the pilot a moment longer before taking inventory of the ocean below. "Your accuracy is what puzzles me. I think you were purposely trying to miss the targets."

Fernando swallowed hard. "I destroyed the freighter. What difference will it make if I failed to hit one of those creatures?"

The Colombian's eyes continued to scan the water. It was possible Fernando might have gotten one of those white dolphins, a smaller one at that. He had seen the tracers kick up a spume close to the creature when it had surfaced, but then the shots had gone wide. He was getting strange vibes from Fernando, reading something in the man's manner to suggest he didn't like doing this.

"Take us back to the ship," Ortega growled hotly.

Fernando nudged the cyclic over, banking the chopper in the direction of the *San Carlo*. Farther away, two other vessels were moving toward it. Both of its sister ships, the *San Diablo* and *San Pinto* were coming fast to join her.

Chapter 26

*D*estiny saw Jake suddenly reel, fighting for breath. She knew the cause. Her mental link with the dolphins had inexplicably come flickering back, and for one brief instant she had felt Achilles' pain. A round from the helicopter had punctured the young albino's right lung. The impenetrable barrier Achilles had erected earlier had come crashing down with the injury, reopening the strange connection the dolphin shared with his human counterpart.

As if in a dream, Destiny watched as Raduyev limped cautiously toward the man she loved, the Bowie knife clutched firmly in his hand. Inexorably bonded to the pod's youngest member, Jake was feeling the full brunt of Achilles' agony as if it were his own, and it was now obvious to Raduyev that his enemy was caught in the grip of some mysterious seizure.

Without giving it much thought, Destiny picked up the machine gun Jake had set aside on the ground, bringing the barrel to bear on Raduyev before he could use the knife. "Stop!" she cried.

The Chechen halted, surprised to see the weapon trained on him.

Destiny waved the gun. "Get away from him!"

Raduyev turned petitioning eyes to Bashir as Jake took in several ragged breaths. "This girl is no more an angel than I am an infidel," he implored. "If she were truly one of Allah's angels, she would have no use of man-made weapons."

Bashir appeared unmoved by the Chechen's entreaty. "Do not attempt to seek my support, Yeslam. I am only committed to those who are righteous."

Destiny stepped closer to the Chechen, pointing the Stoner threateningly. "Back away!"

Raduyev searched Destiny's face for several seconds more before complying, faltering on his injured leg as he moved backward with a contemptible sneer plastered on his face.

Amphitrite stepped to her daughter's side. "We must hurry if we are to save Achilles."

"Go without me, mother," Destiny said. "I'll stay here with Jay Jay."

Amphitrite seemed reluctant to leave, but Bashir intervened before she could contest the matter. "God go with you, Mother Angel!" he urged. "I will remain here with Destiny." He pointed behind Amphitrite and spoke quickly. "You will find a footpath over there that winds its way down through the thorn bush. It will take you to a small ledge where you can dive down into the sea. It is the fastest route to the water."

Anxiety grew on Amphitrite's face as Jake's labored breathing echoed Achilles' distress. She could not delay any longer. "Stay safe, my daughter!" she intoned, turning to take the path behind her at a run.

Destiny moved to Jake's side, continuing to keep the Stoner leveled at Raduyev. Jake had fallen to one knee, his pallor waxen in the light of dawn. Hefting the bulky firearm as best she could with one arm, she placed a hand on his head, attempting to break the bridge connecting him with the young albino. It was no use. She needed oneness with the others in order to accomplish this, and that had all but deserted her.

Raduyev tittered raucously. "So the mighty Javolyn requires the protection of a woman." He kept up his scornful chortle, continuing to back away slowly, grimacing each time he placed weight on the injured leg.

Bashir suddenly shouted. "Keep away from the-"

Destiny spun to see why Bashir had fallen silent. The Palestinian crashed to the ground in a heap. Before she could grasp what had happened, the Stoner was yanked forcefully from her hands.

Destiny stifled a scream. Ternier loomed above her, his eyes bulging as if they would start from his head. Dangling from his neck was the trinket previously worn by Erzulie, the charm blackened almost beyond recognition.

The Colonel stepped away from Destiny, setting his gaze upon Raduyev. "There is nothing to stop you now," he grunted hoarsely. "Send off the missile!"

Raduyev smiled victoriously, limping the remaining ten feet to the launch control. Within seconds, he punched in the numbers that would fire the Rodong. Completing the task, he looked back at Destiny, his laughter causing shivers to go cascading along her bones.

"How long?" Ternier demanded, his voice cutting into Raduyev's glee like the sharpened edge of a knife.

The Chechen stopped his laughter, his mirth changing over to annoyance. "The Rodong's computer must first go through a pre-launch initiation sequence."

"I care nothing for explanations," Ternier roared. "How long?"

"Three minutes!" Raduyev grunted. His eyes abruptly darted to Javolyn like those of an anaconda ready to feast, and he tested the edge of his Bowie with his thumb. "You can have the girl," he said coldly, "but Javolyn is mine."

As the Bell Ranger headed for the *San Carlo*'s helipad, something made Ortega look back at the sea behind him. "Abort the landing!" he shouted excitedly. "Bring us around!"

Fernando followed the order, banking the chopper hard to port.

Ortega pointed wildly. At least nine albino dolphins were converging on the area of sea where Fernando had last fired the guns. Drawing closer to the creatures, more fins could be seen knifing the water.

The Colombian squinted hard. A huge congregation of gray bottlenose dolphins was now visible. "Fire the gun down into that pack!"

"The gun is empty," Fernando said. "We expended all the rounds."

"Show me!" Ortega demanded, staring over at Fernando suspiciously.

Fernando thumbed the firing button on the cyclic stick. On the chopper's port side, the Minigun barrels became blurs of spinning motion, failing to discharge a single round.

Ortega slammed a fist into the control console, his face painted in livid murderous rage.

Fernando spoke quickly, his voice tense as his boss reached for another grenade. "Why kill them when you have the chance to catch the ones with hands. Wouldn't it be better to have the *San Diablo* and *San Pinto* deploy their nets?"

Ortega hesitated, giving the suggestion some thought before shaking his head. "No! The white ones are too fast and far too smart to be trapped."

"Look there!" Fernando pointed out hurriedly. "They're keeping a small one from sinking. If they don't swim away, you'll have enough time to surround them." He pointed again at an adjacent area of sea where a furious jumble of whitewater roiled the water. "And you've got tuna as an added bonus."

Ortega fingered the grenade's pull ring as he watched the scene below. The water appeared stained with blood where a group of white dolphins lingered. Within their midst, a smaller one was being kept afloat. "Alright," he finally begrudged reluctantly, placing the grenade back in its box. "Perhaps coming away from here with live specimens is not such a bad idea."

Keying the mike, Ortega hailed the other ships, giving them precise instructions.

Even in the midst of his pain, Achilles heard Amphitrite's urgent call. *Hold on, young one, do not be afraid. We will bring you back to full rejuvenation.*

With his physical existence now fragile and slipping slowly from him, Achilles answered. *I only fear for Jay Jay.*

Your bond with him has become a liability, Amphitrite replied. *Jay Jay has become debilitated by your suffering.*

Achilles felt his body being lifted to the surface. Natalie was supporting him. Coral and Reef were next to her. Nevertheless, he would require either Destiny or her mother to bring the pod's mental energy into full focus. Destiny, he knew, was more adept at this sort of thing than Amphitrite, but something in Destiny's psyche had changed to deflect his sense of her.

And something within himself had also changed, something that was affecting the others as well. He could not explain it. He only knew it was time to take an aggressive stand against the forces confronting his species if they were going to survive and propagate.

They had resources at their disposal with which to fight back. Their very intelligence could be used as a weapon. Through Jay Jay they had learned of the iniquitous human alliances that had come to the island, a brittle union of differing motivations and ideologies held together by threads of greed, power, and hate. Driving a wedge of distrust between the parties had been easy enough. Strangely, the whales had willingly lent their support. And now there were other things they could put to good use.

There was heartfelt emotion tied into this new perspective, an emerging side of him he never knew existed. Fully surrendering to this emotion went not without inherent risks, however, for he was vaguely aware of the negative consequences that might come of it. A gleaning of intuition suddenly accompanied his pain, and he immediately understood why he had lost all sense of Destiny. She had fallen prey to the same emotion, and in so doing her purity had been contaminated.

Help me to journey into myself, Achilles cried out, *for that is the only way I can bring Destiny back to us.*

Amphitrite's essence reached out to him. *Always remember to cast away the illusion of separation, little one. Only in unison can we attain the higher self, the very power to manipulate the earth's illusion.*

Comforted by these thoughts, Achilles felt his pain diminish. Before him lay the same rainbow presented to Jay Jay, a thing with no distinct location nor distance. And yet, paradoxically, it gave him direction.

Chapter 27

*J*ake gasped, once again able to breath. The strange debilitation gripping him suddenly vanished as quickly as it had come, and before him he perceived the multi-hued band of light arching away from the darkness.

It was then he became aware of the voice echoing across the cosmos. Achilles was calling out to him. *You must hasten to follow the rainbow, Jay Jay. Merge with it and drink of its energy.*

Sensing the urgency in the words, Jake felt himself catching up to the leading light waves pulsating between galaxies. Without knowing why, he instinctively sensed the thing rushing up from the black void to intercept him even before he recognized the danger. Abruptly, he rolled left, letting the surge of energy carry him beyond the glint.

Coming back to his feet he saw Raduyev before him, the Chechen's face twisted into an emblem of hatred. Thrown off balance by Jake's sudden dodge, the man's eyes bulged in disbelief as his Bowie only met air.

"Kill him already!" Ternier screamed in annoyance, continuing to hold onto Destiny with one hand. "He has no weapon."

Jake found the K-bar to be missing from his hand. His knife lay on the ground near Raduyev's feet.

Emboldened by his unarmed opponent, Raduyev eyed Jake disdainfully, his need to destroy prompting him to ignore his injured leg. "You are weak, infidel," he sneered. He reached down quickly to pick up the K-bar. "Does Allah's chosen one make you tremble so much that you cannot hold onto your weapon?"

Jake circled left, awaiting another lunge by the Chechen. Armed with a blade in each hand, Raduyev was now twice as dangerous. But the Islamist was not so eager to rush in this time, holding back and looking for the right moment to make his move.

"Kill him!" Ternier bellowed impatiently. "Kill him or I will shoot him down from here."

"No!" Destiny cried, suddenly turning on Ternier with liquid eyes and clawing at his face with both hands.

Three times larger than the diminutive girl, Ternier sent her sprawling to the ground with a vicious backhand. Stunned by the blow, Destiny lay dazed at his feet, blood trickling from her mouth.

Out of the corner of his eye Jake saw what Ternier had done, and in that instant his rage detonated like a megaton bomb. Disregarding Raduyev completely, he bit back a silent oath and leapt at the powerful Haitian before the Colonel had a chance to react. In the span of a millisecond, he exploded across the four meters separating him from Ternier, his legs seemingly energized by something beyond his comprehension. Caught by sheer surprise at the bold move, Ternier's jaw hung agape in frozen astonishment just as the heel of Jake's right foot slammed him full in the face. Tumbled from his feet by the force of the blow, the Colonel still managed to pull back on the Stoner's trigger. Flames belched from the muzzle, stabbing up into Jake's chest.

In that instant, time came to a standstill and a multitude of voices resounded in Jake's head, but the words came to him as one compressed thought rather than a chorus. *Do not let the darkness deceive your senses, Jay Jay, for it will lead you to foolish presumption.* The words were familiar, he had heard them before. Swept along the rainbow's curve, he glimpsed the same dodecahedron he had seen in the dream as the voices continued to indoctrinate. *Unconditional love is the one true component of all reality, Jay Jay. We give it to you freely, enabling you to see beyond the physical deceptions that trick the unenlightened senses. It is your shield of invincibility. You must cast aside all doubts that you can survive this moment.*

Jake sensed the entire pod behind these thoughts, each separate creature merging to join as one unified higher self, and in that instant he fully understood the truth. The power behind all creation could be his if he gave up the illusion of separation.

A sense of exhilaration washed over him at this discovery, immunizing him from the physical and social forces of the universe. It was a state of omnipotence, cleansing and coming easily to him, for he had never let a fear of death govern his actions. It was this state of oneness with the others that freed him, keeping him from presupposing one's separate physical existence to be the ultimate reality. And by consciously living the illusion, he now had the power to manipulate it.

Joined with the others, Jake stared directly into the Stoner's barrel and smiled. Time had stopped, holding back the flame leaping from the muzzle. He could not be touched.

A look of incredulity transcended Ternier's face as he continued to press down on the trigger. "Why will you not die?" he screamed.

"Maybe your aim is off," Jake growled. Stepping in close to where the man lay, he reached down with one hand and tore the firearm from Ternier's grasp. The Colonel offered little resistance, his expression still dumbstruck. Rearing back, Jake came down hard with the weapon, cracking it butt-first into Ternier's forehead and opening a huge gash. Ternier's arms fell limply to each side, his eyes glazed and frozen in a vacant comatose stare.

Whirling back around, Jake locked eyes with Raduyev. The Islamist appeared white as a ghost. "This fantasy of yours to take over the world has become tiresome," he announced calmly, training the Stoner on the Chechen.

Though seemingly still dazed, Destiny rose to stand beside Jake. "He's punched in the launch code to the missile," she fretted. "It will launch in less than three minutes."

Jake stared stonily at his enemy. "I'll only ask you once to stop this missile from firing." In his tone was the unmistakable promise of death.

Raduyev forced a haughty grin. "It is too late for that. Once the code has been fed to the Rodong, it cannot be stopped."

"Then you leave me only one choice."

The Chechen let out a tense, strained laugh. "And what choice is that?" he asked gruffly.

Jake's reply was caustic. "Sending you off to your mentor the devil."

At seeing the look on Jake's face, a rabid animal growl left the Chechen's lips, escalating into a deep throaty rumble. But even before he could spring in a last-ditch effort to save himself, Jake turned the Stoner loose. The torrent of bullets flashed across the short space separating the two men and flung Raduyev backwards, nearly cutting him in half.

Destiny looked away as Jake pumped one final burst into the Chechen's fallen corpse. Releasing the trigger, Jake stared down at Raduyev's remains and spat. "Consider your debt to Myers paid in full," he muttered quietly.

A sudden groan caused Jake to look behind him. Destiny was kneeling at Bashir's side, cradling his head as he came around. "Are you able to stand, Bashir?" she asked.

Bashir rubbed the back of his head, attempting to rise on unsteady feet. Destiny rose with him, lending support. "What has happened?" he rasped.

"You were struck from behind," the girl said tenderly, her voice edged with concern. "Do you know how to keep the missile from launching?" she went on hurriedly, knowing time was running out.

Bashir continued to rub his head, shifting his eyes to where the missile control box lay. "Yeslam is the only one who has such knowledge."

Jake quickly interceded. "Where's the missile located?"

The Palestinian's eyes fell on Raduyev's riddled body. "About 200 meters from here."

Jake grabbed Destiny by the arm. He had felt the pod's collective mind, now fully aware of what was possible. "You can stop it," he encouraged. "You are the lens through which the others can focus."

Destiny stared back morosely, all traces of the self-assured optimism she had shown him in the past now gone. "Something has happened to me, Jay Jay." Her eyes were wet with moisture, sending forth a frustrated dribbling of tears. "I can't feel the others."

This was not what Jake wanted to hear. Millions of people were about to die.

Chapter 28

*D*estiny affixed Jay Jay with helpless eyes. By falling in love, she knew she had compromised herself. The emotion was unyielding in the way it tugged at her, drawing forth a selfishness within her she never knew existed. Her need to prevent Jay Jay's death had caused her to neglect the others. And even worse, she now realized she had broken the cardinal tenet instilled in her by her mother. She had fallen victim to doubt by presuming the future might actually be unalterable. There was a foolish side to presuming, for it had a self-fulfilling power. The painting back in the Gaia cave was the cause of this. She had inadvertently let her mind wander over unfamiliar terrain, an area of the psyche where pessimism abounded. She had become infected with a belief that perhaps Jay Jay's prophesized death was permanently etched into the fabric of space-time, an inevitable occurrence destined to be unpreventable. And it was this that had brought on the fear. With her mind shackled by it, she had lost her sense of the others.

"You've got to try," Jake urged, gently wiping away the tears that marred her face. "Nothing is impossible. You were the one who taught me that."

Destiny stared hard into his eyes. She could see why Achilles had taken to him so readily. In many ways, the two of them were very much alike. Both were fearless, filled with a natural unstoppable energy that sought to challenge danger at every turn, particularly when the danger emanated from some iniquitous source seeking to mete out injustice and misery. And like his bond-mate, the young albino was now determined to fight back, tenaciously lashing out at evil in an effort to rid the earth of such influence.

Bashir stood nearby, watching Destiny closely. "Allah has given you purpose, my angel. With his power behind you, it is not possible for you to fail."

Something within Destiny began to ease as she pondered this, and she realized the threads of fear that had grounded her in the earth's illusion were beginning to break. Letting out a deep breath she relaxed her mind, feeling the last tendrils of dread escape her.

"I know you can do this if you try," Jake reiterated.

"Trying will not be enough, Jay Jay," she said, her tone harboring pessimism. "Doing will be the only thing that matters."

"Then we will do!" Jake declared. "We will do it together."

Destiny felt herself smiling. She was drawing strength from the way he was looking at her.

Turning to gaze out to sea, Destiny realized others had come into the clearing now. Samuel and his mother, Louwanda, had ascended from the caverns below. She recognized other faces. Most belonged to those abducted from Malique, but among them were two that had abetted Raduyev. One was the man with the bloodhound eyes she had seen down in the caverns, the one called Gullu. Kalid was with him.

Jake started, his eyes darkening as they fell on the two bearded men, and he immediately raised the Stoner, prepared to use it once again.

Destiny grabbed his wrist, her grip surprisingly strong. "It's alright, Jay Jay," she assuaged gently. "These men are not a danger."

"You don't understand," he snapped sharply. He pointed the Stoner accusingly at Sherkhan, not daring to take his eyes from the man. "That one cannot be trusted."

Destiny continued to hold his wrist. "Please, Jay Jay."

Sherkhan separated himself from the milling group, moving off to one side of the clearing where no one else stood. Humbly he faced Jake, his arms drooped resignedly at his sides. "I deserve to die," he said softly, sorrowfully. His manner was remorseful, the embodiment of decisive repentance, and he seemed fully prepared for Jake to kill him. "Not only have I betrayed you and your brothers, but I have also betrayed Islam."

Jake's frosty glare fell away, changing over into a mystified frown. He felt strangely defused by the man standing before him. Surely such a show could not possibly be contrived. Sherkhan's eyes were pathetically rheumy, holding back a flood of unshed tears, and within them Jake sensed the cloud of tragedy. He turned to Destiny, aware of the depth of empathy gathering on her face as she clutched his wrist beseechingly. The grudge he held for the man suddenly seemed insignificant when weighed against what was currently at stake, a thing of infinitely greater importance.

Slowly, he lowered the Stoner, lucidly aware that something within himself had changed, though he couldn't quite pinpoint what it was that now took away his desire for vengeance. Perhaps it had something to do with his interaction with Destiny and the pod, or maybe it was his exposure to their fabulous but cryptic art. By all counts, Sherkhan should pay for his involvement in Myer's death. But within Sherkhan's sorrowful eyes he sensed a crushing despondency, as though some terrible calamity had left the man bereft of loved ones, an extortion of the man's very soul that had caused him to do what he had done. In that twinkling of circumspection, something glimmered vibrantly in one of the back corridors of his mind, and he suddenly saw the pathos behind the man's actions. And with this newfound gleaning he was now convinced Sherkhan had undergone the same transformation as Bashir. The dolphin art affected each person differently, and for some it was able to lift away the shell of the outer persona, revealing the true nature that lay beneath.

Jake met Destiny's earnest stare and gave her a reassuring smile, inwardly ashamed of his brief display of madness. Time was running out. "We've got a missile to stop," he reminded her.

Destiny let go of Jake's wrist and read the faces milling all about her. She had become the focal point of all gazes. Raising her voice, she said, "I'm going to need everyone's help."

"Whatever you ask!" Bashir blurted.

Destiny took a deep breath. "I need everyone to concentrate, to focus your thoughts on one thing."

Those around her began to nod and smile in acquiescence, but it was Bashir who clarified what remained to be said. "A missile is going to launch at any moment, people. We will all carry out God's will by stopping it."

Bashir turned his gaze back to Destiny, presenting her with an encouraging grin. Destiny studied the Palestinian, amazed that he somehow understood what had to be done. Almost at once, a sense of the pod returned, an eager cacophonous buzz resounding in her head.

I am here for you, my daughter.

I, too, Natalie called.

We are with you. It was Coral and Reef.

Our minds will become one, Hermes and Aphrodite intoned.

Let the essence of our thoughts merge into something greater, Apollo and Artemis droned.

Ride my mind and spirit as you ride my back, Hercules rumbled.

As one, all things are possible, echoed Thetis.

We are guardians of the earth's fate, Athena stressed.

And then a twelfth voice nudged her. *Be not without hope, girl, for crystal rain can fall from the darkest clouds.* It was the voice of Jacob. He was reminding her about a passage taken from the writings of Nizami, an ancient Persian poet. There was always hope, even in the darkest hours of adversity.

A multitude of other cetacean voices joined in, soaring into a wondrous heavenly chorus. Like wisps of unyielding love, these various sentiences intertwined and blended, reaching out and latching onto Destiny's central core. Jay Jay was with her, and so was Bashir. Both human and delphine merged, with all distinctions beginning to blur. Slowly, they began to rotate around her, quickly gaining momentum and coalescing into a whirling mass of pure energy.

Intruding its way into this growing collective mind was a growing roar, and in that moment the higher self knew the missile had launched.

In unity with the all, the mind reached out to transcend space and time. Catching a limpid glimpse of her essence at the center of this maelstrom of swirling energy, Destiny's spirit suddenly quailed, gasping out in alarm. Achilles was missing from the whirlpool. And without the young albino, the higher mind, though powerful, would lack sufficient potency to stop the inevitable.

Destiny let out a lamenting cry, unable to focus. *Where are you, my Achilles?* Already she could feel the vortex beginning to dissipate in faltering disarray. Distraught by the mounting fear within her, she called out to him again. *Answer me, Achilles!*

Time hung still as Destiny listened. The roar of the rocket engine clashed discordantly against the rustle of cosmic wind, a foreordained tolling of physical death to those who understood the foreboding sound. Fear was her only enemy now, a thing without form or substance, and yet a formidable antagonist, nevertheless. If she let it, fear would bring on the destruction of millions. Failing to conquer it meant doom to innocents. Once again she was letting fear influence her actions. Once again, she was letting it dictate the fate of the world.

No! she screamed out defiantly, but even then she felt restrained, aware that her protest lacked the conviction to snap the chains of dread. The fear assailed her with a sharp insistent tug, storming her very will, and pulled to the very brink of panic she cried out again. *I will not let you rule me!* But she had great difficulty in throwing forth this singular thought and it oozed out of her slowly as though her mind were mired down in a thick slurry of suppressive mud.

In desperation Destiny barely pulled herself free and focused with renewed intensity, more determined than ever to gather in the eddy of swirling energy. And though it stabilized, instinctively she knew it would not be enough.

But the entities within the vortex rallied her, shouting out in one voice, giving her strength. *We love you, Destiny. We love you as we love one another. Love is the greatest power of all, for herein lies the power to create the highest good, the very power of God. Together we are one, a consciousness that cannot be conquered.*

Destiny harkened the words, letting the energy build. And yet she knew it would not be enough. Twelve key entities were now in place, each positioned on a separate plane of the dodecahedron. But a thirteenth would be needed to accomplish fruition, an entity of absolute purpose. This was something her mother had fathomed long ago from staring into the amulet's crystal, the rule of sacred geometry discovered by the ancients.

A vague presence suddenly entered Destiny's thoughts, a benign splinter of the mind she had often felt from time to time. But now the presence had a face. It was a coffee face, a face that bespoke of the Caribbean. It was a face with wide cheeks and twinkling eyes, a face that teemed with unblemished compassion. All her life she had seen the face, for Jacob had always displayed it in a black-and-white photograph he kept in a glass frame hanging from his cottage wall. It was the face of Esmerelda, Jacob's grandmother, a renowned vaudun priestess.

The face smiled tenderly, radiating a profound kindness. *We have come a long way, my child, and the time is now upon us. Unforeseen circumstances often arise when we stand against evil, sometimes taking those we love on to the next realm of existence.* Esmerelda's spirit sighed deeply, forcing a pinwheel of stars to go spiraling away in the cosmic breeze. *Put your sadness at rest, sweet girl. The Supreme Oneness deems it necessary to intervene. The one you seek is reprieved from moving on, though it is uncertain how long this will last.*

Destiny remained transfixed, trying to find meaning in the words as the face of Esmerelda faded to mist.

And then another spoke in a voice that resonated across infinity. *All that I am is yours,* it said. *Let us create the reality of our choosing.*

Overcome with elation, Destiny recognized the essence behind the voice. Achilles had come to join her. A flame of comprehension suddenly entered her mind. The young albino had sacrificed himself so that Jay Jay could live. And then he had sought refuge somewhere deep inside her, helping her to overcome her fear. Using her as a medium, he had rallied the others into a collective force, allowing Jay Jay to defeat both Ternier and Raduyev.

With Achilles' essence now poised to take them through the dimensional gap, she pressed the cosmic trigger. Almost at once, the maelstrom of coalescing energy imploded, channeling its way through Destiny's being in one explosive, unstoppable surge. And then she knew the missile was no more, its streaking mass vanishing into a singularity on the far side of the universe.

Chapter 29

Climbing from the chopper's copilot seat, Ortega stared at the sky above Navassa Island and frowned. He had seen the missile rise up from the island's surface, only to disappear as if it had never existed. He tried to make sense of what he had just witnessed. The thing had literally shrunk in on itself, the roar of its engine suddenly cutting out. Only a vapor trail remained in the morning sky, and now even that was slowly dissipating out over the sea as though the event had never occurred.

No matter, he thought. For whatever reasons, it was really a blessing in disguise that the missile had failed. Provoking the Americans would have brought too much scrutiny into this region, especially with Ternier wanting to fuel another civil war in Haiti. Though getting involved with the man called Omar had been a mistake, there was the chance he might actually come away from all this with far more than he had originally envisioned. For it seemed that treasures awaited him at every turn.

Still puzzled by the strange event, Ortega pondered his next move. His first priority was to capture as many of those extraordinary white dolphins as he could lay hands on. Already the seines of all three vessels were being deployed, and it would only be a matter of time before he had a sizable contingent of specimens caught up in the nets. From his vantage point up on the *San Carlo's* helipad, he had a clear view of the surrounding sea. Less than two hundred meters from where he stood, he could see several of these incredible creatures floating stationary on the surface, including the small one Fernando had nailed from the air. And if his eyes were not deceiving him, he was certain he had spotted a human female riding a gray one.

This time he would make sure the girl stayed captured. Turning, he impaled Fernando with a nasty glare. "I want this bird refueled and ready to go in the next few minutes. Make sure the gun magazine is fully loaded this time."

Assisted by several crew members, Fernando avoided meeting Ortega's eyes. "I'm moving as quickly as I can, boss," he said appeasingly.

"A snail moves faster," Ortega admonished sharply, his lips curling cruelly. He watched Fernando closely for the next several minutes, making sure the tasks were carried out.

Ortega shifted his attention to the *San Carlo's* tug. Though it was now operable again, he had lost yet another crewman. The diver Omar had placed aboard the tug had been the cause of it. At seeing the destruction of the freighter, the diver had turned on the tug's crew, stabbing one of them to death. Luckily, the two remaining men had reacted fast enough to kill the diver before they suffered the same fate.

As he thought about this, his eyes caught sight of bubbles breaking the ocean surface directly off the *San Carlo's* port side. Probably coming up from the freighter he had sunk.

Disregarding the bubbling water, he entertained himself with visions of all the riches awaiting him. Under the island was a large cache of gold, or so he had been led to believe. And he had not forgotten the stack of boxes Omar had turned over to the Colonel. All of these things he would take for himself once he finished this business with the dolphins.

And then there was the other hoard of gold back in that cove he had raided. He had learned enough from the dolphin hunters to know what those pieces of hardware were used for. The smaller device was a sending unit, while the larger one was a receiver that tracked the coordinates emitted by the sender. He had seen the text message on the receiver, and on it was a mention of gold, including the geodetic coordinates of where it could be found. He had plotted those coordinates on a map, discovering them to approximate those given him by Omar when the Islamist had tracked the dolphins back to the Haitian coast. More gold, it seemed, was to be had back in that hidden sanctuary just below Malique.

Ortega smiled greedily at this knowledge. Maybe he would fly to the cove before he stepped foot back on Navassa Island. Certainly, the escaped dolphin hunters were on their way there at this moment, and the last thing he wanted was for them to reach the place ahead of him and make off with the stash.

The sound of shouting jarred Ortega from these musings. One of his crewmen had moved to the edge of the helipad and was pointing at the water in alarm. The mild bubbling Ortega had noted a few moments earlier had turned into a gurgling, roiling froth. Only now it had expanded, stretching out in all directions.

Ortega looked on in horror, watching the sea all around him erupt into a churning boil. Bubbles the size of the tug were now breaching the surface close to the *San Carlo's* hull. He turned sharply. Pedro had come up from below to stand next to him, and on his battered face he could see fright.

"What is happening?" Ortega bellowed.

Pedro shrugged helplessly. "I do not know."

Spray began to explode from the water as the eruption of gas escalated. A half-mile distant, the *San Pinto* abruptly listed, its bow plunging below the waterline. Further away, the *San Diablo* began to flounder. Ortega could see foaming white water pouring over its decks, and the tug pulling its seine was now gone from sight.

Never had fear touched Ortega the way it tugged at him now. The sea had become perilous. Here was one reason ships were sometimes reported missing in reasonably calm weather. Such disappearances had happened all over the world since the beginning of recorded history. He was familiar with the theory. Fields of methane hydrates resting on the sea floor were capable of periodically releasing vast quantities of methane gas. When this occurred, the water became saturated with so much dissolved gas that the fluid density was diminished to the point where it would no longer provide buoyancy, and vessels caught in such violent discharges were in danger of sinking without warning. Laboratory experiments had conclusively proved that methane bubbles could cause any normally floatable object to lose its buoyancy, but then again, almost any gas could do this.

The flight deck suddenly lurched violently underfoot, nearly plunging Ortega to the deck below. With his heart skipping several beats, he managed to regain his balance and scramble back into the Bell Ranger's cockpit. He had to get off the ship.

Gripped by panic, Ortega yelled out to Fernando. "Get us airborne!"

Fernando started to climb in from the opposite side, but Pedro yanked him back, striking him hard in the head with a closed fist.

Ortega stared aghast. "What are you doing?" he screamed.

Pedro climbed in next to him and began flicking switches. "I will do the flying!" he said. His tone was gruff and challenging.

Ortega felt his stomach rise up sharply as the ship dropped with startling suddenness. The plunge was short, and the vessel jerked back up as though tied to a huge bungee cord.

Flabbergasted by what was happening, Ortega could only watch as Pedro throttled up the engine. There was no time to reprimand Cardoza's nephew for his show of impudence. Consumed with anxiety, he focused on the whine of the turbine as it powered up for liftoff. All around him, the sea was a raging torrent. Already it had risen up to within ten feet of the flight deck.

With heart-stopping abruptness, the *San Carlo* dropped again, making Ortega cringe as angry shouts filled the air. Swiveling his head, he was shocked to see crewmen fighting to climb into the back seats. A vicious melee had broken out among the men.

Pulling his pistol, Ortega swung around, fighting against the seat belts and firing at the nearest man. He did not want the weight of additional passengers dragging down the chopper.

The crewman seemed not to notice the stain of blood spreading rapidly across his chest. Driven by terror and adrenaline, he continued to struggle with the others trying to get aboard. Ortega fired again, this time sending a bullet through the man's temple. But as the man fell, two more crewmen hopped over his fallen body in a bid to climb aboard.

Screaming obscenities, Ortega pulled back on the trigger several more times, dropping each man before he could gain entry to the cabin. He was momentarily pinned to his seat as the helicopter suddenly rose. The sensation instantly subsided, and for what seemed like an eternity, the chopper hung jerkily above the deck as though the main rotor could not get enough bite.

Fearful of stalling, Ortega stared down, almost losing control of his bowels at what he saw. Geysers of foaming white water were practically touching the Bell Ranger's skids. The *San Carlo* was now gone, completely engulfed by a sea of churning froth.

Ortega gritted his teeth, his mind suddenly dredging up one other tidbit of information. Some scientists had theorized that a heavy discharge of a gas less dense than air could bring down planes. And methane, he knew, was one such gas. He could tell the chopper was struggling to stay aloft, unable to get the required lift. And the turbine did not sound right to him, buzzing erratically as though straining to suck in sufficient oxygen to burn fuel. At any moment, the engine could quit. Then the aircraft would drop into the boiling cauldron like a boulder.

Like a man stranded on a gallows, Ortega awaited the inevitable. At any second, the trapdoor beneath his feet would spring open. Like a yo-yo on a string, the chopper bobbed precariously, laboring to remain just beyond the reach of the frothing geysers. Closing his eyes, his mind anchored itself to the wail of the turbine, expecting it to cut out altogether.

Abruptly, the whine of the engine steadied. Suddenly pushed down hard in his seat, the all too familiar sensation made him open his eyes again. They were rising, gaining altitude. Below him, the fountains of foam had flattened. With the discharge of gas now abating, the sea was rapidly calming.

Looking in all directions, Ortega gawked in dismay. All three of his ships were gone.

Wallowing in disbelief, Ortega stared dumbly at the water below as the chopper continued to climb higher. Farther away, the sea remained relatively calm. From his position, he could clearly see the boundaries of the gas eruption. It had only covered an area encompassing his trawlers. But in the midst of this waning effervescence, a small zone had managed to stay undisturbed. And in that zone he could see hundreds of gray forms milling about. Centered among them was a small contingent of albinos.

A gruff voice intruded its way into Ortega's awareness. Swiveling his head, he realized Pedro was speaking to him. "My uncle is going to be very displeased with what has happened," he grunted. On his battered face, Ortega could see the hint of a callous grin.

An image of Cardoza's snarling pet tiger flashed briefly in Ortega's mind, but the anger rising within him quickly supplanted the thought. Dropping his gaze back to the ocean below, he felt the hate fizz up from the pit of his stomach. Though it seemed absurd, he was certain the dolphins were somehow to blame for this recent calamity. "Take us lower!" he hissed, pointing to the heavy congregation of cetaceans off their starboard side. "They did this! I want them all killed!"

Pedro nodded, his manner immediately turning cruel as he nosed the Ranger over.

Uneasily, Ortega watched him manipulate the controls, feeling the chopper respond sluggishly. As a pilot, Pedro was not in the same league as Fernando. Nevertheless, Pedro was the only option he had at the moment. And unlike Fernando, Pedro had a fervid passion for killing.

As Pedro took the aircraft into a wide, bumpy turn, Ortega glanced in the direction of the old lighthouse jutting above the island. He had an unobstructed view of Navassa's eastern side, and close to the shoreline near the northern end he glimpsed a vessel sitting at anchor.

Ortega frowned darkly. Even from this distance, he was certain he had seen that same vessel before. Yes, it had to be Javolyn's. As soon as he finished with the dolphins, he would have Pedro fly them over there for a closer look. And if the boat was indeed the one used by Javolyn, then he'd destroy it. He had enough firepower at his disposal to obliterate all those who opposed him.

Pedro suddenly yelled, looking below him in confusion. "Where did they go?"

Ortega snapped his eyes back to the area where he had last seen the dolphins. The sea was now empty. Angrily, he searched the sea in all directions, whipping his head back and forth before pointing again. "There!" he snarled, motioning furiously at one o'clock. "Ahead of us! Rake the water over there!" He was certain he saw fins break the surface. "They cannot escape us."

Pedro jerked the Ranger's nose down, attempting to bring the aircraft into alignment with the sector of ocean Ortega had indicated.

And though he saw nothing on the surface that suggested dolphins, he turned the weapon loose. Clumsily, the chopper yawed left, shuddering fiercely as the Gatling gun opened up. Added to the drone of the turbine, the sound was deafening. An instant later, a line of spray kicked up on the water directly ahead.

"You're missing the spot," Ortega scolded sharply. With the guns firing, the Ranger's yaw had worsened, swinging farther to the left.

Ignoring Ortega's admonishment, Pedro held down the trigger.

Ortega screamed. "You fool! You're wasting ammunition!"

Pedro continued to fire until the gun stopped chattering. "The gun is not working," he yelled out in frustration. He let up on the trigger before depressing it again, but the weapon remained silent.

Ortega's fury was rapidly reaching its limit. "Idiot!" he bellowed. "The gun stops firing after four seconds. It requires a few seconds to cool before it will work again."

As the chopper passed over the area fired upon, Ortega looked for signs of a hit. At seeing none, he ordered Pedro to circle around. "Sooner or later, they have to come up for air," he hissed impatiently.

Pedro banked the chopper hard. For the next several minutes, Ortega kept his eyes glued to the ocean, his mood growing progressively darker as the chopper continued to circle. It baffled him that nothing showed on the water below.

With his rage now boiling over, Ortega stared back in the direction of the lighthouse. "Head for that boat and destroy it!" he screamed. "I will at least have some satisfaction."

Chapter 30

M at Daniels studied the helicopter in the distance, the growing buzz of its rotor blades making his heart pound heavily. He had been watching it for the better part of five minutes from Jake's boat, fully aware of its destructive capability. And now it was making a beeline directly for the *Avenging Angel*, dropping down low in readiness for what he could only assume to be a strafing run.

Knowing they were in deep trouble, he shouted a warning at the top of his lungs. "Everyone take cover!"

Minutes earlier, Hector had set up the M-60 on its swivel mount, and now Mat stood manning the weapon, looking through the shield of Plexiglas at the oncoming aircraft. He was quite familiar with the sound of a Minigun, and minutes earlier he had seen the chopper rake the sea with a horrendous barrage. He knew he would have only one chance at taking down the helicopter before its awesome Gatling gun had the *Angel* in its sights.

No stranger to such overwhelming odds, Mat pulled back on the sixty's cocking bolt, prepared to defend the vessel as the chopper came closer. It was moving toward him slowly, almost as if those aboard wanted to savor the moment they would unleash the weapon at their command. "It'll truly be a miracle if we survive this," he muttered under his breath.

By nature he was not a religious man, but as he faced down the oncoming aircraft, he began to pray.

Pulled along by Hermes, Jake broke the surface, knowing what was about to happen. Next to him, Destiny sat astride Hercules. The girl appeared incredibly drained from her recent ordeal at stopping the missile, and he intuitively knew she would need time to fully recoup her energies if she was going to undertake a similar feat aimed at negating the danger now closing in on the *Angel*. But time was a luxury they no longer had.

Jake looked down at the creature towing him. "We're only gonna get one shot at this," he said gravely. "You sure you can do it?"

"I will not fail you, Jay Jay," Hermes twittered back. "Hold on."

Jake had just enough time to note the look registering on Destiny's face before his powerful mount pulled him below the surface. "Jay Jay, no-" was all he heard as he was tugged forcefully into the depths. There was no time to debate the issue. And judging from the position of the approaching aircraft, he barely had enough time to attempt what had to be done.

As Hermes descended rapidly, Jake perceived a multitude of gray forms dart out of the way. Without a dive mask, he could not see clearly, but he knew it would not matter anyway. Once he positioned himself, he could even close his eyes.

Hermes suddenly slowed, reaching the nadir of the dive, and Jake released his hold on the albino's dorsal fin. Staring up at the surface, he knew he was deep, perhaps better than 120 feet. But would it be enough?

Keeping his body rigid, he felt Hermes' beak make contact with the soles of his feet. It was now or never.

Hermes took off for the surface, starting the ascent slowly at first to ensure Jake remained balanced. And then Jake felt the dolphin's raw power as the albino accelerated. With his body almost buckling under the explosive surge, Jake strained hard against the pull of the sea, using every muscle in his body to maintain the rigid posture Hermes required.

Gritting his teeth, Jake glimpsed the surface through slitted eyes a split second before becoming airborne. Launched from the water like a guided missile, he could tell Hermes' timing had been perfect.

Converging on an intercept point directly above him was Ortega's chopper, its gun still silent as it lined up on its intended target.

Throwing his arms out in front of him, Jake reached for the aircraft's port-side skid. He caught it just as the pull of gravity nullified Hermes' boost, and hooking a leg over the tubular skid, he grabbed hold of the rear strut and glanced down. Hermes was just entering the water in a perfect dive sixty feet below him. Still sitting astride Hercules, Destiny stared up at him in horror.

With catlike agility, Jake began to haul himself up into the rear cabin, fully aware that the Minigun might be engaged at any second. All the doors on the chopper had been removed, giving him unobstructed access to the back seats. Poking his head up, he could tell the men at the controls were totally focused on the *Angel*, now less than 400 feet away.

The man on the right suddenly swiveled his head around, his expression momentarily frozen in stark surprise at seeing another person aboard the aircraft. Jake reacted swiftly, lunging forward with a closed fist before Ortega could shout a warning. Only halfway into the cabin, he was barely able to reach Ortega's face, and the punch landed without any leverage behind it.

Pulling himself into the cabin the remainder of the way, Jake yanked his K-bar from its sheath just as Ortega turned again. Eyes flaming with hatred, the Colombian twisted savagely in his seat, awkwardly extending an arm. Gripped in his hand was a semi-automatic pistol.

Jake slashed out with the knife, slicing deep into Ortega's wrist just as he pulled back on the trigger. The gun exploded an instant before Ortega hollered in pain, and Jake felt something hot singe his scalp.

The aircraft abruptly lurched, then snap-rolled with such violence that Jake was sent headlong toward the opposite side of the cabin. Only his quick reflexes saved him from being flung clear. Catching the starboard door frame with his left hand, he hung suspended by one arm, finding himself looking back into the cabin as the centrifugal force of a nasty left bank stretched his body out laterally. It was then that he saw the pilot's face glaring back at him, and strangely it did not surprise him at all that the man doing the flying was none other than Pedro.

Jake held on tenaciously, his grip rapidly waning as Pedro tried to dislodge him. Ortega leaned to his right, fighting against his seat belt and craning his head out the side door to stare directly into Jake's face, and in his eyes Jake could see the fires of madness burning fervently. Caught by the slipstream of air rushing past, globs of blood from his oozing wrist dribbled back to spatter Jake's cheeks. Still managing to retain possession of the pistol, a cruel smile came to the Colombian's mouth as he shifted the gun to his left hand, angling his arm around the door frame to get a clear bead on his unwanted passenger.

Jake gazed transfixed, his sense of time dramatically slowing as he looked down at the barrel of the handgun coming to bear on his face. He had cheated death too many times, and now he knew the bill was finally coming due if he did not let go. Preparing to release his grip, the chopper suddenly bucked hard, and Jake became aware of a white blur falling away beneath him.

Jarred by the impact, Pedro jerked the cyclic back to his right, inadvertently veering the aircraft out of its acute bank. Flung back into the cabin by the sudden shift in inertia, Jake found purchase on the opposite door frame before he could be ejected, the K-bar still gripped firmly in his right hand.

Ortega whipped around in his seat, cursing with rage. With the helicopter now on a straight and level heading, Jake readied himself as the muzzle of Ortega's gun poked from between the seats. Another shot rang out, the sound overlaying the whine of the turbine. But this time Jake shifted well beyond the path of the bullet. Plowing through the cabin's rear bulkhead, the round entered the engine compartment. A whine of protest immediately erupted from the turbine, escalating quickly into a raucous shriek, and the aircraft began to shudder giddily.

With his ears ringing, Jake sprang forward, jabbing the K-bar into the back of Ortega's gun hand. The Colombian howled shrilly, withdrawing the weapon but still managing to hold onto it.

The chopper snap-rolled to port a second time, catching Jake off balance again. Hurled back to starboard, he again caught the door frame with his free hand. Finding himself in the same position as before, his body hung precariously from the side of the aircraft. More blood spattered his face as Ortega leaned out into the wind to end this standoff. Once more, time seemed to bog down as the Colombian extended the pistol to blow his head off.

Momentarily disregarding the danger, Jake held on, unwilling to let his fingers slide away just yet. Overcome by a strange sense, he looked down. The frozen smile of an albino was directly below him, rising up as if in slow motion. The smile belonged to Achilles.

Almost mesmerized by the sight, Jake watched as the juvenile protracted both arms and reached for Ortega's gun arm. Reaching the apex of his leap, Achilles' jaws parted.

Ortega let out a harsh cry as the jaws closed on his arm. With bulging eyes, he stared as the pistol was ripped from his hand by one of the juvenile's hand-like appendages. He screamed again, his face racked with pain. Bearing the albino's full weight, his limb was nearly wrenched from its socket. Achilles would not let go, and it was only the seat belt that kept Ortega from being torn from the cockpit.

The Ranger bucked several more times, and Jake caught a glimpse of three more albinos as they latched onto the chopper's tubular skids with their wondrous hands. The aircraft dipped precipitously under the combined weight, and it began to plummet rapidly toward the sea.

In desperation, Pedro fought the controls, pulling up hard on the collective and jerking the cyclic to starboard. The shift in G-force was nearly instantaneous, and Jake was able to haul himself back into the cabin, no longer held in the grip of inertia.

Ortega continued to scream. Forced to bear Achilles' full weight by one arm, his body remained bent at an awkward angle as it was stretched halfway out the cockpit.

The juvenile looked up at Jake, reaching out and giving him Ortega's pistol with his free hand. For one meteoric moment, Jake thought to send a bullet into the back of Pedro's head, but Pedro jerked the stick again. Flung to the port-side of the cabin, Jake found himself pitched forward on his belly, his head jutting out the door into the wind. He could feel the chopper coming out of its turn, and as he looked ahead, he saw that the aircraft had its nose down and was beginning to line up on the *Angel*, now less than forty meters away.

The damaged turbine screeched like a dying animal, making his ears ache. But in that instant the Gatling gun's protruding mechanism lay directly before him and he did not hesitate as the barrels suddenly spun. Flames spewed forth as the awesome weapon discharged in a harsh buzz, throwing out a storm of rounds that kicked up a traveling spume of water. Extending the pistol out in front of him, he fired at close to point-blank range and emptied the clip as the racing geyser sped rapidly toward the *Angel's* bow. The Minigun abruptly ground to a halt as parts of the ammo feed leading from the magazine disintegrated. Seized up, the weapon could not fire.

Jake rose up into a crouch and, looking behind him, spotted the thing he had noticed when he had first climbed aboard the chopper. A box of MK3 concussion grenades was strapped to the middle seat. Lifting the cover, he grabbed one of the cardboard cylinders and pulled the pin, letting the spoon pop free. From the front seat, Pedro pivoted his head around to locate Jake, skewering him with a hateful, enraged glare, but at seeing the live grenade being reinserted back in the box, his face turned an ashen white and a look of utter terror filled his eyes. Opening his mouth, he shouted in desperation, but the shriek of the laboring engine made the words indiscernible.

Jake grinned wickedly, giving the panic-stricken pilot a farewell wave of the hand. And with that he leapt clear of the aircraft, knowing the water was only a short distance away. Dropping feet first, he saw all four albinos plunge with him.

Upon hitting the water, Jake surfaced quickly. Eagerly, he looked up at the dying chopper, watching it yaw erratically. On a collision course with Navassa's nearby cliffs, a trail of dense black smoke billowed profusely from its damaged turbine. Frenzied movement within the cockpit could be seen as the helicopter's two occupants fought frantically to jump clear. Pedro nearly succeeded, but he had only fallen less than a meter when the whirlybird erupted in a huge fireball, and he disappeared in the flash of flame. Bits and pieces of the aircraft fell into the sea, while other burning fragments were strewn onto the karst forming Navassa's shoreline.

Satisfied that the threat had been eradicated, Jake turned toward his vessel less than twenty meters away. Mat and a few others were waving to him from the port railing.

"You are unharmed, Jay Jay?"

Jake swung around, seeing Achilles next to him. Grinning from ear to ear, he reached out and rubbed the dolphin's snout affectionately.

"Only because of you, my friend." He paused, noticing the small scar on the juvenile's back. The wound was almost fully healed. He had felt the pain of it when the bullet had pierced Achilles' lung. "That makes two I owe you."

Upon rejoining the others aboard the *Avenging Angel*, Jake was puzzled. Two people were missing. "Where's Zimby and Hennington?" he asked Mat.

Mat shrugged. "Seems they went ashore."

Jake stared at the nearby cliffs, frowning. "What for?"

Mat shrugged again. "The big guy said he had some unfinished business to take care of."

Jake scanned the escarpment rising up from the sea. Deep down, he knew the reason for Zimbola having gone ashore, though he couldn't understand why the broker had accompanied him. Compounding his bewilderment further was the absence of Destiny and her mother once again.

"Seems we got more company," Mat said.

"Huh?" Jake pulled his eyes from the nearby cliffs to stare in the direction Mat was looking. Surrounded by a small cluster of gray dolphins heading toward the *Angel*, Destiny rode Hercules. Squinting against the sun glare reflected off the water, he discerned three other human forms; two were being supported by several members of the pack while the third was slung across Hercules' back directly in front of Destiny. The girl kept a firm grip on the man, making sure he did not slide off. She still looked exhausted, making Jake wonder if she had anything left within her to revitalize the people she had rescued.

Jake scurried to the rear platform, ready to lend a hand, but Hector, Jacob, and Dr. Grahm were already there ahead of him, stooped low to give assistance. Further away, a few albinos were coming on fast to join the girl.

Destiny shouted worriedly. "Do not pull them from the water just yet. I'll need time to resuscitate these men."

Both Grahm and Hector reached out to grab hold of the two closest men while Destiny focused on the one borne by her mount. Jake could see that all three were unconscious. Destiny's charge, however, was missing an arm. A stubborn flow of blood from the severed limb was turning the water red.

Jake studied the men. Two were from the *San Carlo*, but the one in Destiny's care he did not recognize.

"This one has lost a lot of blood," Destiny said tiredly. "He has other injuries, and it's possible he may not survive."

Jake stared fascinated, watching three albinos nuzzling the comatose man's body. "I'm sure you'll do your best to keep him alive," he encouraged.

For one brief moment, Destiny stopped her ministrations to gaze up at Jake. And in that tiny passing of time Jake imagined he was seeing a heavy burden lifted from the girl's soul.

Ternier lifted the blackened charm from around his neck and flung it aside. The ancient trinket was useless to him. Gingerly, he touched his forehead where Javolyn had bashed him, eyeing his fingertips to see if the bleeding had finally stopped.

Looking around the deserted clearing, his eyes settled once again on Omar's dead body. It was a dismal reminder of what had happened, a stark epitaph to the way his plan had unraveled so quickly. Angered by the sight, he took three maddened steps to the corpse and kicked it savagely in the head.

"Only a truly evil person fights with the dead."

Ternier spun around, shocked to find he was being watched. Zimbola and Hennington stood at the edge of the clearing. He knew at once that it was the big man who had spoken.

"What is it that you want?" Ternier griped angrily, knowing all too well what it was. Out of the corner of his eye, he located the Kalashnikov that had been tossed aside by Omar earlier on. It lay on the ground less than two meters away. Slowly, he began edging toward it.

"Justice!" Zimbola rumbled, his deep bass voice leaving no doubts as to what he had in mind. "We are here to serve justice."

The Colonel sidled closer to the weapon. Rarely had he encountered men larger than himself, and the Jamaican's size intimidated him. "I am a ranking magistrate of the Republic of Haiti. State your business and be done with it."

The giant frowned fiercely, stepping closer. "We are no longer in Haiti."

Ternier leapt for the Kalashnikov. Something akin to a steel vice closed on his wrist as he lifted the weapon, and he found himself staring into eyes filled with loathing.

"You killed Mercades!" Zimbola spat. "And now you will pay for it!"

Ternier gasped, startled by the strength behind the grip. In panic, he lashed out with his other arm, landing a solid blow to the Jamaican's chin and following it up with a knee to the groin.

Zimbola grunted as though pricked by a pin. Shrugging off the blows, he caught the Colonel by the throat to avoid a vicious head-butt. "You will pay," he said in a rumbling snarl.

Barely able to breathe, Ternier felt his feet leave the ground, the giant's thumb pressing into his Adam's apple with terrifying force. Knowing he was about to die, he struck out at the face in front of him, fighting to draw breath each time he struck. Something suddenly crunched, an all too familiar sound he had often heard within his torture chambers. Yes, it was the sound of cartilage being crushed. But this time it was his own larynx that was collapsing. Horrified by this one thought, Ternier felt the darkness close in on him like an onrushing black cloud.

Feeling Ternier's body go limp, Zimbola continued to hold him aloft as he walked him over to where the karst dropped off toward the sea. Bellowing like a maddened bull, he heaved the corpse down the steep escarpment, watching it tumble away.

Chapter 31

*T*he remainder of the day went quickly, with Jake finding himself strapped with numerous tasks. As fortune would have it, however, finding Zimbola and Hennington had not been one of them. Both had returned soon after Destiny's revival of the injured men, each hauled back to the *Angel* by an albino dolphin. Once aboard the sturdy vessel, Zimby's reserved manner was all too evident to Jake, and he did not press him about where he had gone, though he sensed Ternier would no longer be a concern.

Through the efforts of Achilles and the other albinos calculating the effects of wind and drift on a vessel the size of *Relentless*, Jake was able to pinpoint the exact location of Mat's boat, set adrift by Ternier shortly after the Colonel's raid upon the *Angel*. With Mat riding behind him on the waverunner, Jake covered the fifteen miles of open sea in short order, leaving his friend to pilot *Relentless* back to Navassa by himself. Beforehand, both men had agreed that their vessels would be needed to ferry all those abducted back to Malique.

And then there was the matter of the Islamic terrorists. "We have a problem." Jake found himself saying to Mat.

"Tell me?"

Jake sighed tiredly, the strain of the last twenty-four hours starting to catch up with him. "I know you have a report to make about what happened out here, but the last thing these dolphins need is Uncle Sam poking his nose around this island."

Perplexity filled Mat's face. "Why is that?"

"Because they're building a refuge directly under this chunk of rock." Jake paused, seeing the surprise in his friend's expression. "There's much more to this than you're aware of."

"I'm listening."

For the next half hour, Jake told Mat everything he knew about the dolphins and their connection with the island. He left nothing out, apprising him of Ternier's scheme and the Islamist plot. Mat's eyes widened appreciably at the mention of their old nemesis, Raduyev, and the Colombian-Jihadist connection, coming alive further at Jake's description of the Chechen's death.

"So you're telling me these creatures used all that hydrogen gas they've been storing to sink those ships." Mat shook his head in wonder. "Incredible!"

Jake assessed his friend closely. Outside the pod and those of his crew, Mat was the only other person he trusted implicitly. "So what's it gonna be, pal? You tell the story to your superiors like it really is and this place is gonna be crawling in military brass. Once they get a whiff of how unique these creatures are, they'll capture as many as they can, using them as military assets. These dolphins don't deserve that."

Mat turned and stared at the island. "God damn you, Jake. You're asking me to ignore my responsibilities. I've got a job to do."

"I know you do, Mat, and you're good at it. But sometimes circumstances get in the way that force us to draw a line in the sand, and in this case it's a line that cannot be straddled." Jake softened his tone. "Which side of that line you going to take?"

Mat threw his hands up in annoyance, then slapped them down hard on the *Angel's* railing. "Don't press me! I've got to think this out."

Jake knew that tone of voice, realizing he had to back off. A decision like the one he was asking Mat to make was more than just difficult. It might very well change the course of his life. Certainly it would have a major impact on other lives. "I'm going ashore, Mat. I'll show you Raduyev's submarine base if you'd like to see it. I still haven't seen it."

Mat's funk showed a trace of abatement. "I also want to see this dolphin refuge."

Jake smiled. "Whatever you want, buddy."

Led by Destiny, it was nearly midday by the time Jake and Mat reached the cave entrance leading to Raduyev's subterranean base. Having nothing better to do, both Dr. Grahm and Jacob had accompanied them.

"Are the villagers still down there?" Jake asked, adjusting the Stoner's shoulder strap.

"Yes," Destiny said, glancing briefly at the weapon slung over Jake's shoulder. "The danger is long past. Bashir has everything under control."

"And your mother is still with him?"

As if in answer to the question, Amphitrite suddenly emerged from the mouth of the cave.

A loud gasp broke the air behind Jake. "Harriet!"

Jake spun around. Grahm was looking beyond him, staring with his mouth wide open.

For several long seconds, Amphitrite gazed back at the scientist, her face frozen in stoic bewilderment.

"It is you!" Grahm blurted. Overcome with joy, he rushed over to embrace the woman with outstretched arms.

Caught in a fierce hug, Amphitrite continued to appear confused, her arms dangling helplessly at her sides.

The other members of Jake's party stood speechless, captivated by the strange scene unfolding before them.

Grahm relaxed his smothering embrace, holding the woman at arm's length. "It's me, Harriet…It's Franklin." His elation deflated rapidly at seeing Amphitrite's lack of recognition, and within moments his eyes began to mist over. "You don't remember me?" There was an overwhelming crush of emotion in the way the question was spoken.

Amphitrite seemed utterly lost, her manner dull and lifeless as she searched his face. "There…there is a certain familiarity about you," she whispered uncertainly.

Grahm was overwrought with frustration. "I am your husband, Harriet." His words came out in an explosive rush. "You disappeared many years ago. You were reported lost at sea in a hurricane. The sloop you were sailing sank near this island. You were pregnant with our child when it happened." He suddenly paused as he studied her face. "You don't remember, do you?" There was desperation in his voice now.

A pained expression manifested itself in Amphitrite's features, the frustration turning to liquid in her eyes. "There is a blockage to my memory...I...I wish I..." A trickling of tears began to flow down her cheeks.

"It doesn't matter, Harriet," Grahm blurted sympathetically, once more squeezing her tightly to him. "All that matters is I've found you again." He looked down at her face. "The years have been kind to you, my darling. You've hardly aged."

Amphitrite reached up, placing a gentle hand on his forehead. A moment of stillness ensued before a small, startled cry left her lips, and she scrutinized his features as if truly seeing him for the very first time. The trickle of tears streaming down her face began to flow more quickly, and she suddenly hugged Grahm with an unrestrained fierceness. "Yes... yes...I see it all clearly now."

Jake read her expression, envisioning the flashbacks currently consuming her mind. Amphitrite was revisiting the past, the portion of her memory that had up to now eluded her.

"You've lived in Haiti all these years?" Grahm murmured in her ear.

"Yes, my darling, but my life has not been without purpose." She shifted sodden orbs to Destiny before turning back to look deeply into Grahm's eyes. "You should rejoice in knowing that Destiny is your daughter."

Destiny stared incredulously. "Father?" She rolled the word off her tongue as though testing the sound of it. For one dizzy and emotionally charged moment she hung back, caught up in all that the word implied before repeating it. "Father!" The word was shouted this time, no longer alien to her.

A touching scene followed as Destiny flew into Grahm's arms. Raining kisses on the girl's cheeks and holding her tightly, the scientist's voice was choked with emotion. "I knew there was something about you from the very first time we met. Oh, my sweet child, you make an old man proud at seeing what a beautiful and courageous young woman you've grown into."

Jake stood back, not wanting to intrude on this tender reunion. As he looked upon the faces of the others, he could not find a dry eye among them. And while Jacob wore a lopsided smile, Jake could not help but notice a trace of sadness in the Haitian's expression as well.

Several minutes passed before Amphitrite finally pulled away from husband and daughter. Turning, she singled out Jake. "I am told you have been searching for something in these waters for some time now, Mr. Javolyn."

"I'd prefer it if you call me Jay Jay."

Amphitrite smiled, her cheeks still wet with moisture. "As you wish, Jay Jay." She pointed to a stack of boxes partially hidden behind a stand of poisonwood trees. "I believe you will find some of the items you've been seeking in those crates over there."

Jake appraised the pile of crates from where he stood. "If those boxes contain what I think they do, I'm not sure I have the right to take them."

Amphitrite's smile became somber. "If you are not the rightful owner, then who?" Releasing a weary sigh, she added, "This is not a matter of choice for you, Jay Jay. The paths our lives take are often guided by a power beyond ourselves, a force far removed from random coincidence. Certain things are meant to happen in order to clear the way for the future and to keep past events from repeating themselves. The lives of all those who stand here have become entwined, coming together for a common purpose. Where mankind goes from here will be determined by the actions we have already taken and the actions we are yet to exercise. Evil takes many guises, and on this day we were able to defeat it, each of us contributing in our own way."

Amphitrite paused, giving Jake a moment to reflect on the things she had just said. "Take possession of the boxes, Jay Jay, and load them aboard your vessel. A higher authority has deemed it necessary that you be entrusted with these things if you are to go on fulfilling your true calling."

"I'll consider it," Jake said awkwardly. "But right now, I need to have a look inside this-"

Jake suddenly lost his tongue. Others were beginning to climb from the mouth of the cave to stand behind Amphitrite. Apparently, the remaining villagers kidnapped from Malique were coming up to join her. Several of the newcomers carried boxes similar to the ones stacked at the side of the clearing and Amphitrite had them place those additional boxes on the pile. The opening to the subterranean cavern was narrow, only allowing the passage of one person at a time.

When the procession of people finally stopped, Jake looked to Amphitrite once again. "Has everyone been accounted for?"

"Two others will be up shortly. Twenty-two people were taken from Malique and three others from a disabled boat. We will require the use of your vessel and that of your friend to take them all back to Haiti. Will that be a problem for you, Jay Jay?"

"None at all." Jake took a quick head count, suddenly aware that Bashir, Sherkhan, and the one called Kalid were missing. "As soon as everyone's up, Mat and I will go down there to have a look." As he said this, another Haitian emerged from the cave opening.

"I don't think that will be possible," Amphitrite said. There was an apology in her tone.

Mat, who had been standing by in silence, suddenly spoke up. "Why not?"

The ground abruptly rumbled and shook underfoot just as the last person cleared the cave entrance. Less than two seconds later, a cloud of dust spewed from the opening, and Jake realized all the Islamists remained unaccounted for.

Amphitrite stepped away from the cave mouth as the dust began to settle. "An explosive charge has been set off further down, permanently sealing off the tunnel. Access to the cavern is no longer possible."

Jake glanced around sharply, carefully surveying the faces milling all around him one more time just to be certain he hadn't overlooked anyone. "What about Bashir and Raduyev's men? Are they still down there?"

Amphitrite met Jake's eyes, staring back impassively, though her eyes held the glint of mischievous guile. "You have no need to be concerned about them. Their mission is at an end."

"That doesn't mean they're no longer dangerous," Jake objected pointedly. "They have a sub at their disposal."

Destiny interceded. "Bashir is their new leader now, Jay Jay. You have my word that he will not pose a threat to anyone. If anything, the men he commands will now devote their lives to a common good."

"Who is this Bashir?" Mat demanded, staring first at Destiny, then at Jake.

Jake narrowed his eyes wearily, keeping his attention focused on the girl. "What kind of common good?"

"All will soon be revealed."

Jake sighed grumpily, throwing his arms up and rolling his eyes in frustration. It didn't make sense why Destiny continued to remain nebulous and evasive whenever it concerned Bashir.

"Damn!" Mat griped. "Will someone please tell me who this Bashir is?"

Jake tried quelling Mat with a wave of his hand. "Easy, partner. I'll get to the bottom of this." With eyes still clinging to Destiny, he said, "Can I have a word with you in private?"

Everyone stood silent as Destiny followed Jake beyond earshot. "Look," Jake said, "if you say Bashir is not a threat, that's good enough for me. But Mat needs a little more to go on than that. Have you forgotten he works for the U.S. Department of Homeland Security?"

Destiny studied his troubled expression a moment longer. "That's all I can tell you right now, Jay Jay."

"You're placing me in a very awkward position with my friend," Jake grumbled. "As it is, I'm trying to convince him not to report everything that happened at this island. The last thing you want is Uncle Sam probing around here and discovering the extraordinary intelligence of your friends and the refuge they're building."

"I'm sure you'll figure out a way to keep him from doing that. And besides, I can tell Mat is a man of conscience."

Jake was growing annoyed. "Why must you be so vague when it comes to Bashir?"

Destiny's lips curled up in amusement, her eyes provocative and rebellious. "I'm sorry, Jay Jay. I guess I deserve a spanking."

Disarmed by the implication, Jake looked down at her in mock anger. "And I aim to give you one."

The trip back from Navassa went smoothly, with *Relentless* following behind the *Avenging Angel* the whole way. Docking at Malique's main pier, both vessels shed their passengers quickly. Through the healing powers of the pod, both Emmanuel and Lucette Baptiste were well on their way to full recovery, with virtually all their wounds now fully healed.

With Destiny standing by his side, Jake watched the last two villagers step off his boat. Carried between them was a non-Haitian laid out on a stretcher, the lower half of the man's face shrouded in a dense cluster of coarse dark hair, the stump of his right arm swathed in a thick wrap of white surgical dressing. Clutched tightly in the man's remaining hand was something he refused to relinquish, an object from which the man would not withdraw his eyes.

Jake could not help but smile at what he was seeing. He had since learned the bearded man was the captain of the Yemeni freighter Ortega had destroyed. "If Bashir were still here, he would not be very pleased over the way his painting has been appropriated."

Destiny looked up at him. "I don't think Bashir would have raised a fuss in view of what the painting is doing for the man."

"I still find it amazing how this art is able to free up a person's mind, at least in some people." Jake shook his head as if unwilling to accept what was occurring here. "That man had a key role in a sinister plot aimed at murdering millions of people, and now he's docile as a lamb."

Someone spoke behind Jake. "That is because he did not really accept the ideology he had become snared in."

Jake turned, finding himself staring into Jacob's face. "Have you ever considered using these paintings as a kind of acid test?"

"I assume you mean for gauging a person's mettle," Jacob replied absently, his gaze searching out the crowd gathered near the shore before settling on something. There was bleakness in his eyes.

Jake saw where he was looking, noting that Jacob was watching Amphitrite and Dr. Grahm. Husband and wife were holding hands, talking quietly. "Yeah," Jake said. "From what I've seen so far, you can use the art to cull out those that are good from the chronically bad."

Jacob turned back to Jake. "I suppose such use might hold some merit, but then we would be playing the part of judge and jury in assessing a person's true temperament." Jacob expelled a prolonged sigh. "The pod has no interest in judging others, Jay Jay."

Jake weighed the words gravely. "Your venture is going to require many more people than you currently have. The last thing you want is ill-intentioned individuals tripping up your plan. Perhaps it would be wise to lay down certain protocols for recruitment."

Jacob brought his eyes back to Amphitrite. "I'll give your idea due consideration."

Jake located the two survivors from the *San Carlo*. He already knew Fernando and Antonio could be trusted, having seen the way they had reacted to Achilles painting. Both men were standing on the dock next to Mat's boat, engaged in conversation with Chester Hennington. "There's three potential recruits who-"

Destiny tugged sharply on Jake's arm, giving him and Jacob a worried look. "Visitors have come to Gaia, Jay Jay. Hermes and Aphrodite tell me a vessel is anchored just beyond the cove."

"Can they describe it?"

A moment passed as Destiny focused inwardly. "They tell me it's the same vessel you helped the dolphin hunters escape in."

Jake absorbed this information, wondering how Walter McPherson and company had learned about the albino hideaway. But as he thought about it, the answer came to him in a flash.

Chapter 32

Walter McPherson's head felt as if it were going to explode as he stared at the strange art hanging against the wall in the small thatched cottage. Never in his life had he felt so ill. Neither Frank Jaffey nor Ben Loomins seemed to notice as he staggered on unsteady legs towards the door. Stepping out into the sunlight, he stumbled down to the water's edge before sinking to his knees and retching harshly. Dumbly, he stared at the slick of bile laid atop the small wavelets lapping gently over the sand as he gasped for air.

"Whatsa matter with you?"

McPherson looked up, seeing Charlie Loomins hovering over him with the small caliber rifle he carried.

"Are you sick?" Charlie asked when McPherson failed to respond.

McPherson managed to stand erect, fighting to bring an icy stare to his features. It was the face of authority developed from more than ten years in the military. "Why aren't you guarding the prisoners?" He turned slightly to glimpse the two people sitting in the sand a short distance away. One was a man, the other a boy.

Charlie acknowledged the captives. "Aw, they're not going anywhere. I don't think they're gonna give us any problems."

McPherson felt his strength beginning to return. "I'll make the decisions around here," he admonished sharply. "There's a pile of gold somewhere around here, and those two probably know where it's hidden."

"I thought we came here for the dolphins," Charlie said weakly.

"We came here for anything of value."

Charlie looked around to observe his surroundings. "Well, so far all I see are trees and water."

McPherson kept his tone in military mode, projecting the voice of command he always used on subordinates. "Henderson has determined this place to be the home of those white dolphins. Sooner or later, they'll come back here, and when they do, we'll block off the entrance. But until they do, we'll busy ourselves by finding where the gold is hidden." He drew in air to clear his head. "Now I want you to go over there and keep an eye on them until I figure out our next move."

Charlie turned, shaking his head and muttering to himself as he trudged back toward the captives.

With his temples still throbbing, McPherson watched him go. Breathing deeply, he tried ridding himself of the nausea he was feeling. Even thinking was difficult, and he had to focus hard to collect his thoughts. He couldn't understand why Henderson was not here to meet them. Interrogation of the two prisoners had so far proven useless, with both of them telling him that Henderson had disappeared sometime during the night.

Feeling less nauseous, McPherson let his eyes roam over his pristine surroundings. It almost seemed appropriate that such unusual creatures would reside in such an exotic setting. Henderson had text-messaged him on that delphine-locating device, providing him with the geodetic coordinates of this cove and inferring the place to be the actual home of Natalie and others of her kind. Henderson had also indicated there was a rich cache of gold situated here, and if McPherson would help him take possession of it, he'd be willing to share it.

McPherson let out a curse. He did not like going on a wild goose chase, especially in view of the Colombians who would surely be coming here sooner or later. While being interrogated by them, he had tried withholding information about the dolphins. Oh, he had really tried. He had given them his best bald-faced look of incomprehension and innocence, doing his utmost to deceive them. But the one called Pedro had scared him senseless, and he had ended up spilling most of what he knew. And now that he had time to reflect on it, he felt ashamed that Jaffey and the Loomins brothers had been able to suck up the punishment far better than he, disclosing much less than he had eventually blabbed. At one point he had even lied about the whereabouts of the DBT receiver, but the Colombians had eventually found that too, discovering it during a search of their salvage vessel. Unfortunately, the receiver contained a log of all recent transmissions, and it was almost certain his captors would discover Henderson's message.

As McPherson recalled these things, he thought it odd that the leader of his captors was already familiar with this new breed of dolphin. So far as he could tell, the man wanted these creatures even more than he did. But Henderson's revelation concerning a stockpile of gold had added a new twist to the way things were progressing. And if he didn't find it soon, he risked being captured a second time by the men he had escaped.

Something else troubled him. He now knew the identity of the man who had rescued him. Jake Javolyn had been one of the Seal trainees under his watch at the Coronado training facility. At first he had failed to recognize him, and it was only while they were pulling away from the *San Carlo* in the salvage vessel that it had come to him with jarring clarity. The Colombian boss had even spoken Javolyn's name during his grilling of Ben Loomins, asking the bearded individual standing next to him if Loomins' description of the man was accurate. Fearful for his life, however, he had failed to make the connection. But now it was all flooding back. The bearded one had also been a Seal candidate, a Chechen by the name of Yeslam Raduyev and a classmate of Javolyn's during their stint at the Coronado school. He well remembered the bitter rivalry between the two.

And while it baffled him immensely as to how these former Seals had become involved in all of this, he also realized that it had bought him some time. In sailing away from the *San Carlo*, he had seen the eruption of flames engulf part of the vessel, and it was this that had emboldened him to come here directly, giving him hope that pursuit by the Colombians would be delayed indefinitely, presumably by the damage the conflagration had caused.

A conflict of emotions gripped him as he pondered these things. His naval career had been under fire for some time now as a result of not heeding Javolyn's allegations concerning Raduyev during their training at Coronado years earlier. Much to his surprise, Javolyn had gone over his head shortly after the incident, sending a formal letter summarizing his concerns up the chain of command. And then he, McPherson, had compounded the problem by explaining away the incident to his superiors as nonsense, describing Javolyn as nothing more than a Muslim hater. On top of that, he had pulled strings with the top brass, insisting that the Chechen be allowed to accompany Javolyn on that fateful Afghan mission, the one in which five members of the Seal team had died, including Myers and Captain Sheridan. His bad judgement had cost him dearly, placing a major obstacle in his path of advancement.

McPherson sucked in another deep breath, looking dismally about him. If only he could capture this new breed of super-intelligent dolphin, his career might be resurrected. But it was really the possibility of gold that interested him even more, assuming the message Henderson had sent him to be true. Finding such treasure would be an absolute godsend. The inheritance he had received after his father had passed away the year before had been far less than he had hoped for. And now the family fortune was all but gone. With a string of bad investments on his part, the lavish lifestyle he had grown accustomed to since birth was now on the brink of bankruptcy. The little money he had left was rapidly disappearing, most of it going toward bribes and down payments aimed at capturing dolphins with hands.

Glancing back at one of the cottages, McPherson stared in annoyance. What were Jaffey and Ben Loomins doing in there?

The angry frown that began to form on his face abruptly changed to bewilderment. Something was buzzing in the distance. Looking up to locate the growing hum, panic suddenly gripped him. Rotor blades were beating the air, their deepening pitch telling him a helicopter was approaching. He stood frozen, his eyes searching the air above. In moments, he caught sight of a chopper slipping over the cove's southern ridge.

The chopper abruptly flared, hanging in the sky for a short interval as if those inside could better study the lush bowl-shaped amphitheatre beneath them. Moments later, the aircraft dipped lower, the rhythmic flapping of its main rotor growing blatantly louder the closer it came.

McPherson's first impulse was to run, but he realized there was really no place that offered refuge in the oblong confines of the chasm surrounding him. Immobilized by fear, he watched as the aircraft made a slow, almost cautious descent before catching him with a savage down-blast of rotor wash. For a prolonged moment, it hovered ominously over his head before coming to roost further up the beach, its cockpit swinging around to face him just before it touched down. Five bull-necked Latinos spilled from the rear cabin, all of them toting Uzis. Without hesitation, the men rushed at him, their scowling faces showing no signs of friendliness.

Numbed by the intrusion, McPherson could only stand there before being knocked to the ground. Crippled by panic, he found himself looking up the barrel of one of the weapons, its muzzle only inches from his face. Behind the man holding the Uzi, he glimpsed another Latino emerge from the helicopter's co-pilot seat just as the rotors ceased swishing. Unable to pull his eyes away, McPherson stared in awe as the man swaggered closer. Growing up the way he had, he recognized the mien of privilege immediately, for the man seemed to radiate an aura of extreme wealth and power. The Latino came slowly toward him, a man who apparently took pride in his grooming. He was clean-shaven, sporting a shiny crop of jet-black hair punctuated with rich streaks of silver at the sides. His hair was long and neatly trimmed, pulled back austerely into a tightly bound ponytail, with the hint of gel giving it luster.

Chilled with foreboding terror, McPherson gaped dumbly, vaguely wondering how the man was able to wear an expensive, immaculately tailored Armani designer suit in such sweltering heat without sweating.

The impeccably dressed Latino stared down at McPherson as though he were a warden looking at an escaped convict. He seemed satisfied by the fright he was seeing. "My time is very limited," he said. His voice held the inflections of culture and refinement, though his English was tainted with a heavy Spanish accent. He let his eyes linger on McPherson briefly before pivoting his head in all directions to take in the encompassing scenery. "And even more limited is my patience."

The man paused just long enough to let McPherson absorb the underlying threat. "There is a question I have that requires an answer, and you will provide me with this answer without hesitation."

McPherson nodded vigorously, sincerely hoping he would be able to comply. Here was a man used to having his way, and he had no desire to be on the receiving end of more physical punishment. The beating he had suffered at the hands of Pedro continued to haunt him, and from the hooded flat stare the Latino gave him, he instinctively knew the man would bring upon him a penalty far worse than what he had previously endured.

"I am told there exists a treasure trove within this place," the Latino said. "You will tell me where it is."

McPherson spoke quickly, feeling his voice crack under the man's intense strident gaze. "I tried getting that information from the people we found here, but they pretend ignorance. I'm sure they can tell you where it is with the right persuasion."

The Latino's face clouded, and McPherson cringed as though expecting a series of blows to rain down on him. When none came, he risked meeting the eyes of his interrogator, but the man's attention was drawn elsewhere. From the direction of the thatched cottages, one of the man's cohorts was coming back at a brisk trot to join him, rattling something off in Spanish between breaths. Trailing behind him, Ben Loomins and Frank Jaffey were being prodded along by one of the Uzi-wielding gunman.

The Latino nodded gravely, his eyes roaming the cove in all directions once again before settling back on McPherson. "How many people are with you?"

"Two," McPherson blurted. Reading skepticism on the man's face, he quickly added, "Two people are here with me. Two others were already here when we arrived."

McPherson's captor elicited a faint dubious smile. "What about your vessel? I assume the one anchored beyond this cove belongs to you."

"Yes…two men are aboard her."

"Watch where ya jab that thing," Ben Loomins protested stubbornly, turning to glare at the man prodding him forward. He looked down at McPherson, grumbling in annoyance. "I knew it was a mistake to come here."

The Latino barked several orders in Spanish, and within the span of a minute his henchmen herded over Charlie Loomins and the two people he had been guarding. Singling out Ben Loomins, he pointed to the small inflatable rubber boat sitting on the beach a short distance away. Reverting back to English, he said, "You! You will take this boat out to your vessel and bring back the other two men aboard her. Two of my men will accompany you. If you give them any trouble, they will shoot you and throw you over the side for the sharks."

Ben Loomins sighed loudly, shaking his head as if to say what else could go wrong. "Why does this not surprise me?"

It wasn't until the inflatable, pushed along by its puttering little outboard, was well away from the beach before the Latino leader brought his attention back to his captives. With hardened eyes drifting among them, he glowered menacingly. "We will now have a little discussion regarding the whereabouts of a certain treasure. If any of you attempt to lie, deceive, or withhold any information regarding this, you will be taken into the open sea where you will be disemboweled and fed to the sharks."

McPherson shuddered. Instinctively he knew his captor would have no qualms whatsoever in carrying out the threat.

The four men peered down from their concealed position amid dense foliage hugging the chasm's edge. Mat Daniels handed the binoculars to the man on his right. "Recognize anyone besides McPherson and his associates?"

Hennington was still wheezing hard and sweating profusely from the strenuous uphill trek. Physical exertion was something new to him, but Mat admired his determination in keeping pace with the rest of them. Hennington had insisted on coming, offering to help out any way he could. His hands were shaking with fatigue, and he had difficulty steadying the glasses as he sighted on the group of people gathered on the beach well below them. The broker of old had undergone a complete metamorphosis, his former flamboyance in dress no longer in evidence. With his trademark fedora now missing and his clothing in tatters, he appeared completely bedraggled and worn. Nevertheless his voice held a calm dignity when he answered.

"The one in the suit is Rafael Cardoza." During his dealings with the Colombians, he had met Cardoza on two previous occasions.

Mat stared over at Jacob. "Is there a way down there without them seeing us?"

Jacob's manner was grave. "Only one place exists where we'll be visible. It's about halfway down."

Mat didn't like the sound of that, but risks were something he had grown used to, especially whenever Jake was part of the picture. Shouldering the weapon he carried, he said, "Then we best get cracking." Keeping his gaze fixed on the Haitian, he rose to his feet. "You have any objections in leading us down there?"

Jacob managed a small smile. "Follow me!" He was still breathing hard as he began to move along the narrow trail that skirted Gaia's rim. He, Mat, Zimbola and Hennington had covered the distance from Malique to the cove at close to an all-out run in less than fifteen minutes, and his legs continued to burn from the rather steep uphill hike.

"I hope Jake knows what he's doing," Mat muttered half under his breath. "It just seems like too much of a coincidence those people would come here."

"I do not find it to be coincidental at all," Jacob huffed. "Those tuna trawlers belonged to Cardoza. It is obvious someone aboard those vessels sent off a message about this place shortly before their fleet sank."

"But how'd they know where to go?"

"The explanation is simple. The dolphin hunters provided them with this information."

Following behind Jacob, Mat chewed on this. The more he thought about it, the more it made sense. Hours earlier, Jake had filled him in on the missing details he had not known about the dolphin hunters, one of those details being Walter McPherson's involvement. And through the binoculars, he had definitely recognized McPherson sitting in the sand down there, clearly cowed by Cardoza and his gun-wielding goons.

Mat gritted his teeth in anger. McPherson was a pompous asshole whom he disliked intensely. If it hadn't been for McPherson's meddling influence in the Afghan mission, Myers would still be alive. Under normal circumstances, he would have left McPherson for the wolves, but the fact that Myers' kid was also down there with him put a different spin on things and he'd do whatever it took to keep the boy from getting hurt. He owed Myers at least that much, because if Myers hadn't insisted on taking point back in Afghanistan, it would have been he who would have fallen victim to Raduyev's treachery.

Another thought entered Mat's thinking, one that didn't add up, and he voiced it to Jacob. "How would the dolphin hunters know about this cove?"

"We had an informant among us," Jacob said, his tone still reflecting his physical weariness.

"Who?"

"One of Dr. Grahm's assistants must have told them about this place."

"If that's true, then how'd he get that information to them?"

"He probably found a way through some kind of wireless transmission. Dr. Grahm said that Nicolas Henderson is an electronics genius." Jacob stopped speaking momentarily to catch his breath. "Perhaps Henderson is the traitor."

"But you said Henderson's not down there." Jacob had also gotten a glimpse through the binoculars.

"Either he's hiding or they killed him."

Chapter 33

Rafael Cardoza watched the inflatable disappear into the narrow inlet that led to the open sea, his mind dwelling on his nephew's last transmission. Somewhere hidden in this place was a hoard of gold. At least that was what the message had said. Based on some kind of sophisticated hardware hidden under a pillow in Ortega's stateroom, Pedro had discovered information that corroborated the claim of the dolphin hunters.

A dark smile crossed Cardoza's face as he mulled this, for it seemed his instincts not to trust Ortega had been right all along. Placing Pedro aboard the *San Carlo* was so far proving to be a wise course of action. From the communiqués he had received from Pedro, it appeared as though Ortega had his own agenda going. He was puzzled though. Since the last message, he had not been able to reach his nephew.

Turning, Cardoza let his eyes wander over the five captives forced to sit in the sand. Scowling, his gaze fell on Jeff Parker. "Was it you who sent that text message?"

A blank look befell Parker's expression. "Beg your pardon?"

"My people found an electronic device, some kind of receiver. On it was a set of coordinates showing this location, including a message. The message said gold was hidden here."

The first signs of fear tinged Parker's face, and he looked nervously about. "I…have no idea what you're talking about."

Cardoza eyed his closest gunman, then singled out Phillipe. "Take the boy out into the water and drown him."

The gunman tossed Cardoza his Uzi before yanking Phillipe viciously to his feet. Forcing one of the boy's arms behind his back, he wrestled Phillipe out into the water.

Frank Jaffey spoke up as Phillipe thrashed about fiercely to keep his head from being pushed under. "Let the boy go!" He looked imploringly at Cardoza. "The guy who sent the message isn't here."

"Where is he?"

"I don't know."

Cardoza turned his eyes back to the water. "Drown him!"

"Wait!" Jaffey cried out, speaking as fast as he could. "The one you're looking for is Nick Henderson. He knows where the gold is. He's the one who sent the message. We came here to meet him, but he was gone when we got here."

Cardoza nailed Jaffey with a penetrating stare, looking for signs of deception. He was good at reading faces, and from all outward appearances, it looked as though the man was telling the truth. Nevertheless, making an example of one of these people would instill sufficient fear in them to keep them from withholding any more information. And fear was a tool he routinely used in achieving the power he wielded as a Colombian drug lord.

Bringing his gaze back to the water, Cardoza noticed the boy was still putting up an insane struggle. "I said drown him!" he repeated in a deadpan tone.

The man holding Phillipe grinned maliciously, forcing the boy's head below the surface.

Something odd and fleeting touched Cardoza as he watched the order being carried out, almost as though he had been witness to a similar scene here in this setting long ago. But that was absurd, for he knew this was his first visit to this most extraordinary place. Caught in the grip of déjà vu, his mind flitted to his ancestry, a lineage that went all the way back to the Spanish conquistadors. He was familiar with his family history, knowing that a distant relative of his, a bankrupt Spanish nobleman, had been among the first Europeans to sail with Columbus. Coming to this very island seeking to start a new life and replenish a lost fortune, his progenitor had helped eradicate the savages infesting the land, growing exceedingly rich over time. What were they called? Ah, yes, the Tainos.

A strange dawning took hold of Cardoza as he thought about his heritage, and he fantasized that perhaps his ancestor of nobility had killed many of these Tainos in this very place. Yes, perhaps the boy carried a smidgen of Tainos blood in his veins, and now history was repeating itself.

Cardoza smiled cruelly, studying the horror-stricken faces of his captives as they watched what was being done to the boy. The feeling that he had brought about a similar act in this very same place a long time ago was suddenly stronger, and visions of a massacre took hold of his senses.

He was seeing through the eyes of his predecessor, a man who commanded a small army of Spanish soldiers, and the screams of the Tainos being slaughtered in this secluded haven gave him pleasure. Strangely, it seemed all too familiar, a scene perpetuated over and over again in countless dreams he had as a boy, and now he was reliving it once more. Within this cove his ancestor had found a great hoard of gold, taking it from those he had killed. And it was that gold that had laid the foundation to the family estate, handed down from generation to generation until it had eventually established roots in Colombia.

Instill terror in those around you and then take what you want. Yes, that was the family credo he had firmly embraced, solidly indurated within him by genetics, and one he had taken to heart with a reverent passion. Through his efforts in drug trafficking, the wealth and power of the Cardoza estate had grown dramatically, and he would continue to go on taking from others whenever and wherever the opportunity presented itself. Causing the death of others, it seemed, always led to an increase in wealth, and that was something he constantly hungered for with an insatiable yearning. Wealth equated to power, and power was intoxicating.

Shaking off the visions of past carnage, Cardoza looked at his expensive Rolex watch, knowing his 320-foot ultramodern yacht would arrive shortly to drop its anchor just beyond the outer reef. Then he would deploy more men, having them scour this hideaway and the surrounding hills until they found the one called Henderson.

Cardoza snapped his head around, following the sound of a small, startled cry. Only a ripple of water remained where the drowning was taking place. Completely bewildered, he glanced around sharply to see where his man might have gone.

Setting his eyes back on the fading ripples, Cardoza waited a moment longer. When the man failed to appear, he looked to one of his remaining two gunmen. "What happened to Dominique?"

The gunman stared wide-eyed at the spot where Dominique had been moments earlier. "He slipped and went under."

Cardoza was growing annoyed. "Hand your gun to Raoul, Pablo, and go help him!"

With Raoul keeping his Uzi trained on the captives, Cardoza watched Pablo wade out until he was waist deep in water. A passing storm the night before had stirred up the sea bordering the coastline, leaving the incoming tide pushed into the cove a milky white and effectively masking anything below the surface.

Crouching down until his face was just above the surface, Pablo groped around, willing his hands to make contact with something. Doing this for several seconds, he became increasingly frenzied. This quickly changed to maddened agitation.

"What's going on?" Cardoza demanded.

A mix of astonishment and fright solidified on Pablo's face. "They're gone!" he yelled. "They're both gone."

Chapter 34

*M*entally linked to Achilles, Jake had a clear picture of Phillipe's plight. The juvenile's biosonar immediately told him what was being done to the boy. Pulled along by the young albino just below the surface, he had slipped unseen into the cove, coming to Phillipe's aid just in the nick of time.

Seething with anger, Jake reached out with his free hand while still gripping Achilles' dorsal fin with the other. Catching the bully unawares, he caught the thug's right ankle and tugged savagely, sweeping him off his feet and dragging him out into deeper water heel-first. Hermes was right behind him with Phillipe in tow, having snatched the boy from the man's grasp. With both dolphins pouring on the speed, they quickly covered the distance back to the cove's inlet where they rose to the surface. From where they now floated, they were beyond the line of sight of those still on the beach.

With Hermes lifting Phillipe's head clear of the water, the boy broke out in a coughing jag, gagging then gasping for air. Using his grip on Achilles for leverage, Jake shifted his hold on the thug, getting a handful of the man's shirt collar where it met the nape of his neck. He continued to keep him under. The man clawed insanely at the arm restraining him with a strength born of sheer terror. Resolutely, Jake refused to let go, most of his attention focused on Phillipe. Gradually, the boy's breathing steadied.

Only when the thug went limp did Jake pull him to the surface. Another albino swam in to help, and Jake passed his unconscious charge over to Aphrodite.

Satisfied that Phillipe was okay, Jake held on as Achilles dove. Staying submerged, he was whisked rapidly back across the cove. There was still work to be done and he was eager to get on with it.

Cardoza's eyes bulged in disbelief as another of his men disappeared below the surface. Pablo had let out a piercing scream, seemingly fighting against something unseen tugging him under. Tensing with fear, he backed away from the water. When Pablo failed to surface, he pointed his Uzi at McPherson. "You! You are coming with me!"

McPherson sat frozen, his expression ashen.

Cardoza stepped closer and kicked him savagely in the ribs. "Get up!" he roared, all of his previous composure now gone.

Fearful of being shot, McPherson staggered to his feet, his face a mask of pain as Cardoza prodded him toward the helicopter. The chopper's pilot was still aboard, standing by at the controls, and Cardoza motioned for him to crank up the turbine.

Realizing he was the only one among them being led away, McPherson hollered out in panic, his cries of protest competing with the rising whine of the chopper. "I've told you everything I know. The one we found with the boy knows where Henderson is. I'm not the one you want." In desperation, he glanced back at Parker. "Take him!" he begged.

Cardoza looked back at Raoul and gestured, drawing a thumb across his own throat. "Kill him!" he shouted. Raoul nodded back grimly, his gaze momentarily taken from Parker.

Parker reacted swiftly, springing to his feet while Raoul was looking back at Cardoza. In an attempt to save himself, he lunged for Raoul's Uzi, but Raoul knocked him back down before he could get a hand on the weapon. Dazed, Parker found himself looking up into Raoul's maddened eyes, the Uzi aimed at his face. In that instant, Parker knew he was a dead man, his mind reeling in expectation of the hail of heated metal that would take his life. He dropped his gaze in resignation, his eyes coming to rest on Raoul's trigger finger.

Raoul's body jerked. Parker looked back up in surprise, staring into the face of his would-be assassin. The thug's mouth hung open in pained amazement. And then Raoul's head abruptly exploded, and Parker was reminded of something he had once seen. It was the way a watermelon had splattered when he had dropped it from the roof of a building during a prank some years back. Headless, Raoul's body twitched jerkily as it staggered away. Toppling to the ground, it continued to spasm erratically.

Perched on one of the cove's tiered ledges, Mat Daniels stared through the telescopic sight of his SR-25, the target better than two hundred yards distant. The rifle was a sniper's dream, accurate to nine hundred yards, and he had become expert at using such a weapon during his stint in the Seals. He had seen what was about to happen to Parker and had less than a second to react, throwing the rifle to his shoulder and firing in the same movement. The first shot had been too low, catching the man squarely in the chest. Displeased with his aim, he had fired again, this time taking a more deliberate stance and sending the bullet to its intended point of impact. Satisfied with the effort, he watched as Parker rose unsteadily to his feet, safe for the moment. Pivoting the rifle, he sighted on Cardoza, ready to take the drug lord down. The scope was filled with McPherson's frantic image. Get out of the way, asshole! He cursed under his breath. McPherson was impeding a clear shot. The way Cardoza was forcing McPherson across the beach, he might end up hitting the naval captain instead.

Cardoza saw Raoul's head erupt in a pink cloud and instinctively knew the shot had come from somewhere along the ridgeline above him. Almost immediately, his eyes located the source. He could clearly see four men on one of the cove's tiered ledges about midway down, one of them holding a rifle currently pointed in his direction. In desperation, he used McPherson as a shield, hunkering low and keeping a tight grip on him as he wrestled him toward the chopper. Ignoring McPherson's pleas, he shoved him roughly into the aircraft's rear cabin, then followed him in to sit beside him, making sure to keep his captive between him and the unseen sniper. Almost immediately, the chopper rose, climbing two hundred feet straight up before banking hard to starboard. In moments, it cleared the ridgeline overlooking the waterfall and was gone.

Mat lowered his weapon, finding it difficult to suppress a grin. He had to be honest with himself. Saving McPherson had not been very high on his priority list.

With both gunmen now in custody of the dolphins, Jake had Achilles tow him out to the salvage tug. From beneath the surface, he could make out the outline of the small rubber boat tied to the vessel's stern. On his way to the cove, he had seen the small inflatable heading for the tug, two gunmen aboard it with Uzi submachine guns trained on the man steering it.

Jake conveyed his plan to the juvenile. *We'll wait for them to bring the others ashore, Achilles. Then we'll take them by surprise.*

Do not let yourself get shot as I did, Jay Jay.

Jake glanced to his right, seeing Destiny riding Hercules. *You don't have to worry about that. Seals are trained to catch an enemy off guard.*

There may be more danger, Jay Jay. Coral has detected the approach of another vessel. A rotary-winged flying machine similar to the one you destroyed at Navassa has just set down upon it.

Jake gave a mental nod, wrapping his mind around this new development.

Achilles added another thought. *Jacob believes the men we captured belong to the same organization that owns the fishing trawlers we sank.*

Then they've either come for revenge or something else, Jake answered. Projecting his thoughts was becoming automatic now.

A sound from above ended the interplay of thoughts, and instinctively Jake knew the inflatable boat was being boarded again. The tide had changed, improving underwater visibility, and from where Jake hovered below the surface, he could see men climbing down onto the boat's open deck.

Jake waited as the two Uzi-toting gunmen took up positions along the inflatable's bow where they could look back at their three captives. Noting the opportunity, he responded quickly, knowing Achilles was reading his mind. Using the dolphin's backside for support, he pushed off hard with his feet, lunging out of the water and throwing a hand around the throat of each man from behind. Caught completely by surprise, their screams were abruptly squelched as both were pulled backwards into the water. Before they could even comprehend what was happening, Achilles reached out and tugged their weapons away.

Releasing his hold on the men, Jake poked his head above the surface, aware of the bafflement painting Ben Loomins' face.

It took Loomins less than a second to realize who he was staring at. "You again," he muttered, but his tone did not hold the same animosity he had shown Jake before.

Jake found it difficult to withhold a grin. "Yeah, but you could at least say thanks."

Sputtering water, the two gunmen broke the surface, splashing frantically as they struggled to regain the boat.

Jake turned his eyes to the floundering men, then looked back at Loomins. "I can let them climb back aboard if you'd like."

Loomins' countenance clouded. "That's if they're able to do that," he said, waiting for one of the men to raise his head above the inflated gunwale. He let out a grunt as he stomped down hard on the man's head. Though stunned, the man hung on stubbornly, and Loomins had to kick him a second time to make him let go. Knocked senseless, the man fell away, floating momentarily before slipping below the surface. Seeing this, the man's partner treaded water, shifting a fearful gaze from Jake to Loomins.

Loomins eyed the second man contemptuously. "I hope you're a good swimmer, cause there's no way you're getting aboard this boat." He suddenly became aware of Destiny breaching the surface, the large albino bull under her. The man Loomins had knocked cold was slung across the dolphin's back immediately in front of the girl, who kept him from sliding off.

"You should let the sonofabitch drown," Loomins suggested, but to Jake his words lacked conviction.

Jake scanned the sea to the south, quickly spotting the vessel Achilles had warned him about. It was coming on fast, rapidly closing the distance separating it from the salvage tug. The vessel was huge and modern, its sleek hull and superstructure a gleaming white. It was one of those customized mega-yachts fabricated mostly from fiberglass, the kind that only the super-wealthy were able to afford and maintain.

Swinging his gaze back to Destiny, he said, "We better take refuge in the cove." He had no doubts that another fight was brewing, knowing this one would be far more intense and dangerous.

Destiny smiled back serenely. "There's no need to hurry, Jay Jay."

Jake was learning to read the girl well, and on her face he could not detect the slightest hint of alarm.

A loud boom cut through the air, drawing Jake's attention back to the vessel bearing down on them. An expanding spume of water rose from the boat's port side, and upon its deck he could see men scurrying about in confusion. Another explosion followed, this one catching the yacht further back astern.

Jake narrowed his eyes, feeling only mild discomfort from the passing shock waves as they pulsed through the sea. Immersed in water as he was, the blasts might have caused serious injury had the yacht been closer to his present position.

A rush of foaming whitewater a short distance away from the vessel caused him to shift his gaze, and he realized the bow of a submarine was breaking the surface.

"Is that who I think it is?" Jake asked incredulously.

Destiny nodded, continuing to smile. "We now have other friends to join our cause."

Jake kept his eyes trained on the sub as the rest of its hull rose up and stabilized. In moments, the hatch on its conning tower opened and three men flooded out. Even from where he treaded water, he could make out the lines of a shoulder-mounted Stinger missile being brought to bear by one of the men. And then the missile was sent on its way, zipping across the gap separating the sub from its target.

The missile exploded with devastating impact, abruptly turning the whirlybird resting upon the yacht's helipad into a raging inferno.

Holding onto Achilles, Jake scrutinized Destiny appraisingly. "How could Bashir possibly know that boat was a threat?"

"Mother alerted Bashir to the danger before she left the cavern. She had a vision of what was to come." Destiny paused, as if to gauge

Jake's reaction. "Bashir and his followers want to devote themselves to protecting the pod."

Jake stared back at the yacht, watching it for the next minute. Severely holed by the sub's torpedoes, its bilges were straining hard to stem the flow of water rushing into its hold. Slowed by the damage, the vessel was making a wide turn, seemingly preparing to head back down the coast.

With the danger now in retreat, Jake looked back at Destiny. "Tell your mother she's an amazing woman," he finally said.

It wasn't until much later in the day that Jake had a moment with Mat. Walking along the water at the northern end of the cove, Jake fixated his long-time friend with a weighty stare. "So what's it gonna be, buddy?"

Mat unleashed a hefty sigh, avoiding Jake's eyes. He looked to the water instead, gazing at the creatures shadowing them. "You're not making this easy for me, ya know."

Jake turned to follow his gaze. "Listen, Mat, whatever decision you make I'll respect. All I can tell you is that within the coming months some incredible things are going to happen. Call it whatever you want, but I can guarantee it's going to set the stage for a new phase of history on this planet. But in order to make that happen, these creatures are going to need help from people like us."

Jake let that sink in before going on. "These creatures are not here to favor any one government or sovereign nation. Their cause is much too pure and noble to pursue a thing like that. In giving them your support, you'll no longer be abetting any arrogant, self-serving politicians or bureaucrats."

Mat practically laughed. "Amen to that."

"You'll be making a difference if you help them, Mat. A huge difference."

"That's all fine and dandy, pal. But ideologies don't pay the bills. What do I do for income?"

Jake could not help but smile. He could tell his friend was beginning to vacillate. "I can guarantee you the pay will be much better than anything the DHS is capable of throwing your way."

Skepticism etched Mat's face. "How's that?"

Jake turned his gaze back to the dolphins. "These creatures are already exceedingly wealthy. I'm sure they'd be willing to work out an arrangement with you that's more than generous."

Indignation suddenly lit Mat's face. "I'm not some donkey that needs to be coaxed by dangling a juicy carrot, ya know. You're making me out to be some greedy asshole."

"You've got me all wrong, good buddy. Don't forget, I know you way too well to ever think that. And these dolphins will never think any less of you for accepting a lucrative compensation package. Just think of yourself as being a well-paid employee of a budding international corporation. You'll have a compensation package with all types of perks."

Mat paused a moment longer before grinning broadly. "Count me in! With you around, I know things will never be dull."

Later that night, a celebration of sorts took place in Malique. Food and drink were in abundance, and joining the party were faces not indigenous to the tiny coastal fishing village. The atmosphere was jubilant, with wild reggae music filling the air. As if to underscore the festivities, more than two dozen paintings depicting the strange dolphin art were placed in full view for everyone to see.

Now able to walk, the former captain of the Yemeni freighter stared happily at Jacob. "The Koran has an old saying, my friend: 'Saving one life equates to saving the lives of all humanity.'"

Jacob was familiar with the quote. He had read thousands of books, and the Koran was one of them. But he knew the quote was incomplete, for the verse in its full context actually comprised a dire warning, requiring that those who fight against God and his Messengers either be slaughtered, crucified, or their hands and feet be alternately struck off. Earlier in the day he had learned the man's name, and he knew that Abdel believed Destiny, Amphitrite, and the white dolphins to be messengers sent by God. Having now lost an arm, Abdel had shifted his convictions, discarding completely his former allegiance. "What do you plan on doing with your life now?"

Abdel's eyes seemed to gleam with newfound purpose, and he turned them in the direction of Destiny. The girl stood off to one side of the crowd as she talked quietly with the man who had brought him here. "My life is in the hands of Allah's angels. From this day forward, my only wish is to serve them."

Jacob assumed a solemn expression, thankful that men like Bashir and the man standing before him had joined the ranks of sanity. "If that is truly your wish, then perhaps there is a place for you among us. We are in need of people with skills such as yours."

Abdel turned back to Jacob. "It is my understanding that you also serve them."

Jacob held back his amusement. In time, he knew Abdel would come to understand the full context of what fate had led him to. Rather than break the man's illusions, he merely nodded with a smile. Let him draw his own conclusions. "Yes. For a long time now I have served them." And they me, for they have given my life purpose.

Jacob looked around, singling out various faces. All about him there was potential. Already he could envision what Fernando and Antonio could provide. And although Dr. Grahm's presence tended to bring a cloud of sadness to his heart, he knew such sadness would gradually fade in time. There was no disputing the value the scientist would bring to the plan, and he could not deny that having Grahm aboard would only hasten their objectives.

And while Jeff Parker had shown an interest in joining them, Frank Jaffey and the Loomins brothers were another story. They were still mulling Emmanuel's offer. Nicolas Henderson, however, would never be given such an opportunity. The albinos had discovered his body shortly after Bashir had driven off Cardoza and his thugs.

Jay Jay had told him to be wary of Ben Loomins' quick-tempered disposition, but as he observed the man, he could not help but sense a trace of good in him. Perhaps it was possible the dolphin masterpieces had worked their magic on him, permanently defusing any desire within the man to capture dolphins for the sake of profit.

Turning, Jacob located Mat Daniels in animated conversation with Phillipe and the hulking giant, Zimbola. Here was another man with skills similar to Jay Jay's, though he had the impression the former DHS agent's approach to dealing with threats would be a bit more conservative than Achilles' bond-mate. Daniels had already accepted the job as Tursiops' head of security, and Jacob knew the man would take the position seriously.

Jacob's eyes suddenly fell upon Chester Hennington. Amphitrite had briefed him on the man's Tainos heritage, and it was this tidbit of information that made Jacob scrutinize the man with far more than a passing interest. Here was an individual they could surely use, a broker with superb negotiating skills according to the things Javolyn had mentioned about him.

Inwardly, Jacob began to smile about such prospects. Months ago, Amphitrite had revealed visions to him. The current cosmic climate was rapidly changing, telling her a nexus was fast approaching. It was now time to move forward at a faster pace, turning their dream into reality. But for this dream to reach fruition, a team of people would be required for the change to take place. It had started with one thought, one voice, and now others were beginning to echo the cause. Expanded by the imagination of others, hope had come fully into view. Yes, the power of visualization was a wonderful, seemingly magical thing, for it could propel an idea into something tangible and real.

Jacob's musings were suddenly interrupted by a sudden cessation of reggae music, and he realized his cousin, Emmanuel, was about to speak. Emmanuel was Tursiops' official spokesman, and he had an announcement to make.

"May I have everyone's attention, please," Emmanuel shouted. He waved everyone in closer to the makeshift dais he was standing upon. Everyone crowded in to hear what was about to be said.

Emmanuel cleared his throat, presenting a huge smile to the crowd. From where Jacob stood Emmanuel seemed to stand taller, with a sure set to his shoulders, so different from the gaunt and withered slouch of his body when they had first carried him aboard the *Avenging Angel* following his rescue from Ternier's prison. "We are on the verge of great things to come, ladies and gentlemen, what future historians might one day call the beginning of a new phase in human history. For those of you who wish employment with this milestone business venture, your skills are most welcome."

Emmanuel paused momentarily to scan the faces before him, then shifted his gaze to the sea behind him. More than two dozen delphine heads poked above the water's surface adjacent to the village's main pier. The dolphins were also listening intently.

Jacob wore a thin smile, knowing most of the things Emmanuel was going to say. The potential sea colony would be the first of its kind ever, the start of a global enterprise with an earth-saving mission, a union of dolphins and humans working in cooperation.

For the next half hour, Jacob sat back and took in the words.

Chapter 35

*I*t was not until two days later that Jake had the *Angel* anchored off the Devil's Horn. As promised, Achilles had led him back to the exact spot where the unusual coral formation in the shape of a sea turtle lay. Uncharacteristically, Zimbola let out a grunt as he pulled the first aluminum case slung by a rope from the water, setting the heavy container down on the deck with a dull clunk.

Seconds later, Jake climbed onto the swim platform, water dripping from his body as he shed his dive gear. "Let's see what we've got," he said.

Using a pair of bolt cutters, Hector snipped off the partially corroded lock.

Jake looked to Destiny, who was already aboard. She wore a quiet smile as she eyed the container. Turning his gaze back to the box, Jake wondered if his search had finally ended. Perhaps his promise to a departed friend would now be satisfied. "Here's hoping," he said.

The cover resisted him as he pulled it back on its hinges. Tugging a little harder, he felt it break free, and he was immediately greeted by the glint of gold in the early morning sunlight. To be sure, he dug his fingers into the mass of coins filling the box. There were hundreds, perhaps even thousands of them. Here was more of the treasure Mercades Myers had pulled up from the depths better than twenty years earlier.

Jake stared up at Zimbola, unable to hide his glee. "I counted twelve more containers down there. I'll go back down and tie off the rope. We'll bring 'em up one at a time."

"You won't have to," Destiny said. As she finished saying this, something bumped heavily onto the swim platform.

Jake looked behind him, spotting Hercules. The dolphin withdrew his hands from another metal container identical to the first. Within moments, several more containers were deposited onto the swim platform as more albinos rose up from below. Having swum the heavy boxes to the surface only reaffirmed the strength of the creatures, for Jake was sure each case weighed better than three-hundred pounds.

Jake grinned expansively, aware that he now had in his possession most of the treasure Myers' grandfather had previously salvaged from the sea floor. He found it strange that half of it had come to him as a result of what had happened back at Navassa. Also accompanying that portion of the treasure were bearer bonds that had most likely been stolen from the Haitian national treasury during Baby Doc's reign. As yet, he hadn't taken the time to fully appraise the full worth of the bonds, though he was certain it was well in the tens of millions. These would be given to Jacob, adding to the monies needed in launching and operating Tursiops Worldwide.

Turning his attention to Phillipe, Jake noted the look of awe reflected in the boy's eyes at seeing the gold. "I've never told you this, Phillipe, but this is your inheritance."

"Huh?"

Jake smiled, amused that Myers' kid didn't have a clue about the promise given his father. He had purposely avoided getting the boy's hopes up until he had actually recovered the treasure.

"Some of this will go toward your formal education. A hefty donation to Harvard should make it easy for you to get accepted without any hassles. Maybe-"

"I want to stay here with you, Jay Jay!" Phillipe looked horrified at the suggestion.

Jake sighed. "I promised your dad if I found the treasure I'd make sure you got a college education."

"I can stay in Gaia and Jacob will teach me."

"We'll talk about this later."

"I want to swim with the dolphins."

Before Jake could reply, the boy dived over the side. Achilles was right there to meet him, and Phillipe grabbed hold of his dorsal fin.

Jake looked helplessly at Destiny. "Kids!"

The feeling was strange to Destiny. An almost tangible force had drawn her deep into the cave behind the waterfall. Irresistibly beckoned by it, she sensed its unyielding power. The unseen presence was stronger this time, and instinctively she knew the spirits of the Tainos were calling out to her. Like Hennington, Phillipe also had a trace of Tainos blood flowing through his veins. This she instinctively knew, and she thought it befitting how justice had a way of being served. Some of the wealth the conquistadors had gained at the expense of the people they had all but destroyed had come back full circle to the boy.

But it was the man-made chamber the presence wanted her to see, and she dropped the thought of the boy as she stared up at the ceiling. The mud she had smeared over the painting had fallen away, leaving the artwork fully illuminated under the torchlight, and she now understood that the future had changed, for it was not Jay Jay being mauled by a tiger, but another.

Destiny studied the ancient mural for a long moment before hearing someone emerge onto the landing behind her.

Jake followed her gaze, his eyes clouding in amazement at what he saw. "That's Walter McPherson. He was the one who wanted Natalie."

Destiny turned, her long ebony tresses framing an ivory face in the torchlight, and in her expression Jake could see the immense burden that had been lifted. For one prolonged and giddy moment she just stared at him, not saying anything. And then she dropped the torch, coming at him in wild desperation.

Jake winced. The grip of her arms about his neck was surprisingly fierce as she rose up in search of his mouth. Even more surprising was the feel of her lips as they spread over his, shockingly steamy and moist, and Jake found himself responding with a lusting desire as she melted like wax against him, vaguely wondering if his heart might burst. Afraid he might crush her to dust in his embrace, he finally released her, and for several light-headed seconds thereafter, they clung to each other.

"I love you, Jake Javolyn," she gasped feverishly. "I've loved you from the very first moment I saw you." Her eyes shot to the mural showing Jake firing his guns at the retreating helicopter, and she realized she had loved him long before she had met him.

Jake had difficulty speaking, his throat parched to the brink of closing. "I love you, too," he managed to croak hoarsely, and with an aching hunger that took hold of his very being, he pulled her tightly to him again. The feel of her body against his intoxicated him and he was suddenly electrified with wanting, feeling every nerve within him pulsing with an insatiable yearning. And then they made love, an all-consuming passion that seemed to carry their spirits to the far side of the universe. Caught in its grip, Jake sensed a searing bout of light enfold his soul, something good, eternal, and boundless.

Much later, as they strolled hand in hand along the cove's gentle waters, several members of the pod leaped high, seemingly hanging in midair in defiance of gravity as they executed a series of breathtaking acrobatics that bordered on the impossible. But then Jake knew that nothing was impossible.

Destiny stopped and leaned up against him, and Jake sensed the aura of virtue and innocence still clinging to her in spite of their lovemaking. "Oh, Jay Jay, look!" she said breathlessly, pointing. "It's so beautiful."

Jake turned, seeking out the thing that had caught her gaze. The most magnificent rainbow he had ever seen straddled the waterfall. The sun was directly overhead, the light giving stark contrast to the arching hues. He realized a strange quirk of physics must be taking place, for the spray coming off the falls had risen into a golden mist and was interplaying with the sunlight in such a way as to make the individual rills appear like bejeweled necklaces, with each gem coming alive and glinting sharply as the light caught it. Captivated by the sight, he watched as the separate colors pulsed and shimmered as they streaked along their respective bands. And as he followed their paths, he had the impression they were racing to infinity.

He blinked, enraptured even more. The vision was changing, and an instant later he was seeing Achilles' painting all over again, the intricate geometry twisting and snaking and teasing his brain, and he suddenly discovered the underlying lucidity within those brush strokes. It was the rebirth of hope.

He blinked once more, then rubbed his eyes to be sure it wasn't some trick of the imagination. The odd display of light had changed yet again, and he realized the face of a Haitian woman was staring down at him, her expression lit up in a benevolent, omnipotent smile, her orbs twinkling like day stars against the milky blue sky. And then the face dissolved, turning back into a dazzling rainbow.

It was an illusion, he knew. From where he stood, it was a thing with no real location nor distance. Nevertheless, he could not refute its existence, for the direction in which it was oriented was palpable, pointing the way to a possible future.

Destiny had also seen the visions, giving a silent thank you as Esmerelda's essence faded into the rainbow. At this moment she felt strangely fulfilled and complete, as though there was nothing missing from her existence, and for the first time in her life she realized she was truly happy and alive. Squeezing Jake's hand, she looked up into his strong face, and in a sudden intuitive flash she knew that he would continue to carry out his one true calling.

And that was to protect.

To find out what happens next in this on-going saga, read
Part Four of the Dolphin Riders Series -
Dolphin Riders, 2nd Edition
Creation.

Acknowledgments

No one deserves more credit for their support in the writing of this tale than my wife and soul mate, Harriet, my biggest fan. Her indomitable spirit and encouragement were indispensable in keeping me focused on completing a work that could have otherwise gone unfinished, a story that could have conceivably transpired in an alternate universe closely paralleling our own. As the novel progressed, it was always a delight to gauge her reaction, which was never disappointing as I read succeeding entries to her over breakfast each and every Saturday morning.

But the thing that finally compelled me to actually write it was the way Harriet was able to cope with her illness. Harriet is tough as nails and since the year 2000 she's been battling CML - chronic myeloid leukemia - and so far, she's put up one hell of a valiant fight, absolutely refusing to yield to what most doctors would describe as a devastating, life-threatening malady. Thus, she made up her mind long ago to live out a normal existence, avoiding hospitals completely and refraining from seeing doctors as much as possible. Consequently, it was her grit and determination that inspired me to take pen to paper and flesh out an adventure imbued with these admirable qualities of the spirit. In its basic subliminal form I wanted to honor her with something unique, essentially a literary work that came from the deepest part of me, something only I could give her, but something which would reflect her iron will and indomitable strength. This is initially mirrored in the book's opening scene where we find a woman adrift and marooned in a thunderous, tumultuous sea. She is alone and clinging to a piece of flotsam, and the reader finds the woman to be pregnant. By all rights, she should accept her fate and succumb to the elements, but she continues to fight on in the face of overwhelming odds, clinging to and refusing to quit until she has nothing left within her to resist the battering forces of a sea gone mad. Later in the book we learn the woman survives with the help of a dolphin and that her name is Harriet Grahm. And although she has no recollection of her former life, she ends up taking on a new identity, becoming Amphitrite, one of the cornerstone characters of the story. During her ordeal at sea, something incredible has happened to Amphitrite, and her failure to remember her past has somehow given her the power to glimpse the future. Henceforth, she becomes an arrant believer in this power and what the future holds, convinced her visions are real, and it is this ability that spills over and infects the reader to make the story palpable and real.

Writing the novel was a labor of love that took four years to complete. In creating it, I had to constantly challenge myself to come up with new ideas, not always knowing where the story was headed since some of the characters within the developing plot started taking on a life of their own. I only knew I wanted to take the reader on a journey to high adventure, an escape from the often mundane routines of everyday life most of us encounter, and in adhering to this I kept imagining what I'd like to see on the big screen if the novel was ever made into a blockbuster movie.

My heartfelt appreciation also goes out to my daughter, Melissa, for her added encouragement to keep me moving forward with this project. And I certainly would be remiss if I left out her three little progenies, Troy Jacob, Solomon, and the latest addition to the family, Jayna Jocelynne, each of whom provided me with the personality traits and inspiration to create the mischievous impish characters which have now come alive to play an integral part within the sequel to this tale.

And lastly, I want to thank my sister, Barbara, in showing an enthusiastic interest in my creativity. Whenever she picked up the unfinished manuscript, she always seemed to have trouble putting it down, totally absorbed and fascinated by the plot's intrigue and explosiveness.

About the Author

*M*ichael J. Ganas is a licensed professional engineer. Following a stint in the U.S. Army, he earned a degree in civil engineering from Cornell University. Shortly thereafter, his love of the sea prompted him to pursue a career as a deep-sea commercial diver, heading a wide array of marine construction projects. This eventually led him into his current occupation, which takes on the challenges of civil engineering in underwater environments. Having published over twenty technical articles involving marine engineering, he decided on writing his first novel, an epic action adventure titled *The Girl Who Rode Dolphins*, which eventually merited seven literary awards and has since been subdivided into the first three books of the on-going *Dolphin Riders* book series. *Retribution* is the third book in the series.

Printed in the USA
CPSIA information can be obtained
at www.ICGtesting.com
LVHW022308151123
763951LV00025B/61

9 781948 494731